Dear Reader,

What do a mail-order bride, a royal imposter and a small-town spinster have in common?

The answer is Christmas—a time of hope and promise, of family and giving, of celebration and tradition.

And for three unforgettable heroines, a time to find their long-deserved happiness.

For our 1993 Keepsake Collection, authors Curtiss Ann Matlock, Marianne Willman and Victoria Pade have written the stories of three women whose lives are forever changed by the magic of the season.

Take home a copy of our collection today and join these heartwarming characters on their respective journeys of discovery.

The editors at Harlequin Historicals would like to take this time to thank all of our loyal readers for their continued support and to send you and your families our very best wishes for the upcoming year.

Sincerely,

Tracy Farrell

Tracy Farrell
Senior Editor

1993
Keepsake

Stories

Curtiss Ann Matlock
Marianne Willman
Victoria Pade

Harlequin Books

TORONTO • NEW YORK • LONDON
AMSTERDAM • PARIS • SYDNEY • HAMBURG
STOCKHOLM • ATHENS • TOKYO • MILAN
MADRID • WARSAW • BUDAPEST • AUCKLAND

1993 KEEPSAKE CHRISTMAS STORIES
Copyright © 1993 by Harlequin Enterprises B.V.

ISBN 0-373-83261-3

The publisher acknowledges the copyright holders
of the individual works as follows:

ONCE UPON A CHRISTMAS
Copyright © 1993 by Curtiss Ann Matlock

A FAIRYTALE SEASON
Copyright © 1993 by Marianne Willman

TIDINGS OF JOY
Copyright © 1993 by Victoria Pade

CONTENTS

ONCE UPON A CHRISTMAS
Curtiss Ann Matlock

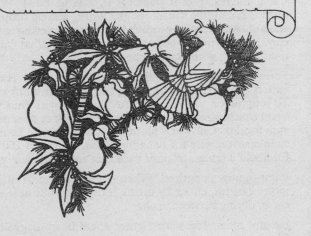

BAKER'S CLAY
CHRISTMAS ORNAMENTS

4 cups flour (plain, not self-rising)
1 cup salt
1¼ cup water

Using fingers, mix ingredients in a large bowl. When mixed, knead like bread dough. Work, adding drops of water if needed, until product becomes the consistency of clay. Store in plastic bag, pinching out only what can be used to work with at one time.

Form shapes either by rolling out and cutting with cookie cutters or knife, or by pinching and rolling like any clay. To join pieces, wet the juncture just a bit with finger or small brush. Keep figures about a ½" thick or less; prick with toothpick in 3 or 4 places to prevent lumps. Insert a stainless-steel wire for hanging. Bake, on foil, at 250° F. for about 3 hours, or until hard. Let cool completely.

Paint figures as desired. When paint is dry, coat in furniture varnish, either by brush or dipping. Use at least 2 coats, drying between each.

Helpful hints: Ideas for figures come from magazines, Christmas cards and tins—from everywhere! A garlic press makes great hair, beards, etc. using stainless-steel wire will allow the hook to last indefinitely. Acrylic paint remains bright longer. Dipping in the varnish instead of brushing it on covers more completely and gives a porcelain-look finish. I store my ornaments wrapped in white tissue paper and sealed inside a plastic bag with a few grains of rice to absorb moisture. There are books on this craft at the library.

Chapter One

Texas, 1875

John was to meet them. Olivia hoped she recognized him; it had been almost four months since she had seen him. She had a tintype of him, quite small and taken some six years ago, but still, his features weren't clear in her mind. Surely he would call out her name.

Will had the canvas flap raised and his head stuck out the window. The rocking of the stagecoach had him holding tight and bumping his head more than once, but such discomforts never bothered a ten-year-old boy. His dark hair whipped around, and his young face was intense, his gray eyes bright.

"It's just a few buildings, Mama." Will glanced at her.

"I told you John said it was very small."

Snatches of sharp, cold wind blew inside. Around Will's bobbing head, Olivia caught sight of steel gray sky, brown grass and bare, scrubby trees. It was the drabbest land she'd ever seen. The lushness of the home they'd left behind flashed across her mind—trees that grew to the sky and pines that kept green all year. And shiny emerald holly, too. John had said there was no holly here.

Henry raised his head from where he'd had it buried in Olivia's lap. She wiped his tiny nose with a handkerchief—she was down to her fancy lace-edged ones—and her hand bobbed with the coach. Henry went to coughing. His chubby cheeks were flushed; he'd suffered a bit of fever for the past two days. Finished coughing, he leaned against Olivia and held tight. Olivia stroked his silky hair, wishing as she had for the past nine days to be where she could prepare him some ginseng tea and a garlic poultice.

The stagecoach slowed, and her heart began to hammer. How did a woman greet a man she barely knew and yet was going to marry? A man she would very soon be sharing a bed with.

What would John think of her? Would he still want her?

Olivia had never been a raving beauty. Her hair, while shiny, tended toward thinness and was the color—exactly, as Cecilia had on occasion pointed out—of a mouse's. Cecilia always was quick to say that she thought mice had lovely hair. Olivia's face was the sort that was simply there. Her features, if of any note at all, being a little pinched. Her eyes were almost lovely, but not quite, being not quite hazel and not quite golden. However, Olivia knew she had about her a certain presence; this was her saving grace. She was a lady and knew how to present herself as one. She could at one moment be timid, the next bold—blowing hot and cold, her father used to say. But she was always a lady, and this gave her an anchor in all circumstances.

That morning she'd donned her best traveling suit—a very expertly made-over one of Cecilia's from before the war. Now it was rumpled and dusty. Brushing at it, Olivia thought of her mother's teaching that a lady was a lady in silk or in sackcloth, it made no difference.

The coach pulled to a stop. Olivia sat there, feeling as if she couldn't move yet, as if her body were still being bounced around as it had for the better part of the past three days.

The door of the coach was flung open, and one of the drivers, a gray-bearded man with a wide-brimmed hat that looked as if it'd been stomped on, said, "This be Esperar, ma'am."

She swallowed, struggled for calm, and caught Will in midflight with "Get your hat, Will."

He jammed his round-brimmed hat on his head and popped from the coach like a cork from a bottle. Olivia grabbed Henry and, with shaking hands, again wiped his nose and fastened his scarf around his neck. The driver lifted Henry down, and Olivia, her heart beating near clean out of her chest, came next. Her legs shook so, she grabbed on to the coach for support.

John? Her eyes searched for his thick, burly figure. She tried to hide her eagerness and her fright.

"This here's the Esperar Hotel, ma'am."

She saw the sign beside the double doors: Esperar Hotel and Café. A man, short and spare, in a rough wool sack coat and ribbon tie rippling in the breeze, stood on the porch, gazing at her, expectant and curious. He wasn't John. She turned. Across the dusty street was a low clapboard building labeled Wild Horse Saloon. She had seen a number of such places in the last few days. Two horses were tied to the rail in front. Surely if John was inside, he would have come out. Down from the saloon was a stable. Two men peered from the open doorway. They had guns strapped to their hips. Neither was John.

Their bags and steamer trunk were left on the hotel porch. The drivers tipped their hats, then drove away. Olivia stood there on the porch with Will on one side and Henry clinging to her skirt on the other, the sharp wind buffeting them all, and watched the stagecoach head off to the south. She felt very much the same as the day she'd watched her house go up in flames.

"I thought John was supposed to be here," Will said.

"I thought so, too," she murmured, and scanned the distance, looking for an approaching rider. There was none.

Her gaze again swept the town, this time noting a nearby building with a drab sign creaking in the breeze. It read The Emporium. Surely a grand name for such a small establishment. Except for the sign, there was no movement at all, nor at any of the houses, five of them, all small, two that were partially adobe.

Where was John?

The wind stung her cheeks, and tears stung her eyes. She couldn't crumble in front of the children. And hysteria certainly wasn't going to help the situation.

The hotel door squeaked, and the spare man in the wool sack coat reappeared. He smiled. "Was someone to meet you, ma'am?" He spoke with a deep drawl, and in a gentle manner.

Olivia nodded, and eagerness rose within her. "Yes. John Carter. Do you know him?"

"Oh, I sure do. Fine man—Monroe Locket's partner." He smiled again, and Olivia's spirits fluttered farther upward, until he added, "But I ain't seen him in...oh, at least three weeks."

Olivia's spirits dropped and slipped clean out her toes.

"John and Monroe's place is 'bout a five-hour ride out," the man was saying. He checked his pocket watch. "The stage was near an hour early today, and John probably got a late start. He'll be along. John's as dependable as they come. Why don't you and the young ones come inside and have somethin' hot while you wait? We can leave your trunks right here. Those skies look threatenin', but it ain't gonna rain."

Olivia accepted with gratitude. Will, always a talker, as his father had been, started right in with, "We're from North Carolina."

"My, my, you've come a fer piece."

Will and the gentleman went on ahead, while Olivia, lifting Henry into her arms, took a last glance down the street.

"Maybe he change-ed his mind," Henry said fearfully, repeating exactly Aunt Cecilia's dire prediction, and with Cecilia's dark inflection in his childish voice, too. Aunt Cecilia was a dear woman, but one filled with several bushels of fear; the war had done that to her.

Olivia looked at her small son and found a confident smile from the place mothers always managed to keep smiles, even in times of great doubt. "Out here isn't the same as ridin' in from Uncle Rupe's, honey. John's just a little late, that's all."

Henry laid his head on Olivia's shoulder. "I wanna go home."

Olivia hugged him. "I know, sweetheart." It seemed the best thing to say, and Olivia was simply too tired to argue.

Suppose something had happened to John? Olivia wondered as they continued inside. She pressed aside the cold fear. There was no use borrowing trouble when one couldn't pay it back.

The Esperar Hotel was like no hotel Olivia had ever seen. It didn't even come up to the level of the Sheehan Boardinghouse back home, which wasn't really any level at all. It was about as small as a cracker barrel and was plain as dry toast, and looked a lot like it, too, being built of weathered wood inside and out. The only color came from blue gingham curtains at the windows.

Introductions were made, and Olivia found herself heartily grateful for these friendly people. The spare man was Oscar Tucker, and his wife, as plump as he was spare, was Selma. "These folks are waitin' for John Carter, Mamma," Oscar Tucker said to his wife, "and I knew you'd want to see them fed while they do." Both smiled broadly and appeared quite delighted to have guests. While his wife hurried away to the kitchen, Oscar Tucker quickly covered the table with a gingham cloth, saying, "It ain't often we get folks such as yourselves who appreciate the niceties."

Olivia, with memories of tables set with pure linen and fine china and silver, said, "At this moment, Mr. Tucker, simply being on solid ground is the most precious nicety in the world."

Selma Tucker returned, bringing two glasses of cool milk, a pot of tea, small slices of fruitcake, and two wet cloths to wipe up with. "This little one looks a bit peaked," she said of Henry.

"He's had a cold almost the entire trip," Olivia said as she wiped Henry's face.

Selma Tucker tutted and shook her head. "I remember our trip, and wish I didn't. We came out from Georgia, all the way by wagon."

"We came by train to Dallas," Will chimed in. "Gettin' here's only taken us nine days all told, and it wouldn't of taken that but we missed a stage."

"Are you-all relatives of John's?" Oscar Tucker asked.

Olivia shook her head. "Not quite." She took a deep breath. "John and I are to be married."

They were surprised, of course. "Well, how nice!" Selma Tucker said after several silent seconds. She smiled. "How nice indeed. John's a fine man."

"Yes, he is," Olivia agreed. And she wished he'd come.

Selma Tucker poured the tea and served the small slices of fruitcake. "My sister sent me the candied fruits from back home," the older woman said, beaming when Olivia complimented on the cake. "I baked up the loaves way back in October for this Christmas a-comin'. And we might as well start enjoyin' and celebratin' right now with your arrival and comin' marriage."

Olivia said, "Thank you . . . it's very kind of you to share." As she tasted the cake, childhood Christmases filled her mind and brought a flicker of joy to her heart. She had packed in her trunk dried fruits— peaches, apples, figs—and looked forward with sweet anticipation to baking them up for their Christmas. If only John would get here. Her fears rose again, threatening to swamp her. Perhaps he wasn't ever going to come, and they were stuck here. Or, worse, what if when he did come he wasn't at all the man she thought him to be? What if it turned out that she and John hated each other?

For goodness sake, she was thinking like Cecilia! And that thought put starch in her spine. She pushed the fears aside and closed the door on them.

The Tuckers told of when they had come to Texas six years earlier, seeking a new start following the hard war years, just as so many Southerners had. Just as Olivia was doing. Oscar Tucker was a preacher, as well, and traveled for nearly a hundred miles around to spread the word. "He'll be the one to hitch you and John," Selma Tucker said happily. "I'm surprised John hasn't spoken of it to Oscar. Were you plannin' on hitchin' right away?"

Olivia shook her head. "We thought we'd wait a couple of weeks." To see if they remained certain, though she didn't say that.

"And very practical that is, too," pronounced Selma Tucker. Naturally curious, she managed to work the conversation around to the trip back east that John had taken the previous summer, and Olivia said yes, that was when she had met him. Mrs. Tucker took that as so romantic. Olivia said nothing about how John had come looking for a wife, nor how she'd been looking for a husband, and they'd struck a bargain more than fallen in love.

Oscar Tucker excused himself to go on an errand over to The Emporium. A daily checker game, Selma confided after he'd gone. Will, having had enough cake and women's talk and sitting still, went out to the porch to keep an eye out for John. Henry crawled into Olivia's lap and went to sleep.

Olivia waited for John, the clock on the sideboard chimed out every fifteen minutes, and her insides began to wind tighter than the clock's spring.

Monroe hadn't wanted to come, and he only had because he'd promised John. Of course, the promise didn't mean that much, because Monroe would have promised his partner the moon at the end if it would have eased John's mind any. Still, a promise had been made—not to mention the woman's trunk had to be sent back. And, too, Monroe had loved John Carter as he never had another human being in all his life.

He pulled his team to a stop in front of the hotel. A shirttail boy sat there atop a mound of carpetbags. Monroe knew he had to be the Pritchett woman's boy, but Monroe didn't speak as he passed him and entered the hotel. He heard female voices in the dining room, hesitated, then went in.

There she was, sitting with Selma Tucker at a table. Her back was toward him, but he knew it was Olivia Pritchett. She wore this highfalutin hat with plumes, such as women of her sort wore and which served no purpose other than to show off. Selma saw him first, and her face lit up. "Why, hello, Monroe..." Her smile faded as she slowly stood. Selma wasn't stupid; she knew there was a reason Monroe had come instead of John.

The Pritchett woman stood, too, and set a small boy to the floor as she turned to face Monroe.

Selma wiped her hands down her apron and said, "Missus Pritchett, this is Monroe Locket, John's partner. Monroe... this is Missus Pritchett."

The woman, her face as pasty as milk gravy, stared at Monroe.

The best way to tell it was straight and quick, so Monroe did. "John died three days ago. Lockjaw."

Chapter Two

Olivia stood gazing out the window into the dusty street. She watched small dust devils and thought: *this has to be the driest place on earth.*

She thought of how it had been raining so much when John had been up in Cherry Creek. She recalled him running through the rain and onto her porch, laughing and saying he liked rain. Then her thoughts skipped to Christmas, and all the things she'd brought for them to have a grand time these holiday weeks. They'd made plans, she and John, and those plans had centered most around Christmas, because it was to have been a new beginning for both of them. Olivia had dreamed of so much for herself and John, but above all for her boys. She had held these dreams for so long, long before John....

"Mama?" Will touched her arm.

She tried to smile at him, tried to bring her mind back to the moment at hand, but it fought her all the way. She was numb, blessedly numb, and her spirit wanted to cling to it. Henry tugged at her skirt, and she thought how she must rally for her boys. She was the only one they had.

"Come sit down and have some strong coffee, dear." It was Selma Tucker. She took Olivia by the shoulders, guided her back to the table and pushed the china cup and saucer close. "Here... I sweetened it.... It'll help to clear your mind...."

Olivia blinked; her eyes were sandy-dry. Her gaze moved to the tall, lanky man with his coat hanging open. He held a steaming cup in one hand and his rifle in the other. He had not removed his hat; it remained pulled low over his forehead, putting his face into dark shadow. That's what he seemed to her—a cold, dark shadow.

Selma Tucker told him to set his rifle aside and sit. He did so but with obvious reluctance. Olivia tried to picture John's face, and came up with a blurry image, a sense of him more than his actual features.

She knew she was sitting there like a woman gone mad. Selma Tucker whispered to Monroe Locket, "Did you have to tell her like that?" Will said, "Mama, here's your coffee." Henry said, "Mama... mama... mama..."

Digging to the recesses of her soul's strength, as she'd long ago learned to do, Olivia took the cup from Will and drank. Then she breathed deeply, commanding her good senses to return. She had her boys to care for. Her eyes met Will's, and she saw the relief flicker there. She squeezed his hand.

"Are you feelin' a little better, dear?" Selma Tucker asked.

Olivia nodded. "Yes, thank you." Her voice came as a bare whisper. She again drank deeply of the coffee, then looked at Monroe Locket. "It was very kind of you to come to tell us. I understand it is quite a ways, and the day is cold."

"Had to be done," the man said. His voice was oddly soft and gravelly at once. There was no friendliness in him.

A well-deep feeling of aloneness swept through Olivia. She was totally, utterly alone in a strange land.

The man said, "I have the trunk you sent out ahead in the wagon, ma'am."

Her eyes flew to his face. "Thank you," she managed. She summoned all the inner strength she possessed. Carefully, she set her cup in its saucer, fighting to keep sanity by clinging to each small, civilized thing. "Mr. Locket, these are my sons—Will and Henry. Boys..." she prodded.

"Hello," Will said sullenly. Henry, his chin quivering, nodded.

The man nodded in return. "Howdy." His eyes met Olivia's, then shifted to his coffee.

Olivia said, "Missus Tucker, could I impose upon you to entertain the children in your kitchen so that Mr. Locket and I may talk in private?"

"Why, certainly. Come along, boys."

Will hesitated and Henry clung to Olivia. "Take brother's hand, honey. Please, Will, take care of your brother." Will took hold of Henry and dragged him along after Selma Tucker.

Monroe was left there at the table with the woman, and felt as awkward as a hell-raiser in church. The woman seemed to have regained some composure, but her hands were twisting one of Selma's napkins into a knot. Just as Monroe shifted himself around to say his piece, the woman spoke.

"How did it happen?" she asked. Her eyes regarded him in a surprisingly quiet way. They were the color of muddy water shot with sunshine.

Bluntly, as he'd spoken before, he answered, "He ripped his hand on a trap 'bout a month ago. It festered some, but not bad." A lump rose in his throat, and he dropped his eyes to the cup that he cradled with both hands. "He got the fever last Sa'urdy, was gone before two sunsets."

"At least he didn't suffer long."

And Monroe said, "Depends on your view of what's quick, ma'am. He spent twenty-four hours like he had an anvil on his chest."

She again stared downward and twisted the napkin. Monroe sipped the coffee and wished it was whiskey.

The woman said, "I'm sorry about John, Mr. Locket. He was a fine, wonderful man."

She started to cry, and resentment, like a searing poker in his chest, gripped Monroe. This woman was alive, sittin' here in a warm room in her Sunday best, while John lay in the cold ground.

"Well now, ma'am, I do reckon that you have plenty reason to be sorry about John's passin'... but you don't need to go pretendin' feelin's for him is one of them, because all the tears in the world ain't gonna get you a durn thing more or less than what he left for you." He pulled a canvas pouch from his coat pocket and tossed it on the table. "John felt obligated to give you this. I don't know what he might have told you, but he weren't no rich rancher or anythin'. This is all the cash he had. And, ma'am, you're now entitled to a quarter of the yearly profits from the LC Ranch. But don't go thinkin' you can eat high on the hog, 'cause profits are like flyin' horses this year." He tossed a folded and crumpled piece of paper beside the pouch. In his mind, he recalled how John had labored to tell him what to put down on the paper. *John... I would have taken your place, if I could have....*

Olivia stared at the man's face hard as carved granite. He had accused her and found her guilty, of what she wasn't exactly certain. She looked at the items on the table, and then back at him. Wild fury burned up her spine and out her tongue.

"That I don't have to *pretend* anything is exactly right, Mr. Locket. I was offerin' you common courtesy and heartfelt sympathy for the loss of your dear friend, something civilized humans offer to each other in circumstances such as this." Her voice broke, then came back low and sharp. "And I'll tell you another thing.... I *cared* for John Carter. I won't pretend we were lovers, but we had the precious regard of people who are lookin' for the same things—and who *respect* each other. Don't you dare belittle that, Mr. Locket!" The last words were bitten out, and her "Mr. Locket" sounded a whole lot more like a curse word, which was exactly as she had intended.

The man sat there, his face a block of belligerence. Ill-kept belligerence, Olivia thought, noting his day-old growth of beard, and that disgusting hat still on his head. Then he averted his eyes. "Well, ma'am, it don't matter one way or the other now."

No, Olivia thought with her ire draining, it didn't. She slowly picked up the crumpled paper, unfolded it and read. "This isn't John's handwriting."

"He was too sick to write.... I wrote what he told me."

She refolded the paper and held it out to him. "I can't take any of it. I wasn't yet his wife."

It was gratifying to see she had surprised him. "John meant you to have it. He felt he'd gone to the bridge with you. And it ain't like he gave you a share of the ranch, 'cause he didn't. It's profits—if we ever get any." His voice was sharp and bitter, condemning her for not taking the offer as he had condemned her for wanting something before.

"And do you ever intend to have any profits, Mr. Locket, or are you simply working your life away for nothin'?"

Through gritted teeth, he said, "We'll have profits, ma'am, in time."

Prodded by the desire to lash out as much as by principle, she tore the paper in half and dropped it to the table. "Profits or no, I can't take this, though I appreciate it, sir. And I wouldn't have expected less of John Carter." Again her eyes filled with tears, and she popped out of the chair and strode to the window, wrapping her arms tightly across each other as if to hold herself together.

The man cleared his throat. "Well, it's your choice, ma'am. None of mine." She heard his chair scrape as he stood. "I'll set your trunk on the porch."

She looked over her shoulder at him, then returned her gaze to the window. "Thank you again for comin', Mr. Locket. And I will keep John's money, for I have no choice. I have very little. However, I assure you that when I can I'll repay you."

A stillness held, and then Monroe Locket said, "No repayment necessary. Like I said, that money came from John."

The thudding of his boots and jingling of his spurs echoed as he walked out of the hotel. The door closed, and aloneness fell around her.

Olivia watched his tall, lanky figure through the window. He walked lightly, even stealthily. The wind tugged at his coat, his battered wide-brimmed hat, and the hair that fell on his collar, but he didn't seem to notice. He was as cold and hard as the wind.

She watched him enter the saloon. You just go ahead and get yourself stinking drunk, mister! she thought. She hoped he'd get a whopping hangover. John had said that his partner was a little rough, but that certainly was an understatement. Monroe Locket was so coarse he could well chap himself. However in this world John Carter, a gentleman, could have been friends with the likes of Monroe Locket was beyond her.

Yet the fact remained that John and this man had been friends, and her ingrained sense of understanding brought pity for him. No doubt the man's rudeness and accusations stemmed in part from his suffering at the loss of his dear friend.

And loss was something Olivia understood only too well, having had her family home burned to the ground, having to bury her father, nurse an ill husband and then bury him, too, only to be left with nothing more than a few family mementos, and no home to put them in.

She rubbed her hands over her upper arms. *Oh, John, I'm sorry for you, but you're dead and gone, and I still have two boys to raise. I still have a life left. Damn you, John, for up and dying!*

She formed her hands into fists, seeking control. Slowly she moved back to the table. Sniffing, she pushed aside the torn paper, took up the pouch and poured the contents on the table. There, amid the money, was the small portrait of herself that she'd given John. And a plain gold wedding band. She fingered it gingerly, choked back tears and turned to the practical task of counting the money. Tears certainly weren't going to see to things now.

There were paper bills, and more in coin—meager indeed. Added to what she had saved, it would get them home—if they were careful about eating.

Home. With something close to pain, she crumpled into a chair. Tears came in a rush, while her heart cried out for the dreams that had filled her mind for the past months. *Oh, John... what do I do now? What do I do?* Her head fell forward, and she sobbed on her arms.

She couldn't indulge in such for long, though, for the boys and Selma Tucker came from the kitchen.

Henry pressed his head against Olivia's, and Mrs. Tucker hovered, clucking her tongue and repeating, "There, there... We all know, yes, we do..."

Will patted her shoulder. "Mama...it'll be all right. I'll take care of you." He, a mere boy, and all his life having to take a man's place. It wasn't right. The fierce protectiveness of motherhood brought good sense creeping back up her spine.

Choking back tears, she straightened, dabbed at her eyes with the well-used handkerchief and began to remove her disheveled hat. "Well, boys," she said with a deep, shaking sigh, "there's nothing for us but to return to Cherry Creek." Will's long face was enough to send her into another spasm of sobs, but she held tight.

"And live with Aunt 'Cilia?" Henry asked, his small voice quavering.

Olivia nodded. "Aunt Cecilia and Uncle Phillip will be glad to have us back, don't you think?" She tried for a smile that didn't quite form.

"Yeah . . . Aunt 'Celia'll be glad," Henry said solemnly.

"No, she won't," Will put in. "Aunt Cecilia don't know how to be glad."

Olivia shared a gaze with her son. Will had a greater understanding of his elderly aunt than she had given him credit for. She put a hand to his shoulder. "But Aunt Cecilia and Uncle Phillip love us."

"Not enough to let us have a Christmas tree," Will said, jutting his pointed chin. "I don't wanna go back. There's nothin' in Cherry Creek but a bunch of old roosters. I can get a job out here. Ol' Ben taught me lots of stuff." He eyed her defiantly, desperately, then pivoted away. "I don't wanna go back!" And he ran outside.

Her son's protest echoed inside Olivia's mind. A knot of fiery rebellion existed inside her, too. She'd made so many plans, cherished so many hopes and dreams, and come so far.

Light was slipping away when Monroe Locket at last came out of the saloon. Olivia had been watching from her hotel room window for over an hour. With her heart pounding, she raced down the stairs. At the door, she paused to straighten her shoulders and wrap her fortitude about her—the same as she wrapped her shawl. She stepped outside.

He was bent over, setting her trunk to the porch. His head jerked up when she opened the door.

"I need to speak with you, Mr. Locket."

Every fiber of her being wanted to turn around and go right back inside. She stepped toward him. The cold breeze tugged at her hair, but her face was hot.

Monroe Locket straightened, gazing down at her from his taller height. His face was in too deep a shadow for her to clearly see it, and that made her even more nervous. There was an aura of hard, cold rock about him.

"I don't wish to impose, Mr. Locket," she began, her voice unsteady, "but my children have come a long way..." She paused, then began again, looking at a point somewhere around his chin. "Missus Tucker informs me that the stage heading north won't be through here for another full week, which would necessitate spending six days and nights in this hotel, and paying for such. I simply don't have the money to do that, and my son has a terrible cold. He's been travelin' with it, and I have had neither space nor the wherewithal to treat—"

"Ma'am, can you come down from the wall?" he said, startling her. "I'm ready to head out and would like to get started before black night."

She took a deep breath, straightened her shoulders and lifted her eyes to his. "Mr. Locket, I would like to stay at your ranch through Christmas."

Even with his features in shadow, she saw his surprise. "You want to come out to the ranch?"

She nodded. "As I said, I cannot afford for the children and I to await the stage in this hotel, and my son needs a place where I can tend him. And we've come a long way, Mr. Locket, to simply turn around and head right back. We'd like to at least see the place John spoke so lovingly about, and we all need rest. I'd like to stay the three weeks until the north stage after Christmas. I can't pay you, but I can clean and cook, and Will can—"

He held up his hand. "Whoa up there, ma'am. You don't need to go gettin' ideas. You were John's log to carry, not mine. And I ain't in the market for a wife. I've returned your trunk and passed along John's money—and the inheritance you profess not to want. That's the end of my responsibility."

And that got her back up. "I do not consider myself and the children your 'log' of responsibility, Mr. Locket, and I'm not askin' to be. And as for marriage—I'm not considerin' that, either. John was an exceptional gentleman, and I don't expect to find that again. And I did not simply *profess* not to want the regular profits."

"Yearly profits."

"Well, I still have no thought of them, though heaven knows I could use them—*if* there were any."

Monroe Locket said, "There will be. And they're yours, so you might as well take them."

"Suppose when the day finally dawns that the ranch earns profits, you send them to me, if you're of a mind," she said, unable to resist the sarcasm. Her father had always told her that her sarcasm would be her downfall. "With that settled . . ." She gazed at him, and he saw the ire in her cocked chin. "I believe John has built a cabin for us, so we would not be takin' room away from you, only the food we eat. It seems a small thing to ask."

"Ma'am, believe me, the best thing is for you to head back right now." He sounded generous, and proud of himself for this tact. "This land isn't a good one for a woman alone."

"No land is a good one for a woman alone," she shot back at him with clarity.

She eyed him; he eyed her.

"Mr. Locket, I have just spent without a doubt the most miserable nine days of my life. The past three and a half cold, wet days I spent being beat to pieces in a stagecoach, and three nights sleeping on mattresses stuffed with corn shucks—if I was lucky—and sharing those mattresses with bugs, and once with a snoring old woman whose breath would have knocked over a horse. Before that I had the pleasure of riding the train, which rocked as if in high seas and where a man almost vomited in my lap. We could not afford a Pullman, Mr. Locket. *If* we slept, we did it sitting up. And now you are telling me I must turn right around—without even glimpsing the cabin that John built us, the place where we had focused all our hopes and dreams—and take my person directly back on all that? And do it with a sick child?

"Now, sir, not only can I not afford to pay for room and board, but with that week's delay here, the children and I would find ourselves spending Christmas on that damnable train or waiting in some damnable train station. My sons have suffered enough upheaval and disappointment without totally ruining their

Christmas. Can't you recall what Christmas meant as a child, Mr. Locket?"

"Ma'am, I never was much of a child, and I didn't know about Christmas."

"Then that should give you pity on children," was her snappy reply. She breathed deeply. "I'm askin' for a bit of kindness. Has no one ever given you that? Are you without indebtedness to a single soul?" She paused then, and her eyes both dared and beseeched him.

"Ma'am, did anyone ever tell you that you could tongue tomatoes off the vine?"

That set her off-balance, and she puzzled over it for a moment. Then she countered, "I realize I have a weakness for talkativeness, but I assure you I will restrain myself if you will let us come to your ranch. We have come too far not to even view the place where we were headin'."

He gazed at her, and she sensed his weakening. "There's just me and a hand out at the place. Folks might talk."

"People always talk."

"Ma'am, if you come with me, you'll have to go right now and stay the night on the range." He seemed awfully proud of that tact.

But Olivia countered, "Our bags are sittin' ready, just inside the door. I'll get the children."

"Wait!" He gazed at her, then sighed. "Never mind. Might as well wait until mornin'. First light, and you-all better be here, or I go without you."

"Yes, Mr. Locket. And thank you."

He turned on his heel and stalked back across the street, without a tip of the hat or a by-your-leave.

Olivia sighed deeply. She had gotten what she wanted.

Chapter Three

The woman was there with her young'ns waiting for him. "You said dawn," she said, as if criticizing him for being tardy—or prideful that she was waiting. He saw that in the tilt of her pointy chin. She wasn't a looker, but there was something striking about her. Monroe could see why John had been proud of her; John felt the same about the woman as he had about the rams, which didn't seem much how a man was supposed to feel about the woman he was to marry.

"Yes, ma'am," he said as he stopped the wagon.

She looked at him expectantly, and he deliberately stayed put. He was taking her to his ranch; he wasn't going to load her bags. But shame goaded him when she and the shirttail boy began to do it alone, so he got down and did it. Besides, he had to do the big trunk.

To Monroe Locket, women were a necessary evil, especially out in this land, which wore a man down and would turn a woman into dust. This was a man's land was how he figured it.

Monroe had loved a girl once, a golden-haired gal, back when he was barely old enough to shave. When he'd gone away to war, he'd given that golden-haired gal his savings in gold coin, his matching set of gray geldings, and his heart; she was to safekeep all. When he returned, he'd discovered she'd married the miller, and Monroe's money had gone to buy furniture for their clapboard house, and Monroe's grays were pulling the miller and her around in a buggy. He hadn't fallen for a woman since.

A couple of times a year he went down to San Antone and visited a house there, but mostly he did without; he was building a ranch. When John started hankering after a woman's touch, Monroe had advised him to go down to San Antone for a few days and forget about marriage. But John had wanted a wife, and being a methodical man, he'd checked out women when he'd gone on the trip east to purchase some breeding rams for the ranch. John had found a breeded ewe for himself, Monroe guessed. As certain as he was that the woman had been going to marry John for his ranch, he was equally certain he would accept her because John had been his friend and partner.

But now John was dead, and Monroe was alone. He thought how he'd pretty well grown up alone, orphaned at five. Only now this seemed hard to take.

The woman rode along beside him and kept bumping up against his shoulder. Roads here weren't anything more than well-traveled tracks, less than that the farther out on the range they got. Nothing like she was used to back in Carolina, that's for sure. Mizzuz Pritchett came from a prominent family, and Monroe thought it somewhat comical that she was riding along with him, because her family probably wouldn't have allowed the people he came from to enter her front door.

They weren't going along five minutes, and she began to chattering. *It was certainly windy down this way... like the sandy beaches were, she'd been there once... Were the trees shaped that way because of the wind?* He said yes. She got the idea and shut up, too.

Olivia thought Monroe about as hard as granite and as prickly as a porcupine with indigestion. He related to his horses with more warmth than he'd given her or the boys. He had agreed to have them under duress, and he certainly wasn't going to make them welcome. And that was the crux of it, she thought a little guiltily. She *had* imposed herself and the boys upon the man. And she was properly sorry, or at least she was trying to be, and she promised herself to be as unobtrusive to Monroe Locket as possible during their stay.

The day had dawned with a cold, blustery wind and clouds spread like a thin coat of pale gray paint. After awhile the clouds had cleared but the cold wind remained. Olivia's wool cape over her traveling suit was barely enough, yet she refused to let on and remained sitting straight and tall. She was relieved that the boys were snug in the rear of the wagon beneath the buffalo robe that Oscar Tucker had provided. Will didn't stay beneath it much; there was too much for him to see.

All around them the land stretched as tan and coarse as a potato sack, so very startlingly different from her home back in Carolina. The blackjack and post oaks were stumpy, as if sun-parched and wind-worn. Occasionally, in low areas, they came upon groves of what Olivia thought of as 'real' trees—cottonwoods, sycamores, willows. But there were no kingly pines. A few scrubby cedars and an occasional patriarchal live oak provided the only green. Every so often a bird fluttered or called, but mostly it was as if they'd decided to hide out. And where at home there were always scents—tangy pine, sweet boxwood, winter damp—here the air was completely scentless, as if the wind had come and blown every single smell away.

"Been a dry fall," Monroe Locket said when she commented on it all.

When they rode out of the timber area, the land rolled into grassy hills with winter-bare brush that Monroe Locket called mesquite trees. All of it was near colorless as any dead thing, and as brittle as dried seasonings. In many places the earth shown through, about like skin through ragged holes. There were no neatly plowed fields, no orderly woods, no deliberately formed roads. It was raw and wild, and Olivia thought it beautiful.

Above them the sky stretched wide and seemed close enough to touch, and below stretched land so vast it made Olivia realize how vulnerable and puny she really was. The openness made life seem bigger and grander. Gazing at it all, Olivia felt a quickening inside. She was so very glad to see it after all.

They stopped to rest one time beside a small stream. Monroe Locket hopped down and went straight away to see to his horses. Olivia looked at him. He wasn't going to help her down from the wagon; he hadn't helped her up—Oscar Tucker had.

"Mama, can I go look around?" Will asked eagerly.

"I suppose." She looked at Henry, who was gazing from the wagon, as if contemplating. "Would you like to go with Will?" she asked.

"Guess so."

Will frowned, but then a good-natured smile took its place as he helped his little brother from the wagon. Olivia cautioned them not to go out of sight.

"Bushes can hide us," Henry said seriously, and Will tugged him along.

Awkwardly, in her thick skirts, Olivia climbed to the ground. *There, that would just show that man!* She took a step, wobbled and grabbed hold of the wagon. Every muscle and joint cried out. Then she saw Monroe Locket look her way. She straightened her back and, as gracefully as possible, went to the rear of the wagon to unpack the refreshment Selma Tucker had kindly provided.

Though Monroe Locket made a fire for hot coffee—for which Olivia was heartily grateful, even if it did taste more like muddy water—they didn't linger. In less than an hour, they were packing up to leave again. Will helped with the horses, while Henry, very tired now, remained with her as she packed away the foodstuffs. She tucked Henry beneath the buffalo robe, then climbed up onto the wagon seat, feeling she was learning how to do it.

They hadn't gone a mile when she spotted the pecan trees, two of them, with pecans thick across the ground.

"Oh, stop, Mr. Locket!" she cried, and was jerked forward as he quickly pulled up. "Look—pecans!"

"Ma'am, I don't have time to be fritterin'," the man protested.

But Olivia was already climbing from the seat. "We'll be quick. Will, come on. Henry, you stay in the wagon—keep under that robe. Give me the sack."

She hurriedly dumped the remainder of their food from the tow sack, and she and Will went to scooping pecans off the ground. Will jumped to catch a low-hanging branch and shook it to bring more ripe pecans raining down. The next instant Henry had wriggled down to join them, and they all laughed. As Monroe Locket gazed morosely from the wagon seat, Olivia thought of her private vow not to annoy him. But she simply couldn't pass up these riches.

Will helped Henry into the wagon bed, then together he and Olivia lugged up the sack of pecans. Olivia hurried to get back up on the seat, for she sensed she had sorely tried the man's patience. She took hold, placed her foot on the step and struggled to pull herself up. Suddenly Monroe Locket's hand jutted down and gripped her wrist. His hand was bare, strong, thick veins bulging beneath tanned thick skin. She looked up—into dark, vibrant, beautiful eyes.

For an instant, she froze. Then his hand tugged and, using his strength, she went on up. With him balancing her, she stepped into the box and lowered herself onto the seat. Still, he kept hold of her. She didn't pull away. Then they were staring at each other, Olivia again looking into his vibrant eyes, with irises so dark no pupil showed and rimmed by long, silky lashes. Those eyes seemed to hold a deep, secret wisdom.

Something passed between them. It flickered in his dark eyes and brought a warm, tingling flush over Olivia.

He let go her wrist, and Olivia faced forward. He slipped on his gloves, and Olivia straightened her skirt. He snapped the reins and clucked to the horses, sending the buckboard again bumping along.

Now that they had at last looked at one another, Olivia and Monroe Locket kept looking. Olivia smiled once when catching him sneaking a glance at her, but he didn't smile in return. She didn't sneak her looks so much; she looked openly, or at least as much as she could and not appear improper. Her impression of him changed. Where she had thought him scruffy, she decided he wasn't. He had handsome features beneath that hat—a rather square face, high cheekbones, a straight Greek nose. His mustache was his pride, she thought, because it was thick and full and shaped just so. And normally he shaved the rest of his face, because his beard could be no more than a few day's growth. All in all, there was the sense of a singular man about Monroe Locket.

"How much farther, Mr. Locket?" she asked.

"'Bout an hour as the crow flies...two as the pig walks."

"Are we goin' as the crow or the pig?"

His eyes slanted to her. "The pig." He didn't grin.

Will scooted up behind the seat. "Are those things cactus, Mr. Locket?"

"Yep."

Olivia leaned over and saw the thorny plants here and there, jutting up out of the grass. She'd always thought of cactus as growing out in a desert.

Will asked, "Can you eat those cactus? I've read people can do that."

"I'd advise peelin' it first," Monroe Locket said.

"We don't have any cactus up where we come from, so I haven't seen any before," Will said. "But we got blackjack oaks, like these. We have all kinds of oaks back home—black oaks are real common. Lots of willows, too, and elms, and pines. Look! It was a snake, Mama, but it's gone now."

"Shouldn't snakes be hibernating?" Olivia asked, peering at the ground as if she might see one.

"At home they are. But I just know it was one. Watch out, Henry, or you'll fall out at a good bump. Are snakes out here, Mr. Locket?"

"Can't say I know all."

"What kinda snakes you got down here? Are there a lot of rattlesnakes? We got cottonmouths up there. You got those down here?"

"We got snakes that'll plant you," Monroe Locket said flatly. "Boy, you're 'bout burnin' my ears. Give it a rest, okay?" That shot Olivia up straight, and she tuned up to tell Monroe Locket a thing or two.

But Will said easily, "Sure." He wasn't the least fazed by the morose man.

Olivia realized her son had the right attitude. She had no right to be irritated with Monroe Locket. He had brought them along, when he would rather not have, she thought, reminding herself to try and not be a thorn in his side.

They all rode along in silence. Olivia's thoughts returned to all the plans she had made. A woman's dreams spun in the quiet solitude of night. William had been a good husband, though he had returned ill from the war, and she had spent a good deal of their years together caring for him. Her dreams now sprang from the best parts of those years and the lack in them, too. She imagined herself in a kitchen of her own, cooking for her man. She'd done the cooking at Aunt Cecilia's, but it had been Cecilia's kitchen and home, and Olivia had had to abide by Cecilia's rules, which were many. Olivia imagined cleaning and scrubbing and making beautiful a house for her man and their children. She imagined sharing coffee and the sunrise with her man, imagined walking hand in hand with him while the sun set. She imagined sewing a quilt for their bed. She anticipated sleeping with her man, and she imagined them lying intimate together, touching. She imagined her man as both passionate and gentle. She had told herself she wasn't a young innocent this time. This time she knew what she wanted from a man. This imagined man possessed a strong, healthy body, was of medium height and weight. She knew him to be kind, sturdy and reliable, maybe even a little proud, for such seemed to suit the male species.

Yet, truth be told, her imagined man had never taken on John Carter's face. Not once. He had remained featureless in her mind, as if seen through several layers of cheesecloth, no matter how hard she tried to conjure him.

It was the wagon stopping that brought her out of her deep thoughts. Three riders approached at an easy lope. Olivia's interest quickened. How nice to meet other people!

And then she saw Monroe Locket lift the rifle from its place at his feet. Carefully he laid it across his lap. His hand remained around it, his finger near the trigger. His expression didn't change, remained perfectly stoic, yet there was a sharpness about him, as if he were ready to begin firing in an instant.

Olivia's heartbeat pattered. She checked the boys, seeing Henry curled beneath the buffalo robe and Will watching eagerly.

The men pulled their horses up quickly, aggressively. They were, like Monroe Locket himself, very Texan, with wide-brimmed hats, heavy leather coats and boots. They wore, as well, leather coverings over their legs. One of the men moved his coat to reveal a gun on his hip, and Olivia knew he'd done it deliberately. During the war, even some after it, Olivia had seen such hardened men. But not at all these last years in quiet Cherry Creek, where the only time a man had a gun was when he went hunting.

"Howdy, Locket." The man in the middle spoke; he seemed in charge. Shifting his gaze to Olivia, he touched his hat. "Ma'am."

Olivia nodded politely. She noted him as a little past middle age and with a hint of the gentleman about him. Yet he didn't introduce himself, and Monroe Locket made no offer to do so, either, which definitely was a lack of manners.

The man's eyes focused hard on Monroe Locket. He leaned on his saddle horn and said, "Heard about John Carter. I never wish a man misfortune, and I'm sorry about your loss."

Monroe Locket simply nodded. The two gazed at each other. The animosity was thick as dark sorghum.

"Heard you and John brought in rams now, and you're goin' into the woolly business in a big, permanent way."

"Big and permanent as life, I guess."

The other man smiled thinly. "Might not be too permanent then, eh?" He shifted in his saddle. "We're all cattlemen up here, Locket, and you knew that full well. You're askin' for trouble, bringin' woollies in here."

"I paid for my land, same as you Burnham, or anybody else. What I raise ain't nobody's book but my own."

The man called Burnham narrowed his eyes. "You're passin' on my land now, Locket, and that's okay. But I'm not likely to let you pass a herd of those woollies over my grass—and neither are my neighbors. You're gonna have a hard road to market."

"A lot of what you and a few others keep callin' *your place* is free range, and I have as much right to it as anyone."

"Lew Jones's section isn't free range."

"He ain't wrote from up north to say I can't use it."

The man stared hard at Monroe Locket. "I was here first, Locket, and I intend to fight for my cattle... if I have to. And every other rancher around feels the same. If we have to, we'll run you right out of here. Even if it's in a pine box."

That stopped Olivia's breath in the back of her throat.

Monroe Locket took so long to answer that it seemed everyone was holding their breath. Then he spoke low and cold. "I'm not takin' anything from you or anybody else. But if you want to try and run me out or bury me under, you go ahead. I don't think you're gonna find it too easy." The next instant he clucked to the horses and snapped the reins, sending the team out smart and Olivia grabbing hold of the seat. He gave no backward glance.

Olivia did. With her heartbeat skipping over her ribs, she twisted to see if the riders were going to come after them. But they raced away in the opposite direction. She looked at Monroe Locket's hard-set profile. "That man threatened you—and it certainly sounded like bodily harm."

"It was."

"Because of sheep?"

"I think it's more because they ain't cattle, and I ain't a cattleman."

Olivia puzzled over that, and Will said, "I guess we'd better keep a lookout for them comin' back."

Monroe Locket said, "Always need to keep an eye peeled in this country, boy."

Olivia didn't like the sound of either statement. "Those men don't like sheep?"

"Nope."

"For heaven's sake, why should they not like sheep?"

"They're cattlemen."

"I'm sorry, Mr. Locket, but that answer doesn't serve. Why should this Mr. Burnham care if you raise sheep?"

Monroe cut his eyes to her. "Didn't John explain any of this to you, ma'am, when he asked you out here?"

"Well . . . he said there was some conflict with some neighbors over use of the land, but he acted as if it were of small consequence."

"John was a solid man, but he did have a habit of lookin' on the bright side of everything," Monroe

Locket said. Just when Olivia was about to prod him
for an explanation, he spoke. "Cattlemen make up all
kinds of reasons for not likin' sheep, but in this case it
has to do with the misguided beliefs that the critters
smell, kill the grass, and spoil waterin' holes...plus the
fact that I was a blue-belly in the war; Albert Burnham and the rest were Dixie-singers."

Olivia pondered that for a moment. "John said you
were a Tennessean, Mr. Locket."

He cut his eyes to her. "Yes, ma'am. So's Albert
Burnham."

"I see." And she did, all too clearly. It was the same
bitter, life-choking nonsense that she had hoped to
escape by coming to Texas. Apparently there was no
escape. "The war's been over for ten years," she
murmured to no one in particular.

"Yes, ma'am, it has," Monroe Locket said quietly,
his eyes straight ahead.

Henry popped up. "Mama, I have to go potty."

Olivia's small watch pin read almost two o'clock by
the time the ranch buildings came into sight. She
strained to see, her spirit suddenly soaring with relief
and gratitude. The end of the horrible journey at last.
Thank you, God!

The structures were grouped in a glen of willows,
cottonwoods and a grand live oak. John had said they
had a spring. From John's description, she placed
each building. The largest, of stone and log, was the
barn, with a number of corrals surrounding it. Behind it, where she couldn't see, would be another lean-
to for sheep. The next building in size, also of stone
and log, was the house. It was really two separate

structures connected by a dogtrot. That was what John had called the porch in between. She could clearly tell that one half of it was newer than the other—it was the cabin John had built for her and the boys. Then there was a small log dwelling, a hut for hands. And the privy. There were more than a dozen horses in the corrals, a cow beneath a tree, and chickens about the yard, but Olivia didn't see any sheep.

"Where are the sheep?" she asked.

"Out eatin'," Monroe Locket said. "Pretty hard to keep four thousand sheep penned up."

Olivia couldn't imagine that many sheep. John had never told her.

A small, shaggy and mottled dog came racing forward, greeting them with happy barks.

"Hi, Belle," Monroe Locket said, and there was actually a warmth in his voice.

"I'm gonna walk the rest of the way." Will jumped from the wagon before Olivia could advise caution. The dog pranced and ran with him.

"I wanna go, too!" Henry cried, but Olivia wouldn't let him jump from the moving wagon, and the man made no offer to stop.

Olivia gazed at the ranch buildings. It was all so primitive compared to the home she'd grown up in, her family's elegant plantation home, Wild Cherry. Or even the smaller white house she'd shared with William after the war. And Cecilia's and Phillip's house on Main Street was a grand mansion by any standard. The elegance of it flashed in stark contrast through her mind.

However, as Monroe Locket pulled the wagon to a halt in front of the house, she thought there was something uniquely beautiful about this place. Its beauty lay in the solidity of it, the peace of it.

A man waited for them. He was old, a Mexican man, with leathery skin and a curious but friendly smile. He helped Olivia from the wagon. "*Buenos días, señora*... Hello..." he said, his eyes sparkling. "Welcome."

"Thank you, Mister..."

"Luis." He bowed slightly, then moved to help with the unloading.

Henry dropped to the ground from the rear of the wagon and ran to join Will. Olivia called a caution. Trying to find strength for her weak, shaking legs, she moved beneath the porch. Sandy dirt floor here. The door to the cabin on her left stood open, revealing a wooden floor inside and a large iron stove connected to a stone fireplace chimney at the far end. The stove's firebox was open, and the flames inside danced merrily. She gazed at the fire, the warm room, and every fiber of her being longed to go inside. But the knowledge that she was a stranger here, an uninvited guest, brought a sudden, stark shyness.

"This is the place John built for you and the boys," Monroe Locket said gruffly, drawing her attention.

Carrying two of her bags, he pushed open the door of the opposite cabin and went inside. Olivia followed. He plopped her bags beside a bed built into the far corner. It was covered with a multicolored quilt, roughly made, yet clean and bright. There were two small pillows of blue striped ticking.

Monroe Locket indicated a skinny tree-limb ladder. "There's a loft...couple of rope beds up there for the young'ns. Hope you brought blankets."

Olivia nodded absently.

The room was half the size of the bedroom she'd had at Cecilia's. It had chinked log walls, a split-rail floor and a rock fireplace at the end. There were two windows, with small but true glass panes, a rather rough dresser and a lovely rocking chair. Glancing around, Olivia thought this place was rough and crude, but as solid as the ground upon which it stood. And it would have been her own. She was so glad to have come to see it.

The man started toward the door.

"Mr. Locket!" Olivia called and waited for him to turn. "Thank you, sir, with all my heart."

He gazed at her, his eyes dark and intense. For a long moment, they looked at each other. Olivia felt a warmth rush over her, hard, fast, and urging.

"I have to ride out to check my flocks," he said tersely. "Luis will be here to look out for you and the boys. You should have everything you need in the main cabin." He indicated the cabin across the dog-trot with a bending of his head.

"We shall be quite comfortable," Olivia said.

With a nod, he turned and left.

She hurried to the door. She watched him walk in long, firm strides to the barn. He appeared to be hurrying *away* from her more than *toward* anything that was calling him.

Twenty minutes later, through the window, she saw him riding away, trailing a packhorse. He had not stopped to tell her goodbye. Though of course there was no reason why he should.

Chapter Four

Luis was still at the table working with leather in the murky glow of an oil lamp when Olivia came into the cabin, bringing what was left of Henry's ginseng tea and the bowl of water she'd been bathing him with.

"Are you stayin' up all night, Luis?"

He smiled faintly. "I sleep little these days of my old age. And I stay here tonight, while Señor Monroe is gone, to be near if needed. How is the small one?"

"Sleepin', finally. The fever turned an hour ago."

She cleaned the cup and emptied the water from the bowl, setting both neatly on the sideboard. They were her own rose-blossom china; they looked pretty, all white and shiny against the darkly stained sideboard. She ran a hand over the smooth, burnished wood that caught the low glimmer of the lamps. It was a plain piece, but very finely crafted.

"Do you know where Mr. Carter or Mr. Locket got this, Luis?"

He looked up from his leather working and nodded. "*Oh, sí, señora.* Señor Mon-roe, he make that. And the rocker, too," he said, with a wave, indicating the rocking chair sitting beside the great iron stove. It was exactly like the one in the cabin Olivia and the boys were sharing. "He like to do the woodworking. Señor John, he do the big things—the barn, your cabin. Señor Monny, he make the fine things—the doors an' furniture. Is nice, no?"

"It's very nice." Olivia ran her gaze over the room, noting the squared windowsills and doors, the plain but well made furniture. Wearily she lowered herself into the rocking chair, testing its bottom and finding it lovely. She rested her head back and rocked. Monroe Locket knew what he was about in rocker building, she thought, for the chair moved smoothly. She recalled his big, rough hands and wondered that they could craft such lovely things.

"The *señors* were a good pair," Luis said thoughtfully, his gaze on the leather strips he worked. "Señor John, he plan for all the big things—Señor Monny, he handle the little details. Señor John have the idea to bring thousands of sheep up here from the south to build a biiig ranch." He spread his arms. "Señor Monny, he handle all the little things of doing it—the food, the herders, the trail to follow. They good together. Señor Monny misses Señor John, and he mad at the world now." He nodded sadly.

Olivia thought of John. Though she could not recall his face, she could remember his goodness, and her heart ached for things that could have been. And, she thought with sudden clarity, if she could miss what could have been, how much more Monroe Locket must miss what actually had been. Great pity for him touched her.

"I make this for Señor Monny," Luis said, and held up the braided leather.

"That's beautiful work, Luis." She peered closer. "I've never seen such work. What will it be?"

"A bridle... It is a craft of my people. I learn from my father, and he learn from his. I make it for Señor Monny's Christmas, to cheer him." After a pause, he lifted his eyes to Olivia. "Your coming will cheer him, too. He thinks not, in his anger, but it will. And me, too. You make wonderful soft breads—bis-gets." He smiled broadly. "Good, like Señor John used to make. Señor Monny, he love those."

"Oh, he does?"

Luis bobbed his head with seriousness. "You make a bunch, and we will all have a little peace around here."

During Monroe Locket's absence, Olivia put her energy into cleaning and dressing the cabin that had been inhabited only by men, who gave little thought to such things. She settled in like a happy swallow in a season's nest, never mind that at the end of this short season, she would leave. For this short time, the cabin needed her, and she needed to be needed.

The cabin's store of dishes was meager, so Olivia brought a few pieces of her own from her trunk and arranged everything neatly in the small area kitchen. She scrubbed the floors and polished Monroe Locket's furniture to a high sheen. She washed the tiny windows, and she whipped up curtains for the windows with the extra calico she had brought; nothing fancy, just something to add color and brightness. Something to leave when she was gone. She hoped, too, to please Monroe Locket with all that she did. He would see she was a capable woman, not a bit of weak fluff that was of no use.

Why she should care what he thought gave her pause.

Each day Will shadowed Luis and joined in helping to do the chores, getting mini-lessons in Spanish while he was at it. Henry spent most of the first day in bed, and much of the second day playing with the dog. He'd never had a dog so close before; Cecilia hadn't allowed one for fear of disease.

Preparations got under way for their Christmas celebration, too. This year they were to have a tree. Will could recall having a tree, but Henry could not, for such was another thing Cecilia forbade. Luis said other *Americanos* of the region used the green cedar. Olivia and the boys planned to decorate it with ribbons, cookies, and figures formed of flour clay. The second evening after arriving, when Henry was better, Olivia brought out the large lump of 'clay' she had made from flour, salt and water, and she and the boys began forming stars, sheep, angels—anything they could think of. Even Luis joined them. Olivia was in charge of making the angel for the treetop, though she received numerous 'suggestions' from the boys. The figures were left on the edge of the stove to bake and harden overnight.

They were happy, the three of them, with their new friend Luis. It was as if they were vacationers on an island of perfect dreams. It was, Olivia thought, a time of perhaps coming as close as she ever would to her private dream, and she would enjoy it.

It was with Monroe Locket in mind that Olivia made biscuits each morning and evening and watched for his return. He came on the evening of the third day, he and his horses black silhouettes against a fiery setting sun. She recognized him instantly by the easy way he sat in the saddle. Luis and Will ran to meet him.

"Come on, honey," Olivia said to Henry. "You can set a place for Mr. Locket."

Her skirts swirling with her movements, she got the plate and utensils for Henry, then pulled biscuits from the oven, poured a cup of coffee and set it beside Monroe Locket's plate at the end of the table where the large chair sat. She was running a last survey over the table when he appeared in the doorway.

He looked at her, and she looked at him.

His beard was thicker, full and black, and the whole of him, from his battered hat to his worn boots, was covered with a sheen of dust. He held a rifle at his side. But it was his eyes, dark and beautiful, that captured her attention—and caused her to run a hand up to her hair, tucking loose wisps back into place.

"Welcome, Mr. Locket."

The woman stood there, looking as shy and uncertain as a schoolgirl. Something tugged inside Monroe. He'd put off returning for an extra day because of that stirring he felt deep inside whenever he looked at her.

Monroe nodded to her. "Hullo." He set his rifle aside, removed his hat and coat, and hung them on the hook. Then his eyes took in the room. There were curtains at the window, and the window glass was so clean as to not be there at all. Everything was clean, even the oil lamps. The table had white china plates on it, all neatly set with white cloth napkins, none of it belonging to him. Didn't hardly seem like his home, as if he'd been swept clean away with the dust.

The woman stepped forward to the corner of the table. "I've made lamb stew from meat in the storeroom." She paused, then added, "And biscuits, too."

"Sounds good," he allowed. He'd smelled the tantalizing aromas on the way in, and his mouth was already anticipating the taste, though he wouldn't have said. Furtively he looked at her.

"I have warm water for you to wash in," she told him, nodding toward the basin. "And that towel's for you."

As if he'd needed coaxing to wash, he thought sharply. He might be a backwoods hill boy, but he knew about washing. Though he didn't usually go to the trouble of heating water to do it. He wasn't about to remove his shirt, not with the woman there, but he did roll up his sleeves. The warm water felt good. She stood at the stove, stirring the stew, and he felt her glances. It was awkward.

When he'd finished drying his face, she said, "I've poured you coffee," and pointed at a steaming cup at the end of the table.

He moved slowly to sit. At least she'd put the coffee in his enameled mug. It was good coffee, too. And then she brought the bowl of steaming biscuits to set right in front of his plate. He started to tell her the coffee was good, but stopped. He didn't want to start getting all friendly. The woman was as different from him as day from night. And she was only staying a few weeks.

Still, the brew relaxed him. He sat back and watched her move. She was a plain woman, but all woman, and she moved with an unconscious sway of her hips. Suddenly realizing the warmth swirling in his groin, Monroe averted his eyes.

Will and Luis came in, lugging a large, cloth-wrapped bundle between them. One of three sheep carcasses Mr. Locket had brought back, Will informed Olivia as they went into the stone-walled back room to stick it in a barrel with salt. They would bring in the other two after supper, he said, chattering all the while he and Luis washed and even as they took their places at the table. He was full of himself, feeling strong and grown here, surrounded by strong, grown men. Olivia didn't pay him much attention until she heard, "What are you gonna do about them killin' your sheep, Mr. Locket?"

She plopped the jar of honey she was carrying to the table. Monroe Locket looked over his coffee cup at her.

"Some sheep were killed?" Olivia asked.

"They killed twenty-five out of one flock," Will said, proud to do it. "Came in and shot up the camp, caved in the roof of the shepherd's hut. They're tryin' to run Mr. Locket off—like the Yankees done us."

"Will!" Olivia said sharply. "That war is over and done."

"Can't rightly point the finger at exactly whose doin' the damage," Monroe Locket drawled, looking straight at Will. "Let's just say we got some men runnin' around pesterin' my flocks as a way of makin' their point. Now they've made it, I doubt we'll have any more killin' of sheep. Are we ready to eat, ma'am? My stomach thinks my throat's been cut."

Will opened his mouth, and Olivia shushed him, took a seat beside Henry and bowed her head for prayer. Silence fell over the table. She peeked at Monroe Locket and saw him staring at them all. The boys and Luis had their heads bowed deeply. Olivia closed her eyes. "Bless this food to the nourishment of our bodies, and thank you, Lord."

When she lifted her head, Monroe Locket had a biscuit in hand and was dipping honey upon it. His eyes came up to meet hers. "Where'd the honey come from?" he asked.

"I brought it from home."

His eyes lingered on hers before returning to the plate in front of him.

As they ate, Will again brought up the subject of the sheep killing. Monroe Locket sidestepped the issue with a bland comment and then went on to tell about some Indians he'd seen while out on the range. Soon he had Luis telling stories of the 'old days,' getting himself off the hook so that he didn't have to talk much at all.

He ate two helpings of stew, five biscuits with honey and an enormous bowl of bread pudding, and finished it all off with three cups of coffee, with honey added to that, too. Olivia felt she'd learned a valuable secret in discovering Monroe Locket had a very strong sweet tooth.

After the meal, Olivia cleared the table, Luis and Will saw to the sheep carcasses, and Henry fiddled with the flour clay at the table. Monroe Locket lounged in his chair at the far end of the table, rolling himself a cigarette. More than once her eyes met his through the thin silver smoke twirling up from his cigarette.

It came to her with startling clarity that he was looking at her as a man looks at a woman. It had been a long time since anyone had looked at her like that. Or perhaps it had been a long time since she had *noticed* anyone looking at her like that.

"Could you turn that lamp up, Mr. Locket?" she heard Henry ask. "I can't hardly see my star."

She glanced around to see Monroe Locket lift the lamp from where it hung on the single tree above and set it to the table near Henry. "Does that suit ya, boy?"

"Yes, and my name's Henry," Henry said quite righteously.

Olivia smiled. Her youngest was small, and so quiet most paid him little attention, but he could make himself known when he wished.

"My brother's name is Will. You should call us by our names, like we do you."

At that Olivia whirled to scold, but clamped her mouth shut as she saw Henry lifting the flour-clay star he was working on, showing it proudly.

"I'm makin' a star. See? We already made five, and now we got to paint 'em. We're gonna hang 'em on the tree."

Olivia returned her hands and eyes to the wash-basin, but tuned her ears to the two at the table.

"What tree?" Monroe Locket said.

"A Christmas tree. Don't you know 'bout Christmas trees?"

"Yeah . . . I heard of 'em."

"Have you ever seen one?" Henry asked pointedly.

Out of the corner of her eye, she saw Monroe Locket nod. "One or two."

"You never had one?" Henry asked, clearly astonished.

"Never had occasion," Monroe Locket said.

She glanced at him, then returned to scrubbing the skillet. The legs of his chair scraped the floor, and she whirled around. Their eyes met.

He said, "I'd best go see to night chores." He took up his coat, hat and rifle, and left.

Olivia returned to scrubbing her pan that no longer needed it, and thought of how Monroe Locket had looked at her. His looks had reminded her that she was more than a widow with two children. His looks had reminded her that she was a woman, with all the wildly rippling rivers of womanly hopes and dreams flowing through her.

John's gazes hadn't done that. No one's gazes had done that in an awfully long time.

And then she tossed aside her rag with high annoyance. Right now she did not need to be reminded of her womanliness! Not now, when there was no answer for any of it!

Olivia was alone in the main room; Luis had gone to his hut, and the boys were snug in their loft.

Carefully she damped the fire in the iron stove for the night, making certain live coals would be left for morning. She left the coffeepot on the hottest part of the stove in case Monroe Locket wanted more before bed. Quickly, and almost furtively, she pulled three leftover biscuits from where she'd slipped them in the sideboard, wrapped them in a slightly damp cloth, placed them in a clean pan and set them near the coffeepot. Lastly, she placed the flour-clay stars and rather misshapen sheep she and Henry had made that evening at the edges of the stove.

Then she lingered, finding little things to keep her, enjoying the silence and neatness of the room. And waiting, too, for Monroe Locket to return.

She had just decided he was spending the night outside when the door opened. "I waited to speak with you, Mr. Locket," she said quickly.

He set his rifle aside. "Yes, ma'am." He smacked his hat on the hook and shrugged out of his coat.

Olivia wet her lips. "I wanted to tell you how much I appreciate you letting us stay these days. Henry is much improved. And Will is having the time of his life. It has been good for us all to have the opportunity to see the place John and I had made so many plans for. To have come so far and not seen this place... Well, I'm glad I could see it. Thank you for allowing us to come."

Her fulsome appreciation made him feel absurdly proud and awkward at the same time. He gave a small smile as he crossed to the stove. "Ma'am, I don't think I did much *allowing*. You had taken the studs and were set to come, and I had education enough to azzle out of your way." He poured himself a cup of coffee and then looked up to see her gazing at him with amusement.

"You do have a most colorful way of speaking, Mr. Locket."

"Southern hill talk, ma'am."

Her eyes lingered on his, and he saw understanding there. There was a lot more to this highfalutin woman than he'd thought at first. His gaze drifted to her breasts, and then he saw her catch him at that. She didn't look away though, pretending. Not this woman; she looked him full in the face.

She said, "Good night, Mr. Locket," in the fashion of a woman to the manor born.

"Good night, Mizzuz Pritchett."

Inside her own cabin, Olivia closed the door and leaned against it for a moment, then moved to stare into the low-flickering flames of the fire. She understood what was happening between herself and Monroe Locket as attraction, but it all seemed so unfathomable. Monroe Locket was certainly different from John Carter. Different from William, by a long shot. Different from any man she had ever known.

He was . . . well, he was coarse, in a way. Her eyes moved to settle on the warm patina of the rocking chair's arms. Wood that Monroe Locket had shaped so finely, and with great care. Certainly not coarsely. She thought again of how he had gazed at her, and a vibration shimmied down to swirl in the intimate parts of her. She put a hand to her flaming cheeks. For so long, she had shut away these feelings. Damn him for waking them! She would not have such a man as he— not by a long shot!

The next instant, a strange sound jarred her out of her musing—a deep roar. It was the muffled sound of Monroe Locket bellowing, "Mizzuz Pritchett!"

Before she could reach the door, he was pounding on it. She yanked it open. "Mr. Locket, my children—"

"Mizzuz Pritchett!" He loomed over her, and she shut her mouth. "You can be busy as a bee in a bottle all over this place—the cabin, the barn, the privy, even Luis's place. They can all be your play-pretties in the remaining days you are here. But by damn, leave my sleepin' quarters alone!" His voice was like a powerful crescendo.

"But I only cleaned—"

"I don't want it cleaned! I want it left be! Do you understand?"

Olivia swallowed and nodded.

"Good." He strode back across to the opposite cabin.

Olivia said quietly, "But you needn't shout about it, sir. All you needed to do was tell me."

Monroe Locket stopped in the doorway of his cabin and stiffened. Olivia thought, if it was a fight he wanted, she could give him one as rich as her biscuits. However, without turning to look at her, he entered his cabin and closed the door with a solid thud.

"Mama, what's goin' on?" Will called from the loft.

Olivia told him to shush and go back to sleep. She was too worn out for white-washed motherly explanations. As she lay in bed, a great astonishment stole over her. She could not recall speaking to anyone in the past four years with as much spirit as she had spoken to Monroe Locket. She had heard that people who came out here grew stronger.

The sheet beneath Monroe was crisp and smelled of sunshine, as did the wool blankets covering him. The woman was taking off quite a bit more than he'd offered, to his mind. She'd come in here, acting like this was her place. Like she intended to make it her place. Well, if she thought he'd step in for John, she might as well think again!

Though why in the world she might think that was beyond him. Surely she couldn't want this lowly cabin and way of life that much. That just didn't add up. John had said she came from a fine home and fine people back in North Carolina. She hadn't been destitute.

Olivia Pritchett was a lady born and bred. Monroe hadn't often been around her kind, though he'd seen enough in his time to recognize one when he saw her. Maybe such as Olivia Pritchett had fit with John, who after all had been a tuckyhoe Virginian from a solid family. But such wasn't the kind for a poor orphan boy from the backwoods.

Dawn was a rose glow when Olivia moved across the dogtrot to the main room. The air was sharp, but the clear sky and the faint scent of moist earth promised a warming. Timidly she rapped on the door. When there was no answer, she lifted the latch, feeling as hesitant and unwelcome as a mouse in church and with the urge to run right back to her own room and stay there until it was time to return to Esperar. However, between now and then she and the children had to eat.

Monroe Locket wasn't there. A pot of coffee sat on the hot stove. It was fresh. Two of the three biscuits she had left were gone. Olivia smiled at that and poured herself a cup of coffee.

She carried it to the window. The sky was like glass, and the golden glow of a rising sun made black silhouettes of the barn, trees and shrubs. She saw Monroe Locket then—a bulky black silhouette far out at the edge of the grass, standing before John's grave. His head and shoulders were bowed, as if from a great weight. Everything about him said loneliness.

Olivia watched him until he strode away to the barn. Then she pulled her shawl tight, took up a cup and strode off to get buttermilk from the cool box kept in the spring. She would need buttermilk to make fresh biscuits for breakfast.

Chapter Five

Monroe Locket was a reticent man and said very little that day to anyone, as far as Olivia could see. He did, however, eat plenty of her biscuits, at both breakfast and supper. She didn't make any for midday dinner, for she didn't want to wear a good thing out. At each of the meals, Luis made a point of complimenting her on her biscuits. "Umm-mmm, señora. You make the best bis-gets in the world. Doesn't she, *patrón?*" he said to Monroe Locket, who answered with a simple nod.

Later that morning, with her hands already scrubbing shirts in the washtub, Olivia told Monroe Locket she'd gladly wash his clothes, as she was doing Luis's, if he'd bring them to her. "It's a warm day. I'll do your long-handles, too, if you want." He went into the back room and returned with three pairs of trousers, five shirts, numerous socks, and his long underwear that he'd just removed, giving them to her with a mumbled and red-faced "Thank you." She discovered she'd bit off another job, too, because there was plenty of mending to be done on his clothes.

Will tagged after Monroe Locket and Luis, and Olivia allowed it, but Henry she kept near. He helped her clean and bake Christmas bread and wash clothes, and then he played with the black-and-white dog. When the sound of hammering came from behind the barn, he wanted to go see what it was about. He grabbed Olivia's hand, pleading, "Hurry, Mama... hurry..."

Behind the barn, at the far end of one of the corrals, they found Will and Luis digging a trench nearly three feet wide and so far about a foot deep. The earth was so hard they had to pick at it. Monroe Locket worked off to the side, building something with wooden planks.

"We're makin' a dippin' vat," Will told her. "Mr. Locket's sheep have scab, and they have to be dipped." Then he went on to tell how they were going to make a long vat to hold the dipping solution that the sheep would run through. "All the sheep are gonna have to be brought up." His young face was eager beneath his wide-brimmed, low-crowned hat that was no longer the neat head covering he'd worn to town back home.

Henry wanted to stay with his brother and the men, but Olivia wouldn't allow it. She was afraid he would get hurt somehow. "You come with me and help me bring back cool water for them to drink," she cajoled. As they walked to the spring, Henry spied mistletoe high up in the branches of the live oak tree. "We'll have Will get it for us later," Olivia promised.

"And a tree, too. We gotta get a tree."

"We'll get a tree, honey. It's too early yet, though."

That evening at supper, he asked Monroe Locket, "Does it ever snow here?"

Monroe Locket, who'd barely said two words during the meal, finally said, "Once in awhile."

"Does it get deep?"

The man clearly hadn't expected another question. He swallowed and said, "Not much more than ankle-high. Sometimes we get a blizzard and drifts waist-high. It'll come a killin' cold for a day or two, then warms up and melts off."

"Do you think it'll snow for Christmas?"

"I don't know all, boy."

"My name is Henry."

"And it's a button-poppin' name," Monroe Locket replied, surprising them all.

The following morning, just after Olivia pulled two pans of biscuits from the oven, Monroe Locket said he was riding out to the flocks. He pocketed two of the biscuits and said he would return in time for supper that night. Olivia was annoyed by his high-handed manner in grabbing the biscuits and running off, but then she had to chuckle at herself for her imagined governorship over both her breads and Monroe Locket—and at Monroe Locket for making certain he got breakfast biscuits before he left.

The day was a near repeat of the previous one, with all of them working until the middle of the afternoon, when Luis called for a siesta and Olivia for naps. Will protested that he was too old for a nap, but Olivia said she intended to have one, so he would get a rest, also.

She enjoyed thirty minutes of true sleep, awoke feeling chipper as a spring bird, and went across to the main cabin to plan the evening meal. She was just checking the crock of milk when she heard a shout. It was actually no more than a sharp, fear-filled yip, but Olivia's motherly ears tuned. Something told her it was Will, though she didn't quite believe it. Every sense alert, she walked out the door to look around the yard. The cry sounded again at the same instant she saw the shiny bay horse running around the large corral, with Will atop it, flopping around like a rag doll.

Her heart leapt up into her throat, and for an instant she froze. The bay horse ran, and Will pulled on the reins, hollering, "Whoa! Whoa!"

Olivia broke into a run for the corral. "Will! I'm comin', Will! I'm comin'!" she called, not fully aware of what she said or even what she would do, simply knowing she would do something. She slipped between the corral rails, and too late she realized she was waving a towel as she went. The horse, eyes rolling, veered. He slowed for an instant, and she thought he was going to stop, but he simply sprinted off again along the corral rail. Olivia saw that one of the reins was dragging the ground. Will was hanging on to the saddle horn and bouncing as if on some crazed spring.

She lifted her skirts and raced after the two. "Will! Will!"

But there was no way to catch the horse in the huge corral. As reality broke through, she stumbled to a stop, chest heaving and heart pounding, her mind and eyes casting frantically about for some way to stop the horse.

Then she saw Monroe Locket vaulting over the corral fence. Olivia started shouting for him to get back up on his damn horse and save her son before he was killed—or words to that effect.

Monroe Locket didn't bother with a horse. He put himself in the path of the steaming locomotive of a horse, and when the animal slowed and veered, he lunged for the horse's head and grabbed him by the bridle. Stock-still and openmouthed, Olivia watched as Monroe Locket seemed to flutter in the air like a leaf and then was skimming the ground like a flat rock across smooth water. The horse, with Monroe Locket and Will still attached, came at last to a stop at the corral fence.

Monroe stiffly picked himself up. His heart pounded ninety miles an hour, and he was painfully reminded of the bayonet he'd taken in the leg during the war, and that he wasn't eighteen any longer. Then he saw the woman running toward them, dish towel flying. The horse's eyes rolled, and Monroe grabbed the rein with one hand and held a hand to the woman with the other. "Don't run."

She stopped, then came forward slowly. Her chest was heaving. Her frantic eyes fell on the boy, who was quivering like a plucked bowstring. His mother took hold of his leg. "Will? Oh, Will."

The boy looked like any boy who might be looking at the painful end of a switch. "I'm sorry, Mama... I'm sorry, Mr. Locket. I just wanted to show ya I could ride."

"Well, you picked a hell of a horse to do it on," Monroe muttered. And yet he was proud of the boy. This boy knew how to turn a hand to most anything, and when he didn't know, he jumped in and tried anyway.

"I thought he seemed friendly.... He let me catch him up, and all...." The boy's voice quavered.

"Never mind," Olivia Pritchett said, finding her crisp voice again. "We can handle scolding later. Just get down now." She reached to help him.

"Stay up there, boy," Monroe commanded.

The woman whirled on him. "He most certainly will not."

"If he gets down now, the horse will have won, and the boy will always hold a doubt inside." This was where a man's hand was needed, and Monroe wondered if the woman could understand that.

"He's *my* son," she said.

Monroe looked up at the boy. "What do you want to do, Will?"

Will's eyes skittered to his mother. It was as if he were trying to hold together the ragged edges of his spirit. "I wanna try, Mama," he said in a voice filled to brimming with fear.

Monroe watched Olivia Pritchett do battle with her motherly fears. Then, back straight as a plumb line and gripping the towel, she stepped back out of the way. Monroe thought it was probably one of the hardest things she'd ever done. He had the odd urge to touch her, to console her somehow, but there was no way he could.

He led the horse, with the boy still on top, away into the adjoining small, round pen. Olivia Pritchett followed, stood and looked over the board fence with wide, worried eyes.

Monroe positioned the reins in Will's hand and adjusted the stirrups all the way up for his shorter legs. Then he began instruction, patiently, quietly. The boy listened closely and soon had the horse walking around the edge of the pen. "I'm doin' it!" he cried with a wide grin.

"Sure you are," Monroe said, knowing exactly the way the boy felt. He looked around to see Olivia Pritchett walking away toward the house. She'd made it through, too.

The following morning, when Olivia entered the main room, she found Monroe Locket sitting at the table. She hadn't expected that. Each of the previous mornings when she'd come in he'd had his coffee— and her leftover biscuits—and had already gone out to begin chores, as if by unspoken agreement he was leaving the cabin for her.

She stopped in the doorway. "I'm sorry, Mr. Locket, I didn't mean to disturb you." And she started to back out.

But he said quickly, "You're not. Come in. I, uh, got coffee made, and I've already milked the cow, so there's fresh milk." Then he returned his attention to the book opened before him on the table.

Olivia crossed the room, poured her coffee and dipped a bit of the milk into it. When she turned, her eyes lit upon Monroe Locket's powerful, virile hand, curved absently around his cup, which she saw contained as much milk as it did coffee. Her eyes lingered on that hand. His head came up, and their eyes met. Fearful of him reading her sensuous thoughts in her eyes, Olivia whipped around and pulled out the flour bin. Of course, she thought, it was her imagination that his gaze lingered on her.

Monroe Locket spoke. "I think you're gonna find you bit off a lot to chew in comin' out here, ma'am.

The first flock will be up this evenin', and we'll start dippin' tomorrow. We gotta make hay while this weather holds—and do a lot of prayin', 'cause if we get cold comin' down, I'm likely to lose half my herd. We'll be workin' from first light to last, and you'll have at least one more man and two more dogs to feed every day.''

"There was a time, Mr. Locket, when I cooked for my husband, a hired hand, the children, two grandparents and three aging friends, *and* any traveler my husband happened to invite. I think I can manage.'' She dipped flour onto the surface of the sideboard. She felt his gaze, but didn't look around, not wanting him to know she felt anything at all. However, when minutes ticked past, and he said nothing more, Olivia ventured, "What exactly is scab, Mr. Locket?"

"It's a disgustin' affliction that causes boils and open sores and the fleece to shred off the sheep about like skin off a snake." She turned to see him rake his fingers roughly through his hair. "You see, those rascals who've been comin' in and shootin' up my sheep camps have used that as an opportunity to drop in scrubs already infested with scab. They knew it'd be a job to shoot all my sheep—and none of 'em were mean enough they wanted to slaughter meaninglessly. So they figured if they could ruin my wool crop, they'd make me go bust, and I'd have to give up."

"And why don't you?" she asked. "Why don't you give up? Those men infect your sheep, they *kill* your sheep. And they surely sounded as if they might come after you next."

He shook his head, and his jawline tightened. "What I got here is mine, and I'll keep it. A man tends to feel that way about something he's built up from nothin'." His tone implied that she had no idea of what he spoke.

"My father didn't build his home from nothing, but he loved it just the same," Olivia said sharply. "And he burnt up in that home." His eyes came round to hers. "General Sherman didn't stop at Atlanta, you know. He came right up through the Carolinas, and he destroyed everything in his path. Don't you dare act like I don't know about buildin' and losin' and buildin' again, Mr. Locket."

His eyes searched hers. "I understand how your father felt," he said quietly.

"I understand how he felt, but I also understand that if he'd not been so proud and determined, he would have been with us to help us stay alive."

They stared at one another, and Olivia refused to give.

Monroe returned his eyes to the book in front of him. It was hard to get his words out. "I'm assumin' you can read, Mizzuz Pritchett."

"Yes." She nodded and glanced at the book, perplexed by the question.

He swallowed and made himself look into her eyes. "Well, I can't. I did good to put down John's words on that paper I gave you—and he told me the spellin'. John always did the readin' for this outfit.... I can pick out some things, but it's important that I have the formula for the dip right. If I don't, we can burn our hands and kill the sheep. I got two shepherds that can read—one in Mexican, the other in Basque, which gives them pleasure but don't feather my nest. I'd appreciate it if you'd read this to me." He might not be able to read, but he wasn't such a fool as to not ask for help when he needed it.

Wiping her hands on a towel, the woman moved to stand behind him and looked down at the book.

He placed his finger on the page. "Near as I can tell, this is what I need to know."

She looked over the page, then said, "Yes, this is about scab." She slipped beside him on the bench, close, but careful not to touch. She began to read aloud. The first was about the disease itself, advice and cautions. When she came to the formula for the dipping solution, she helped him to read the words himself so he would have them in memory. She never made him feel ignorant, and that made him humble.

She finished reading and sat back, looking at him. "Do those men hate you more because of the sheep, or because you were a Tennessean who fought for the Union?"

He gave a wry grin. "All of it, I guess. Most people that keep sheep down in these parts are foreigners, no matter that half of them were here before the rest of us. I'm talkin' of the Mexicans, ma'am, and there's a lot of feudin' between them and the *gringos.* Then there's sheepmen from New England, who ain't considered much less foreign, and Germany, Scotland and England. Most of the cattlemen are from here in Texas or the Southern states. Few of 'em ever kept sheep, and they can't understand 'em, nor the men that keep 'em. Sheepmen and cattlemen dress different, work different, think different. Such as that is bound to rub against each other."

Her golden eyes gazed at the far wall, as if remembering. "One of the reasons I was hopeful about bringin' Will and Henry out here was to get them away from the awful bitterness left by the war," she said, more as if expressing thoughts rubbing deep inside her than speaking to him. "Even after all these years, so many back home seem to live on what-ifs. Their lives have been changed and few for the better. The resentment sets like a sore, lookin' fine on the outside but festerin' underneath and spreadin' like a poison to the next generation." She sighed. "I guess there's no gettin' away from it, though."

"There's no gettin' away from life," Monroe said.

Her eyes swung around to his. They gazed at each other, and all thoughts of resentments and broken dreams and sheep faded like cold shadows before shimmering sunlight. She saw his eyes drop to her lips, and a hot flush swept her from head to toe. She thought perhaps he would kiss her. She *hoped* he would kiss her.

He turned and shut the book. "Thank you for your help, Mizzuz Pritchett."

"Thank you, too, Mr. Locket. Especially for what you did for Will yesterday."

He glanced at her, nodded and moved quickly to the door. "Give a holler when you're ready for everybody to take an' rake." Then with a faint grin he clarified: "When you're ready to eat."

"You do that on purpose, Mr. Locket."

His dark eyes rested on her, and she saw the slight sparkle of a sheepish grin in them. "Yes, ma'am. I guess I do." He left, closing the door quietly behind him.

Olivia sat for a moment, staring at the door. Her fingers tightened around the towel, and she recalled that she had hungry mouths to feed. Her gaze fell to her hand. It was work-worn, no longer that of a young girl who had been served her breakfast and who'd had nothing more strenuous to do than lift her hoopskirt over her head.

She was a woman now, she told herself, and didn't need to be getting carried away by foolish girl dreams. She and Monroe Locket could no more make a pair than a feisty heifer and a stubborn ram.

That evening, just at twilight, Will came running to find Olivia in their cabin. "Mama! Mr. Locket says hold supper, 'cause the sheep are about here. He says I can ride out with him to help bring them up. Can I?" He fidgeted with excitement, and his eager expression begged her.

"I suppose, but—"

He was off and running before she could finish. She went out into the yard to see him already riding away with Monroe Locket. He'd had the horse all ready before he came to ask. The *both* of them had had that horse ready—the very bay that had run away with Will two days earlier!

Worrying over Will and that dang horse, Olivia kept lookout, with Henry right beside her. Twenty minutes later, they saw the first sheep come into sight over the low rise to the west. The sheep crested the rise and spilled across the land like gray, foamy beer spilling across a table. They meandered here and there, yet followed the lead sheep, which had a bell around his neck. Will hemmed them in on one side, and the dog, Belle, hemmed them in on the other. Another dog came into view, and in amazement, Olivia and Henry saw it jump up and cross the thick and flowing herd by jumping from one sheep's back to another. On and on the woolly animals came, flowing into the yard, pushing at each other to find water at the long troughs. Some ran on for the spring creek, bleating, bunching, and sending the horses into a tizzy.

They were not sheep such as Olivia could ever recall seeing. Many of these had horns curling back from their heads, and their wool was shaggy and thin. She began to spot those with sores and ragged fleece—the scab Monroe Locket had spoken of.

A man on foot came into sight. He appeared what Olivia would have imagined a shepherd to look like, with a worn slouch hat and a colorful fleece-lined vest, and carrying a crooked staff. But this gentle shepherd also had a rifle slung over his shoulder.

Lastly came Monroe Locket, riding horseback very slowly, with the coral rays of a setting sun behind him. The proprietor of his kingdom, Olivia thought as she watched him.

Will pushed his horse through the sheep toward her. "Mr. Locket says he hopes you made extra biscuits, 'cause there'll be one more for supper."

"You tell Mr. Locket it won't hurt him any to share his biscuits," Olivia replied.

Chapter Six

The sheep filled the corrals and overflowed into the yard. Those outside the corral were fenced on one side by a bolt of worn calico that was stretched from the house to the cottonwood tree to the end post of the nearest corral. On the other side, the dogs formed the fence. Quite soon the woolly critters lay down and appeared content.

Olivia took dinner out to Monroe Locket, who kept guard in the doorway of the barn. He'd made himself a comfortable seat out of two sacks of grain. She gave him his plate and a basket containing four biscuits wrapped in a cloth.

"Thank you, ma'am," he said. He unfolded the cloth. "Thought I was suppose to share my biscuits."

"You are. There won't be any left over for you to snack on in the mornin'."

"I'll try and bear up," he said with a nod, then bit into a biscuit.

She wrapped her shawl around her and looked at the sheep. "I've never seen sheep like these. They look more like goats."

"They're *churros*," Monroe Locket said, munching on a biscuit. "Old Mexican sheep. Their wool is coarse and don't weigh as much as feathers, but these critters are tough enough to live off sand and air. The point of those merino rams John bought up your way is to give us the best of both animals."

Olivia's eyes strayed to the rifle lying beside him. "If you can keep them alive. Do you think those men might come in here, shooting more sheep?" Apprehension gripped her.

He shrugged. "This is a prime opportunity for them, and I'm just bein' ready and givin' Neron a break."

Neither of them spoke for a long minute. Olivia lingered, indulging in a few moments of being there, alone with him beneath the sparkling stars. The night air nipped at her, and she wrapped her shawl tighter. Longings she only half understood and wished she didn't tugged at her.

Monroe watched her covertly. A nagging worry had come upon him; she wasn't a woman for this kind of life. He said, "If there's any shootin', you and the young'ns get up in the loft and stay there. No one's gonna bother you, and no bullets are gonna go through those logs." After a moment he added, "Did I speak plain enough for you?"

"Yes. I understand." She gazed out into the darkness of the night, as if to see men lurking there, waiting.

And then Monroe said very quietly, "Do you understand that you're quite a woman, Mizzuz Pritchett?" It was another warning.

She slowly turned her head and looked down at him. He gazed at her, steadily, then purposely allowed his eyes to skim downward over her body. She didn't move, but he knew she was feeling the same things he was. A lady she might be, but she was first a woman.

"Good night, Mr. Locket." She started away.

"Yes, and a fine idea that is," he said.

Olivia headed for the cabin, almost running. Yet she wasn't running so much from Monroe Locket as from desires that she'd never before felt, and that were at once wonderful and terrifying.

That evening, Neron, the shepherd, played his guitar for them. Of medium height, he was a handsome young man, with dark skin and black hair and eyes, and one of the most magnificent mustaches Olivia had ever seen. It spread grandly upward whenever he smiled, which was quite often. The vest he wore caught Olivia's eye, too. It was of a durable, woven wool, backed with fleece for warmth and adorned with colorful ribbons and embroidery. It had been a gift from his mother when he left to come to America, he told Olivia. He was Basque, he explained to them, and therefore both a great shepherd and a great guitar player. Luis pointed out that the guitar was a Spanish heritage, but Neron waved that aside. "I will play for you some music of my people," he said in his heavily accented English.

Olivia had never before seen a guitar played so, like a fine concert instrument. And Neron's was a beautiful voice, never mind that they couldn't understand a word of his language, which wasn't at all like Spanish, or even the bit of French that Olivia knew.

The music soothed and uplifted them all. Olivia went to open the window and door in the hope of allowing Monroe Locket full access to the lovely sounds. Luis sat back in the rocking chair, a smile on his face. Will looked at the ceiling, dreaming. Captivated by Neron's flying fingers and the flying notes, Henry kept edging ever closer to the man. When Neron finished his fourth piece, Henry asked, "Do you know any Christmas carols?"

Neron frowned with puzzlement for an instant, then smiled. "Ah..." And he began to strum. It was "Silent Night," Olivia realized with dawning joy. He began to sing, and they all joined in, each in his own language, until English, Spanish and Basque were mingled in lovely melody. As the last note drifted off into the night, Olivia looked up to see Monroe Locket standing in the shadows of the dogtrot. He looked at her, long and deep. Then he turned and disappeared into the night.

After she had tucked the boys into bed, Olivia pulled out the brown wool shirt she had made John as a Christmas present and began to gently remove the stitches. John was gone, but there could still be use for this shirt.

In the first whisper of dawn the following morning, while the sheep still drowsed, Monroe Locket, Luis and Neron—and Will, too, who filled barrels with water from the creek—began the work of mixing the dipping solution. At last, when all arms ached from hauling water and the sun began to peek over the horizon, the sheep were prodded through the narrow chutes and into the vats, where they swam through to the end. When they found their footing again on hard ground, they shook and then bounded away to graze under the loose guard of a single dog.

Will was like a worker bee, shuttling between the men and the barn, fetching, lending a hand, occasionally manning a pole to push the backs of the sheep deep into the lye solution. Olivia brought coffee, then water as the day warmed. Worried about the lambs that had to go through the strong solution, she brought cloths to dry them. Of course, the men thought this pampering silly, but Henry enjoyed helping her. She cooked a big lunch, which the men ate in fifteen minutes. Then there were not only more dishes but also extra wash to be done, for inevitably the men and Will got the lye solution splashed on them. When their clothes became soaked, she insisted they change, for it wasn't good for the solution to set long on human skin.

Henry kept sneaking away from Olivia to play with lambs at the edge of the herd and to entice the dogs away with treats. Olivia pulled him back to the house with her twice. The third time she went looking for him, she came upon Monroe Locket in the act of snatching him up and giving him a swat to his bottom, while saying something like "If you don't stop your devil-mintin', boy, I'm gonna clean your plow."

Incensed, Olivia flew at him. "Don't you dare!" She drew Henry behind her. "He's a little boy. He's naturally drawn to dogs and lambs."

"He's a spoiled young'n. I've told him twice, and he's old enough to understand what's said to him."

"No one understands you half the time," Olivia shot back as she lifted Henry into her arms.

"Keep the boy away in the house," Monroe called hotly. "Can you understand that, ma'am?"

Henry yelled over her shoulder, "My name's Henry! And Santa Claus's gonna bring you coal!"

For that Olivia gave him a good scolding.

The men worked until they could see no more, and then finally came to supper. Everyone, even Will, was too exhausted to talk much. Still, after dinner Neron played them a few songs. When he would have left, Henry asked, "Will you play 'Silent Night' again, mister?"

And again Neron filled the air with the magic of the song.

Two more days of work from first light to last, and the flock was finished and guided back out to the range, leaving the homestead strangely quiet. As if a storm had come and gone. Monroe Locket sent Luis to rest for the afternoon, but he himself kept working with Will's help, repairing fencing and dabbing tar to the seams of the vat that had sprung a number of leaks. Olivia worked to get her kitchen in order again and to get a head start on cooking for the next round of days. It was some time before she missed Henry.

She found him up the live oak tree. He'd been trying to reach sprigs of mistletoe. "Will wouldn't get it," he said, little tears dribbling down his cheeks.

Olivia, her heart fluttering, gazed up at him. He seemed so small and so far up. "Well, come down, and I'll ask Will to get it now."

But Henry shook his head. "Can't. My foot's stuck."

There was no choice but go up and get his foot unstuck. With expertise recalled from childhood, and the awkwardness of a full-grown woman, Olivia went up the tree. Under her breath, she cursed her full skirts. With grunts and gritted teeth, she persisted until she reached Henry. One look down and her head swam, so she made certain not to look again.

Henry's heel was caught in the fork of two strong branches. Olivia pulled, which didn't work, so she tried to wiggle his foot out of his boot, which also didn't work. She tried to pull the branches away from the boot, but still Henry's foot stuck fast. When at last she saw Will in the yard, she called to him.

After his initial surprise at seeing his mother up a tree, he said, "I'll get Mr. Locket. He'll be able to do it!"

"No, Will! Wait—" But he was already racing away.

Of all the sights Monroe had ever expected to see, Olivia Pritchett up a live oak tree was not one of them. He pushed his hat back and gazed up at her. He wasn't a man to laugh easily—born straight-faced, John had always said. Monroe considered laughter all the sweeter when saved for exceptional occasions. This was one of those occasions, and laughter welled up from deep in his belly. The next instant, he tried to choke it back, because the woman's fiery gaze said he'd best not laugh.

"Henry's foot is pinched," she said primly.

Monroe couldn't say a thing, or his laughter was going to pop out.

He handed Will his hat and went up the tree. He had to squeeze past her. His back rubbed her back, his thigh rubbed her thighs, and he didn't try to avoid it one bit. The opportunity was too prime. He thought he'd burst from both laughter and arousal. Wasn't much to freeing the little boy—he simply pulled on both limbs and gave the foot room enough to ease free. Olivia Pritchett glared at him. A man who might be ignorant but not stupid, he knew to keep his mouth shut. He helped little Henry back down out of the tree, then wondered if he needed to go back up for the woman. He wasn't certain he should speak of it.

"Mama...will you get the mistletoe?" Henry called up to her.

"Yes, I will try."

"I'll come and get it, Mama," Will called, but Olivia Pritchett shook her head.

"What in the hell do you want with that?" Monroe asked, mystified.

And Henry told him righteously, "For Christmas. It's a blessin' on the house, and if you stand under it, someone's supposed to kiss you."

A bunch of nonsense, in Monroe's opinion. Speaking of kissing embarrassed him. But he said, "I'll come up and get it," because the woman had no business doing it.

However, she jutted that little pointed chin of hers and said, "I'm up here. I'll get it."

Monroe watched, not at all certain, but not knowing what to do with this woman, either.

Gingerly Olivia moved higher, very conscious of Monroe Locket down there gazing up at her. How undignified she felt! Still Henry looked so hopeful that she couldn't back out.

"Ma'am, that limb looks a little pitiful," Monroe Locket said.

"I'll just brace on it." She shook the smaller branch with the mistletoe and wondered why mistletoe had to grow up at the tops of trees, anyway. She wished she had a stick to knock it down. She shifted and inched up, straining to reach the pale leafy parasite.

The next instant, there came a loud crack. The limb upon which she had braced herself gave way, and Olivia fell. She bounced off branches and limbs, screaming, grappling and clutching. She ended up with her arms wrapped around a stout limb, the rest of her body dangling. Her heart pounded in her ears so loudly that it took her several seconds to hear Monroe Locket speaking to her.

"Let yourself drop now, ma'am. I'll catch you. See? I got hold of you." His hand closed around her ankle. "I'm here. I'll get you."

Shaking like a sheet in high wind, Olivia let go and fell into Monroe Locket's arms. "Oh!" She pressed her face into his neck and held on to his shoulders with all her might. He carried her all the way to the cabin.

Henry came shouting, "You got it, Mama! You knocked the mistletoe down! You okay, Mama? I love you, Mama."

Monroe ordered Will to stoke up the fire and Henry to run to the spring for fresh water to make Olivia coffee. The boys scrambled into action. Carefully Monroe set her to her feet, but he held on to her, because she looked like she was going to faint. She sank down onto the end of the table bench and put her face into her hands.

Totally at a loss, Monroe crouched in front of her, ran his hands over her shoulders looking for damage, and picked twigs and leaves from her hair. Her hair was falling all down around her, and she still didn't lift her face from her hands. Monroe wished she would, and wished she would speak. His heart was near beating out of his chest, and he felt sick when he thought of what might have happened.

"Can you find your breath, Olivia?"

She raised her face then and found his eyes brimming with concern. The spectacle of what she must have looked like up in that tree and then falling from it flashed across her mind, and she began to chuckle. Poor Monroe looked like he feared she'd lost her mind.

"I'm fine, Monroe. Thank you so much for catchin' me."

"You sure saved Mama, Mr. Locket," Will said.

A crooked, self-conscious grin spread his beard. "Yeah, well, I couldn't have her stove up." He surveyed her again, and his eyes focused on her breasts. Her pulse quickened. His eyes came up to hers; his face reddened. "You've ripped your shirt," he said, and, looking downward, she saw the rip in her bodice. He straightened and ordered Will to remain with her for a few minutes, then left, murmuring something about daylight skimmin'.

His voice saying her name, *Olivia,* echoed in her mind.

Late that night, when Monroe came in and closed the door, a piece of the mistletoe fell on his head.

"What the hell—?" He pulled the sprig from his hair and looked up at the bunch fastened above the door, and then over at the woman.

Luis, rising from the rocking chair, chuckled. "Which one of us do you want to kiss you, Señor Monny? Isn't that what little Henry says we are to do, *señora?*"

Monroe glared at him and tossed the sprig to the table. He'd never been at ease with speaking about things so intimate as kissing. Especially when he'd been thinking along such lines so much lately.

Embarrassed, Olivia said, "It's also for the blessing of the house. I'm sorry... I guess I didn't tie the bunch tight enough." She grabbed up the sprig and deposited it in her apron pocket, out of sight, and returned to preparing things to be ready for the morning's breakfast.

For several minutes, Luis and Monroe Locket discussed the dipping, which would begin again tomorrow, when another flock was to be brought up. Luis bid them good-night and left.

After a few more minutes, it occurred to Olivia that she and Monroe Locket were very much alone.

As if drawn by a magnet, she turned her head to see him at the stove, lifting the coffeepot. Their gazes met, then skittered away like two frightened rabbits seeking shelter from a raging tiger.

"It's only an hour made," she said, not mentioning that she'd made it especially for him. She reached for a cup, turned and handed it to him. Her eyes lit on his hand as he took the cup.

"Oh, Monroe—your hand!"

He held it out, looking at it as if for the first time. Between spots of tar, it was cracked to bleeding in places, as was his other. "It's the lye."

"Let's put lanolin on them." Olivia rummaged in the cabinet where she'd seen the small tin of ointment.

"It's nothin'." And he waved her away.

"Now, don't be a child. Give here." He did, and she rested his hand in the palm of hers and began dabbing on the soothing goo. "You're the one who keeps your hands so much in the solution. You need to find a way to keep that to a minimum. Perhaps we could coat your hands several times a day. It shouldn't be of any inconvenience to your work."

When he said nothing, she raised her head. Her eyes met his, and her breath caught in her throat. His eyes were deep and dark and hot. He reached for her, and she dropped the lanolin tin. There came a roaring and swelling within her, a tide of desire dragging her into his arms. And then he was kissing her, hard and demanding, and she was matching him all the way.

They broke apart at the same time.

Olivia gasped for breath and looked at him in shock.

Monroe shoved her from him and said tersely, "I'm sorry... I shouldn'tna done that." God and heaven above knew he was asking for a barrel of trouble. This wasn't a woman a man could take to him for a few hours or days of pleasure and then send away.

Her golden eyes stared at him. "The mistletoe did fall on you," she said, then added hesitantly, "and I quite liked it."

"Lady, you'd better know you got a bear by the tail. I ain't been with a woman in some time, and I hope you can appreciate what that means." And he didn't care how blunt he was being with her—she had to be scared into her senses.

She straightened her spine and lifted that little chin. "I know exactly what you mean, sir. And before you get the wrong idea, I only meant that I'm not such a prude I can't admit to enjoyin' one little kiss, nor such an innocent that I'll pretend it was something more. That was all I meant."

Monroe stared at her, and she at him. Then he said, "Well, Olivia, it may have been one little kiss, but one little spark can start a bonfire to burn down a man's house." And he got himself out of there.

Shame washed over Olivia, and anger, too. She grabbed hold of his chair, dragged it over to the entry, climbed up and yanked the mistletoe from above the door. How could she have kissed him like that? *Like some wanton!* Stomping back across the room, she threw the mistletoe into the trash barrel. What in God's green heaven had come over her to say what she had? He must surely think her some . . . some pain in the neck now—a festering sore in his side! *And she didn't want to be anything at all to him!*

Unexpectedly, she found herself in tears. She brought the back of her hand to her cheek and felt the heat lingering there. And lingering, too, was the manly scent of him, the soft scratchiness of his beard, the silkiness of his hair beneath her fingertips, the hard power of him pressing against her. The sweet, wild abandon that he had made her feel. Lord, forgive her, but she simply couldn't be sorry for experiencing that.

* * *

Seco brought in the second flock. Luis's grand-
nephew, he had dark hair, wore a wide sombrero and
a colorful wool poncho. He was so young his mustache was quite thin. Luis assured her that Seco was a
man of nineteen. Too young to face the responsibilities and threats of shepherding a flock, Olivia thought,
her gaze lingering on the rifle he carried. And then she
recalled that her own William had been only eighteen
when he'd gone to war.

The long days of dipping sheep continued. Feeling
pressed by the imminent winter weather, Monroe
started at the first bare light and kept it up two hours
past sunset, working under lamps and torches. The
cold temperature would take a heavy toll among the
sheep wet with the dipping solution. But once started,
he couldn't stop. It would be either the cold or the scab
that got his herd; he'd take his chances with the cold.
A couple of times he worried about Will working hard
as a man right with them, but he didn't know how to
forbid the boy without hurting his feelings. As often
as he could, he gave the boy easy jobs to do—feeding
the horses, guarding the sheep.

One morning dawned cold and damp enough for
them to build a roaring fire in the stove, as if Mother
Nature were reminding them this was winter. Bundled
in coats, the men continued the dipping, and thank-
fully, the day warmed. Five lambs and three ewes died
that day, though, from the cold. They were lucky to
lose no more.

Olivia did her share and then some. She made large
meals, cleaned up afterward, and washed twice as
many clothes in order to keep the men and Will dry.

She brought coffee and snacks to them, doctored lambs and the men's hands, which dried horribly from the solution, as well as cut and bruised from the work. She was on her feet from the time she rose until after drying the last supper dish.

After each evening meal, she would bring out the paints she had brought—a precious treat from Uncle Phillip. She, Henry and Will would paint their flour-clay figures, each peering closely beneath the sooty glow of the oil lamps. For the angel that would have the position of honor at the top of the tree, Olivia mixed a very thin water-and-flour mixture and coated her. When dried, the angel took on a certain patina.

Monroe always took the first watch in the barn, but Luis and Seco would linger in the great cabin, both deciding to try their hands at painting a flour-clay star. And they would all sing Christmas carols. It was Henry who began it by singing his own broken rendition of "O Come, All Ye Faithful." Seco recognized it and began singing, too.

After Luis and Seco had retired and Olivia had gotten the boys to bed, she would remain awake into the late hours. Sitting in the rocker in their cabin, she would stitch on the brown wool fabric that had been John's shirt in the murky light of the lamp until her eyes burned and her vision blurred.

Olivia realized that Christmas would soon be upon them, and gradually the magic of the season slipped into her spirit.

One afternoon she and Henry walked out of sight of the homestead, through tall winter-dried grasses and up and down hills. The sun was bright, and birds twittered here and there. It was beautiful. Olivia and

Henry sang Christmas carols and danced. Oh, how Henry made her laugh! They came upon a small grove of sycamores and gathered the buttonballs from the ground because Henry thought they would be great decoration. Olivia found the dead vines of wild gourds and traced them to the gourds themselves—a wonderful find! The small orange and yellow gourds joined the buttonballs in her apron pockets. On their return to the cabin, they cut long green limbs from several cedar trees, choosing many bearing the tiny purple berries. She and Henry agreed it was every bit as good as pine and holly.

The sun was hovering on the horizon, and they were singing "O Come, All Ye Faithful" when they came around the bend in the creek and caught sight of the homestead. A few more yards, and the cluster of men came into view. There were horses—four, five, six— she counted, and the saddles were empty. Fear crawled up Olivia's spine.

"Stay here, Henry."

"Why? What is it?"

"Do as I say!" Her tone froze Henry in his tracks.

Her heart thumping, she walked faster, peering over and around the horses. At the same moment that she heard the thudding of fists, she saw that Monroe and Seco were being beaten. Luis and Will were held aside by a man with a rifle.

Fury flashed through her like greased lightning. She broke into a run that sent her sunbonnet flying. "No! No!" she screamed.

Chapter Seven

She flew at them, brandishing the cedar limbs. "Let them go! Let them go, I say!" She smacked the man who had the rifle stretched in front of Will, going at him with a vengeance. He cried out and threw up his hands, trying to protect his face from the cutting cedar. Then she went at the others. She had no idea of her actions, no thought of fear. The raging fury of a woman protecting her own drove her.

Feeling someone lay hands on her from behind, she whirled and lashed out with the remaining cedar limb. The man fell back, as did the others. She glared at them. They stared at her, openmouthed.

"How dare you! How dare any of you!" She pointed at Will. "That is *my* son! You have raised a gun to *my son*." She pounded a finger on her breastbone. "And, by God, I will not have it!" Her gaze came to settle on the one face she recognized—that of Albert Burnham, the man who had threatened Monroe on the trip out to the ranch. "We are visitors here, sir!" she said to him. "Is this the way you treat visitors in this land? My son has nothing in this ridiculous fight of yours. He is innocent. A boy, and this is what you show him." She shook her head. "Have you no shame? Have you come so far into the wild that you go wild yourselves? My, my, aren't you fine ones—you with your guns, and holdin' a man's hands behind his back to beat him...two, three on one. Oh, let me tell you, if any of you ever had any honor, you lost it long ago!" She straightened her spine and glared sternly at them all in the manner of a lady born and bred and proud of it.

One of the men started to speak, but Albert Burnham motioned to him, and he clamped his mouth shut. As one, the men fell away and mounted up. They remained for a moment, their bitterness dripping like cider vinegar, yet they didn't challenge her.

Albert Burnham spoke. "Ma'am, I apologize for any upset your son may suffer from this. We didn't mean him any harm."

"I'm afraid I can't forgive at this moment, sir. Though I find it encouraging that you have the spark of a civilized human left in you. I shall trust that you-all will wait to come and murder Mr. Locket and burn down his ranch until Christmas has passed and myself and my sons are safely away from here."

"There warn't no murder goin' on here!" one of the men said with a blast.

Olivia looked at him. "Oh? Then what is it you plan if Mr. Locket does not give in to your demands?"

The man who had spoken looked down at his horse, and no one else said a thing.

She moved away to Will and wrapped her arms about him. Henry came running, and she enveloped him, too. She did not turn to watch the men ride away, only listened as the echo of the horses' hooves faded, and silence, broken only by the faint bleating of the sheep, took full rein. She held tightly to her sons.

"Well, Olivia, you sure gave 'em thunder and lightnin'." Monroe's voice was muffled. She turned to see him spitting blood and helping Seco to his feet. As Luis moved to pick up a rifle lying in the dust, she saw even his face had not escaped unscathed.

Her gaze met Monroe's. Blood dripped into his eye and ran down his nose.

It came to her then, what she had done. As she swept them with a glance, she felt the blood drain from her head and out her toes. Her legs got weak as water, and she sank. With a lunge, Monroe caught her just before she hit the ground.

Olivia regained a semblance of her composure, though Monroe's hand remained supporting her elbow all the way into the cabin. With shaking hands, she put the kettle on and focused her attention on stoking a fire, while Will lit in with a colorful narrative of the happenings.

"I turned around, and there they were, guns pointin' at us!" His voice rose with excitement.

"Will...you go see if you can help Luis with the sheep," Monroe said.

"No!" Olivia put her hand on Will's shoulder. She couldn't bear him to be out of her sight, and her eyes told Monroe so. "Get me some more cloths, Will."

Her entire body wouldn't stop shaking, and she dug deep for her remaining shreds of fortitude. When she turned around, she found Henry there. She grabbed him to her for a precious instant.

Will brought the cloths, saying, "I thought for a minute they were gonna shoot Mr. Luis, 'cause he was the only one had a gun. I'm sure glad they didn't."

Olivia poured water into a bowl and carried it to the table. Monroe took one of the cloths from Will. Automatically seeing to the youngest first, Olivia turned to clean and dress Seco's face. "You will still be handsome when it heals," she told him, and he grinned, then winced in pain.

Will kept up his recital of the happenings. "Mr. Locket, he just told 'em he wasn't leavin', and boy, I thought they were gonna kill all the sheep. Then this fella started in on Mr. Locket. When Mr. Locket got him down and was poundin' him, they all jumped in."

Monroe felt like he'd been run over by buffalo. His anger had faded; he wasn't one to stay mad long. But he felt like a fool for not being ready when they came. Maybe he'd truly never believed they would.

He felt his face with his fingers. One eyebrow had been busted open, and the cheekbone below his other eye was swelling, turning purple, he imagined. His lips were cut, it appeared he had at least one cracked rib, and his knuckles were raw.

Olivia came and stood in front of him. Their eyes met, hers demanding no nonsense. He surrendered the cloth to her without protest. "At least one of them didn't go unscathed," she said in a low voice for his ears alone as she dabbed at the cut above his eye.

"Two of 'em," he said, with more than a fraction of pride. "Pretty sure I broke one nose."

He watched a grin slip over her lips. Then her gaze moved over his face, and tender pity filled her golden eyes to overflowing.

"I've had a lot worse, Olivia," he said, and the concern on her face warmed his heart.

She nodded, averted her eyes, as if embarrassed. "If you get lye on these, it's gonna burn like fire," she said, tending his hands. "Now, get your shirt off, and let's see if I can wrap your ribs. They'll feel better."

He stared at her. "You done this sort of thing before, ma'am?"

"Before Sherman burnt our home, we welcomed hurt soldiers—from either side. And I nursed my husband for four years."

"I ain't your husband," he said as he unbuttoned his shirt.

Without expression and not looking at him, she said, "No, you're not."

Monroe didn't know what he'd expected from her, but he didn't think he wanted her to say it like that—without any feeling at all. While she worked quickly and expertly, wrapping him tightly with gauze, he gazed down at her shiny hair and inhaled the womanly scent of her. She didn't so much as look at him, though, and when she was finished, she went about the business of cleaning up.

When Monroe, bent with pain, would have led them out to begin work again, Olivia insisted they all have bread and jam and coffee. They must have some rest, some time to catch their breath, no matter that time pressed in on them. She even poured a cup of coffee for Will and ignored his puzzled and questioning looks, for she'd always said he was too young to have coffee.

And then the men went back to work, and only Olivia and Henry were left in the cabin. "Will we still have Christmas?" he asked her, his eyes wide and round and worried.

"Oh, yes, my darlin'." She swept him into her arms. The final thread of composure was fraying, and she frantically tried to hold on to it.

"I'm going to tell you a secret, Henry. I can tell you, because it's something you already know." He searched her eyes. She said, "Christmas is not something we *have*. Christmas is something that *comes*—always—and can no more be held back than can each new day. Christmas doesn't depend on man or anything he does or doesn't do, because he never brought Christmas in the first place. It doesn't have anything to do with things goin' on in the world. It makes no difference if there is snow or not, or if people are fightin' each other or loving, or if greens are hung or the walls remain bare, or if there is turkey and pudding for dinner or just beans and corn bread. It doesn't even depend on Santa Claus and his gifts. None of that brings Christmas or keeps it from coming. Just like one day follows another for people rich or poor, mean or kind, Christmas comes to everyone in the world. Why, you could lie right in your bed over there in the loft, and still Christmas will come to you. The secret is that a person has to believe in Christmas or it simply passes him right by. Comes and goes and is never seen. And this isn't a secret a person can be told about—it's something a person must learn for himself. You must allow yourself to see Christmas when it comes—and then nothin' can take it away from you, honey. And you already know that. You believe in Christmas, so it will come to you."

His eyes shone with bright understanding—the pure belief of a child. Then he looked very solemn. "You learned that in the war, didn't you, Mama?"

"Yes, Henry, I did."

She smiled, and inside she felt herself cracking. "Now go see if you can find some of those cedar limbs that can be used. See? I still have the buttonballs and gourds in here." She drew them from her apron pockets.

He ran from the cabin, eager again.

The last fine thread of Olivia's composure snapped, and she laid her head to her arms on the table and sobbed. She cried out of relief and gladness that everyone was safe, and because of how close their brush with violence had been. And she cried because she knew to be true what she had told Henry about Christmas, but she wasn't sure she could believe anymore. She cried because of all the pain and anger and hate in the world, and because she was so mad at those men who had come in here and threatened their happiness. She cried because of what might have been and what she wished could be.

"Olivia."

It was Monroe's voice, soft and gentle. She hadn't heard his footsteps over the racket of her crying. She tried to choke off her humiliating sobs, but simply couldn't. His hand touched her shoulder, and the bench gave with his weight. The next instant he had pulled her into his arms. She clutched him and cried against his warm, strong chest. He held her, rocked her softly and stroked her hair, all the while murmuring things she didn't understand at all but found comforting beyond words.

For the past eight years of her life—since William had gotten so sick—it had been Olivia doing the comforting of others; no one, until now, had comforted her. This moment, she needed Monroe Locket, and he gave what she needed.

At last her sobs faded, leaving her drained, yet with a blessed numbness. "I'm sorry," she said as she pulled away, averting her face and wiping her cheeks. *Oh, Lord, what he must think of her!* "I just..." She couldn't explain; she didn't understand herself.

He handed her a cup towel, and she dabbed at her eyes.

"You know, Olivia, you are one hell of a joe darter."

"I hope that's somethin' good," she said and sniffed. She lowered her towel and made herself face him.

"Oh, yes, ma'am. That's somethin' unsurpassed." The admiration shining in his eyes brought a flood of joy to her heart.

And then a warm tenderness spread over his hard face. He brought his hand up, slipped it beneath her drooping hair and cupped the back of her neck. He pulled her toward him, and she met him. They kissed. It was a kiss tender and warm and shattering. He lifted his head, gazed at her with heated eyes, then kissed her again, this time hard and deep and hot, sending fire racing through her veins.

Her head was spinning when at last they broke apart and she gazed into his battered face.

Monroe tenderly rubbed his rough thumb over her lips. "I ain't one bit sorry this time, Olivia. I meant to enjoy that, and I did. Thank you."

"You're welcome, Monroe," she answered breathlessly. Her hand rested on his flannel-covered arm. For a long moment he placed his over it and gazed down at it.

Slowly, stiffly, he rose, and, holding his hurting ribs, he left. Olivia sat there, with the scent of him all around her, her lips still burning with his kiss, and her body echoing with longing. Lingering now, too, was the will to go on.

To bring order to her world again, Olivia scrubbed the stove and worktable and eating table. Then she snipped the best of what was left of the cedar limbs, dug out red ribbon, and she and Henry hung their greens around the cabin and over into their sleeping cabin, too. Lastly she brought from her trunk one of the red candles she had made for Christmas Eve and placed it on the table. Then she fried up lamb chops and fall potatoes, heated fat seasoned beans and wild onions, and baked two big batches of golden biscuits. By the time the men came in for dinner, all was ready, and Olivia felt herself again. She was rewarded for her efforts by the smile on each one's tired face. All except Monroe, who looked at all the greenery, then stared first at the candle and then at her. And the look on his bruised and broken face said very clearly that he was putting distance between them. It was as if their closeness of hours before had never been.

Supper was a subdued affair, even with Will. Olivia, self-conscious, avoided looking not only at Monroe, but at everyone else, too, not wanting anyone to guess the passionate feelings stirring within her. She did not speak to Monroe, nor he to her.

What conversation there was of course revolved around what had happened that afternoon. Various courses of action were discussed as to how to get retribution and what to do if the men came again.

Monroe Locket glanced at Olivia. "I doubt they will be showin' their faces anytime soon. Not after the preachin' Mizzuz Pritchett gave 'em." He almost smiled but had to wince from the pain.

It was cold enough that night to cause the dipping solution that hadn't dried to freeze across the backs of many of the sheep. At first light, the men again bundled up to continue the work. After an hour, Luis returned to the cabin for coffee. He huddled over the stove, and she heard him praying for the warm weather to hold. "I think we gonna see some snow soon, *señora,*" he told her solemnly.

However, by that afternoon it was again shirt sleeve weather, and though the night again got cool and again they lost some stock, the following day was almost balmy. Seco's flock was finished, and the men appeared about finished themselves. Seco and his dogs slowly moved the sheep out, Luis retired to his cabin, and Monroe came in long enough for coffee and biscuits that Olivia had made especially for him. She wanted to rewrap his ribs but didn't dare ask. She looked at the droplets of water in his hair as he dried after washing and at his bruised and battered face, and something within her ached to hold him. Henry was there with them, and Monroe kept his distance.

"I'm gonna miss these biscuits, ma'am, when you and the boys go back east," he said, looking her straight in the eye.

She thought of when he'd kissed her. She could think of nothing to say other than that she would miss him and this place more than words could allow. But she wouldn't humiliate either of them by saying that.

The following day, at midmorning, Monroe and Will made ready to ride out to meet the last flock. "I wanna go, too," Henry piped up.

Olivia of course said no and tried to divert him by telling him things they would do to get ready for Christmas, which was a mere two days away now. And then Monroe broke in. "The boy can go. He can ride Barney, and I'll lead him."

"But he's only five," Olivia protested.

To which Monroe said flatly, "He's long overdue. Best time is here and now, with me."

And so Olivia allowed Henry to go. She watched the three ride away, then went inside to channel her worry into baking Christmas sweets. She was pulling her second batch of sweet biscuits from the oven when Luis came hurrying in with Belle at his heels and rifle in hand. "Riders come. Please, *señora,* the window."

Olivia hurriedly closed one shutter, then peered out around the other. Luis stood inside with the door cracked enough to point the rifle out. Two riders came into view, and Olivia recognized them: Albert Burnham and the man who had held his rifle on Will and Luis that day.

They rode slowly to the cabin, stopping their horses far from the door. "I came to talk, Locket," Albert Burnham called.

Luis opened the door another inch. "Señor Locket is not here."

After a moment, Albert Burnham said, "You give Locket a message for me. Tell him I don't want trouble. I'm willin' to buy him out and pay him top dollar. Tell him that."

Impulsively Olivia hurried to the door, flung it open and rushed out, Luis right behind her. "Would you like to come in for coffee, gentlemen?"

Both men stiffened with surprise. Then Albert Burnham nodded. "Yes, ma'am."

Luis looked wide-eyed at her. She cast him an encouraging smile and stripped off her apron. As Albert Burnham stepped through the door, he swept his hat from his head. Then he poked his companion into doing the same. The younger man looked as uncomfortable as if he were entering an enemy camp. Burnham, however, was a man in control. A man whose pale eyes showed him to be very nearly fearless, and as hard as the ground upon which he walked.

"My name's Albert Burnham, ma'am. This is my top hand, Dave Wills."

Olivia gracefully inclined her head. "Very nice to meet you gentlemen. I'm Olivia Pritchett. Please... have a seat." The men settled at the table. Olivia went to the sideboard. Luis moved to sit in the rocker, but kept his rifle in hand.

Olivia made polite talk while she assembled her best china, which she'd gotten out just that morning. "You two came at just the right time. I've just finished baking sweet biscuits for bread pudding." Out of the corner of her eye she saw the men staring at the pan of bread she'd set on the end of the table to cool. "I've been baking for Christmas, as I imagine your wives are doin'." She brought the dishes to the table.

Albert Burnham said, "I'm a widower, ma'am, and Dave ain't married."

Olivia lifted out biscuits with a knife, set them on plates. "And do you have children, Mr. Burnham?"

"Two boys... same as you," he said gruffly. "But they're 'bout grown now."

Olivia passed the two men and Luis sweet breads and filled their cups with fresh coffee and cool cream, all of it served in white china with delicate floral sprigs and silver trim. Albert Burnham and Dave Wills thanked her and, with mouths full, praised her sweet biscuits.

"Monroe Locket is sure a lucky fella to be havin' you here, ma'am," Dave Wills said fervently, then turned near as red as a holly berry.

Albert Burnham said, "You said you was just visitin', Missus Pritchett. Where are you from, may I ask?"

"North Carolina. I, too, am widowed. I was to marry John Carter. My sons and I didn't learn of his passin' until we reached Esperar. It came as quite a shock, and Mr. Locket was kind enough to allow us to come here to rest and to give my boys an opportunity to celebrate their Christmas here, rather than spend it on the long trip home."

"My condolences 'bout John, ma'am."

"Thank you. More coffee Mr. Wills?"

Dave Wills nodded eagerly. Olivia poured coffee for both men, plying them, she decided, more with pride than conscience. A woman used what she had to make men see the light, she thought. "I am ready to accept your apology for the incident the other day, Mr. Burnham."

His eyes, startled, came to hers. Then he nodded.

Olivia cut out another biscuit and placed it before him, saying, "This offer to buy Mr. Locket's ranch... Does it come from you alone, or, as well, from the other men who were here beating Mr. Locket to a pulp the other day?"

Again Albert Burnham's pale eyes flew to hers. "Four of us ranchers have pitched in. We're offerin' cash, ma'am, top dollar. For that matter, Locket can keep his sheep and take the money and them with him out of here." He looked her straight in the eye. "I'm tryin' to avoid any killin', Missus Pritchett. If you have some influence over Locket, you should use it."

"Oh, sir, I would be the last person who could influence Mr. Locket. He is his own man."

Albert Burnham gave a crooked smile as he forked a piece of sweet bread into his mouth. "Ma'am, any woman that can cook like you do would have a great influence over any man." A sparkle touched his pale eyes. Olivia met his gaze and saw understanding there.

"You know, Mr. Burnham, I would find it an honor if you and your sons and Mr. Wills here and any of those men from the other day—and their families, too—would come to join us in celebrating Christmas."

Albert Burnham's pale eyes popped wide, and Dave Wills choked on his coffee. "Come to celebrate, ma'am? Here?" Albert Burnham asked.

"With the sheepman?" Dave Wills blurted.

Olivia said, "I had been plannin' a party—I've been baking and baking for it. And a party would be even more festive with more people." She looked into Albert Burnham's eyes. "We would so enjoy havin' you join us for Christmas dinner, sir. It would be a prime opportunity for you to speak to Mr. Locket about your offer—and to apologize directly to my sons," she added, completely unashamed.

Albert Burnham's eyes said he wasn't fooled one bit by her manipulation. He looked thoughtful and then said slowly, "My sons and I will be proud to come, ma'am. Dave here can speak for himself."

"You can count me in, ma'am," Dave Will's answered as he ate his last bite.

Albert Burnham rose, and Olivia asked, "Will you invite the other ranchers for me?"

"Yes, ma'am," he said slowly, "but I can't offer no guarantees." He took up his hat and paused. "You have reminded me of my heritage, Missus Pritchett, and I thank you."

"It has been my pleasure, Mr. Burnham."

"Oh, *señora,* you are a wise one," Luis said as they stood together and watched their visitors ride away. "Perhaps, God willing, it will work."

"It's all we have, Luis, because Mr. Locket is not about to take all the gold in California for this place. He'd rather be planted here," she said, using Monroe's own term.

Barely an hour later, the sheep came flowing over the rise. Eagerly Olivia ran toward them. She stopped, shielded her eyes against the sun and watched. Will came into view, and then Henry and Monroe, with Monroe trailing Henry's horse. A niggling worry dropped away; her sons were safe. Last to come into view was a bulky man bringing up the rear and carrying a lamb on his shoulders. What a sight they all made!

Olivia waved. Will and Henry waved back, as did the gentleman carrying the lamb. Then Monroe kicked his horse ahead, bringing Henry's horse with him, Henry bouncing precariously atop the thick-legged animal. Monroe stopped as he came to her. Henry cried, "I didn't fall off, Mama."

"Good for you, Henry!"

"He did well," Monroe said, and Henry beamed. Then her gaze fell on the fowl dangling by its legs from Monroe's saddle. "Got one on this side, too," he said, and unhooked both, dropping them down to the ground in front of her. "Turkeys for Christmas dinner." His bruised face was quite proud.

"And we got a tree, too, Mama! Will's draggin' it! See?"

Olivia grinned at both of them. "That's wonderful, because we have neighbors comin' to join us for a Christmas party."

Chapter Eight

William and Luis, helped by Henry and three dogs, settled the herd, while Monroe and the herder, Halsey, came in for coffee and a bite to eat. Halsey was a jovial New Englander whose attire appeared to consist of rags mended together. A battered tweed sailor cap covering shoulder-length white hair topped it off, giving him a ragamuffin, eccentric air. He came singing, not stopping until he was right next to Olivia. He called Monroe "Captain" and Olivia "Madame."

After she'd put coffee and leftover butter-fried sweet biscuits in front of the two men, Olivia, carefully choosing her words, told of Albert Burnham's visit.

At Mr. Burnham's offer to buy him out, Monroe raised his eyebrows and said, "Well, that takes the huckleberry off'n the bush." At Olivia's invitation to Mr. Burnham and the other ranchers to join them on Christmas Day, his eyes narrowed. "You what?"

She said brightly, "I invited them all to Christmas dinner. Mr. Burnham has accepted and promised to ask the others."

Monroe grew threateningly quiet. Halsey pushed up from the bench, saying, "I think I'll take me coffee outside an' check on the woollies. I thank ye greatly, madame, for the refreshments." And he beat a retreat out the door, his frayed coattail flying, his voice stirring into song.

Monroe scraped back his chair and stood. He was mad as fire. "And if you ain't the head hen steppin' high!" He stared at her, not fazed one iota by her cool golden eyes. "Did it ever occur to you that this is *my* place, and that maybe I wouldn't want those that had beat in my face comin' to partake at my table of the food that maybe I ain't cooked but I have provided? Did it ever occur to you that maybe you should *ask* me?"

She jutted that little pointy chin of hers. "You weren't here, and I felt it of more import to take the opportunity than to wait for instruction."

"The more *import* here," he said, throwing the fancy word back in her face, "is the fact that this ranch is mine—not yours to do with as you wish!"

"You have given me a quarter of the profits. That does give me an interest."

"You *refused* the profits!"

"I care about this place." She faced him stubbornly, then looked away. "I'm sorry. I overstepped my bounds. I just thought..."

"You just thought you'd meddle. You're a high-handed woman, Mizzuz Pritchett."

Her face and chin came high. "If you will let me finish, Mr. Locket."

He clamped his mouth shut and waited. He could practically see the smart words forming as she squared her shoulders.

"I knew you were not about to sell. You are far too stubborn. Therefore, there is a good chance you may be killed. Mr. Burnham mentioned as much. However, it has been my experience that it is much harder to kill someone after having shared a meal and conversation with them. What the situation needs is for you men to get to know each other—for those men to see that Union or Confederate, sheep or cattle, you are all the same."

Her gaze challenged him, and he let her have some facts. "While your intentions are good, ma'am, there is a prime chance those men could come into our welcomin' arms, draw down on us and hold us hostage while they kill my sheep and burn me out, without us bein' able to fight back."

He watched the emotions cross her face: disbelief, followed by uncertainty, followed by cracking pride. That gave him a slice of pleasure and then pain. He hadn't wanted to hurt her... but she shouldn't be meddling in things she knew nothing about!

Sighing, he went to the window and gazed out. "This ain't North Carolina, Olivia, with settled men and a law set down straight."

"I'm sorry, Monroe."

He tried to resist, but her small, contrite voice seemed to seep into his heart. He looked over his shoulder to see her proud shoulders slumped, her little pointy chin quivering. He gave a large sigh. The woman did something to him, by damn. "It was my pride talkin'," he said, raking his hand through his dark hair.

"Do you really think they would do as you say—draw down on us?" The words sounded funny coming out of her genteel mouth.

His anger spent, he began to think. "A couple of those yahoos would turn on us in the blink of an eye...but Albert Burnham's a tall-walkin' man. If he says he's comin' for a party and talk, that's what he intends. And anyway, the thing's done now, can't be changed." His spirits rose, and he looked at her. "And if the others want trouble, we'll find a way to be ready for 'em. A party is sure somethin' we ain't tried." He grinned crookedly. "Let's have a roasted lamb to serve with those turkeys, Olivia...only we won't tell 'em it's lamb 'til after they've had their fill."

Sparkling joy filled her eyes, then curved her lips, and they shared the daring. Monroe almost laughed. But then she took a step toward him, and he saw the wanting on her face. He felt it inside himself—a powerful, fearful thing. He got hold of himself, grabbed his hat and headed for the door. "Day's a-wastin', and there's sheep need dippin'."

He left, fairly running out the door. By God in heaven, he was ignorant, but he wasn't stupid. He had no business getting tangled up with her. He wasn't her kind, she wasn't his. She might be finding things to her liking right now, but soon enough she'd grow to hate this hard life and hard land, and she'd be off to the east, or giving him hell if she couldn't go. And he didn't want a wife!

The following days Olivia cooked three meals a day and brought refreshments to the men as they worked. She tended various cuts and bruises on the men's hands and on the lambs. She washed and mended clothes. And in between she prepared for Christmas.

Though she had never had to ready a fowl for baking—old Ben had always done that chore at home—Olivia gamely dipped the turkeys in hot water and plucked the remaining feathers, getting nearly as many on herself as off the turkeys. Will came away from the sheep dipping long enough to help fix the tree on a stand. Then Henry and Olivia clipped soft wool from one of the lambs and pasted it as hair upon their treetop angel. Standing on a chair, stretching to place the angel, Olivia almost knocked over the tree. Henry hung the rest of their flour-clay ornaments.

"Look, Mama! Look!" he cried when finished. The flour-clay ornaments were magical splotches of color on the green limbs.

Then Olivia brought from hiding gingerbread men and sugar cookies to hang, too. Luis added two small silver crosses. Halsey brought three large bronze coins—Indian Peace Medals that he'd won off some Cheyenne braves up in the Nations, he told them. Through a hole already in each, he ran strands of Olivia's red thread for hanging them on the tree.

Henry gazed with awe at the tree. "It's beautiful."

"It is that, lad," Halsey said. The next instant he broke into singing, "O Christmas tree, O Christmas tree..." and led them all in the song.

Monroe stared at the tree, and the boyish wonder Olivia saw in his dark eyes struck deep in her heart. He said nothing, however.

The next morning, Will drew her attention to the addition on the tree of four freshly polished brass bells. "They were in the barn," Will told her.

"They're wagon bells, and they were black as night." They looked at each other, knowing Monroe Locket had been the one to clean and add them.

Before dinner on Christmas Eve, Olivia had the bread pudding and pecan pies made and had readied the boys' best shirts and trousers. That afternoon, catching Halsey's voice singing, she hummed carols, running one into the other as she baked dried fruit sweetmeats, starched and ironed the best of the shirts Monroe had given her to wash, as well as a broadcloth shirt with patches on the elbows for Halsey. Luis requested his shirt done without starch.

That evening, after Monroe had taken his place on guard, Halsey led them all in singing carols. What Halsey didn't have in tone, he made up for in volume. They sounded atrocious, but a good time was had. Soon, however, Henry, anxious for the arrival of Christmas morning, dragged Will off to bed, and the men left, too.

Alone at last, Olivia pulled from the bottom drawer of the sideboard the gift she had worked night after night to make for Monroe. She had turned John's brown wool shirt into a thick quilted vest. Fashioning it after the one Neron wore, she had adorned it with colorful embroidery and edged it with blue satin ribbon. She had wrapped it in layers of cheesecloth fastened with twine.

Hurrying furtively, she slipped into the storeroom and over to the bed she had not touched since the night Monroe had forbidden her. The blanket was neatly spread. Olivia laid her gift upon it and at once almost snatched it back for fear Monroe would hate it, or be embarrassed that she'd given him something. Then, lifting her chin, she pivoted and left it there.

The boys' gifts she had brought with her from Carolina: a buck knife with sheath for Will, and a sketch pad with charcoal pencils for Henry. Cecilia and Phillip had given each boy a pair of socks and a red flannel shirt. Each of these things was wrapped in pale brown paper, and Olivia laid them beneath the tree. Olivia also had Christmas stockings for them, and she had made a stocking for each of the men, as well. These she filled with cookies and sweetmeats. She realized that she had used nearly all of Monroe's store of sugar, as well as the sugar and honey she had brought with her.

The entire time she was working, she expected Monroe to come in. Part of her wished that he would, yet another part of her was grateful he didn't. This night brought fully all the raw loneliness hidden within her heart. If Monroe did come now into the dim cabin, where they would be alone, she wasn't certain what her reaction would be. She just might throw herself at him.

The following morning beneath the tree had been added a slingshot labeled for Will and a small whistle labeled for Henry. Without a name but carved with an intricate *O* on the top, was a small, smoothly rubbed and polished rosewood box. Olivia knew that Monroe had made them all.

When Henry placed the box in his mother's hands, her gaze flew to Monroe. Hiding the joy he felt inside, as fearful of it as he would be of a bear gone mad, he said, "Since we can only dip till noon, we'll get started. You can bring us out a bite, if you're of a mind." And then he left, turning his back on all the feelings inside him.

"*Feliz Navidad, señora,*" Luis whispered and placed in Olivia's lap a braided leather hair adornment.

Halsey came in quickly. "Happy Christmas, madame," he said, and he gave her a small bundle of sassafras roots, tied with woven threads.

Then Henry and Will came with their gift: a jar of honey, complete with honeycomb. "I had to wiggle in the tree and get it, 'cause Will was too big. And I didn't get stung, not once," Henry said proudly.

Olivia hugged the boys to her, and her emotions welled up from her heart and poured down her cheeks. How much her boys had grown and changed during these few short weeks.

For the party, Olivia wore her buff-colored brilliantine trimmed with satin-bound rose scallops. Though eight years old, it was the only dress she owned that wasn't a hand-me-down. She wondered what Monroe would think of her in it. For such a special occasion, she wore her mother's dangling pearl earrings. Though she would not have admitted it aloud, she thought them very sassy and hoped Monroe would, too.

Outside the air nipped, as it should on Christmas Day, Olivia thought. The sheep bleating in the corrals seemed appropriate, too. From the main cabin wafted the heavenly aromas of a Christmas Day—baked meats, rich coffee, sweet pastries. Will and Henry, in starched shirts and with hair neatly combed, were sitting quietly at the table. They grinned excitedly when she came in. "You look beautiful, Mama," Will said. "Like a princess," Henry said.

"And you two are my princes," she said, laughing and feeling as gay as a young girl.

She enlisted the boys' help in setting out the dishes, a mixture of her china and Monroe's tinware, and making the final preparations. All the while she waited eagerly for Monroe. She thought she heard him moving in his back room, but couldn't be certain. She told herself not to be a child; she had never been beautiful, and in any case, none of it mattered.

When the door to the back room opened, Olivia swung around. Monroe stepped into the room. Their eyes met and then skimmed over one another, shyly and boldly at once. His wavy hair was combed but remained unruly, wonderfully so. His mustache and beard were neatly groomed. He wore a white shirt that she hadn't seen before—and the vest she had given him!

Her gaze came back to his face to see a smile there, and admiration in his eyes. "You look gingham-pretty, Mizzuz Pritchett."

Pleasure, strong and sweet, swept her. "And you are very handsome, Mr. Locket."

He put a hand to the vest. "This peacock vest sets me off." He'd never had anything made just for him by a woman's hand. He'd never had anything so fine as this, never dared wear anything so flashy. But this vest suited him fine.

His sparkling eyes held hers, and a delicious, captivating joy wrapped around them both.

It seemed at once both became aware of the boys, standing side by side and staring. Monroe cleared his throat and mumbled that he had to check the stock, then strode across the room and out the door. He hadn't bothered with his hat, and felt naked.

Olivia grabbed up a cup towel and told the boys to go across and bring the rocking chair and the smallest of their trunks to use as a chair.

She drew on an apron, then stilled thoughtfully. The way Monroe had gazed at her echoed to her marrow. She would never, ever forget that look, nor the feelings it had stirred. She had felt beautiful.

Albert Burnham, his two sons and Dave Wills came on horseback. The two younger Burnhams were strapping, brash young men in their late teens. Right after them, in a wagon complete with harness bells, came Ely Chapman, a very stern man, his wife, Mary, a very timid woman, and teenage daughter Fanny, who was a little hard of hearing but neither stern nor timid. George Hillard, surely the toughest-looking man Olivia had ever seen, came with the solemn Purvis Malcolm and his family of three young boys, who had never seen a Christmas tree and were enthralled.

It was Albert Burnham who told her that Tee Thatcher was the only man who had not come. "Don't much miss him," he muttered.

As each guest arrived, polite greetings were exchanged, but then everyone clammed up and stood as if ready to fight. Soon the room was as full and as ready to explode as a can of beans gone bad. Luis and Halsey were absent, and having a good idea they were at someplace they could come in shooting should the need arise did not reassure Olivia, any more than did Monroe and Ely Chapman being the only two men who did not have guns on their hips. She went to plying everyone with coffee and hot apple-peach punch and friendly chatter, but no one seemed about to warm, even though the room was hot as Hades. Even Henry and Will stood aloof, off to the side beside Monroe, eyeing the Malcolm boys. Olivia wondered if she was going to end up right smack in the middle of a fracas and had visions of throwing herself on her boys to protect them. When George Hillard pulled out a flask of whiskey and took a good swig, her patience with coarse behavior reached its limit.

"Mr. Hillard, I must ask you not to drink in this house today. It is the Lord's birthday, and there are children present." She had to say it, and she didn't regret it.

George Hillard and everyone else stared at her as if she'd gone mad, and she figured she had with the idea of this party in the first place. She didn't understand these people—guns on their hips, minds set to fight.

Monroe speaking at her shoulder caused her to jump. "Out of respect for the ladies, Hillard, let's cut the dust outside." He pulled a liquor bottle from a cabinet, pressed past Purvis Malcolm and out the door. All eyes swung to Albert Burnham, who slowly stood, tipped his hat to Olivia and Mrs. Chapman, and followed. The other men filed out behind them.

Olivia sprang to the window, and Mary and Fanny Chapman squeezed in beside her. Will and Henry and the Malcolm boys cracked open the door and peeked.

Fanny Chapman said loudly, "Pa's got his shotgun in the wagon."

Olivia watched the men cluster around the Chapman wagon. They were solemn as funeral directors. Her heart thudded. Monroe was alone, with no gun. The men, their faces set hard, passed Monroe's and George Hillard's bottles. Monroe rolled a smoke, lit it and then stretched the match to the cigar Albert Burnham tucked between his lips. She saw Monroe speak. "I wonder what they're sayin'?" she whispered.

Mary Chapman spoke into her daughter's ear. "What are they sayin', Fanny?" Then she told Olivia, "Not hearin' too good, Fanny's learned to read lips right well."

Olivia and Mary glanced from the men outside to Fanny.

Fanny said loudly, "Monroe Locket said Missus Pritchett went to a lot of trouble cookin', and he don't want her riled, 'cause he don't want to deal with a wet hen—I think that's what he said. He just asked everyone to put their guns in the wagon. Albert Burnham..." She frowned, then smiled. "He said it would be a sin to waste Missus Pritchett's good cookin'. Pa...he says it's Christmas."

Albert Burnham removed his gun belt and laid it in the back of the wagon. The other men followed suit, then passed the bottles again.

Olivia looked from the men to the women beside her. "Ladies, will you join me in servin' our Christmas dinner before the men are soused?"

Mary Chapman smiled, growing valiant right before Olivia's eyes. "We'd be proud to, Missus Pritchett."

Fanny put a hand to Olivia's arm and spoke loudly. "I suggest we put blankets up on the ends of the trot and move the tables out there. We're all gonna puddle in here."

Olivia said it was a fine idea. She looked around to Will, who, being the tallest, was peering over the heads of the other boys out the door. "Will." He jumped and spun around. "You go tell the men we'll be eating in ten minutes and that we need help settin' up in the dogtrot. The rest of you boys start draggin' out these chairs."

"Missus Pritchett," the eldest of the Malcolm boys said, "I think we should tell you that this least one here is our sister Lolly, and she's a girl."

A good time was had by all. In time, Luis and Halsey joined in. Halsey, setting his rifle aside, said, "We figured we were missin' out on a good thing."

"Luis!" George Hillard greeted the old man somewhat sheepishly, obviously thinking of the trouble of days ago. However, the two knew each other from long ago, and George Hillard proclaimed that he and Luis were the only true Texans at the table.

Still later Neron appeared; Monroe had instructed him and Seco to bring their flocks in close enough to have all the men together for a short while. Seco was watching two flocks, and Olivia sent the boys out with a filled plate for him.

Olivia's food was much praised. The three big pans of biscuits she had made were left empty. The lamb roast was consumed, too, all but Albert Burnham eating it. Olivia suspected Mr. Burnham knew what it was, though he said nothing. Wisely, Monroe remained silent on the matter.

One of the Burnham brothers brought out a harmonica and Neron his guitar, and the two played carols while Halsey led all in song. The young men struck up lively tunes, and Mr. Chapman and his wife began to dance. Fanny asked the other Burnham brother to dance, and then Albert Burnham came over to Olivia.

"You are quite good, Mr. Burnham," Olivia said as he whirled her around the dirt-packed floor.

"As I said, you remind me of my heritage," he answered—a little wistfully, Olivia thought.

Monroe appeared beside them. "I'd like the pleasure," he said to Albert Burnham. Olivia's heart skipped a beat at the challenging look in Monroe's dark eyes. Albert Burnham grinned dryly, nodded grandly and backed away. Monroe's hand took hers. His arm went around her waist, and he whirled her around. He avoided her eyes. She longed for him and tried to hide it.

The sun was only a golden glow in the west when the guests departed, each adult with a loaf of Olivia's fruit bread, and the children with dried fruit jumbles, which Olivia admonished them to save for the morning.

As Mary Chapman's husband took her hand to help her into their wagon, she stopped and came back to Olivia. Her once-timid face was alive and glowing. "You have been to us all about like that angel who came to the shepherds on that first Christmas, proclaimin' peace on earth. Thank you." She hugged

Olivia tightly, and then, blushing, hurried back to be helped up into the wagon. Olivia blinked back tears.

Albert Burnham and his group were the last to leave, and before he mounted up, Mr. Burnham took Olivia aside. "Ma'am, I'm straight-talkin' an' straight-livin'. I enjoy a cigar and a drop of whiskey now and then, but I don't get drunk. I have a two-story clapboard house—five rooms with pump water inside. If you will marry me, I'll provide you with your own buggy and a servant. All you'd have to do is cook and keep my house." His eyes softened, and he gazed at her intently.

Olivia stared at him, completely speechless.

"You could think about it a couple of days, maybe come see my place."

But Olivia smiled gently. "I am most honored, Mr. Burnham, that a man such as yourself would think of me...but I cannot marry you. I'm...I'm sorry." And she thought how she was letting her chance to stay in Texas slide away.

She stood and watched the men ride off into the twilight, with the day's happenings swirling in her heart. Behind her Monroe said, "You make the most powerful food in the world, Olivia."

Olivia got the boys to bed early, for it had been a big day, and they were exhausted. After they had said nightly prayers, Henry insisted on singing "Silent Night" one more time. His eyes were closed by the time they finished. He mumbled to Olivia, "Christmas came, Mama."

Olivia kissed him. "Yes, honey, to all of us."

She climbed down from the loft, sat on the bed and took up the small treasure box Monroe had made her. The wood was as smooth as fine ivory, warm as heated honey. She continued to caress it, savoring it.

Christmas had come, she thought. And it had been most wonderful for her sons, just as she had wished. She thought of Will proudly cutting limbs with his buck knife and aiming rocks with his slingshot, and Henry drawing pictures and whistling tunes with his little whistle. *We had a good Christmas after all, John. I'm sorry you missed it.*

And now, she thought with a sigh, their stay at the ranch was almost finished. Four more days was all they had, and then Monroe would take them to Esperar to catch the stagecoach. She didn't want to think about it. Thinking of the coach ride and sleeping on those horrible, dirty mattresses at the stops was enough to wilt all the spirit Christmas had brought her.

She thought then of Albert Burnham. Oh, my, but life was full of surprises. She had let go her chance to remain in Texas. But she simply couldn't marry Albert Burnham. She could never again make a bargain marriage as she had intended with John. No...not now that she had met Monroe Locket.

She thought of going across now to finish straightening the main cabin. But no, she and Mary Chapman had cleaned up everything that was truly important. The real reason she wanted to go over was to see Monroe. She did need to thank him for her gift, she told herself most practically, and then her heart laughed at her foolishness. She simply needed to see him, because the loneliness was eating away at her.

Because hope had risen from some place, she thought as she caressed her treasure box.

She had not expected to find him sitting at the table with a cup of coffee and still wearing his vest, she noted with pleasure. He was munching on a biscuit, with two more on a plate in front of him.

"Monroe Locket, did you hide out those biscuits?"

"I plead guilty, ma'am, and I won't be stingy."

She laughed at that. He took up the coffeepot that was on the table and poured coffee into an extra cup that was setting there, too. He had been waiting for her, she realized with dawning joy and spiraling hope.

Slowly she moved to sit at his right hand. He didn't look at her, he just sipped his coffee. The murky glow of the three lamps above glimmered on his dark hair. She breathed deeply and stretched her tired legs. Pleasurable peace and quiet wove around them.

"This jam is mighty fine," he said. "What is it?"

"Fig . . . from our tree back home."

"Most people bring clothes and tools when they're headin' to a new home. You brought fancy food."

She smiled softly. "It was all for Christmas." She sipped the steaming coffee and recalled how she had kept tucking into the trunk one more jar of sweet, one more package of fruit. Remembering aloud, she said, "Celebrating this Christmas was to be the start of a new beginnin'—for John and me and the boys." She looked at him, shy but having to speak. "Thank you, Monroe, for the treasure box. It's about the prettiest thing I've ever seen. But most of all, thank you for allowin' us to have this Christmas. We live nicely at home. At least we're well fed and my husband's aunt and uncle see us well cared for. But Christmas for that family has been a time of bitter memories for many years now. One of their sons died on Christmas during the war, and Aunt Cecilia won't have a tree in the house, nor any kind of merrymaking. This...this time was special for us, and I think the boys and I may have found a new beginning after all."

She hadn't meant to tell him all of that, but it felt good to have done so.

His gaze flicked to her, then back to his coffee. "I saw you talkin' with Burnham before he left. Are you gonna hitch up with him?"

The question popped her mouth wide. "How did you know he asked me to marry him?"

"He spoke to me earlier about it, wanted to know if I had any objections," he said, and Olivia felt cold disbelief. Then he raised an eyebrow. "Are you gonna marry up with him?"

Outrage, like a creeping thing, slipped up her spine. She set her cup to the table with great care. "He asked you if you had objections? And you said you didn't?"

His eyes flicked to hers, then back to his cup. "I told him I had no claim on you. You had been John's."

Those words added fuel to the fire. "That's right...as I recall you used the term 'John's log to carry.'" His eyes widened. "Well, let me tell you, Monroe Locket, I am not some...some log that you can say you don't want, and then offer to a neighbor!" She stood, knocking over the bench. "I'm going to be gone soon enough—you needn't try to *foist* me off as soon as possible!"

"I wasn't foistin' you. He asked for you. And are you?"

"No, I'm not!" She turned, and her skirts got all tangled around her legs. She jerked them straight and headed for the door.

Monroe stood. "What are you gettin' in a swivet about? What'd I do?"

She whirled at him. "I'm not some piece of ranch equipment that can go to the highest bidder, Monroe Locket. I'm not some fancy stove one of you ranchers can bring home to stick in the kitchen to give out biscuits!" She turned, and again her skirts got all wrapped around her legs.

"I never said you were anything like that. I told Burnham you were your own woman, and he'd have to ask you."

"How wonderful of you, thinkin' of me!" Tears blurred her vision. "Oh!" She clamped her teeth against profanities, flung open the door and raced across the dogtrot.

Monroe called after her, "Why in the hell did you tell him no, if you want to live in Texas?"

She slammed the door and threw herself across the bed, muffling her sobs in the pillows. *He didn't want her. He didn't want her at all.* The thought echoed painfully.

Chapter Nine

Olivia hadn't consciously known the direction of her feelings until Monroe said what he did about not having any objections to Albert Burnham proposing marriage to her.

He wouldn't care at all if she should go off married to another man.

That had been a sword to her heart, pain so real she'd thought her heart would burst. She knew then, in the midst of her shattered dreams, that she had fallen in love with Monroe Locket. That the faceless man in her dreams had begun to take on features at long last—and they were Monroe's features. That she had fallen in love for the second time in her life. This time with the full love of a woman grown. And she had, deep down, been hoping—yes, even expecting—him to ask her to stay and marry him.

But he did not want her.

As she rose and dressed the following morning, she prepared to face Monroe. He must never know her feelings. No one must know. She would not have the humiliation.

The men began dipping the sheep again at first light. When they came for breakfast, Olivia strove to act natural, though she felt most awkward. She greeted everyone pleasantly, even Monroe, though she did not meet his gaze. Nor did she again find occasion to speak to him. The most he said to her was "Is there more coffee?" What he had said about her not being his "log" to carry and having no claim or objections to her marrying Albert Burnham kept echoing in her mind and stirring anger in her heart. Unable to sit at the table, she rose and began scrubbing pots.

Among themselves the men talked about this day being the last for dipping the sheep. Seco had already moved his flock west, and Neron had moved to the northwest. Halsey would move south the first thing in the morning. Will wanted to go along with Halsey for an overnight, but Olivia absolutely refused, so sharply that Will gave her a strange look.

She decided to leave the cedar limbs up around the cabins. They remained alive and green, and she took comfort in that somehow. But at midmorning she and Henry "undressed the tree," as Henry put it. He was sad to see it go. "We won't ever have another tree," he said, with a face a yard long and tears glistening in his eyes.

"Oh, yes, we will," Olivia said. "Next Christmas."

"Aunt Cecilia never let us have a tree."

"When we go home, I shall get a job and we shall have our own house, and we shall have a Christmas tree for the entire month, if we so desire." The words poured from Olivia before she thought that perhaps she shouldn't have spoken them. She didn't want to raise Henry's hopes and not be able to fulfill them. Yet, once spoken, the words seemed to give her strength.

"What job will you get, Mama?"

"Well . . . perhaps I can get a job as a cook. Everyone certainly seems to like what I cook." She thought how Cecilia would have a gigantic hissy fit about a woman of the Pritchett family doing such a thing.

"Will says he can work, too, and I will find something to do," Henry said very seriously.

"You will help me," Olivia said brightly.

She had thought her boys had changed, but perhaps she had done more changing than anyone. She had not realized until now how the rancid bitterness and outdated mores held by Cecilia and Phillip and the rest of the family had so wrapped around her as to hold her captive with them. Now, however, she had broken free and was determined to go ahead in her life.

Monroe found Olivia alone, preparing to put dinner on the table. Her eyes came around to his for a split second, and then she turned her rigid back and focused on stirring her bean soup. She was still angry. Monroe wasn't quite certain what he had done; women were a foreign species to him. He walked toward her, but she kept on ignoring him. He stopped at the sideboard, three feet away from her. He stared at the graceful line of her neck. Funny how he'd thought her plain. She wasn't. Her hair was like silk, and her skin like creamy velvet. He felt at a loss. He didn't want her to be angry with him.

He said, "We won't be havin' dinner at noon. Those dark clouds in the north mean a norther comin', so we'll be at it to finish in the next couple hours. Thought I'd take out coffee, though." And why he was in here, hankering after a woman, when he had important work on the line, he couldn't fathom.

She nodded. "It's made. And I can put the last of the cheese in these hot biscuits." She moved to the worktable. Monroe remained where he was.

"Olivia, I never had it in mind to be *foistin'* you off on Albert Burnham. What I was, was tryin' not to stand in your way. Albert Burnham is a wealthy man for these parts. His house ain't no backwoods couple of cabins but a proper house, with a stove in the parlor and fine furniture from Tennessee, too. With Burnham you and the boys would have just near every comfort you did back in Carolina. And he's a good man, like John was, though it galls me to say it."

Her face came around slowly. For an instant he was appalled to see tears in her eyes, but she quickly looked down into the boiling pot of beans. Again she took up the spoon and began to stir, and quite hard. Monroe felt totally inept, and cursed his foolishness for ever coming in to speak to her.

She said, "That was most kind of you, Monroe, to think of our welfare. I misunderstood, and I apologize for my outburst, though I must say that I'm not a woman who can have her head turned by a pretty house and a few comforts. I cannot marry Albert Burnham."

An odd relief touched Monroe. He shifted his stance. "Well, I admit that Albert Burnham ain't got John's style," he said, "but he makes up for it in other ways. And, while I ain't aimin' to pull up a pulpit, I have to point out that you did come all the way down here with the aim of gettin' a home and a husband and father for the boys."

"My wants go a lot deeper than simply for any human in pants," she said quite sharply. Swift as a pecking hen, she wrapped a thick towel around the coffeepot and shoved it at him. "You can take this out. I'll bring out the biscuits and cheese in a minute."

She clearly meant for him to get out, and he did. He had a ranch to run, and didn't need to keep getting himself sidetracked with this woman!

Olivia sliced the biscuits and cheese with a fury, thinking that Monroe Locket's brain was thick as leftover cream gravy. Her shoulders sagged. He simply didn't see her need, because he didn't feel about her as she did about him. That was all. He had been courteously thinking of her and the boys' welfare. That she wished for far more from him than common courtesy was no fault of his.

The darkness to the northwest approached, and just as the last sheep was run up out of the dipping vat, the first snowflake began to fall. The wind rose, and a true blizzard bore down on them. Olivia, with the wind tearing at her wool cape and the scarf wrapped around her head, helped to get the cow, squawking chickens and wet lambs and ewes into the barn. As uncomfortable as she was, she had to laugh at Henry and Will, who were delighting in the driving snow. She had not ever expected to see Henry robust enough to do so, and, worriedly, she quickly got him inside to dry by the stove.

After supper, in their sleeping cabin, Olivia, Will and Henry peered at the window. All beyond was black night, but they could see the snow piling on the sill. Olivia opened the window wide enough for the boys to scoop up handfuls. They squeezed the wet, heavy snow in their palms.

"Maybe it will snow so much we can't get into Esperar for the stage," Will said.

Olivia eyed him. "If we didn't go this week, we would have to go two weeks from now. We can't stay here forever, Will." She felt so sorry for disappointing him.

"Why can't we stay?" Henry asked, in all innocence.

"Because this place belongs to Mr. Locket," Olivia said. "Now let's say our prayers, and you boys can go up to bed." She moved over to sit on the bed.

Henry scrambled up beside her. "Won't Mr. Locket let us stay? I thought he liked us. He was nice on that day we went ridin', and he's helped me with the whistle Santa Claus left me, and I saw him kiss you."

It was Will's turn to give her an eye. Olivia, not about to ask which kiss Henry had seen—not about to speak about the kiss at all—said, "Mr. Locket does like us, but that doesn't mean we can stay. For one thing, it is improper for an unmarried man and woman to live together. Now, say prayer."

They repeated their nightly prayers, Will including Neron and Seco in his God-blesses, Henry God-blessing every animal on the ranch.

Then Will said, very practically, "Why can't you marry Mr. Locket, just like you were gonna marry John Carter?" Both boys stared at her.

"Because Mr. Locket is not of the same mind about marriage that John was." She directed him toward the ladder.

"Couldn't you just ask him about it?" Will asked. "I'll bet he'd think it was a good idea. He sure likes your cookin'."

Olivia thought if she heard about her cooking one more time, she was going to scream. "No. Good night, boys."

She lay awake staring into the coals of the fire, her mind dwelling on Will's last comment. She imagined herself asking Monroe to marry her. It was very easy to imagine doing. In her dream all went wonderfully, romantically, and he swept her into his arms and told her he loved her. However, she'd learned long ago that dreams and reality rarely went hand in hand.

The blizzard was long past and the sun peeking up into a clear, frosty winter sky the following morning, when Halsey and his two dogs moved the sheep out. By nine o'clock the sun was warming the ground, and by noon the snow was confined to the shade. Olivia was hanging wash on the line, warming her hands every couple of minutes beneath her arms, when she looked around to see Purvis Malcolm riding up.

"Good day, Mr. Malcolm. How nice to see you." Refraining from the unbecoming act of warming her hands beneath her arms, she tucked them into the pockets of her apron. "Mr. Locket is out behind the barn."

The man dismounted from his short and scraggly horse. His eyes, set deep in his bony face, flickered shyly to hers, and he snatched his battered hat from his head. "I didn't come to see Monroe, ma'am. I came to speak with you."

That took the huckleberry off the bush, as Monroe would have said. Olivia finally remembered her manners. "Please come in for coffee, Mr. Malcolm. I'm sure you could use it."

"Yes, ma'am . . . I could."

He was neatly clothed in what appeared his best flannel shirt, vest and duck pants. His hair had been combed, though his hat had wrecked that. He was about as bony a man as Olivia had ever laid eyes on, and he fairly crackled with nervousness. He sat at the table and, while drinking his coffee, responded to Olivia's polite inquiry as to his and his children's welfare and comment upon the weather. Then he got to the point of his visit. He told her his children were good young'ns and no trouble. Lolly hardly made a sound. He had cabins just like these, with stout floors but without a stove, though he would go to San Antone to get one. . . .

From the first sentence, she knew what he was about. She forced herself to look directly at him, to listen with the highest respect to every last word and not reveal her growing horror at the fact that she would have to turn him down. She knew it had cost him dearly to come to her, and she knew he'd done it mostly for his children. He, a skinny, bent man, was a man among men.

He told her of his fine dappled-gray mare and his buggy, and of having enough cash put by to buy pretties for the cabin. All of that would be hers, if she would come and marry him. He ended by saying, "My children need motherin', and I would certainly be proud to have a good woman such as yourself as my wife. I don't beat women," he added, and all the while he spoke, he twisted his hat on the table.

Olivia tucked away a smile at the last part. The dear, dear man. "You honor me, sir, with your request. I must have a few moments alone to consider." She went to the storeroom and sat on Monroe's bed, and thought, if only *Monroe* would ask her...

When it seemed to her that enough considering time had passed, she returned and turned him down as gently as possible. "Your children are lucky to have such a father," she told him, and he seemed to walk much taller when he went out to mount his horse. He rode away quite straight-backed.

Monroe had seen Purvis Malcolm arrive and then go into the cabin with Olivia. He sent Will to check on his mother, and Will reported that Purvis Malcolm was sitting at the table all by himself. "I didn't ask him why," Will said. Monroe debated and at last headed for the house, just as Malcolm was riding away.

He went to where Olivia was hanging clothes. "Was that Purvis Malcolm?" It was a foolish thing to ask, because he knew it was—what he wanted was to know what had gone on, why Purvis Malcolm had come to visit her. He didn't care for his suspicions.

"Yes."

He waited for her to elaborate, which she deliberately didn't do, forcing him to ask, "What did he want?"

"To ask me to marry him." With swift movements, she pinned the edge of Will's shirt in place, bent, took up her wash basket and headed for the house.

"Well, I hope you turned *him* down. All he's got is calamities."

She whirled around. "Purvis Malcolm is a fine man—a man not too proud to admit he'd like a woman's touch!" She stalked to the cabin, leaving him staring after her.

He wondered if she would actually marry Malcolm, and a great ache flowed over him. *Well, he didn't care! No, sir, he didn't! And he wasn't about to ask her about it, either!*

Olivia harbored a threadbare hope that Purvis Malcolm's proposal would stir Monroe to action. But three days later, over an hour before dawn, he was loading their trunks and bags into the back of the wagon. Olivia was surprised to see he had shaved—and had had a rough time of it, because he'd opened some of the small cuts that remained on his face. With furtive glances, she saw that the bruise beneath his eye was now only a shadow. His mustache was neatly formed. She wondered if he'd attended to his appearance for her, but it didn't seem likely. He was very distant, saying little. They hadn't spoken more than a dozen words at once to one another in the past two and a half days. Both had held to polite reserve.

Uncountable times, Olivia had thought of asking Monroe Locket to marry her in the same manner Albert Burnham and Purvis Malcolm had asked her. What did it matter who did the asking, and what did it matter whether he married her for love or for her biscuits? After they were married, he would come to love her. Surely he would. But fear and pride held her back.

Once he'd come up to her as she tended John's grave. She'd said impulsively, "Monroe..." and everything inside her had frozen with timidity.

"What is it, Olivia?" he'd asked, curious, inviting—even, perhaps, eager.

But she'd shaken her head and said, "Nothing... Excuse me." And she'd fled. As long as she didn't ask, she would not have to face the finality of his no and could go on hoping, all the way into Esperar. And beyond.

The day looked much as it had when she and the boys had first arrived in Esperar, cold and blustery, the sky washed with gray. Olivia wore her wool cape and traveling suit she had arrived in, her plumed hat, and had fastened her mother's dangling pearl earrings to her ears. She felt she needed the sass they gave her.

Choking back tears, she bid Luis goodbye. Will shook his hand. Henry, who'd grown very fond of the wise old man, flung his arms around his waist. Will offered his hand to help Olivia into the wagon seat. My, how he had matured during these weeks! He helped Henry up into the back, and only then did Olivia see Monroe bringing the bay gelding. He helped Will to mount up, then came over and hefted himself up into the seat beside Olivia. He didn't look at her and was as distant as the blue mountains. He snapped the reins, and they were off.

Olivia turned. She hadn't meant to but she couldn't restrain herself. She waved at Luis, who stood waving back. And she tried to implant in memory the look of this place where she had come to know a stronger facet of herself and her sons. Where they had spent the best Christmas of their lives. Where she had fallen in love.

Then she faced forward and sat straight, with her cloak wrapped around her traveling suit.

Five hours and even the boys said little. When Henry asked to ride with Will, Olivia allowed it. She also allowed them to ride off some distance, to enjoy themselves in the manner of *vaqueros,* while they could.

It was midday when Monroe stopped the team in front of the hotel. He hurried around to help her from the wagon, but she didn't wait for him, jumping down herself. She wouldn't look at him, and Monroe felt almost as if she'd already left him.

"I can take the boys with me to the livery," he told her. "I'll arrange with Ross to have your big trunk freighted back. And I'll wait to see you on the stage," he added, feeling self-conscious about what she might think.

She simply nodded, lifted her skirts and went into the hotel. He watched her swaying feminine movements until the door closed behind her.

It was Henry's voice that jarred him back to the moment. "Can I sit in the seat with you, Mr. Locket?"

Monroe spun around and saw the boys staring at him. A glance at Will, and he knew the boy had noticed him staring after his mother like a lovesick ram, Monroe thought, embarrassed. Henry regarded him expectantly. "Yeah, sure... Climb on over."

Monroe got up beside the young'n and flicked the reins, sending Joe and Barney toward the livery. Will helped him see to the team, and Henry took care of graining them, while Monroe moved over to help the boy unsaddle the bay gelding. He looked down at the boy's dark silky hair and thought how he'd gotten real used to the boy being around. He was damn sure gonna miss the boy—and the little one, too. These boys were what he'd want his own to be . . . if he ever had any.

"Mr. Locket?" Will said in a very low voice.

"Yeah?"

"Do you think you'll ever be married?"

Few times in his life had Monroe ever been so surprised. "Why in tarnation would you wonder about something like that?"

The boy's eyes swung to his. "Well, it was just a thought," he said with a shrug, as if there were more to say but he wasn't saying it.

Despite himself, when Monroe walked to the livery door, he paused and scanned the hotel windows, wondering about Olivia. Wondering what she would say if he asked her. It was the only way he could get her to stay, and heaven knew he didn't want her to leave.

He felt a great relief at having admitted that to himself at last.

Olivia had taken a room in which to rest and refresh herself. An hour later, from the window, she saw the stagecoach, a small moving dot far out upon the grassland. Without hurrying, she placed her hat upon her head, took up her small purse and carpetbag in one hand and lifted her skirt with the other. On the stairway she met Henry and Will racing up.

"The stage is comin', Mama." Will appeared mixed between reluctance and the natural excitement that any travel would bring a boy. He took her bag, and Henry took hold of her hand.

Selma Tucker came bustling through, smiling. She gave Henry a small sack containing some fruitcake and apples. Grateful, Olivia passed the older woman the last of her rosewater, and then the two women exchanged hugs. There came the sound of the stage stopping out front. Selma pressed her toward the door. "Oh, dear... Here you go. That Gilbert won't wait on God himself."

Will held the door open. Olivia saw the coach and Oscar Tucker tossing their bags to the driver, who was stowing them in the boot. She looked for Monroe. And then there he was before her. She gazed up into his dark eyes. She thought she saw warmth there, and longing, too. She almost asked him then if he would have her, but the words wouldn't come past her pride. And she didn't want to embarrass him.

Then, very gently, he took her arm and escorted her and Henry toward the coach. The door was open, and a portly gray-haired man in a suit and a bowler sat inside, staring out at them.

Monroe bent and looked Henry in the eye. "Be good for your ma, Henry." He ruffled Henry's hair, then lifted him and set him inside the coach. He and Will gazed at each other. Monroe stuck out his hand. "When you get sixteen, if you still want to come, you'll have a job at my place. You're a good hand."

Pride glowed on Will's face, and Henry cried, "Can I come, too?"

To which Monroe, actually grinning, said, "You come first chance you get, Henry."

In a very manly fashion, Will shook Monroe's hand. "Thank you, sir, for teachin' me to ride . . . and stuff." His eyes blinked rapidly, and he grew embarrassed.

"You bet. Take care of your ma."

Will climbed inside the coach, and then it was Olivia's turn. The driver called impatiently, "Time!"

Olivia searched Monroe's eyes. Every cell in her body cried out for him to speak. To ask her to stay.

He said, "I thank you, Olivia, for all you did." His lips formed into a crooked grin. "You're sure a joe darter."

She managed to smile. She tried to speak, to tell him of the love in her heart, but the words wouldn't come.

"Ma'am, either get in or move away, 'cause we're leavin'," the driver ordered from his seat.

Olivia remained mute, because she knew she would burst into sobs should she try to say a word. She placed her foot on the step, and Monroe took her arm to help her inside. She paused, turned her head to look into his eyes, only scant inches from hers. Then, in a burst of bold, devil-be-damned passion, there in full view of everyone, she threw her arms around his neck and kissed him with all the pent-up emotion and fire inside her. A kiss to say what her lips would not. A kiss to remember for a lifetime.

When she broke away, she turned, took hold of the door and slammed it shut behind her. She sat in the seat and stared straight ahead. She could not bear to see his face, and couldn't face the inquiring stares from her sons. The driver's voice rang out, and the coach jerked and took them racing away.

The stage's dust was still swirling around him by the time Monroe came to his senses. The first thing he saw was Selma Tucker shaking her head at him. "You're downright stupid if you let that gal go, Monroe Locket."

"No, ma'am... I ain't stupid," he said as he broke into a run. His horses were stabled, but George Hillard was just coming out of The Emporium to get onto his horse, which was tied at the rail. Monroe called, "George, let me use your horse!"

He didn't give George time to say yea or nay, but pushed the bigger man aside and started the horse after the stage at a lope even before he was fully in the saddle. George always had enjoyed good horseflesh, and this one flew across the ground.

Monroe's heart pounded in his chest as he closed in on the stage. He hoped the horse didn't hit a hole and break both their damn necks. At least not before he had a chance to tell Olivia how he felt about her. He guessed she'd left him little doubt as to how she felt. Everything inside him was whooping for joy.

He yelled to Gilbert, who looked around and then slowed the stage. Will's head poked out the window, and Monroe waved to him.

"Mama! It's Mr. Locket!" Will cried.

"Lemme see." Henry pushed beneath his brother.

"What is it? A bandit?" the portly gentleman across from them cried.

"It's Mr. Locket," Henry told him righteously.

Olivia turned cold and then hot. Through the open window in the door she was amazed to see Monroe riding at a breakneck speed up alongside the coach.

The next instant the coach halted, sending Olivia nearly pitching headlong into the portly gentleman's lap. She thought she heard Monroe calling her name. Hope rose like a bird in flight, and she began to cry.

"Hey, Mr. Locket!" Will called, popping open the door even as the coach still rolled.

Olivia grabbed him. "Will! Be careful!" But he was out and away, Henry scrambling to follow, leaving the door banging in the breeze. The drivers were hollering something, and the portly gentleman was fearfully muttering about a holdup.

And then there was Monroe in the door, reaching for her. He took hold of her hand and pulled her out and into his arms. He held her a moment, then slid her down his body until her feet touched the ground. He cupped her face, sweeping away the tears with his thumbs. She gazed up and saw the love shining in his beautiful dark eyes. "Oh, Monroe..."

"I'll never be anythin' but a rough ol' backwoods cob, Olivia. I ain't got the education and wealth of Albert Burnham, nor whatever it was that you saw in Purvis Malcolm, but I can give you what they never could...which is to say that I love you, darlin', not just your biscuits."

And then he kissed her, and they both let their hearts speak far more than words could ever say.

* * * * *

A Note from Curtiss Ann Matlock

Dear Reader,

Our Christmas tree is put together in a traditional ritual. First, my husband is in charge of putting on the beautiful angel and the lights. Then the ornaments are hung, beginning with the most precious. I hang the glass ball dating from WWII, which was my mother's, and our son begins with our collection of baker's clay figures. Each figure is admired and the memories of making it recalled.

The Christmas stocking ornament with toys was the first piece my husband made. It requires a strong branch, because he made it so thick. It's sort of lumpy, too, because he didn't prick it. But aren't real stockings lumpy? Then there's the bear with our son's initials on his chest; I made it when our son was four. And there's the murky brown teddy bear that was one of my son's first efforts, and the Christmas tree he did when he was five that showed great improvement in his talent.

Let me assure you that we have created some lovely pieces, too. There are the five brightly painted rocking horses, a mustached toy soldier and a snowman with top hat and broom.

Making things from baker's clay is an art that dates to Egyptian times. Our ornaments are all eight to thirteen years old now. They can last indefinitely, but without a doubt, the memories made with them last a lifetime.

I wish you a Merry Christmas that makes a good memory.

Curtiss Ann Matlock

A FAIRYTALE SEASON
Marianne Willman

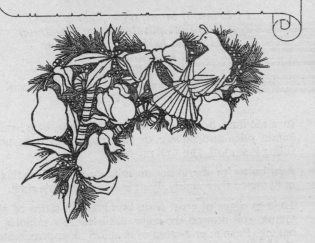

For my aunts, Helen Wojcik and Ruth Clark,
with love

In the South, this traditional dish is often called "Chess Pie." Unlike cakes and cookies, you can alter pie recipes. (The basic pie changes from kitchen to kitchen.) It's fun because you can experiment and tailor the ingredients to your taste.

MARIANNE WILLMAN'S SUGAR PIE

1 1-lb box of brown sugar (light or dark)
4 eggs (may use equivalent in egg substitute)
¼ cup milk, half and half or cream
1 tsp lemon juice
1 tsp of flavoring
4 tbsp butter or solid margarine, melted and cool
1 unbaked 9" pie shell

In a medium bowl, combine brown sugar, eggs, milk, lemon juice and liqueur or flavoring. Beat well, until filling is smooth and well mixed.

Add butter or margarine to mixture slowly, beating it until mixed thoroughly. Pour into unbaked pie shell.

To keep edges of crust from burning, put strips of aluminum foil around the edges until last few minutes of baking. Bake in preheated oven at 325° F approximately 45-50 minutes.

Cool slightly before cutting. Serve warm or cold, plain or with ice cream—vanilla, pecan, pralines and cream—or whipped cream or whipped substitute. (See what I mean? Lots of fun.)

Note: For a more candylike texture, add more brown sugar, decrease eggs to 3. For a more custardy texture, add 2 more eggs (or the equivalent in egg substitute) for a total of 6.

Chapter One

The Princess Irina Christina of Merkelstein was in a terrible temper. Her shrill voice, in impeccably accented English, had assaulted Ellen Shepherd's ears all the way from their hotel to the pier.

"Olga will suffer the consequences of her inefficiency. That ungrateful wretch! After all I have done for her! I shall dismiss her from her post at once! Why, were I in my own country, I would have her in chains for such incompetence."

The carriage turned onto the quay. The breeze coming off the water was brisk, bringing with it hints of colder weather to come. Christmas would be white in England this year. Ellen, called Nell by her nearest and dearest, pitied poor little Olga, who had been the princess' private secretary for the past year. It wasn't Olga's fault that the time of sailing had been changed and the princess had come down from London, so late she had almost missed the scheduled sailing.

Lifting her fine gray eyes, Nell saw the *Pride of Paradise* riding at anchor at the end of the wharf. Ribbons of steam curled from the red-painted stacks amidships. The luxury steamship was in the final stages of preparation to weigh anchor for its transatlantic crossing. With fair weather, she would be in the Leeward Isles on Christmas Day, beneath a hot tropical sun.

She touched the brooch at her collar. It was a circle pin of white gold with marcasites surrounding a gray opal. It had belonged to her mother. Nell had never imagined spending Christmas so far from home, on foreign shores. In happier times, when her parents were still alive, Christmas had always been a fairytale season, filled with laughter and love. She stifled a sigh.

Those days seemed like something from a fading dream. Young women forced to make their way alone in the world and to provide schooling for beloved younger brothers, found daily life far removed from that of storybook heroines. If Nell had been blessed at birth by a fairy godmother, that magical creature had failed to materialize thus far.

The sight of the ship brought home the reality of her predicament. She cast a wary eye at the sturdy figure beside her, swathed in frilled emerald satin, with masses of curls of an improbable oxblood color. The princess, never in the best of moods, was working herself into a frenzy, muttering imprecations in her own vowel-thickened language. Poor Olga was in for it!

Suddenly Nell wished she had the nerve to order the hackney driver to stop so that she might jump down and vanish into the drifting fog along the docks. Four hours in the princess' company was enough to make an angel want to throttle the woman! *And,* Nell thought wryly, *I have never been mistaken for one yet. Not with my impetuous nature.*

If she had not been so desperate to get to the island of Antigua, *nothing* would have forced her into her present plight. She had taken the position of companion to the irascible princess in order to gain passage to the West Indies. Thank God it was only temporary. Still, two weeks at sea with the dictatorial royal would be two weeks of purgatory. Or, more likely, unadulterated hell.

Nell smoothed the black braid on her plain gray traveling dress, a habit she exercised when something worried her deeply. Olga was such a quiet, mousy little creature, and her English was not always understandable. Where on earth would she go, alone and friendless in a foreign country, and what would happen to her if she was indeed dismissed without references? The picture her imagination conjured up was not a pretty one.

Nell knew how difficult it would be. She had gone through lean times herself after losing her comfortable position in the Wimbly household when that dreadful Peregrine Wimbly tried to kiss her on the back stairway. Though the incident had been none of her doing, the Wimblys had sent her packing posthaste, afraid their darling son and heir would contract a mésalliance with a mere governess.

She was distracted from her worries when the hackney stopped near the gangplank. She glanced up to see Olga at the rail, her small face pinched and white. The Princess Irina spied her secretary at the same time. Her thick features sharpened, and her small eyes grew harder than stone. There was not the slightest sign of mercy in her look, and Nell knew that nothing she might say would have any impact. Olga would be dismissed on the spot, without a qualm. Her Royal Highness had made it quite clear that she considered servants such as Nell and Olga to be on the same level as stray dogs and cart horses.

Nell slipped a card from her reticule. If all else failed, Olga might apply to the Reverend Michael Matcham and Mrs. Matcham for aide. Michael and Nell were cousins, and he and his sweet wife had never failed her in time of need. They had even offered to sell the Regency sideboard that had been his grandfather's to finance Nell's journey. She had refused as delicately as possible. Next to the Matchams and their six children, the proverbial church mice were extremely well-off—and the sale of that sideboard might some day pay for the education of their promising young sons.

The groom let the steps down for them. As they exited the carriage, Olga came down the gangplank to meet them, struggling to keep her pince-nez from falling. She was an unprepossessing woman at the best of times. Now, with her pale hair loose from its bun and the tip of her nose an unbecoming shade of red due to a cold, she looked like a white mouse peering out at a menacing world from behind her gold-rimmed spectacles.

"I vas so vorried," Olga exclaimed. "I am so very glad that you have arrived in time despite everything."

The princess whirled on the poor girl. "Incompetent fool." She raised her umbrella as if to strike the girl, but Nell stepped between them. Irina Christina lowered it, but the look she gave Olga was murderous. "If I had missed the sailing, it would be all your fault, you...you *imbecile!* In the past, people have been thrown into the dungeons of Merkelstein Castle for less. Remove your belongings from the ship. You arc relieved of your position.''

Olga blanched even whiter. "But...but..."

"If you do not do so immediately, I shall have the steward throw them over the side of the ship when we leave port."

The princess was about to go up the gangplank when she noticed a teamster loading up luggage next to a piling. She stiffened, recognizing one of her green leather trunks, the Merkelstein crest emblazoned upon its sides in gold.

"You there! What are you doing with my trunk?"

The teamster ignored her and hoisted the trunk on the back of the wagon. "Stupid peasant!" Princess Irina Christina shouted, adjusting her many-plumed hat like a knight adjusting his helm before entering the lists. She advanced down the pier toward him with a martial look in her eye, wielding her spike-tipped umbrella like a weapon to cleave a path through the crowd.

Olga's thin body shook. "Vat vill I do? I have no friends in England, and novhere to go."

Nell put her arm around the girl and slipped Michael's card into her hand, along with the few pound notes she had managed to save. "You are better off away from that horrid creature. Go straight to this address. The Reverend Mr. Matcham is my cousin. He will help you."

Olga's blue eyes brimmed over. "You are so good. So kind. If ever I can repay you, Miss Shepherd—"

The ship's steam whistle sounded, a deep, shivery hoot that assaulted Nell's ears and rumbled through her bones. "I'll help you gather your belongings. Go to my cousin, and try not to worry."

As they boarded the ship, she felt another qualm. The waters looked rather rough. Never having sailed before, Nell had no idea whether she could tolerate a sea voyage. She was fine in an open carriage, but was invariably ill on the stagecoach that ran from Bath to London. The idea of bobbing like a cork all the way to the Caribbean filled her with unease.

Or perhaps this discomfort was merely a result of the tide starting to turn. Even at anchor she could feel the rise and fall of the ship beneath her feet. The rise and fall ... rise and fall ...

Nell grimaced and closed her eyes, but that only made it worse. She opened them quickly and took a deep breath. If she got seasick before they even sailed, she had no doubt that the princess would leave her stranded on the wharf. And she had to get to Antigua, regardless of what she had to endure in the process.

Her younger and only surviving brother, Harry, was a budding botanist. He had gone there the previous April to visit friends and study the flora of the island paradise. His cheerful letters had arrived with regularity until September, when they had ceased abruptly. Her two letters to him since then had both been returned marked Address Unknown. Her numerous inquiries had proved fruitless.

Harry had vanished.

A chill settled over her heart. What could have happened to him, alone on foreign shores? Her hands clenched together. Harry had to be all right. He simply had to be.

Suddenly there was a loud commotion down on the wharf—a high-pitched squeal of alarm that could have come from an irate pig, and a donkey's loud bray, followed by more squeals, and curses in a thick masculine voice. Olga, pausing by the rail, had an unobstructed view. She waved agitatedly to Nell.

"Hurry! The princess...she has suffered an accident!"

They ran down the swaying gangway and made their way through the crowd of interested onlookers. The princess lay sprawled on the wharf amid a welter of shiny but very dead fish, her red wig half-off, and a good deal of her lace pantalettes showing. The crowd was too busy debating why she was lying there to help.

"Had a fit o' some kind," a sailor announced. "Started shouting about how she was a 'princess of the blood' and 'off with his head' and such. Next thing I knew, she was all foaming at the mouth."

"Nah, the old bawd is dead drunk," another fellow affirmed. "Proper paralytic," his companion agreed.

The princess came out of her swoon. Her pale gooseberry eyes filled with cold fire. "What are you looking at, you silly fools? Stand away, I say!" She tried to rise, but fell back, gasping. "Oooh! My leg!"

Nell reached her side and took the woman's hand in hers. "What is wrong, Your Highness? What has happened?"

The princess snatched her hand away and whacked Nell across the arm with the handle of her umbrella.

"You stupid girl! What do you think has happened? That filthy peasant and his wretched donkey have broken my leg!" She tried to move, and her eyes glazed over with pain.

The crowd looked around for the vendor and his cart, but they had vanished into the mist. The thin man jabbed his friend with an elbow. "Told you she was drunk."

"Never could abide a doxy what can't hold her gin," his friend replied.

They were no help at all. Nell spied a swarthy fellow in a uniform with Pride of Paradise embroidered on the jacket. "Tell the captain what has occurred, if you please." She turned to Olga, who had just joined them. "The princess is suffering from shock. I will stay with her while—"

"You will do nothing of the kind," the princess snapped, stirring to life once more. She broke off to moan just once. "I am still in command of my senses. Where is my maid?"

A buxom woman in a dark traveling gown stepped down from the second carriage, which had just arrived with the rest of the princess' baggage. "Ah, there you are, Anna. You will stay with me until help arrives. And you, Miss Shepherd, will go aboard that accursed ship and pack up the rest of my belongings. At once. Olga will help you."

The princess shifted her bulk and winced. "Oh, oh! My poor leg! Oh, the shipping company shall hear from me! Letting rabid donkeys run loose... As for the scurrilous fellow whose stupidity caused the accident—clap him in irons!"

While the princess bellowed and threatened, an interested crowd gathered. "Cor, 'ow she does go on! Regular fishwife." They drew closer to see what might come of this promising spectacle.

Nell was torn between obeying her employer's orders and leaving the injured woman to the care of her maid, who spoke no English. Olga's eyes were filled with pleading. "Please do as she says," she whispered. "Perhaps she vill not dismiss me from her service now. And see, here are the kind sailors come to help us."

Even in her dismay, Nell knew that Olga was right. At least one of us will be employed, she thought. But, sorry as she felt for anyone with a broken leg, she would not stay on herself for more than a few days after seeing the princess comfortably settled. She would get to Antigua, even if she had to stow away on the next ship out. At the moment, that appeared to be her only chance of gaining passage.

As Nell rose, a deep voice cut through the commotion. "Now then, what has happened here?"

The crowd parted before a man in a thick traveling cape. He was tall, wide-shouldered and as splendid as a prince in a fairy tale. He took the situation in at a glance. "Stand back," he ordered the onlookers. "Give the lady some air."

They obeyed with alacrity. Even the fog seemed to pull back from his imposing presence. Nell glimpsed straight brows and chiseled features beneath gleaming gold hair and caught a faint scent of cherrywood pipe tobacco and clean, masculine soap as he passed. He knelt beside the princess and assessed the situation. His movements were quick and sure as he examined the princess.

Wan light, streaming through the shredding mists, fell on his thick golden hair like a benediction. He was quite the most handsome man that Nell had ever seen. He stripped off his cloak and draped it over the princess' prostrate form to ward off the chill air. His aura of command soothed even that agitated creature. "At last," she muttered, between curses and moans, "someone who will take charge!"

Indeed, Nell felt the same certainty. He was a man born to command.

The gentleman addressed the princess. "Madame, it is clear that you require the immediate services of a physician. Until then, I shall try and make you as comfortable as possible."

He signaled to two men nearby. "Fetch a board. We must carry this poor lady to the shipping office and out of this dampness before she takes a chill."

"Yes, Mr. Kincaid." They hurried away.

Nell was glad to let the decisive Mr. Kincaid take over. He seemed to know what he was doing. She stood aside and waited while they lifted the princess onto a board and carried her off. Anna paced silently beside her mistress, adding a somber dignity to the scene. The steamship gave a loud, mournful hoot that shook the dock beneath the soles of Nell's half boots. She turned to Olga. "We had best get aboard and pack everything up quickly."

They hurried off and ascended the gangplank together. Nell cast one glance to the wharf, but Princess Irina and her Prince Charming were out of view. A dank mist was rolling in from the water as they went along the deck. The wind had picked up, and the rocking of the ship was more noticeable. Up and down... and up and down...

Nell tried not to think about it. Olga dabbed at her eyes and blew her nose. "Vat vill you do now, Nell?"

"I don't know, short of finding a magic carpet or a fairy godmother to whisk me to Antigua! But I won't despair yet. I shall find a way to get there, come hell or high water."

Olga blinked at Nell's language. "You are very vorried about your dear brother." She tucked her handkerchief away briskly. "Are you a churchgoing voman, Nell?"

"Why, yes."

The other woman's face cleared. "Then ve must pray and all vill soon be vell. My *nonna* alvays said that honest prayer, coupled vith some sort of—how you say, a sacrifice, or giving up of something special, yes?—that it vill open the very gates of Heaven. And most especially now, in the blessed season of Christmas."

Her earnestness struck a responsive chord in Nell. In the press of daily life, struggling to make a living, she had not always kept the outward forms as well as might be expected of the daughter of a noted biblical scholar. Her slim fingers touched the opal-and-marcasite pin at her collar. It was the only thing she had of any value, and that was mostly sentimental; surely Mama would understand Nell's sacrificing it to help her only surviving son.

"This bauble is not worth enough to pay for my passage," she said, "but if there is truth in what you say, Olga, and I find another way to reach Antigua, I shall sell it and give the proceeds to feed the hungry on Christmas Day!" Nell glanced about the chamber. "But for now, we had best begin packing."

As they reached the staterooms belonging to the princess, there was a shuddering beneath their feet. It almost seemed as if the ship were alive. Something clanked deep in the bowels of the *Pride of Paradise*. Nell wondered if she would ever get used to the constant throb of the engines.

"Here is the cabin," Olga announced, and opened the door.

The princess had taken the finest suite aboard. The walls of the stateroom that served as private salon were paneled in white, with gilt trim and hangings of royal blue brocade. The furniture was upholstered in the same deep color as the hangings. Each of the huge portholes was banded in shining brass. To Nell, they looked like picture frames enclosing canvases of sky and sea.

Moving, shifting, sea. Up and down and up and down and side to side to side...

Nell looked quickly away. It was almost impossible to see the elegant furnishings of the suite for all the trunks, valises and bandboxes. And so many more still waiting upon the dock! She hardly knew where to start. So many garments to clothe one person!

Olga took charge. "My things are still in their trunks, thank heaven. I vill begin here in the parlor, Nell, if you vill pack up her highness' bedchamber. Oh, but I almost forgot—I must tell them ve vill not be sailing..."

She left the cabin, and Nell went into the next room. It was only slightly smaller than the parlor, but even more crowded—a vision in ivory and gold, with a curtained bed built into an alcove, and a medallion of frolicking cherubs painted on the ceiling. The air seemed close.

Nell went to the porthole to open it. The view of the heaving water changed her mind. Through the glass, it looked as though the horizon were rising and lowering even more quickly than a moment ago. The very floor seemed to shift beneath her feet. Nell grasped at a boudoir chair for support and planted her feet, trying to ignore the living sea beneath the *Pride of Paradise.*

She picked up a traveling gown of garnet merino and folded it in silver tissue. The color was all wrong for her employer, with her high complexion and too-red hair. The princess seemed to have no eye for fashion, other than its expense. What lovely fabric, so rich and soft and warm! Not so many years ago, when her father was still alive, Nell had worn lovely garments, too, although never anything so fine as this.

As she turned to replace the gown in the trunk, Nell caught sight of herself in the mirror. This shade of red was perfect for her own dark hair and luminous gray eyes. It brought color to her pale, porcelain complexion. She put it away quickly. Such things were not for an impecunious ex-governess, a mere paid companion.

A pall settled over Nell. If she hadn't left her position with the Wimblys because of their eldest son's uncalled-for advances, she would have had enough money put by from her quarterly salary to pay for her passage despite the princess' unfortunate accident.

Her gloom deepened. She would have to find another way to get to Antigua, and as soon as possible. Perhaps when she'd finished the packing, she could inquire of the purser as to whether there was any way she could work in exchange for her passage to the Caribbean. It made her feel queasy just thinking about what might have happened to Harry in a strange place, so very far from home. Her stomach lurched. Was it from worry, or merely the motion of the ship?

Up and down and up and down and side to side to side . . .

Nell took a deep breath and tried to ignore the shifting of the floor beneath her feet. She packed up the warm cloaks, shawls and gloves first, then the delicate lingerie from Paris, which had never even been taken out of the box. The nightgowns and peignoirs were new, as well. The princess had gone on a royal shopping spree. Nell blinked back a tear. Why, the price of any one of them would have gotten her to her destination. And the thought of what they had cost made her queasy, too. A light sweat broke out on her brow. She should have refused the kippered herrings at breakfast this morning.

Then she saw the hangers swaying in the trunk, although the gimbaled light overhead didn't appear to move at all. Nell realized it was the up-and-down motion of the ship that was making her light-headed and ill. And if it was this bad in port, how much worse would it be on the high seas? It had never occurred to Nell that she might be so bad a sailor. She was almost glad she wasn't setting out on the *Pride of Paradise* after all.

Suddenly the floor seemed to jump up to meet her. She tried to brace herself, but stumbled and fell to her knees. The design in the carpet rose and fell, rose and fell... Her stomach followed the same motion. Nell pitched forward on her face. The vibration of the engine came up through the floor, along with assorted whirs and bumps. Another sharp lurch. Nell no longer cared. She wanted only one thing: to get off the ship—now!

But, try as she might, she was unable to raise her head from the carpet. The short nap felt harsh and prickly against her cheek. With an effort of iron will, she pushed herself up, and moved less than an inch before she fell back with a muffled groan.

Nell moaned through clenched teeth. The laws of the universe had been contravened. Gravity pressed her down, yet she felt curiously weightless, as if at any moment she might go flying dizzily up to the ceiling. She held on for dear life. It grew steadily worse. After a while, distinctions blurred. Up and down no longer existed. Although she felt hot, a cold sweat beaded her forehead and upper lip. Her whole body became damp and clammy with effort. When the floor bucked and heaved, she dug her nails into the carpet's thick nap and clung to it as if it were a life preserver.

For an eternity Nell wallowed in abject misery. Darwin's theories were knocked all awry as she was reduced from human status to that of an amoeba, quivering like jelly in the primordial ooze. She had no idea how long she lay there. Time lost all meaning. Nations rose and fell. Aeons crept by with glacial slowness while Nell fought to keep down her breakfast of kippers and eggs and cold kidney pie. Weak and desperately ill, she prayed that someone would come to her aid.

Her prayers were finally answered in the form of Olga, who slipped into the stateroom munching on a chocolate biscuit. Nell opened her eyes, shuddered in revulsion, and closed them again—but not before seeing Olga whirl around twice, arms outstretched like a dancer from the Covent Garden Ballet.

Olga noticed Nell's prone body for the first time. "Oh! How you startled me!" She danced closer. "But vat are you doing down there, Nell? Have you lost a button?"

"No," Nell mumbled between gritted teeth, "but I am likely to lose my breakfast—violently—if you keep... dancing about like a dervish."

She paused as the ship heaved. Sweat broke out on her brow anew. Olga vanished, then returned with a cold cloth for Nell's forehead. "Poor, poor Nell. Vat can I do to help you?"

"Help me... get off this damned—er, this *ship!*"

Olga knelt down beside her. "But no! You cannot disembark."

"I... *must!*"

"No, I mean that vat you say is not possible!"

Nell's eyes snapped open. Olga was positively beaming. Her hair had escaped its tight and unfashionable chignon to curl in little cloudlike wisps about her temples, and her mouth was no longer clamped in a thin, anxious line. She looked carefree and ten years younger as she leaned closer. "The ship has sailed vith the tide. Ve are under vay."

"Vat? I mean, *what?*" Nell croaked.

"It is true, dear Nell. Marvelously, vonderfully true." Olga leaned down and smiled happily. "Ve are far, far out at sea."

Chapter Two

Nell squeezed her eyes shut against a world gone suddenly topsy-turvey. This time the queasy effect was not solely due to the motion of the ship. "You must...have them return...to port at once," she gasped.

The ship rolled suddenly with a long swell, and Nell moaned aloud. There seemed to her aching brain to be neither up nor down nor sideways. Within seconds she succumbed to another severe bout of mal de mer. It left her hoping for death or dry land—whichever came first. Vaguely, she was aware of the other woman's voice coming from a long distance. A small vial of emerald-green fluid was held to her lips. She fought against drinking it, but Olga was relentless. At last Nell choked it down. Within minutes she felt very warm. Her limbs became weightless and she felt herself floating away on a rosy pink cloud. Floating, warm and secure, into the arms of welcome sleep.

Olga looked down at her with a curious blend of sympathy and scarcely concealed exitement. "Poor Nell," she murmured. "Do not vorry, I have everything under control. You vill feel so very much better vhen you avaken. And all our problems vill be solved."

When Nell regained her senses, there was a gap in her memory. She was totally disoriented by her strange surroundings. Instead of the narrow iron bed beneath the eaves of her past employer's home in Grosvenor Square, she was tucked up in silk-and-satin luxury. The airy ivory coverlet over her was trimmed with deep borders of Belgian lace, and her head was cradled by a pillow of finest down. Frolicking cherubs danced overhead. She blinked. *I have died,* she thought, *and gone to heaven.*

But no, heaven would be filled with the joyous singing of an angelic choir. There were no sounds except for the throb of the ship's engines, and a voice humming nearby.

Nell pushed herself up, thinking that this was merely a particularly realistic dream. But when she turned her head, Olga was still hovering beside her.

And still beaming.

It all came rushing back—the princess and her accident, the elegant steamship rising above the pier, the terrible illness, and the fact that they had set sail. Nell realized that she longer felt the rise and fall of the ocean.

"Are we back in port?" she asked, as relief flooded her veins.

Olga composed her hands before her, as if offering up a prayer. "No, thank the good Lord. Ve are out on the bosom of the great Atlantic, many, many miles from novhere."

Nell jerked fully upright, and was immediately sorry. She pushed back waves of vertigo. *"I beg your pardon?"*

"Oh, it is quite true. Ve sailed from England vith the tide, two days ago."

With supreme effort, Nell swung her legs over the side of the bed. Her weakness amazed her. Two whole days! No, surely this was indeed a dream. It cost her a moment of dizziness, but she managed to stand and stumble to the porthole. The floor felt quite real beneath her bare feet, and the brass that framed the glass was smooth and cold to her touch. She peered through the porthole.

It was true. Pallid dawn light tipped the pewter waves with silver. Waves that rolled endlessly to the far, and vastly empty, horizon.

She looked away quickly. That was a mistake. The room spun, and she grasped the back of a chair for balance. Her head felt as if it were stuffed with cobwebs, but she was, thank the merciful heavens, completely cured of her seasickness. Her gaze alighted on the center of the carpet, where a diminished pile of green luggage lay, each piece stamped in gold with the royal crest of Merkelstein. The scene on the dock came back to her in a rush.

"The princess..."

"Ah, yes," Olga murmured. "You need not vorry. She vas taken avay to her hotel, vith a physician in attendance."

Nell's insides were quivering, but her brain was as steady as ever. "And *we* have sailed in her stead! What has the captain to say about our predicament?"

Olga dusted an imaginary speck from the top of a bandbox, not meeting Nell's eyes.

A flutter of dismay danced in Nell's stomach. "You *have* explained the situation, have you not?"

"Er... not quite. But have no fear. I vill think of something to tell him."

Olga smiled ingratiatingly. Her complacent attitude was beginning to annoy Nell. "I don't know why you are so happy," she muttered. "We shall be in the very devil—er, in quite a fix—when this is sorted out."

"Bah," Olga said in reply. "Ve have almost two veeks before ve dock in Antigua."

"Two weeks," Nell groaned. Suddenly the confines of their stateroom seemed to close in upon her. She felt as if she were suffocating. "I need fresh air to clear my head. I must think."

Olga took one look at her white cheeks and obligingly fetched her a hooded cloak of sapphire blue wool lined with miniver. "There is a sheltered place just outside near the rail. Ve vill be unobserved there."

"I would rather be alone," Nell replied, in her firmest "governess" voice. Olga acquiesced. Nell slipped the cloak on and tied it securely. She was so desperate to escape to the outside that she didn't care that all she had on beneath it was a night shift of fine embroidered lawn. None of the other passengers were likely to be about at such an early hour.

She opened the door to the corridor and went out into the gray and silver dawn. There wasn't a soul in sight. The scene, after the bustle she remembered before departure, was silent and eerie. She might have stepped onto the deck of a ghost ship.

Nell breathed a sigh of relief. Gliding silently along the deck, she stopped at the first sheltered place along the rail. Youth and a strong constitution stood her in good stead. Her strength was returning rapidly.

Although the eastern horizon was edged with faint pink light, the moon rode low in the slowly lightening sky. Its beams marked a path of light across the sea, as bright and shiny as a puddle of mercury. She leaned over the rail. Somewhere ahead lay a softer clime—Antigua—rising from warm Caribbean waters—and the mystery of Harry's disappearance.

Much as Nell regretted her present circumstances, she was glad now that the ship had sailed while she was incapacitated. For once it seemed that fate was on her side. She gripped the rail tightly, closed her eyes and tilted her face to heaven. *Please God, let me find Harry. And let me find him safe and well.*

A sudden roll of the ship fetched her up against the rail, hard. Instantly, a strong arm wrapped itself about her waist, and Nell found her face pressed against a coat of brushed wool. She gasped and tried to push away. She might as well have been pushing against a granite boulder. Panic sharpened her voice.

"Unhand me at once, if you please."

The man obeyed so abruptly that she staggered back a step. "You needn't shriek in my ear," he said in a deep and aggrieved baritone. "I feared that you were about to fall overboard."

Nell stiffened. That voice! And did she discern a faint scent of cherrywood tobacco? Her heart did a somersault inside her chest. For a horrible moment she imagined that her companion was the same dashing man who had come to the aid of Princess Irina on the pier. Then she got a good look at him and could have laughed at the contrast.

He was almost as tall as the rescuer, and had a thick shock of hair beneath a very odd woolen cap. His hair was a wild shade of red, matching the thick handlebar moustache adorning his upper lip. He had a plaid scarf wound around his neck, and the light reflected off a pair of wire-rimmed spectacles perched on his nose. Mild blue eyes peered down at her from behind the thick lenses.

"Allow me to introduce myself. I am Professor Smith, lecturer at the University of Collingham on the diseases of domestic animals." He coughed theatrically behind his gloved hand, then wound the muffler more tightly around his throat. "You must excuse me. I am recovering from a dreadful malady, contracted in the course of my research. It almost proved fatal."

"Brain fever, no doubt!" Nell replied with asperity. Her heart was still thumping like a tambourine, and she hadn't forgiven him for frightening her so. "That is the only reason I can imagine for your inexcusable behavior!"

"Madame, you appeared either in danger from a fainting spell or about to throw yourself into the sea. I caught you, a bit roughly, perhaps, but only to keep you from tumbling overboard."

Nell was chagrined. She could understand why he'd jumped to that conclusion. Perhaps she had reacted too strongly. After all, he had thought that he was saving her life. "Forgive me for speaking so sharply. Although your action was completely unnecessary, it was kind of you, and—"

"Kind? Kindness did not enter into it," he replied shortly. "I am anxious to reach landfall as soon as possible. This chill, damp air is disastrous for one of my delicate constitution. If you had fallen overboard, a search would have been initiated, delaying our journey needlessly."

Nell was appalled at his smug self-centeredness. She drew herself up with dignity. "Surely you speak in jest, sir. I cannot believe that anyone would consider rescuing a passenger lost at sea a 'needless delay.'"

Was there a twinkle behind those thick glass lenses, or was it just the play of light off the sea? Nell could not be sure. The gentleman coughed and looked away. "I am recuperating from a severe illness. On the advice of my personal physician, I am wintering in the West Indies, and am anxious to reach them before I suffer a severe relapse."

Nell eyed him from head to toe. His jaw looked square beneath the heavy muffler, his nose was straight, and his mouth was half-hidden behind the walrus moustache. There was vitality in his posture, despite the drooping shoulders of his baggy tweed coat. The coat was so large that she imagined he'd lost a good deal of weight during his recent illness.

Still, he didn't look like the type to have sickly tendencies, as far as Nell was concerned. However, there were two things that she had learned in her years as a governess and companion. Firstly, no person—no matter how strange in behavior—should be judged on first acquaintance. Secondly, most people proved, upon better acquaintance, to be even odder than she'd originally thought.

And there was something definitely odd about Professor Smith.

The corners of her mouth lifted in a tiny smile. Perhaps her life experiences, from beloved only daughter to overworked governess to unappreciated companion, had made her cynical. But there *was* something very peculiar about this fellow. He looked healthy as a draft horse, in fact. She almost told him so, but experience cautioned against it. Her last position but one had been as companion to a hypochondriac, and she knew better than to chance getting the professor started on an endless litany of complaints. A year in the employ of Miss Hollomby, whose illnesses kept her from doing only those things she did not want to do but never prevented the elderly spinster from doing anything she'd set her stony heart upon, had been enough to last Nell a lifetime.

At that exact moment, the professor removed a huge handkerchief from his pocket and sneezed loudly into it. "Good heavens!" he exclaimed in evident dismay. "I fear this cool sea air has caused a flare-up of my bronchial complaint."

"Indeed, I wonder why you are on deck at all."

"I might ask the same of you, madame. It is all of 5:00 a.m."

It might have been a trick of the light, but Nell thought his eyes sharpened and glittered behind those obscuring lenses. A shiver ran up her back, as if a goose had walked on her grave. It is only the brisk breeze, she told herself, drawing her cloak around her more tightly.

"I am growing cold and will retire to my own cabin, and I would advise you to do the same," she said wickedly. "The air is quite chill, and the shock might prove fatal to your delicate system."

Again she saw that spark of light in the man's eyes. Then his mouth thinned. "Ah, I see that you are a woman of good sense. I will take your warning to heart, madame, and have a hot rum toddy and a fresh flannel for my chest before seeking out my bed once more. But you must allow me to escort you to your cabin first."

There was no way of avoiding it. Nell took the arm he offered and let him walk her back. He was very clumsy and stepped on her feet twice before they reached the door to the stateroom parlor. Although he appeared surprised that she was ensconced in such luxurious quarters, he didn't comment upon it. Nell breathed a little easier. "Good night," she said, and opened the door.

"Good night, madame." He bowed and tottered away, sneezing into his handkerchief as she went inside.

Nell closed the door quickly. What a very strange man! It was just as well that he was the kind of fellow to be so wrapped up in his own sniffles and sneezes that he had no time to give her another thought.

Or was he?

Something about him disquieted Nell. Perhaps it was that elusive gleam she thought she'd seen in his eyes. She paused with her hand on the handle, then suddenly opened the door again. It swung in silently on efficiently oiled hinges. Nell stuck her head out.

Her companion of only moments ago was clearly outlined as he moved through the spears of moonlight slanting across the deck. His former mincing totter had given way to long, easy strides. For a few seconds she thought it was a trick of the shadows.

No, she realized shrewdly, her eyes had not deceived her. Nell smiled grimly as she closed the door and latched it. Professor Smith was either playing the role of invalid to elicit sympathy, or he was completely mad. Since neither character type appealed to her, she made a vow to avoid him for the rest of the crossing.

By the bright light of day, Nell wondered if she'd dreamed the strange encounter. She found the cloak tossed over a chair where she'd left it—or had that been part of the dream, also? Nothing seemed real. Certainly not her present situation.

She checked the ormolu clock on the dressing table. It lacked ten minutes to eleven—well past breakfast, and almost time for luncheon. To her immense surprise, she was ravenously hungry.

She washed and dressed in a plain but suitable outfit: a black skirt, a white shirtwaist and a gray tweed jacket. The circle pin of opal and marcasite pinned to the lapel gave her courage. Although, if Olga was right and Nell's prayers were indeed answered, it would not be in her possession two weeks hence. It gave her a pang to think of parting with it, yet its loss would be for a good cause. Her mother would have understood.

A winged insect buzzed tinnily at the porthole, bringing Nell out of her reverie. She turned to see sunlight flashing off its slender wings and needle-thin, iridescent blue body. It seemed determined to force its way out. Nell felt sorry for this tiny creature trapped in a world of which it had no understanding and little hope for survival.

"There's no safety for you in escape," she said with sympathy. "Nothing but lonely ocean as far as the eye can see. You are far too small and delicate to survive out there. You must stay safely aboard until we reach the Leeward Isles."

As if it had heard her and understood, the insect suddenly flew up in a blur of fairy wings and out to the salon. Nell followed its flight. While she'd slept, the cabin steward had laid the corner table with two settings of heavy silverware and Meissen china edged in burgundy and gold. Crystal goblets caught and trapped the light in myriad facets, sending the arcs of tiny rainbows across the fine porcelain plates. Each piece, she noticed, bore the royal crest of Merklestein.

Olga entered the salon, yawning. Like Nell, she was already dressed, and her gown of soft azure twill was kind to the washed-out blue of her eyes. She pulled up short when she spied Nell.

"How very gray and somber you look. I think perhaps you might vant something gayer for your first day in company." She ducked back into the room and emerged shortly with a gown of antique gold silk and bronze braid trim over her arm, trailing a wake of pleated bronze ruffles. "Much more suitable, don't you agree?"

Nell stared at her. "Are you mad? That is one of Princess Irina's gowns."

A dimple appeared in Olga's cheek. "Ah, but you are here and she is not. And—"

A knock at the door interrupted them. Olga crossed the floor and opened it. A steward and waiter entered with a draped cart bearing an assortment of dishes with ornate silver covers. He bowed solemnly. "The luncheon you ordered, Lady Levitskaya."

He began lifting the covers. Nell goggled at the many dishes from her place on the sidelines. There was food sufficient to feed a hearty family of four—with enough left over for the next day's luncheon. Two bottles of chilled French wine reposed in a chased silver container.

The steward recited the menu: "Chilled asparagus consommé. A fricassee of capon with capers and white sauce, sugar-cured ham with cloves, *haricots verts avec champignons,* and *pommes à la francaise.* For desert, a lemon torte, brandied cherries *en compote,* and raspberry trifle. If the princess requires anything else, you have only to ask."

Catching Nell's eye, Olga waved the hovering waiter and the steward out. "I shall take care of everything," she said firmly, almost pushing them out the door.

As soon as it was shut again, Nell pounced. "The princess? Lady Levitskaya? What on earth is going on?"

A flash of something akin to panic flickered in Olga's eyes. Before she could answer, there was another knock. She opened it hurriedly as Nell stepped back into the bedchamber. A handsome ship's officer, distinguished in his elegant uniform, made a formal bow to Olga.

"The captain's compliments, Lady Levitskaya. If the princess is recovered from her indisposition, he would like to give a champagne reception in Her Highness' honor at nine o'clock this evening."

Olga clapped her hands in delight. "How charming of Captain Creighton. Fortunately, the princess is indeed *quite* recovered. Ve shall be most happy to attend the reception."

He bowed again and said something in reply before departing, but Nell was too stunned to take in his words. Her ears buzzed like the wings of the iridescent insect perched beside her on the apricot glass shade of the unlit lamp.

Olga closed the door and almost skipped toward Nell, her hair coming out of her severe chignon in little wisps. Nell realized that Olga was much younger than she'd originally thought. And definitely mad as a hatter. "Did I hear you say—?"

"Yes! A champagne reception! In honor of the princess!"

"Olga, have you lost your mind? What is this 'Lady Levitskaya' nonsense? And what do you mean by saying that Princess Irina will join the captain's table?" Another thought struck Nell—right in the pit of her already churning stomach. "And why doesn't he know that she remained behind, due to her unfortunate accident?"

Olga went from pink to very white and back again. "The time has come to explain all to you. I vas so frightened I did not know vat to do or say," she said in a quick, disjointed fashion. "You see, dear Nell, I vas not able to tell them *anything!* I forgot all my Engleesh—every vord of it—and they did not understand me. Not one tiny vord. And then I saw it vas too late. The ship had already veighed anchor. I vas even

more afraid." Her voice lowered to a ragged whisper.
"In my country, people are thrown into the dungeons
for less than this."

Nell rubbed her forehead. "Oh, why didn't you tell
me? What a horrid fix we are in, to be sure."

The older woman's thin hands twisted and knotted
together. "You vere on the floor, too ill to help. So I
did vhat I had to do. Please do not be angry vith me."

"Well, there is only one solution." Nell drew herself up unsteadily. "We must reveal the truth—at
once."

"Oh, please . . ."

Nell shook her head at the other woman's distress.
"We have no choice. Any fool will soon realize that
the Princess Irina Christina of Merklestein is not
aboard the ship."

"No, they vill not," Olga interjected.

"You cannot pretend that she is here and keeping to
her cabin for the entire voyage! Especially not after
saying that the princess will make a dinner appearance."

Olga straightened her shoulders and looked Nell
squarely in the eye. "But the princess *vill,*" she said
quickly. "Everything vill vork out. You need not fear.
I have it all arranged."

Nell had a sudden, horrible feeling that events had
just moved beyond her control. "What on earth do
you mean?"

Olga's face was suddenly suffused with a desperate
hope born of desperation. "You must trust me," she
said earnestly. "All vill be explained. Tonight ve vill
join the distinguished captain in his private quarters.
Leave all the arrangements to me." She dropped into

a deep curtsey at Nell's feet. *"Your Most Royal Highness."*

"What?" Nell squeaked.

Olga plainly saw the shock in Nell's eyes. "Only a few short days," she pleaded. "If you tell the captain, Miss Nell, ve vill be in terrible trouble. Perhaps he vould even send us back on the next steamer ve pass bound for England. And then you vill not get to Antigua to search for your poor brother."

Nell hadn't considered that. Her brain reeled. Every day lost narrowed the chances of her picking up Harry's trail. But to aid and abet Olga's fantastic scheme...

"No," she said flatly. "I cannot be a party to this deception."

Olga took in a breath and shuddered. She then played her best card. "Once ve reach Antigua, I shall be safe. Othervise..." She dabbed at her reddened eyes with a wadded handkerchief. "You are a free voman, Nell. You do not understand how it is in my country. Ve have no rights. And those who incur the displeasure of the ruling family...ve have no hope. I can never go back to Merkelstein now, on pain of death."

Something in Olga's voice held the ring of awful certainty. Nell felt herself trapped as effectively as the little winged insect that perched on the lampshade a few inches from her face. Like that fragile, bewildered creature, she had no choice now but to sail on, without any guarantee of safety at journey's end.

Chapter Three

The captain's reception for Merkelstein's princess was set for 9:00 p.m., a compromise between the early hours of the ship's officers, who were at their business with the sunrise, and the late hours of the moneyed classes, who danced till dawn and slept till noon. Nine o'clock felt far away to Nell, but the minutes flew by with twice normal speed. Or so it seemed. The mantel clock chimed nine all too soon.

Olga, dressed in spring-green taffeta with a gauzy pink overskirt, with a pink plume fastened amid her pomaded curls, looked like a rare botanical specimen plunked down in the middle of the stateroom. And the change in Nell was just as startling.

Earlier Olga had made a few strategic alterations in a magnificent scarlet silk gown to fit it to Nell's slender waist, although the greater part of the task had been done ahead of time. "I saw the necessity in advance, and had nothing else to do vhile you vere so ill," she had said brightly. "I am quite experienced vith the needle."

She gave the skirts another tug and turned Nell toward her reflection in the tall looking glass. She adjusted her pince-nez and smiled. "There, you see? Every inch the princess, no?"

"No!" Nell fidgeted while Olga adjusted the slight train. Despite her denial, she had to admit that the lovely red gown suited her figure and coloring. She had never worn anything so fine in her life. She could live comfortably for several months on what it had likely cost. And the jewels!

A great star-shaped ruby and diamond brooch was pinned to the deep corsage that showed off Nell's pearly shoulders, and a lavaliere of huge rubies on a diamond-studded chain rested just above the revealingly low neckline. The gems were complemented by matching drop earrings and an enormous ruby-and-diamond ring worn over her elbow-length gloves. Several diamond bracelets circled her wrist, one studded with rubies and emeralds, and a tiara of white gold and diamonds rested on her coiffed hair.

"How splendid!" Olga declared. "These jewels do not show to such advantage on the princess. Never should a redhead vear rubies. On you, dear Nell, they are stunning. You look like Cinderella, going to the ball."

Olga's compliment helped Nell cope with what her mother would have considered a vulgar display of wealth. Of course, the rules of ordinary good taste did not apply to the highest stratum of aristocratic society. If truth be told, the rich crimson glow of the rubies and the diamonds' glittering brilliance momentarily blinded her. She felt splendidly regal.

But when she looked in the mirror, all she saw was plain Miss Ellen Shepherd, erstwhile governess and companion to the elderly, who would surely be exposed as an imposter, clapped in irons and thrown into the hold before the day was out.

"I do feel like Cinderella," she admitted ruefully. "Or, rather, like Cinder Ellen. But while the fairytale Cinderella merely returned to her previous life in the scullery after the ball, I am likely to end up in a much less desirable place."

"Bah! Ve are breaking no laws. And you must not say such things, dear Nell, for our escort vill be here at any moment."

The waiting was worrisome. Nell paced the blue-and-gold-patterned carpet of the salon to work off her nervousness. The scarlet silk of the Princess Irina's fashionable dress rustled like the sound of scandalized whispers with her every step: *"Imposter, imposter, imposter."*

She stopped beside the inlaid game table and sighed. "This won't work, you know. It is a mad scheme, and bound to fail."

Olga went white again. "Oh, do not say so! Everything depends on you. If you do not go through vith it, vat vill happen to us?"

"What indeed?"

The ship's officer arrived to escort them to the reception. There was admiration in Lieutenant Neal's handsome countenance as he bowed to Nell. In other circumstances, she would have felt pampered and beautifully feminine in such a fabulous ensemble. Instead, she felt like an actress in a bad farce. Steeling her nerves, she gave in to the inevitable. She accepted the spangled shawl that Olga draped gracefully around her shoulders, and the three of them went out into the corridor.

The reception was held in a long salon on an upper deck. The open double doors gave a good view of the immense chamber. It was paneled in walnut, although much of the wall space was covered by brown velvet draperies tied back with gold cords and tassels. In the background, a quartet of musicians played delightful strains of Mozart pieces. A look of pleading from Olga spurred Nell's courage. She lifted her head and went in.

Twin brass chandeliers spilled warm light on the guests. Nell looked about in dismay. She had envisioned an intimate soiree, instead the salon was as full as it could hold. But perhaps it would make her role easier, for with so many people, there would be little chance of intimate conversations that might prove her downfall.

The women were grandly gowned for the occasion, and decked out in their finest jewels. The men provided a leavening note in their black evening dress and crisp white shirts. The captain spotted Nell and went to greet her. Before he was halfway there, every single person in the room had noticed her arrival and every eye was turned her way. The music abruptly stopped. A hush fell over the room, changing to the buzzed murmur of lowered voices. Butterflies danced a wild mazurka in Nell's stomach. What had she gotten herself into? She was every bit as mad as Olga to have ever agreed to this!

But there was no going back now. The music began again, this time playing a slow and ponderous tune. Nell realized with a start that it must be the national anthem of Merkelstein. She felt her face flame with embarrassment. She knew that she was ill-prepared to play her part. And the longer she tried to carry it off in public, the more certain was her exposure, and the disaster that would surely follow.

Nell came to a decision there and then. The only way to play it safe was for "the Princess Irina" to vanish from view. After the reception, she would retire to her stateroom, and stay there for the duration of the voyage. Olga would have to announce that the "princess" had succumbed to another bout of seasickness. Nell could see no other way out of this untenable situation.

Unpleasant as it would be to stay cooped up for so long, that was infinitely preferable to the alternative. But first she must get through the next few hours safely.

The captain and his officers tendered their bows. Nell extended her gloved hand regally, and Captain Creighton bowed again over it. "We are honored by your presence, Your Highness."

He was a fine-looking man, with a firm but kindly air. Nell liked him at once and was chagrined at having to deceive him. The captain was equally pleased with his royal passenger. He had heard rumors of the arrogance of Merkelstein's princess. They were obviously untrue. "Permit me to present my guests to you," he said charmingly.

Another gentleman had been watching Nell with keen interest. He stepped forward for an introduction. "Mr. Hugh Kincaid," the captain said in surprise. "I didn't expect that you would be joining us this evening."

"How could I pass up the chance to meet our enchanting and beautiful princess?"

Nell turned and received an unpleasant jolt. Prince Charming stood beside her. Her gray eyes widened in alarm. The man, tall and wide-shouldered, with thick golden hair, was the same Mr. Kincaid who had come to the rescue when the real Princess Irina was injured on the pier. Her stomach sank.

"Your Highness." Smiling to show a row of even white teeth, he clasped her extended hand. He was strong, and the heat of his touch burned through her gloves to her skin. She wanted to snatch her hand back before she melted.

Common sense rescued her from her startlement. Nell's instincts had always been sound. Now they went on full alert. She tried to smile and respond politely while her mind was in complete chaos. She couldn't very well make a scene. It was only guilt at her masquerade that made her so jumpy. She tried, although her thoughts were panic-stricken, to recall what had been said at the time, and if either she or the princess had announced their identities to him then.

Hugh Kincaid looked at her sharply. She'd gone very pale. He slipped his arm around her shoulders. "The princess seems to be overcome with faintness," he said in his deep baritone. "Here, madame. Please sit down and regain your strength."

Without so much as a by-your-leave, he escorted Nell to the sidelines, where gilt ballroom chairs were ranged along a wall. He sent a steward to fetch a glass of champagne for her, and deposited Nell in an alcove flanked by tall columns and a miniature forest of potted palms. Up close, his eyes were as dark as sapphires.

"You should have known you couldn't cover it up," he murmured in her ear.

"I beg your pardon?" Nell could scarcely hear the sound of her own voice over the wild tatoo of her heart. "I have no idea of what you are referring to Mr. Kincaid!"

He smiled blandly. "Why, with all due apologies for my American abruptness, madame—and my admiration for your courage—you should have known that you were still so weak from your indisposition to cover up the fact."

Mr. Kincaid's voice was smooth, and showed just the proper degree of concern, but Nell was alarmed by the sparks that shone in the depths of his deep blue eyes. Could it be...was it...*laughter?* No, that was impossible.

She thanked him as he took a glass of champagne from the steward and handed it to her. There was something dangerous about Mr. Hugh Kincaid, Nell decided. He saw too much. She would have to avoid him just as assiduously as she planned to evade that dreadful hypochondriac, Professor Smith.

The next half hour passed in a blur of names and faces. Only a few stood out from the rest. There was a keen-eyed lady named Mrs. Grant, who ran a progressive school for young women, and a celebrated portrait painter whose work Nell had seen exhibited. The tall gentleman in formal evening dress but wearing a jeweled turban was an Indian rajah. His eyes were dark and liquid, with mysterious depths to them. Her meeting with him went smoothly, as did the introduction to Lady Culpepper, a dignified aristocrat traveling with her young granddaughter.

Lady Culpepper was a thin matron in silver gauze, with faded blond hair, an aura of weary elegance, and a rope of large and lustrous pink pearls. They wound twice around her throat to cascade down her flat bosom to her narrow waist. While Nell was no connoisseur of fine pearls, she was sure the necklace was worth a fortune.

"Allow me to present my granddaughter, Miss Boynton," the Englishwoman said. "Gwendolyn is about to make her debut in polite society."

Nell took the girl's hand in hers. "How do you do?"

Gwendolyn stammered something incoherent and blushed to the roots of her nut-brown hair. It was evident that she wished she were elsewhere. The girl was neither plain nor pretty, and clearly suffered from acute shyness. Worse—from a fashionable point of view—she had none of Lady Culpepper's style or her wordly air. What she did have was a sweet smile and a pair of wide and innocent brown eyes that reflected her emotions like a mirror.

"I am hoping that my dear Gwendolyn will acquire a bit more countenance from expanding her horizons through travel," said Lady Culpepper.

"I—I have a friend in Antigua," Gwendolyn blurted out. Lady Culpepper shot her a quelling glance. The girl blushed hotly and fell silent, looking down at her tightly clasped hands.

They moved away, and Nell hoped the shy little creature wasn't in for a scold from her redoubtable grandmother. Nell realized that she'd lost track of

Olga during their conversation. There she was, that traitoress, flirting with the ship's purser, over the rim of her champagne glass!

Nell's flutter of panic grew stronger when a silver-haired gentleman with a large diamond stickpin paid his respects.

"Grand Duke Alexi of Ermarnia," the captain said by way of introduction. "Perhaps you are already acquainted?"

Nell was shaken. Ermarnia was a small state near the Austrian border—not very far, she feared, from Merkelstein. She held her breath as the grand duke beamed down at her.

"Unfortunately, our paths have not crossed before today. I regret deeply that I have not yet visited your fair country, Princess Irina. Now, more than ever."

She blushed at the charming compliment and greeted the next person in line. The minutes flew by quickly. Nell managed to carry off her role without having a long conversation with anyone. After dinner she would skip the ball and retire immediately to her suite.

And *stay* there until they reached port.

Only a few more minutes until she could escape, Nell thought, counting them desperately. Then a late-comer arrived.

"Ah, there you are, Professor!" the captain said jovially over Nell's shoulder. "I am so glad you feel well enough to join us this evening."

"My apologies for being so tardy," Professor Smith said from somewhere behind Nell. "At the last minute I felt a bronchial condition coming on. I was forced to steam my throat and prepare a tea of slippery elm and cherry bark to ward off pleurisy."

Nell cringed as she caught a glimpse of a dark evening coat too large in the shoulders, and small spectacles with wire rims beneath a shock of thick, bright hair. Then Professor Smith stood before her, stumbling over his own feet in the process. He smelled of peppermints and brilliantine, and his collar points were too high for either fashion or appearance. His mustache seemed even shaggier than before, as if it had taken on a startling life all its own.

His eyes were still hidden behind their heavy lenses, yet they swept over the assembled guests with a peculiar intensity. They paused when they reached Nell. He didn't appear to recognize her from their meeting at the ship's rail. As the captain introduced them, Nell watched him with a stab apprehension.

"Ah...the Princess Irina Christina of Merkelstein..." Professor Smith said, his voice bland. He favored Nell with a stiff bow. "You cannot imagine how I have been looking forward to this very moment."

The professor smiled down at her. Behind the tiny circles of glass, his eyes were as mild as an April morning. But then his fingers closed around hers like the bands of a steel trap. Nell was startled. Who would have guessed that they held such strength?

As the professor bowed over her hand, his spectacles slipped down his aquiline nose. Suddenly unmasked, his eyes were not at all the weak and watery orbs that she'd glimpsed through the lenses. No, the irises revealed were an intense and burning blue, like the hot August sky. A ripple of alarm ran through her body. She felt as if she'd had a pitcher of ice-cold water dashed in her face.

He dropped her hand and pushed the spectacles back in place. The glint of fierceness in his eyes was replaced by a benign beam of pure goodwill.

Perhaps it was only the strain she was under, but for those few, startled seconds, Nell had felt that the very air throbbed with danger. *You are being a silly fool, Nell Shepherd,* she told herself briskly, *seeing even this poor, self-imagined invalid as a bogeyman!*

She gathered her scattered wits. "You are an American, Professor?"

"Yes, ma'am. Or, rather, Your Highness. You must forgive me for my breach of etiquette. We Americans are shockingly informal."

"But that is one of the most charming things about them," the grand duke said. "Do you not find it so, Your Highness?"

It took Nell several seconds to realize that he was addressing her. She felt her cheeks grow warm. "Yes, indeed," she murmured.

The professor adjusted his eyeglasses and addressed her as she lifted her glass of wine. "Have you visited the United States in your travels, Your Highness?"

"I, uh..." Nell shot an imploring glance at Olga, who had drifted closer. Olga shook her head slightly. "No," Nell answered quickly. "I have not. I hope to soon, however."

The conversation turned to the grand duke's adventures during his two visits to New York and Boston. Nell didn't hear a word of it. Her heart was hammering so loudly it deafened her. How had she ever let Olga convince her that she could carry this off? Despite the other woman's nonchalance, she wondered if there were laws against what she was doing?

And what the punishment might be.

When she became aware of her fellow guests once more, the talk had turned to another subject: a string of recent jewel robberies. "And," Lady Culpepper was saying, "when the train reached Paris, they discovered that the thief had made off with Madame Archambeau's famous diamond choker, her emerald earrings, and the Fabergé egg the tsar had given to her, as well."

Olga's eyes were round with interest. "But that is impossible. If they were traveling by private train, with their own servants, I do not see how the thief could get aboard to take Madame Archambeau's jewels."

"That is the most scandalous part. In Vienna, Madame Archambeau had met a young English couple, members of the minor nobility, and invited them to join their party. They left the train at Lyons without incident." Lady Culpepper's voice lowered dramatically. "It is now suspected that they were common thieves, passing themselves off as aristcrats."

Nell had just taken a swallow of champagne, and she choked on the delicate fizz of the bubbles. Professor Smith clapped her on the back so hard that she almost spilled the remainder down her cleavage. He took the glass from her hand and whispered, for her ears alone, "You will have to be more careful."

Nell's heart did a slow somersault. She recovered quickly. "I beg your pardon?" Her voice mixed just the proper amount of puzzlement with icy hauteur.

"Much better," he murmured. The professor sent her a glance over the rim of his eyeglasses, then turned away to set the empty glass down on the tray of a hovering steward. What a very peculiar man, Nell thought.

"There will be dancing in the ballroom shortly," the captain announced. "I must, unfortunately, return to my duties." His genial gaze went from the rajah to the duke and ended with the professor. "However, I am sure that you gentlemen will escort the ladies there for me, and fill up their dance cards, as well."

They thanked him for the enjoyable evening. The duke, as the highest-ranking male, assumed he would escort Nell, who, in the guise of a princess of a ruling house, was at the head of the list of female guests. In the shuffle, however, the duke was somehow edged out of the way by the professor, and found himself at Lady Culpepper's side. He offered the dowager his arm politely, but eyed the professor through his monocle with an affronted air.

The professor was too busy stumbling over an inconvenient chair leg to notice. He righted himself, managing to save his spectacles from falling off his nose, and bowed to Nell. "I shall be pleased to offer you my arm, Princess Irina."

Nell had no choice but to accept his escort. He sensed her unwillingness. "Let me assure you, Your Highness, that I will not trod on your toes more than is unavoidable."

She thought she spied a twinkle behind his glasses, but it was gone in an instant. Probably a flash of light, Nell decided. She didn't think Professor Smith had either the wit or the sense of humor to joke with her.

She placed her hand in his arm. "I shall hold you to your word, sir."

They went into a corridor carpeted in deep blue and antique gold with the trident-and-crown emblem of the Triton Line woven into it. The walls were paneled in an exotic wood the color of raw honey. Pools of light along the way were warmed by the gold opal glass shades of the lamps. They were held aloft by bronze mermaids wearing the Triton Line crown on their streaming hair. Nell was awed. All this for a simple corridor. She had never imagined that such luxury could exist within the confines of a ship. Then again, this was a ship catering exclusively to the wealthy and aristocratic, and its hold was filled with luxury goods, not hopeful immigrants.

She realized belatedly that she was staring. And Nell doubted that Merkelstein's haughty princess would stare if the corridor were paved with diamonds. A definite gaffe on her part. She slanted a look up at Professor Smith and caught him watching her sharply. Her heart bounded within her chest. How much had those blue eyes noticed?

Her escort lurched suddenly and almost tripped over his own feet. "Beg pardon," he exclaimed, fighting for balance. Nell relaxed. She almost laughed at her fears. Why, she doubted he could see much past the end of his nose.

The ballroom was on the next deck and they could hear the music as they ascended the carpeted staircase. Three huge crystal chandeliers lit the chamber, which was lined in gilt-framed mirrors from floor to ceiling.

"Is this not delightful?" Olga whispered excitedly in Nell's ear. "You are Cinderella, gone to the ball." She waved her hand as if she held a fairy godmother's wand in it. "Who knows vhat magic the enchanted night might yet bring?"

"I know," Nell replied tartly. "We shall end in rags, working in the scullery—or whatever it is they call a ship's kitchen."

"The galley," Olga said. "You must have more faith, dear vone. Remember, this is the Christmas season, the time when angels roam the earth, and miracles occur."

Her simple optimism didn't have the desired effect. Nell glanced at their splendid reflections in one of the gilt-framed mirrors. "Miracles are for those far more deserving than two masqueraders like ourselves."

Olga merely smiled.

Almost immediately they were surrounded by their newfound admirers. Nell found herself swept off by the rajah and the grand duke in rapid succession.

Although she searched the room with every circle of the waltz for Mr. Kincaid, Nell looked in vain. Her only consolation was that he wasn't dancing with some beauty in his strong arms. She knew he was single, but perhaps there was a fair fiancé waiting for him at home in America. The thought was like a splash of cold water.

What am I thinking of? He is quite above my touch. And even if he had shown the slightest interest, it would only have been for "Princess Irina Christina," not a poor nobody governess such as myself.

The dance ended, and the grand duke bowed over her gloved hand. "Your Highness, would it be far too presumptuous if I begged to have the honor of the next dance, as well?''

She favored him with a smile over her fan. ''Indeed it would, as well you know. However, if you will fetch me another glass of champagne, perhaps we might sit this dance out together.''

''But of course!''

He went off with alacrity. The moment he turned his back, Nell ducked behind one of the potted palms. She didn't want to dance and she certainly didn't want another glass of the sparkling wine. What she wanted most was to get away from the heated ballroom, the press of people, and her own sense of disappointment. Cinderella had gone to the ball, but there was no prince.

She opened the first door she came to that offered escape, and found herself in a small conservatory. The potted plants and trees were black silhouettes against a blazing universe of stars. After the overly warm ballroom, the air was cool as satin. A silky breeze touched the bare skin of her arms and shoulders like an invisible shawl. At the far end of the conservatory, she discerned a pair of French doors and went toward them.

The glass doors opened onto a small, sheltered balcony overlooking the rear deck. The air was as fresh and heady as champagne after the stuffy interior. Nell stepped out, heedless of her hair coming loose in tiny wisps about her face. The scene was so lovely it seemed unreal, like a romantic stage set. The sky was spangled with thousands of stars. The wake of the ship was a train of frothy lace across the dark velvet of the sea. Somewhere, back along the way, lay England. In the opposite direction, the tropical islands awaited the ship's arrival. Her heart beat a little faster. Once she was in Antigua, she would surely be able to get news of Harry. Tears shimmered in her eyes, half-blinding her.

Nell turned back toward the conservatory and ran into a broad chest clad in evening dress. Two hands steadied her shoulders. She smelled bay rum and she looked up into a handsome and familiar face. It quite took her breath away.

"Mr. Kincaid! Whatever are you doing out here?"

He released her and made a bow. "Not finding you inside, I came through the doors in search of you. And I might ask the same of you, Your Highness. Surely it is too cold for you out here? You'll catch pneumonia."

A tiny shiver ran through Nell. "You are right, of course. But I have always loved the night sky, and I let my enthusiasm carry me away."

"I understand completely. It is fascinating to watch the old and familiar stars change their patterns as we head south."

His voice was low and warm. It lured Nell into an indiscretion. "My grandfather was an astronomer," she said without thinking. "He taught me all the constellations when I was a mere girl. I had hoped to follow in his footsteps one day."

"And which grandfather was that?"

The sudden sharpness in Kincaid's tone had sent a warning prickle up her spine. "Ah, er...a great-grandfather on my mother's side," she mumbled.

Nell was annoyed with herself for letting his nearness make her drop her guard. Olga's careful coaching had not prepared her to embroider the princess' past with anecdotes from her own. Nell only hoped she hadn't somehow betrayed them both. She needed to distract her companion, and quickly.

"Look overhead." She tilted her face to the umbrella of glittering stars overhead. "Have you ever seen anything so beautiful or so mysterious?"

"Never," he answered softly.

With a shock, she realized he was looking down at her instead of up at the night. Even in the dimness of starlight she could feel her cheeks burning.

Kincaid tilted his head. "You are a most unusual woman, Your Highness. I would imagine that princesses grow inured to the most fullsome compliments, yet you are blushing like a schoolgirl."

"It was the dancing," she said quickly. "It is much too warm inside tonight for such exertion."

"But not out here." Kincaid bowed and there was an odd, dancing light in his eyes. The music came to them faint but clear. "Madame, may I have the honor of this waltz?"

He held his hand out to her, and Nell seemed powerless to refuse. His fingers closed over hers, warm and strong and strangely possessive. The strains of "Tales from the Vienna Woods" filled the conservatory as he drew her close. One arm encircled her neat waist, holding her lightly as he guided them through the intricate steps.

Nell's mind was awhirl. Dancing with the duke had been pleasant. Dancing with Mr. Kincaid was like waltzing on a cloud. She was thoroughly caught up in the moment. They swept effortlessly around the conservatory, the tails of his evening coat and the skirts of her ball gown billowing out behind them as they swirled and turned and spun in time to the lilting music.

Around and around and wilder and wilder they went. Pearly light shone on his hair and the firm lines of his cheek and jaw. Nell was suddenly robbed of breath. She had wished for a prince, and she had gotten one. Laughter born of sheer exhilaration rippled from her in a merry peal. No matter how preposterous the situation, she was enjoying it to the utmost.

For a few giddy moments, she forgot all her troubles. There was only starshine, and music, and the scent of bay rum mingling with the dew of violets in her own perfume. Then the waltz ended on a high, bright note. Hugh Kincaid's eyes were warm and intense as they looked down into hers. Instead of relinquishing her, he tightened his hold on her. Nell's breath caught in her throat. He looked as if he meant to kiss her.

He did. His head dipped to hers, and his fingers cupped the back of her head as his mouth came down against her lips. Softly at first, a mere brushing of mouth on mouth. Then his encircling arm drew her hard against him.

The touch of his lips, so gentle a few seconds earlier, turned hard and hot. Nell knew she should protest and draw away. She was helpless to move at all. Nothing in her chaste experience had prepared her for this. His kiss was a flame, searing through her thin defenses. All her notions of proper and ladylike behavior went up in smoke. There was nothing but the stars and the two of them. Then there was only the kiss.

It was nothing like Nell had expected. She'd imagined her first kiss would come from a young man to whom she had first become betrothed. It would be a tender and demure touching of lips; an action to be followed shortly thereafter by flowery phrases and pledges of undying esteem. Hugh Kincaid's kiss was neither tender nor demure. It was ruthless. It challenged and demanded, exhilarated and frightened with its intensity. And it was followed by another kiss as fierce and possessive as the first.

At first Nell was stiff with surprise, but then she melted against him. She had always prided herself upon being a levelheaded woman. At the moment, however, she didn't know up from down, and would have been hard-pressed to recall her own name. To her surprise, she realized that her arms were twined around Kincaid's neck. She couldn't remember putting them there. Dizzy and giddy and filled with wild joy, she gave herself up to the kiss.

His arms tightened around her, crushing the ruffles of her silk gown against his chest. Her ribs felt bruised by the power of his embrace, and the diamond-and-ruby lavalier pressed painfully into her skin. She gave a little yelp of protest. He released her instantly. Nell was still dazed, and her legs were weak as water. It seemed the most natural thing in the world for her to cling to him for support.

Kincaid looked down at her in the silvery light, and she saw a series of expressions flit over his strong features. First there was surprise, then frowning speculation. Last of all came suspicion, followed by a careful blankness that left her feeling shut out and very much alone. "You are either very innocent," he said fiercely, "or damnably clever."

Nell gasped. His brutal words stung. She reached out her hand to slap his cheek, but he caught her wrist. For a long moment, he stared down at her. Tears formed in her eyes.

"Perhaps I've made a mistake," he said, frowning.

"You most certainly have!" She jerked free and fled the conservatory. To her surprise, she was on an outside deck, not in the ballroom, as she'd planned. All the better. She didn't want anyone else to see the sparkle of tears in her eyes. As she reached the stairs, she heard the ship's bell begin to chime out the hour. Midnight.

Nell blinked away her tears. So much for Olga's talk of Cinderella. The fairy tales had gotten mixed up somehow. She'd wished for a Prince Charming and gotten a frog. And a mannerless one, at that. The real Prince Charming would never have kissed his princess until her mouth felt bruised. How dare Kincaid take her in his arms and kiss her without a by-your-leave!

How *dare* he! Why, if it had happened in Merkelstein, the real Princess Irina Christina would have had him clapped in irons for his audacity. But, a small voice whispered in her mind, if it had been the real princess out on deck with Hugh Kincaid, it was highly unlikely that their dance would have ended with a kiss. There was some comfort in that.

Nell stumbled in her haste. The frosty starlight glittered on the hundreds of crystal beads encrusting her shoes, so that they looked to be made of spun glass. Nell entered the suite in a wistful mood. She half expected her splendid gown to change before her eyes into a tatter of rags.

As she removed her borrowed jewels and silken gown, she stripped away her disguise, as well. The gilt mirror of the dressing table reflected an ex-governess turned unwilling adventuress. Nell met the gray eyes of the imposter in the looking glass with fortitude. She straightened her shoulders, though her heart felt forlorn. She couldn't wait for the masquerade to be over.

She shucked the jeweled slippers off. For a penniless young woman such as she, there were no fairy godmothers, and no glass slippers.

And, she thought sadly, her Cinderella story would have no happily-ever-afters.

Chapter Four

Nell's head began to throb and she suddenly realized how very tired she was. After changing into one of her own flannel nightgowns, she climbed gratefully into the comfortable bed, decked out with Princess Irina Christina's embroidered Irish linen.

Once esconced in the luxurious bed, Nell expected to fall asleep from sheer physical exhaustion. Yet her mind was startlingly awake, and filled with restless energy. She counted sheep in vain. Each fleecy beast that leapt over the stile in her mind's eye bore a startling resemblance to the princess—frowning in indignant disapproval.

Opening her eyes, Nell stared at the ceiling through the dimness of the room. It was not only the leaping images of the princess keeping her awake. Hugh Kincaid also haunted her thoughts. She feared that his keen eyes and sharp wit would soon uncover her deception. And she feared her confused reactions to him. He was a very dangerous man. At least where unworldly—and, she had to admit, naive—ex-governesses were concerned.

Another problem keeping her awake was her part in Olga's sorry scheme. The truth of the matter was that Nell was living a lie and saw no way to extricate herself from it. She, who had been raised to esteem honor and despise falsehood.

Another truth—just as difficult to deal with—was the fact that by her masquerade she had forfeited any chance of seeing Hugh Kincaid's regard for her blossom into anything more. She wasn't quite sure what he'd meant about her being either a total innocent or damnably clever, but she knew in her bones that the attraction was mutual. Instinct also told her that it might have had the potential to ripen into something more than an idle shipboard romance.

Nell wondered what he thought of her and her precipitate flight from the starlit deck. She had reacted to his kisses like a silly, inexperienced young woman.

Which, of course, she was.

Her mouth still burned from the touch of his lips on hers. She felt like Sleeping Beauty, awakening from a hundred years' sleep. *I am still mixing up my fables,* she thought wearily. But then, she felt very mixed up indeed. By becoming part of Olga's hoax, she had tangled herself hopelessly in a web of lies. She dashed away a traitorous tear. Another followed, leaving a warm trail down her cheek. Nell buried her face into the pillow and wept her heart out.

She wept all the tears she'd stored up from all the sorrows she had never been able to properly mourn over the years. The shock of her parents' deaths, following so closely upon one another, and of being thrown out of the only home she ever known—penniless, to boot—had been severe. But Nell had had to be strong for Harry, a sickly schoolboy at the time, and to find immediate work to secure a roof over their heads and food for their bellies—not to mention their futures.

The tears came hot and fast. She wept for her brother, who was full of sweetness and intellectual brilliance and who had gone to the West Indies on holiday with high hopes of securing a teaching position, only to disappear from the face of the earth. A hundred possibilities, all of them horrid, jostled into her crowded thoughts.

And when the storm of deep grief ended, leaving her drained, she found there were even a few tears left for Miss Ellen Shepherd, who had gone straight from girlhood to adult responsibilities without once having tasted the heady champagne of romance.

And likely never would. Cinderella's night at the ball had been short and not very sweet.

Hugh Kincaid had danced with her only because he believed her to be the royal princess of Merkelstein. And if her real identity was discovered? She deemed it highly improbable that someone of his elevated social circle would take any notice of an impecunious ex-governess. When she was unmasked in Antigua—as surely she must be—even that slight hope would vanish forever, like dew on a summer's day.

Nell dabbed at her eyes. How disappointed her parents would be in her woeful lack of character: worrying over Hugh Kincaid and fearing retribution once she was unmasked, when she should be asking heaven for forgiveness. Somehow, the coming of Christmas made her fall from grace seem all the worse.

By the time the clock struck two, Nell was in a positive ferment of remorse. Sleep seemed as remote as the moon. After rolling over a dozen times in as many minutes, she imagined that she would still be lying there, counting her iniquities, when Olga returned.

However, when Olga did tiptoe in later with a secret smile on her lips, Nell was fast asleep. Exhaustion had claimed her, and she was dreaming of places and people dear to her heart from oh so long ago.

Nell wandered down a dim, dream-shrouded hall. Soft voices and bursts of bright laughter lured her on. She opened the door of shining gold at the end of the hall, and found herself magically transported back to the old vicarage. She went in, shutting the door behind her.

It was perfect. The smallest details, long forgotten, were there, unchanged by time. The wallpaper was just as she remembered it, silver and white scrolls against a background of rich cream. The tier table, centered with a crystal dome enclosing wax roses, stood in its accustomed place beneath one of the long windows. Oh, and there was her mother's cluster of green-and-purple Venetian glass grapes, brought back from her parents' honeymoon trip. The Christmas tree stood in the bowed window, trimmed with white candles and crimson ribbons, chains of gilt and silver paper, and myriad tiny red blown-glass balls fashioned into clusters of holly berries against green glass leaves. Someone had turned the lamps down low, and the snowy tapers upon the fragrant branches were lit.

Delighted and astonished, Nell turned slowly to view the rest of the room. Her heart gave a great leap of joy.

The rosewood sofa, which she knew had been sold off, was restored to its former place near the hearth, and her mother sat there, embroidering with a golden hoop.

"Come in, Nell, dearest. We have been waiting for you."

Papa was in his high-backed chair, lighting his faunite pipe. He puffed out a fragrant cloud of smoke. "Listen, Nell. Can you hear the carolers coming up the walk?"

"Why, yes!"

The strains of "It Came upon the Midnight Clear" floated outside on the clear, bright air. Through the sheer lace at the windows, Nell could see snowflakes drifting down like feathers shaken loose from the wings of hovering angels.

"Mama, how beautiful you look! And Papa—so young and handsome."

They smiled at her. "Harry and the others are just back from sledding. Ah, here they are now."

Nell surveyed the room in wonder. Everyone was there: Mama and Papa, Harry and Jonathan and dear Aunt Eloise. Even Grandfather and Grandmother Thompson, looking as young as they had in their wedding portrait. Voices were raised in cheerful exchange. A door opened behind Nell and admitted one more person to this cozy family scene.

"We have a special guest this evening," Mama announced.

Nell pivoted slowly. Smiling across the room at her, his eyes sparkling like dark sapphires against his tanned skin, was Hugh Kincaid. She held out her hands and went to welcome him. . . .

"Nell, darling..."

"Nell, darling?"

Her eyelids fluttered open, and the cozy drawing room vanished.

Olga bent over her, looking at Nell by the light from the bedside lamp, which she had lit. "I have had such a vonderful evening," she said. "So romantic. First the grand duke, and then the oh-so-handsome Captain Creighton. I must tell you all about it!"

With a groan, Nell rolled over and put the down pillow over her head. "Go away," she said crossly.

"Vell, if you are going to be so peevish, I vill vait until morning!"

Olga swirled off in a rustle of skirts, turning off the lamp on her way out. Nell tried unsuccesfully to recapture her wonderful dream. After tossing about, she drifted at last into deep and dreamless sleep.

In the warm morning light, still wrapped in the happy aura of her earlier dream, Nell decided her situation looked slightly brighter. She decided that she must carry off the masquerade, if only so that Mr. Hugh Kincaid would never know of her folly. She breakfasted with Olga in the stateroom, continuing her lessons in what she would have to know to keep up the masquerade properly.

"There is too much to remember," she protested. "It is inevitable that I will make a mistake sooner or later."

"Hopefully, later." Olga adopted a stern mien. "You must remember, dear Nell, that you are royalty. As such, you may make any number of faux pas, and no one vill look askance."

Nell sent her a bemused glance. "Do you mean that the rules of ordinary politeness do not apply to princesses of the blood, or that royals are so eccentric that no note is taken of their manners?"

Olga beamed. "Both. You catch on quite vell. Now, say for me the members of the royal house, both living and dead, of the past two generations."

With a groan, Nell recited the convoluted bloodlines of Merkelstein's royal personages, and their links, however remote, to the nobility.

After another quarter hour, Olga deemed her protégé ready to make another public appearance. "Do not look upon it as a test, but a challenge," she said encouragingly.

"Yes," Nell agreed, lifting her chin. "We might as well be hung for sheep as lambs."

"Vhat? Hanging sheep? Who vould do such a silly thing?" She eyed Nell over the rim of her pince-nez. "Is this vone of those curious English customs? Or are you just pulling the vool over my leg?"

It took Nell several minutes to control her laughter. She explained, as best she could, what "pulling the wool over one's eyes" and "pulling one's leg" meant. "Nor," she added, "are the English so peculiar as to actually send farm animals to the gallows."

Something crucial appeared to have gotten lost in the translation. Olga continued to look horrified, and Nell gave it up as a lost cause. "The sun is shining, and we have been cooped up here all morning. Let us go out for a stroll along the deck."

They started out for the sun deck to enjoy the increasingly mild weather. Admiring glances followed their progress. Olga looked quite elegant in yellow wool piped with brown velvet, and Nell was splendid in a walking dress and matching jacket of white merino cut in a nautical style with navy trim and jaunty gold braid.

The sky was incredibly clear, and the sea as blue as lapis and netted with golden light. Under any other circumstances, Nell would have reveled in the glory of the day. She was not as sanguine as her companion that any errors on her part would be overlooked. Like her confidence, her resolution wavered in the bright light. She wished that she could end this farce by making a clean breast of it—but to whom?

Captain Creighton was bound by the laws of the sea, and he was certain to be very angry with them. A shudder passed through Nell at the prospect of spending the rest of the voyage confined to quarters—or worse.

The only other course of action would be to divulge her dilemma to Hugh Kincaid. A man who had kissed her by moonlight would not be ready to throw her to the fishes so easily, would he? Nell knew that he might despise her for her part in the charade, but at least he would know that she did have some degree of integrity.

But there was Olga's fate to consider.

No matter how her inclinations urged otherwise, Nell could not and *would* not be responsible for the dire consequences that exposure would cause her newfound friend. Having seen something of the Princess Irina Christina's temper, she could well imagine what terrible punishment Olga might endure. No, despite the clamoring of her conscience, she would have to see this through to the last act.

The attendant snapped to attention when they reached the sun deck and hurriedly set out two chairs for them. The location was rather too prominent for Nell's taste. There was a place around the corner that offered protection from the wind and curious passersby, as well as an unobstructed view.

"I would prefer to sit in the alcove near the rail," she said.

"Yes, Your Highness. At once, Your Highness."

The attendant was so flustered as he tried to move the chairs that he blundered into the path of a man rounding the corner. There was a sudden shout, a flurry of folding chairs and tweed, and a hurtling figure came crashing down at Nell's feet. A tin of peppermints hit the bulkhead and opened, spilling white lozenges everywhere.

A pair of small blue eyes blinked up at her from behind a pair of wildly askew spectacles. She knelt beside him. "Professor Smith! Are you all right?"

A look of chagrin twisted his features. He reached up and pushed his eyeglasses into place, then assured himself that his cap was still on. He touched its brim. "My apologies, Princess Irina."

"Tut, tut," Olga clucked. "Vhat a singularly clumsy young man."

Nell blushed at her friend's frankness; in fact as Professor Smith tried to get up he didn't realize—or rather, didn't see—that the hand with which he was reaching for the deck, was instead poised over thin air and the ocean far below. He clattered to the deck and knocked his head against the teak rail with a solid thunk. Her best governessing instincts came to the fore.

"Perhaps, sir, it might be wise to have your eyes examined again as soon as possible. I believe that a change of lenses might be in order."

"Nonsense," he said, clapping his hat more firmly down on his head. "I can see perfectly well." He stood up, apologized again to Nell and Olga, then made a hurried bow to the ventilation tube, which he'd evidently mistaken for the white-uniformed attendant, and blundered back the way he had come.

Nell's eyes crinkled in laughter. "Poor man. The bruises on his shins must be permanent." Yes, there was certainly something very odd about him, although he seemed perfectly harmless. Olga's thoughts were running along the same lines.

"Perhaps he is a man of genius. I have heard that such people often live in a vorld of their own imaginings, rapt in their higher thoughts. That vould account for his profound clumsiness."

Nell laughed and took her chair. "If the professor is wrapped up in his imaginings, they probably have more to do with pills and potions and whatever malady he chooses to have at the moment than genius."

She picked up one of the books Olga had fetched from the ship's library. It was one of Mrs. Alter's adventurous romances, which were prime favorites of Nell. Olga was not in the mood to read. She tipped her hat over her face and promptly went to sleep. Nell immersed herself in the tale of an English general's daughter and her forbidden love for a dashing Scots laird.

A soft voice jolted her from her reading. "Your Highness, forgive my boldness in speaking to you without an introduction..."

Nell looked up from *The Wild Rose Among the Thistle*. A thin man with a kindly air, a fringe of silver hair and twinkling blue eyes stood before her, hat in hand.

"I am the Reverend Mr. Mitchell, vicar and choirmaster of a small church in Devon," he said quickly, encouraged by her smile. "I shall be conducting the shipboard choir on Christmas Eve, and we are short of members. I understand from Lady Levitskaya, that you are gifted with a particularly lovely voice."

Nell glanced around. Olga was now nowhere in sight. "Lady Levitskaya is very kind. I have sung with the village choir, but—"

She broke off, realizing what she had said. Mr. Mitchell took her pause for modesty. "Singing with the villagers! How perfectly delightful, my dear princess. I am gratified to know that you, despite your royal blood, do not stand on ceremony in the worship of the Lord!"

Inwardly cringing, Nell was persuaded to agree to attend rehearsal that evening before dinner. Mr. Mitchell went off, properly pleased to have snagged a royal patron for his choir. Nell sank deeper into self-recrimination. It seemed that every time she opened her mouth she made her situation worse.

Olga came bustling back. "I see that you have spoken to the so nice Mr. Mitchell. You vill sing vith the choir, no?"

"No thanks to you. How could you put me in such an untenable position?"

The other woman sank into the deck chair beside Nell. "Ah, but you see, I also vill be singing. It vill be quite festive and put us in the spirit of the blessed Christmas season, is that not so?"

Nell, remembering Mr. Dickens' novel, made the only suitable reply that came to her. "Bah, humbug!"

Olga was already leafing through in her own book and ignored her, but Nell did receive a startled look from a young married couple strolling by with their three children. She pretended not to notice.

The breeze had picked up by afternoon, and the dancing surface of the ocean was so golden-bright it was almost impossible to look at it. "Goodness," Olga exclaimed. "I have forgotten to fetch the songbook I vanted to give to Mr. Mitchell. I vill meet you there."

"Very well." Nell came around the corner of the promenade deck and almost collided with someone coming the other way.

"What the devil—?" Hugh Kincaid caught her by the shoulders to keep her from pitching sideways. His mouth turned up in a surprised smile. "Oh! I beg pardon, Your Highness."

"I beg yours," she stammered, and blushed to the roots of her hair. After their encounter in the conservatory the night before, his presence rendered her awkward and tongue-tied. "The light blinded me. I— I hope I didn't tread on your toes?"

He pulled her into the shade of an overhang. "If so, I didn't feel it. Where are you off to in such a hurry?"

"To the rehearsal for Mr. Mitchell's Christmas choir. I am already late."

But escape was not to be so easy. Kincaid took her arm. His smile grew warmer. "Let me escort you then. I have been hoping for an opportunity to apologize for my behavior yesterday evening."

Nell had been hoping to avoid any mention of it. She was blinded, not by the dazzling sun on water, but by the warmth in Kincaid's eyes when he looked down at her. It robbed her of breath. She almost stumbled over a ring set into the deck, but Kincaid held her up effortlessly

Once again she was amazed at how strong he was. The muscled arm beneath his coat sleeve was as solid as steel, although proximity to industrial metal had never caused the internal reaction that was occurring inside her at the moment. Everything was melting. Her heart had grown to three times its usual size and threatened to burst from beneath her tucked bodice. She put her hand up to shield her face.

He was instantly concerned. "Have you something in your eye?"

He pivoted so that her back was to the bulkhead. A moment later he whisked out a handkerchief of snowy linen and tilted her chin upward with his other hand. Her gaze met his. Something happened in that split second. At the touch of his hand, the universe shrunk until there was nothing in it but the two of them. Nell felt little fizzles of warmth in her chest, and a deeper, slower heat in the pit of her stomach.

Kincaid dropped his handkerchief and cupped her cheek with his hand. "Do you know what you do to a man with that wide-eyed look?" he murmured. His finger traced the curve of her cheek and the line of her jaw. "Do you know how truly beautiful you are?"

Nell scarcely took in his words. He was so close, his warm breath stirred her hair. She felt giddy and light-headed. Staring up into his deep blue eyes made her even more so. As he moved even closer, she clutched at the lapel of his coat. Kincaid groaned and swept her into his arms.

His mouth found hers. As kisses go, it was a bomb-shell. The deafening roar in her ears was like the thunder of cannon fire. Rockets burst inside her, lighting her up from the crown of her head to the tips of her toes. The lingering heat of his lips blazed through her, fusing her thoughts into an incoherent mass.

Nell was oblivious to everything else. Everything that was not Kincaid, that is. She was excitingly aware of his firm arm around her, his fingers splayed against her back. Of his hard chest and the heat of his body and the subtle, enveloping scent that was his alone. Of his mouth, pressing yet again on hers, urgent and possessive, breathless with passion.

Or was that her? She was lost in his kisses, whirling up in sensation—and then plunging down like a stone when he suddenly pulled away.

Her cheeks were flushed, but he was pale. He straightened his cravat and gave her a rueful smile that didn't quite reach his shadowed eyes. "I hadn't planned to do that again," he said harshly. "I suppose in your country I would be hung for such an act of lèse-majesté."

That brought Nell up short. She remembered, just in time, that he thought she was a princess. Would he still have kissed her if he knew she was plain Ellen Shepherd, with neither a sou to her name nor a drop of royal blood in her entire body? She knew the answer. If he knew the truth, he would think her an unprincipled adventuress.

Her roiled emotions got the better of her. Without warning, her eyes filled with tears.

Kincaid smothered an oath and relinquished her. "Forgive me. Once again I've acted like a damn...like a complete fool."

Before she could find her voice, he bowed and was gone. Nell managed a croak directed at his retreating back. Kincaid had disappeared into one of the salons. She remained by the bulkhead for some time, trembling and trying to rearrange her disordered thoughts. She had imagined kisses as tender. Gentle touches that warmed the heart yet left the body unmoved. Kincaid's ardent, masterful kisses had forever disabused her of such ridiculous notions.

With all the will in the world, she could not prevent him from kissing her again if he so decided. Nor, she realized hotly, would she want to do so. It was a moment of revelation. All her life she had heard whispers about fallen women, and wondered at their foolishness. For the first time in her short life, she thought she had begun to understand a little. With a man like Hugh Kincaid, lovemaking would be something wonderful.

After composing herself and brushing out the crushed collar of her dress, Nell went to join the others at the rehearsal. She arrived breathless, with rosy cheeks and gray eyes aglow.

Olga, peeking over the top of her hymnal, was very pleased to see it. What dear little Nell needed was a kindly patron to look after her affairs. A fairy god-mother of sorts.

Olga quite fancied herself in the role. It wouldn't take much doing. After all, Nell already had the gowns and jewels, the tiaras and diamond slippers—and, quite possibly, an interested prince. All she needed now was just a teeny touch of magic.

Chapter Five

For Nell, the next several days passed in games of shuttlecock and shuffleboard, afternoon teas and anagrams, and the wonderful indulgence of reading undistrubed for hours at a time. The evenings were spent dining and dancing and putting on elaborate, costumed charades. To her intense disappointment, Hugh Kincaid took no part in any of those activities. He divided his time between the card room and the smoking room.

Instead, Nell found herself courted and flattered by the Grand Duke Alexi, the rajah, and a German baron, none of whom interested her in the least. Nell realized that even the most wonderful ball in the world would be boring if the one person you most wanted to dance with didn't attend. She wished she knew the reason for Kincaid's avoidance of her.

One morning, the rajah had startling news to offer over breakfast in the white salon, news that quite drove Hugh Kincaid from her thoughts. There had been a robbery aboard the *Pride of Paradise* the previous evening. "The pattern continues," he announced softly. "We should not have sailed on the

Triton Line, I fear. You ladies must take precautions to safeguard your valuables."

Captain Creighton joined them just in time to overhear. Nell set down her delicate porcelain cup. "Is it true that there has been a robbery?"

"I regret to say that it is, Your Highness. We are taking measures to apprehend the thief and restore the stolen property."

He explained that while the Grand Duke Alexi was engaged in an evening of cards with his friends, a thief had broken into his stateroom and robbed him of several irreplaceable items.

Gwendolyn Boynton and Lady Culpepper joined them, all agog. "I was told that the most costly item stolen was a Fabergé creation—a cunning little flower of white enamel with gold, rose pearls and rubies, that opened into a clock. It was to have been a gift to the governor from the prince of Ermarnia."

The captain was clearly chagrined to find his aristocratic passengers so well-informed. The diplomatic repercussions and the loss to the line would surely be devastating. His gaze took in the entire table, then stopped at Nell.

"A quiet investigation of the passengers is already under way, under the supervision of Mr. Kincaid and Professor Smith. I know that you will all cooperate with them fully. First, they will be looking for any discrepancies among the passenger list. Never fear, we shall soon uncover the culprit. Meanwhile, I would advise you all to have your jewels deposited in the ship's safe until we reach Antigua. Especially you, Princess Irina."

"Bah!" exclaimed Olga, with an airy shrug. "The Princess Irina Christina is not afraid of thieves!"

"Nevertheless, it would be wise to heed my advice." He appealed to Lady Culpepper, as a woman of good sense. "Surely you will see the necessity of having your pearls locked up in the safe?"

The Englishwoman considered his suggestion, but discarded it. "The circumstances are quite different, really. The grand duke was away from his quarters when the thief struck, and, you see, I never remove my pearls except at bedtime, when they reside in a special case beneath my pillow. I defy any thief to try and take them!"

Though he was plainly unhappy about being overruled, Captain Creighton had no way of forcing them to comply. He bowed stiffly. "Let us hope that none of you have reason to regret your decision."

"I will protect you, ladies, should the need arise." The rajah took Nell's gloved hand and raised it to his lips. His dark eyes shone. "It would be the greatest honor I could hope to attain."

"Nonsense! These ladies are perfectly capable of taking care of themselves," another voice said.

They looked up just as Professor Smith joined them. He was wearing a thick coat of houndstooth wool with a matching cap, even though it was quite warm in the salon, and brandishing his amber-headed cane in the rajah's direction. Unfortunately, it connected with a vase of flowers, knocking it over and sending a rush of water into the other man's lap. The rajah leapt to his feet, stifling an oath. The look he shot the professor would have burnt a lesser man to a crisp. Or perhaps, Nell thought, only a more observant one. The professor didn't appear to have noticed the little accident he'd caused.

"In any case," he announced, "I have promised Captain Creighton that I will help him catch the scoundrel responsible before we reach Antigua."

"And how do you propose to do that, sir, *fall* upon him?" the rajah bit off viciously. He sent the other man a withering look and stomped away to change his trousers.

Professor Smith merely shrugged. "I shall do whatever is necessary, no matter how repugnant I find it."

"How very brave of you," Nell said drolly. After a few encounters, she was becoming used to the way the professor's mind worked. He did not disappoint her.

"Not at all. I am a man in urgent need of peace and quiet! This constant hubbub, with people searching through cabins and tramping up and down the decks at all hours of the night, is upsetting to my delicate nervous system." He coughed, wheezed, and pushed away a lock of springy red hair that had fallen over his eyes.

"Oh, dear. My throat is developing a tickle. Why, I have sneezed twice in the last hour. A sure sign of an impending attack of some kind. However, once the thief is caught, things will return to normal."

He gazed at Nell through his thick spectacles. "Someone aboard the *Pride of Paradise* is not whom he—or she—pretends to be. I will soon get to the bottom of it. You have my word, Your Highness, the thief *will* be caught."

Nell was uneasy. The investigation into the theft made her position even more tenuous. If her impersonation was discovered, she would surely be a prime suspect. She felt the snare of lies she and Olga had spun tightening about her. Oh, if only she'd told the truth from the start! Her Cinderella dream was quickly turning into a nightmare.

The theft was the main topic of conversation for the rest of the week, which flew by quickly. The other area of interest was the entertainment for the Christmas celebration. Nell's resolution to retire to her suite for the duration of the voyage had been foiled by Olga and the Reverend Mr. Mitchell.

Word of mouth, increasingly balmy weather, and the inevitable boredom of a two-week crossing combined to provide much greater interest in the Christmas program. And when the opportunity to be presented to the Princess Irina Christina of Merkelstein was thrown in as a treat, Mr. Mitchell found himself with an embarrassment of volunteers. What had begun as a simple choir of carols and winter festival songs, blossomed into a full-scale pageant before his delighted and disbelieving eyes. Nell was too busy to worry, except in the wee and silent hours of the night.

An overcast and windy afternoon found her in her salon, idly turning the pages of another novel. Soon it would be time to go to rehearsal. The seas were rough, but the pitching of the ship no longer bothered her in the slightest. She was glad to be out of the public eye for a few hours. She toyed with a necklet of topaz and pearls. The ongoing investigation into the theft and into the background of the ship's passengers was making her fidgety. That, and a growing sense of unease that she had been missing something significant—something that didn't quite add up.

Olga sat across from her on the settee, making last-minute adjustments to the ruby silk evening gown that Nell would wear for the Christmas festivities. The minutes ticked by in companionable silence. She had just threaded her needle again when the ormulu clock bonged out the hour. Olga glanced up in surprise

"So late? Come, ve must go to the rehearsal," she said, setting aside her needlework. She smoothed her skirts and drew on elegant gloves of straw-colored kid. "Ve must set an example for the others."

Nell put aside the book she'd been reading with a smile. "I declare, you are as much a tyrant as the princess ever was."

She put on a fetching little feathered hat that matched her gown of rose and gold tafetta, and her gloves. She caught their reflection in the looking glass above the console table. She and Olga made a fine pair, Nell thought. That was it, she realized. Her brow puckered. How could a mere secretary afford such a wonderful wardrobe?

"How very splendid you look, Olga," she said slowly. "Surely that yellow walking dress is as fine as anything in the princess' own wardrobe?"

"Ah, yes..." Olga glanced in the mirror and smoothed a frill into place. "My favorite day dress. This lace, it is made only at the convent of the Sisters of Divine Mercy in Bruges. The silk is from the Levant."

Nell's heart sank. "I am surprised that your wages would cover such a great expense. Judging by my own meager salary, the princess is not the most generous of employers."

Olga blushed. For the first time since Nell had known her, she seemed at a loss for words. "A—a castoff," she said finally. "Princess Irina, she did not find the color pleasing vhen the seamstress delivered it. And, of course, since I am so handy vith the needle, I vas able to alter it to fit me."

"How very fortunate."

And how very clever Olga must be, Nell thought as they left their stateroom, since the skirt of the dress was without a seam or ruffle from waist to hem—and Olga was a good eight or nine inches taller than the princess. Yet how else would an impecunious secretary be able to own such a wordly wardrobe? Dismay fluttered in the pit of Nell's stomach. After all, what did she really know about Olga?

Nothing.

Not even how long had she been in the princess' employ. The flutter in her midsection stilled and became a cold, heavy ball of lead. Could Olga be the jewel thief, masquerading as a secretary?

Then Olga smiled and tweaked a ruffle of Nell's gown into place. Her eyes were as happy as a child's, and just as guileless. Nell smiled back. *It is just my overwrought imagination,* she told herself. *Olga is sweet, generous, excitable, and very clever with needle and thread. She is a bit eccentric, no doubt, but she is no more the jewel thief than I am.*

They went through the red salon and down the corridor to the room where the rehearsals were held. Nell was glad to be busy. At least, by immersing herself in plans for the Christmas choir, she managed to avoid

Hugh Kincaid quite easily. In fact, he seemed to be avoiding her. Except for his appearance at dinner or luncheon, she rarely saw him. Not so Professor Smith.

"Halloo! Princess Irina!"

Nell heard him hailing her from somewhere out on deck, and cringed. The hypochondriac had attached himself to her like a limpet, and not even the rajah's sauve but pointed comments had kept him away. Nell had come to dread that first glimpse of bright red hair at the far end of the deck. It was uncanny the way a man who could scarcely see to keep from tripping over noticeable items on deck—coiled ropes, chairs, and his own two feet—could manage to spot her when they were at opposite ends of the ship.

She expected to hear him come up behind her at any moment. Short of gathering her skirts and bolting through the nearest door, there was no way of escaping him. Nell didn't hesitate. "Quickly!" she instructed Olga.

They ducked into a salon that had been set up for cards. Several of the ladies looked up as they hurried through, and two rose and curtseyed. Nell felt guilty avoiding the professor. For all his imagined illnesses, he was really quite harmless. He reminded her of a clumsy, eager Saint Bernard puppy, falling all over himself and everyone else in hopes of receiving a little attention.

Unlike most of the confirmed hypochondriacs that she'd met, he had a sympathetic ear for others' problems. He had befriended shy little Gwendolyn Boynton, and more than once he had sheltered that hapless damsel from the sharp tongue of her acerbic grandmother.

As Nell came out on the opposite deck, she saw the young lady in question near the rail, on the receiving end of a scolding from her grandmother. The dowager's clipped tones carried to Nell's ear. "If Mr. Kincaid asks you to dance with him tonight, then you must, child. It doesn't matter if you like him or not. What matters is if *he* is taken with you."

Gwendolyn seemed to shrink inside her wide navy collar. Nell's heart went out to the girl. It seemed to her that Lady Culpepper had wanted an exotic and dazzlingly colorful butterfly of a granddaughter and had been given a delicate, silver-winged moth instead. With all the goodwill in the world, Miss Gwendolyn Boynton could never be what Lady Culpepper expected her to become.

"She expects me to make a grand marriage," Gwendolyn had confided one morning as she and Nell strolled around the decks together. "I should like to please Grandmama, but you see, I am not a very grand person. What I would really like is to marry a curate or scholar and live in a darling little cottage in the country, with masses of flowers and an herb garden! I do love plants and flowers, and even Grandmama says that I have a green thumb, expecially with roses and ferns. And I should like to have chickens and geese and perhaps a pig or two... although I don't particularly like cows, they are so very large... and I would never, never, *ever* again have to attend anything grander than one of the subscription assemblies in Nethergate!"

It had been a wonderful little speech, full of fire and passion. Nell had seen quite a new side of Miss Boynton. She didn't think that little Gwendolyn would get her wish, however. The redoubtable Lady Culpepper, having failed at firing her granddaughter off properly in London, seemed determined to foist the unwilling girl up on some wealthy colonial planter who was in the market for a blue-blooded wife. If she did so, it would be a disaster. Gwendolyn would be utterly miserable.

Upon reaching the red salon, Nell took her place between Olga and Miss Felicity Andrews, a lively young American woman who was an illustrator of children's books. Lady Culpepper and Gwendolyn drifted in a few minutes later. The girl's face was still red from her grandmother's lecture, and Lady Culpepper seemed distracted. They joined the chorus with Olga, a Mrs. Winkler, the bursar and the grand duke. Three more ladies bustled in, apologizing for their tardiness, and took the booklets the choir director handed them.

The rajah sat in on the rehearsal, but took no part. Instead, he contented himself with sending long, smoldering looks in Nell's direction, causing her to trip over her verses more than once. Mr. Mitchell rapped his baton for attention.

"Where is Professor Smith? Is he not coming to rehearse?" Mr. Mitchell asked petulantly. "He did promise to join us today, now that we are ready for the men's solos."

Hugh Kincaid entered, as if on cue. "Professor Smith sends me in his stead. He has succumbed to a bout of fulminant bronchial quinsy, and I have volunteered to take his place. A new finding in the investigations into the grand duke's missing articles delayed me."

Alexi stepped forward anxiously. "How are your inquiries coming, sir? Have you any news you might share with us?"

A dangerous spark danced in the depths of Kincaid's eyes. "I will only say that we are very close to a solution. A number of interesting things have come to light. The thief has gone among us in disguise."

Nell's heart stopped, then began beating again, so strongly that it sounded in her ears like thunder. Kincaid's gaze reached her, paused imperceptibly, and went on. "The mystery will be solved and the thief placed in custody before we reach port. You may count on it."

An excited buzz filled the room. Nell was unsettled but the Grand Duke Alexi smiled. "You are a man of your word, Mr. Kincaid. When this is solved, you shall have my undying gratitude."

The Reverend Mr. Mitchell was also relieved, but for other reasons. "Well, now that it is almost settled, we may get to the more important matter of our rehearsal."

He bowed to Kincaid, almost rubbing his hands in glee. "We are honored, sir. I was just about to cast the roles. You may have your choice of singing as Gaspar or Melchior. Captain Creighton has kindly agreed to play the role of Balthazar." He held out a packet of notepaper. "Perhaps you would care to take a moment to go over the little script I have put together."

Kincaid's dazzling smile blazed out. "I have already reviewed the professor's music sheets. I would like to take the role of Melchior—providing that the

Princess Irina sings the duet with me." His gaze met Nell's. She had no power to look away.

All eyes were on her as Kincaid bowed. She flushed, but agreed. Mr. Mitchell took a seat at the piano forte and played the melody for Melchior's song. Kincaid caught it quickly, and filled the chamber with his rich voice. The words were simple, but their meaning was timeless and sincere.

"Angel from heaven, what gift shall I bring
to honor the Babe, the newborn King?
What shall I take with me when I do call
upon the Babe who is Himself
the greatest gift of all?"

His voice was warm and golden. The vibrant timbre of his tones echoed in Nell's bones and sent a tingle of appreciation down her spine. The rest of the cast broke into applause when he finished.

Mr. Mitchell favored him with a slight bow and turned his attention to Nell. "And now, Your Highness, you will sing the next verse in response to Melchior's question. The third and fourth verses are the duet." He handed Nell a sheet of music written out in his precise hand, then went through the tune once. "And now..."

She picked up the bright thread of melody, her voice as sweet and pure as crystal bells:

"Gold and jewels and great treasure trove
Pale in splendor beside truth and love.
If you truly wish to honor the King,
These are the gifts that you must bring:

Love and truth.

Her voice broke on the last line. The Reverend Mr. Mitchell waved a hand, and a steward was instantly at her side with a glass of lemon-barley water to soothe her throat.

"We must keep you in good voice—so lovely a voice, too—for the next three hours," the choirmaster told her.

It was the longest three hours that Nell could remember since coming aboard the *Pride of Paradise*.

After a confused beginning, the presentation came together quickly. Mr. Mitchell was in transports of ecstasy. His little group had talent, enthusiasm and sensitivity—qualities his choir at home had only in half measure, he said. Inspiration struck.

"If the weather is clement, as surely it will be, we shall arrive from the balcony deck and proceed into the ballroom. With the stars behind us, it will be quite a dramatic entrance. Do we dare—? Might we go up to view the area? Perhaps it will stimulate our creative efforts."

The grand duke clasped his hands in emphatic agreement. "Yes, you will never view the beauty and mystery of the night as you will at sea. Is that not right, Captain Creighton?"

"That is so. On clear nights I like to go up to the topmost deck, above the bridge. The stars are larger and more brilliant than on land...so near that it seems you can touch them."

The company was charmed by his description. Gwendolyn put a hand on Lady Culpepper's sleeve and looked at her with soft, dark eyes, like a spaniel's. "May we go up and see them, Grandmother?"

"Why, I see no reason why we shouldn't do so, now that rehearsal has ended for the evening. The air is quite warm, and there will be enough time to dress for dinner."

The grand duke smiled down at Nell and offered her his arm. "If I may be so bold, madame?"

"I should enjoy it very much," she replied. She wanted to see the stars, and she was glad that the grand duke's actions had forestalled Kincaid as he stepped toward her.

They trooped out on deck and up a series of stairs. "Really," Lady Culpepper said in an aside to Nell, "I am most surprised that the professor gave his role over to Mr. Kincaid so readily. I am sure, Your Highness, that there is some antipathy between the two men."

Nell was startled. "What brought you to that conclusion?"

"Mr. Kincaid and the professor rarely attend the same affairs. When one is present, the other invariably leaves. I noticed it at the champagne reception in your honor, and again at the ball. It is plain that they dislike each other, and mean to avoid one another for the duration of the voyage."

Nell's brow puckered in a frown. It was true.

They went through the ballroom, where the great chandeliers were unlit, and through the conservatory to the balcony beyond. As they arrived at the rail, someone quenched the fairy lanterns on either side. The glory of the stars sprang out against an indigo background. Nell was dazzled. They stood beneath a canopy of blazing diamonds, some clustered in bouquets of scintillating light, others strung out across the sky like glowing garlands.

Nell didn't know how long she stood at the far side of the dark deck, utterly entranced. As her eyes adjusted, she made out shining darts of blue and green and red. She wanted to reach out and gather in the stars by the handful.

Someone joined her, and Nell turned her head. Olga was standing beside her with a finger to her lips. Her eyes were brighter than the stars overhead. "Dear Nell, you vill never believe! Captain Creighton vill be in Antigua for several veeks. He has asked if he may call upon me vhen ve reach Antigua. Of course, I have told him yes."

Nell stared at her in horror. "Olga, once we reach the islands this charade will end. He thinks that you are a noblewoman. When he learns the truth..."

Olga grinned in the moonlight. "And the truth must be that I am Lady Levitskaya. Vhat else? Surely you vill not be so cruel as to inform him othervise?"

Before Nell could reply, the night was shattered by high-pitched cries of alarm. It took a moment for her to realize that it was Lady Henrietta's voice. "Oh, good heavens! My pearls—the Culpepper pearls are gone!"

"Here, light the lamps!" someone said.

An instant later the stars faded as warm yellow light flooded the area. Lady Culpepper stood in the center of the circle like some tragic queen, clutching her shawl against the bodice of her gown, where, only moments earlier, the fabulous pearls had hung.

"What utter effrontery! The Culpepper pearls have been stolen from around my very throat!" she exclaimed with great indignation.

Kincaid was at her side immediately. The air crackled with tension. "You are sure, madame, that you haven't left them in your stateroom?"

"I am not senile, Mr. Kincaid. I had the pearls around my throat less than five minutes ago. Someone has slit the string and taken them!"

Kincaid took charge. "Please remain where you are until we can search the area."

Captain Creighton was very upset. "You see what comes of vanity and not heeding my warning," he told Lady Culpepper sternly.

She bristled with outrage. "I had no idea that anyone would *dare* to do such a thing to *me!*"

The area was searched, but to no avail. After conferring with Kincaid and his first officer, Captain Creighton let the passengers leave to dress for dinner. "We can't very well search them. These aristocrats live by their own rules."

"Yes, there would be hell to pay if you even suggested it," Kincaid agreed. "We must use subtler means to unmask the thief."

A great weight settled over Nell as they went to change into evening dress. As they unlocked the stateroom door, she tried to recall where she had last seen Lady Culpepper with the pearls. "I am certain she had them on when the lantern was shuttered."

"Yes," Olga agreed. "I saw them myself. Such lovely, lovely pearls. It vould be a shame if they vere not found."

A sigh escaped Nell. "It certainly would. We are in a terrible fix."

"But ve have nothing to do vith this."

Nell shook her head at Olga. "It looks very bad. There is only one stairway leading there."

Nell's face was pale in the lamplight. "The only people on the balcony at the time were ourselves, Mr. Kincaid, the captain and the first officer, the grand duke and the rajah, and Lady Culpepper and her granddaughter. If the thief were an outsider, he would have had to come right past us. No one did."

Olga didn't understand. Nell wrung her hands. "Oh, don't you see? If there was no outsider present, then *the thief must be one of us!*"

Dinner was subdued that evening. The ladies looked quite prim without their glittering jewels, which had been carefully locked up in the ship's huge safe. Dancing had been planned for afterward, but few were so inclined. The musicians played while the passengers stood around in tense knots or drifted away to their staterooms early.

They next few days were horrid. The day before Christmas dawned in golden light that promised fine weather ahead. Nell, unable to sleep, had wrapped herself in a gauzy shawl and had gone to the rail to watch the sunrise. The air was soft and sultry and the sea glittered like molten gold. Birds swooped and soared on the breeze, a sure sign of land ahead. Tomorrow they would reach Antigua.

Her reverie was disturbed by the sound of stealthy footsteps approaching. There was no reason for such furtiveness. Could it mean that the thief was on the prowl once more? She craned her neck. If she could get a glimpse of him in action, she might be able to help Lady Culpepper regain possession of her fabulous pearls—and divert suspicion from herself.

The footsteps stopped, then came on with a rush. Instinctively, Nell ducked into the shadow of a vent stack. Something dropped with a light chinking sound, and she heard a smothered oath. Then she thought that she caught a gleam of red hair in the faint dawnlight as the figure searched the deck for something he had dropped. What was Professor Smith doing, skulking around the ship? Why was he acting so mysteriously? Nell gasped. And why was he dressed all in black?

He straightened up quickly and cast a suspicious look over his shoulder in her direction. Nell held her breath. He didn't see her. The professor disappeared into the deeper shadows. Something sparkled and shone in his hand just before he was lost from her view. It was all very strange, Nell thought. What on earth was he up to?

She waited, listening cautiously, for several minutes.

Suddenly Nell wished she was safely back in her cabin. Perhaps she should tiptoe away while he was occupied with whatever he was doing...

Just as she was about to start forward, a shape moved out of the shadows once more. She blinked. How could she have been so mistaken?

It wasn't the professor at all. It was Hugh Kincaid.

She knew him at once by his walk and the quick, athletic grace of his movements. He stepped through a patch of light, and a shiver ran through her. It was definitely Hugh Kincaid, but she could not make out any identifying features. He was wearing a mask over his eyes. He slid along the edge of the shadows and vanished up the companionway.

Nell's heart was pounding so hard it seemed to shake her body. She stayed hidden for a few minutes, gathering her courage, then slowly crept toward where he'd been hidding. She had to know the truth.

What was it that she'd glimpsed? Jewelry or coin or plate? Nell went past the stairway and found a blank steel wall. The deck was empty. She reached out, and her fingers came into contact with a small grill. It was loose, and came away in her hand. The warming light fell upon something that glittered in the dim interior.

Slowly, carefully, she slipped her hand inside the small space the grill had covered. A puff of warm air startled her, and she realized that the grill covered part of the ship's ventilation system. Gingerly, she tried again. She almost squeaked in alarm as her fingertips grazed something furry. Then, with heart-sinking realization, she knew what it was.

Nell grabbed it firmly and pulled it out. It was a man's wig, bright as fire. Then she found a crumpled shooting cap of checked wool, a bushy mustache, still sticky with spirit gum on the reverse side, and a pair of wire-rimmed spectacles. She held them up to her eyes.

The cold glass felt molten in her shaking hand. She blinked and took them away, her mind whirling with incredible possibilities. If worn by someone with excellent eyesight, such as herself—or Mr. Hugh Kincaid—they would distort everything and make objects appear quite small and very far away. She dropped them suddenly, and heard a telltale tinkle of broken glass. When Nell stooped down to retrieve the spectacles, she found that one lens had shattered into dozens of saw-toothed shards.

It all made horrible sense to her now. "Professor Smith" had always managed to find a reason to retire early, and Hugh Kincaid had always arrived late. Their "avoidance" of one another. They were of the same height and roughly the same build. Nell understood why she'd twice almost mistaken the hypochondriacal professor for the sophisticated Mr. Kincaid, since they were one and the same man.

She realized dumbly that the perfect disguise for a sneak thief would be as a bumbling, stumbling professor who couldn't manage to walk along the deck without either falling or knocking something over. Who would suspect Professor Smith? The disguise was diabolically clever.

Her fingers were stiff as sticks, and terribly awkward. She shoved the items back into their hidden recess and replaced the grill. She was sickened by her discovery and wanted to weep. There was only one logical conclusion: Hugh Kincaid, the man who haunted her virginal dreams, was the jewel thief. Her heart froze into a lump of ice and cracked into a thousand pieces.

She turned swiftly and walked back the way she had come.

Chapter Six

Nell fled to the safety of her cabin, barely holding back the tears. Her fairytale season had gotten all mixed up. She had gone from Cinderella at the ball to Sleeping Beauty, awakened by her first kiss. Now she was Sister Anne, fleeing the terrible secrets of Bluebeard's tower room. And, like Sister Anne, she cursed her own curiosity.

She burst into the salon and looked wildly about for Olga. Instead, she found Gwendolyn Boynton sobbing into one of the tapestry pillows on the sofa, as if her heart would break. "Oh!" she exclaimed when she saw Nell. "Oh, oh, *oh!*"

Nell went to her. "What is wrong, Gwendolyn?"

"Ever-everything! Grandmother!"

The girl was hiccoughing with every sob now, and totally unintelligible. Nell thought she made out a reference to Lady Culpepper and Hugh Kincaid. She gently took the pillow from Gwendolyn's hand and put her arms around the girl's heaving shoulders. "There, there, have no fear. Your grandmother cannot force you to receive attentions from Mr. Kincaid. You leave him to me, poor child! I shall have plenty of things to say about him to the right people. Yes, and I shall have an earful for Mr. Kincaid himself."

"Do you, now? How opportune."

Nell looked up in alarm as Hugh Kincaid came out of her boudoir. He was still garbed in black from head to foot, and the mask dangled from his fingers. Gwendolyn froze, then shot up to her feet. "Mr. Kincaid! Oh, no!" She looked around like a frightened rabbit, then dashed from the room.

Nell decided to follow, posthaste. She had barely started toward the exit when he forestalled her by planting himself firmly in front of the cabin door. He was as wary as a panther—and as dangerous.

"Stand aside," Nell ordered in her most imperious manner. She was glad that her voice wavered only slightly.

"I think it would be in your best interest to stay and discuss a few things with me, madame."

She drew herself up, summoning all the dignity she could muster. "The only person I will be discussing anything with is Captain Creighton."

As she lunged for the door, he reached out like lightning. Her wrist was caught in his iron grasp. "Not so fast, Princess Irina, or whatever your real name is."

He smiled at her gasp. "Oh, yes. I have known all along that you are an imposter. You see, I have been acquainted with the Princess Irina for some time. And, of course, I am aware that she remained behind in England due to an unfortunate sequence of events. You are an enterprising lady to have taken advantage of them at such short notice."

Nell felt her face burning with mortification. She went on the attack. "And I, sir, am aware of your various identities as both the fumbling Professor Smith, and the nefarious thief who robbed the grand duke and Lady Culpepper of their valuables."

There, that had surprised him. He frowned. "What tricks have you up your dainty sleeve, Miss—?"

"Shepherd. Miss Ellen Shepherd. As to tricks, I can explain my masquerade as something rooted in innocence, while you—"

The door swung open, and Captain Creighton stepped in. His face was very somber. Nell brightened immediately. "Oh, I am so glad to see you, Captain!"

Kincaid let go of Nell's wrist. "A bold little baggage, isn't she? And caught with Lady Culpepper's pearls, red-handed."

"What?" Nell couldn't believe her ears. "I do not have Lady Culpepper's pearls!"

"Enough of these games," Kincaid said angrily.

He picked up the tapestry pillow that Nell had taken from Gwendolyn and reached under its braided edge. He extracted a rope of luminous pink pearls, the same pearls that Nell had last seen adorning Lady Culpepper's spare bosom.

"I think we all recognize these," Hugh Kincaid announced. He turned to Nell. "There is your jewel thief, Captain."

His voice seemed to come from very far away. The room spun giddily about her, and Nell clutched at the table to keep from falling. The last thing she remembered was the floor rising up to meet her.

Nell's humiliation was complete. Not only was she thought to be a wicked imposter and a jewel thief, but she, who had always prided herself upon her strength of character, had fainted dead away.

Since recovering, she'd been locked in the princess' suite of staterooms, alone. Olga must be locked in her bedroom, as well. Hours had passed without a word of what was transpiring or an opportunity to give her side of the story. Not that it was likely to be believed, under the circumstances.

Nell paced the room in agitation. It galled her to think that Kincaid had fooled her so badly. That she had been tricked by a few kisses into believing that he...that he... And, to make it worse, he had tried—quite succesfully—to pin the thefts on her. That was the cruelest blow of all. How foolish she had been to let her heart be stolen by a pair of blue eyes and a few passionate kisses. Why, she had almost imagined herself in love with him. The man was an utter cad!

She could only imagine what stories he had told to exonerate himself and place the blame upon her innocent shoulders. It didn't bear thinking about. The suspense of waiting was terrible. Suddenly she heard voices, and a key turned in the lock.

Kincaid entered with Captain Creighton. She was aghast at his effrontery. "Why hasn't this man been taken into custody?" she demanded heatedly. "Or has he thrown his disguise overboard and hidden his ill-gotten gains?"

"Madame," the captain announced, "you have some serious explaining to do."

"I shall be heartily glad to do so. In fact I have been waiting to speak to you these past four hours," Nell snapped.

He ignored her tart tone. "Before proceeding further, I must ask you to present your papers of identification, and those issued for the journey."

Nell stiffened. "My papers! Why, the Princess Irina had them, since I was a member of her entourage."

Kincaid frowned. "Then she must have them still."

The implications hit Nell. She had no proof of either her identity or citizenship. "What will happen now?"

Captain Creighton looked suitably grave. "You have quite a problem on your hands. It's quite possible that the authorities might refuse to let you disembark, and order you back to England. We will come to that later. Now, regarding the matter of Lady Henrietta's pearls . . ."

"I have no idea of how they came to be hidden in my—er, the princess' stateroom." Nell lifted her chin. Her cheeks were flushed, and her eyes were sparkling with indignation as she faced the captain. "You will have to appeal to Mr. Kincaid for that information. It is he who is your jewel thief! No doubt he is the same villain that has been preying upon the passengers of the Triton Line these past weeks."

"Mr. Kincaid?" Captain Creighton shook his head. "Nonsense."

"There is proof, if only you will look. Inside the grill by the number six vent pipe, you will find the red wig and eyeglasses belonging to 'Professor Smith.'"

Nell turned to Kincaid, who was watching her with a smile tugging at the corners of his mobile mouth. "Can you deny, sir, that you and Professor Smith are one and the same man?"

Kincaid's smile widened to a grin. "No, I cannot. What a clever little minx you are. How did you catch on to me?"

She drew herself up stiffly. "There, you see? He admits it. And what reason could he have for such a disguise, other than to rob your passengers?"

"So that is your opinion of me." Kincaid stepped forward, a hard look in his eyes. "You are a fine one to talk of disguises, Miss Shepherd."

Nell had the grace to blush. "My reasons were innocent ones. By the time I recovered from my mal de mer, Olga had already told everyone that I was the princess. I did not want her to come to grief over it. You may find me guilty of brashness, Mr. Kincaid, but aquit me of any wish to do harm—unlike yourself. Captain Creighton, if you are a man of sense, you will immediately clap Mr. Kincaid in irons, before he can escape with his ill-gotten goods."

Captain Creighton choked suddenly. But no, Nell realized, he was...he was actually *laughing!* She looked at him as if he'd lost his mind.

"Mr. Kincaid is not a th-thief," he said, almost doubling up with laughter. "M...Mr. Kincaid is—is..."

"A villain and a brass-plated liar!" Nell supplied.

"Not at all. He's—he's—" And Creighton was off again, whooping with mirth.

Nell edged toward the door. The captain was either mad or intoxicated. She didn't intend to stay around long enough to discover which. Unfortunately, Kincaid was there to cut off her retreat.

"What the captain is trying to say, my dear Miss Shepherd, is that I am the owner of the Triton Line."

She gasped. One look at the captain's face told her it was true. A twinkle shone in Kincaid's breathtaking blue irises.

"You must admit that it would certainly be ill-advised of me to go about robbing my passengers if I wish to keep their custom. And I assure you, I have not done anything of the kind. Someone, however, has been doing it with alarming frequency." He smiled. "I decided it might be wise of me to spend some time incognito in hopes of discovering a clue to the thief's identity. And what better disguise could I find than that of a nearsighted, bumbling hypochondriac? One whom most of the passengers—including yourself—would go to any lengths to avoid?"

Nell's color rose and fell with stunning rapidity. On the one hand, she was relieved to know that Hugh Kincaid was not the criminal and had not set her up to take the blame for his actions, but on the other hand, it made her case look much worse. She looked down at her hands. There was no answer there. Nell took a deep breath and looked Kincaid square in the eyes.

"I realize that things look very bad for me," she said quietly, "but I am not the jewel thief."

The door opened, and Lady Culpepper and Gwendolyn Boyton entered. The girl's face was as red as her grandmother's was white. The dowager's spine was ramrod-straight as she sent Nell a chill, aristocratic look. "Painful as this is, I must exonerate this unfortunate young woman of having taken my pearls."

"I did it! I took them," Gwendolyn blurted out. Then she burst into tears.

"What my granddaughter means," Lady Culpepper said, "is that she is the one who hid the rope of pearls in the cushion found in this room. However, she did not steal them."

She paused and the silence in the room was profound. Even Gwendolyn's sobs had ceased. Lady Culpepper cleared her throat. "The actual Culpepper pearls were quietly sold two years ago to pay my late son's gambling debts. The pearls I have been wearing are fakes. Excellent ones, if I do say so."

The older woman's voice quavered, then grew firm once more. "When I learned of the jewel thief preying on the Triton Line, I decided to pretend that my pearls had been stolen. You see, the insurance on them has never been canceled." She lifted her chin. "The Culpepper fortunes have not fared well in recent years. I intended to use the money from the insurance to fund my granddaughter's debut in colonial society. I meant to throw the false pearls overboard at the first opportunity."

Gwendolyn hiccoughed to life. "I c-couldn't l-let her do it! I saw Grandmother slip her pearls off and put them into her reticule. I had guessed that her finances were not in tune, and knew that she was doing it to underwrite my debut. I knew the ship would be s-searched, and I was s-so afraid. I hid them in the pillow I was embroidering."

"And so," Kincaid said sternly, "you thought to blame the princess instead."

"Oh, no," Gwendolyn wailed. "I came to ask the princess for advice. She had been s-so k-kind to me. But then you arrived and spoiled it all. I didn't know what to do, and I was afraid you would think it strange if I took the pillow with me, so I left it here. I thought that no one would dare search the princess' rooms.

Then I could come b-back for them later and pretend I'd found them hidden somewhere."

Lady Culpepper hung her head. "I wouldn't have gone through with it. A Culpepper could never be party to such a crude deception. Of course, by the time I came to my senses, Gwendolyn had taken the pearls and hidden them." She sighed, but lifted her chin and faced the captain and Kincaid. "I am a foolish and wicked woman."

Kincaid smiled. "Foolish, perhaps, but not truly wicked. I would say that your besetting sin is pride, madame. But it is counteracted by the great love you have for your granddaughter. So much love that you thought you would do anything to secure an established future for her in society."

The dowager's thin lips twitched in a parody of a smile. "You are a very astute young man."

"Then," Kincaid continued, "perhaps you will heed my advice. Gwendolyn is a shy and bookish young lady. The life you propose for her would bring nothing but unhappiness."

"Oh, yes!" Gwendolyn breathed. "I don't want a grand marriage, Grandmama. Truly I don't."

Lady Culpepper embraced the girl. "Hush, child. I know. I have learned my lesson. There is plenty of time for you to decide your future. We shall take each day as it comes."

Kincaid's smile was warm. When they faced him, he schooled his features and gave them a severe lecture on the virtues of truth, honesty, and the courage to live up to them.

Although he didn't look at Nell, she knew the message was for her, as well. She wanted to sink through the floor. Her instincts about him had been right. Kincaid was the kind of man you could take your troubles to and be sure of support and guidance. Why, oh, why, hadn't she trusted him and gone to him with the truth in the beginning?

She frowned suddenly. "But if you aren't the thief, Mr. Kincaid, and Lady Culpepper's pearls weren't really stolen, there is still a mystery to be solved."

"It has been solved." Kincaid came to her side. "While you were locked up here, we managed to catch the thief trying to break into the rajah's cabin. The Grand Duke Alexi—real name Alfred Perkins—is now residing in the ship's brig."

Nell was startled. "The grand duke? But what of the Fabergé clock stolen from his cabin?"

Kincaid's grin spread. "The Fabergé clock that no one but the grand duke had ever seen? I'm afraid it was as much a figment of his imagination as his noble blood. The real Grand Duke Alexi is a child of eight or nine years. I met him in Vienna last year. And I had my eye on the bogus grand duke from the start. What I needed to learn was where he hid the stolen items in order to get them off the ship without discovery."

Nell's anger grew. "Then you knew all along that I was innocent, that I had stolen nothing!"

Kincaid took her hands in his. "I had no idea of what you were up to, my dear, but I'm afraid you have stolen something, whether you intended to or not." He lifted her hands to his lips and kissed them. "You see, my very dear Miss Shepherd, you have stolen my heart."

Nell's hands trembled in Kincaid's strong gasp. Her eyes were suddenly filled with stars. She scarcely noticed when Captain Creighton escorted the others out and she was left alone with Kincaid. "If you knew I wasn't the Princess Irina, why didn't you expose my charade?"

"You interested me. I was intrigued as to just what your game was. Tell me, did you look to make a grand marriage? Is that what your little masquerade as the princess was all about?"

Nell shook her head. The time had come to tell him everything. "I am a penniless former governess trying to reach Antigua in order to search for my younger brother, who disappeared there three months ago. Harry is a scientist, and quite unworldly. Anything might have happened to him!"

She poured out her story from start to finish, including the return of Harry's letters and her fears for Olga, which had led her to go along with the mad scheme. "The past few days have been purgatory. I would give anything to put them behind me."

Kincaid eyed her quizzically. "Regrets, Miss Shepherd?

"Many, sir. I must confess," she added, "that it is a great relief to unburden myself. I have always been a truthful person and it has gone sorely against the grain to live such a lie the past two weeks."

"And what do you regret, specifically?" He put his arms around her and tilted her face up to his. "This?"

His mouth came down on hers softly, but with a barely repressed hunger. His kiss robbed her of breath, of thought. Nell was floating in the air, her mind reeling with delight. "Or this?" he murmured, trailing kisses along her cheek, her jaw, the graceful curve of her throat.

His gentle insistence and her own yearning were too much for Nell. She made a soft sound of protest. He stopped at once, but kept his hands on her shoulders. His face was tender and serious. Nell was a trifle breathless, and her heart was pounding beneath her silk bodice.

Kincaid smiled down at her. "You don't regret my kissing you, do you?"

"Oh, no!"

"Do you want me to kiss you again, darling?"

"Oh, yes . . ."

He did. Thoroughly. His strong arms molded her against his chest until their hearts beat to one rhythm. His mouth was ardent upon hers, tasting and teaching. Nell had always been a quick study. She returned his kiss with a surprising degree of enthusiasm. This time it was Kincaid who groaned. Ardor blazed into passion, catching them both unawares.

Olga came in in a rush and stopped short, staring at them. "Vhat are you two doing, standing around kissing at such a time? It is Christmas Eve, and the Reverend Mr. Mitchell is vaiting for us to begin the Christmas festival."

Nell's face flamed. Kincaid seemed strangely short of breath. He recovered first and offered his arm to Nell. "We have a good deal to discuss, my dear, but I don't want to keep Mr. Mitchell waiting."

She stared at him and put her hands on her cheeks. "I couldn't possibly take part now. The scandal . . ."

He grinned. "My darling Miss Shepherd . . ."

"Nell."

"Nell. No one knows the truth of your identity except the captain, Lady Culpepper and her granddaughter. As for Mr. Mitchell, he wouldn't care if you were a beggar from the London streets or the queen of Sheba. What he does care about is your lovely voice, and its place in his beloved Christmas program. Now, unless you wish to disappoint him and the rest of the passengers, I suggest you change into your gown and we make haste to the ballroom.''

A half hour later, Nell, Kincaid and the rest of the choir were entering the darkened ballroom from the starlit conservatory, with only the light of their candles to guide them. The room was scented with pine garlands that had been kept fresh in the ship's hold and were now draped effectively along the walls. The sweet strains of the familiar carols filled the air as they took their places. One by one the lanterns were lit to frame them. The little play began.

This time, when Nell sang that truth was the gift to give the infant King, she held her head high. Her gaze locked with Kincaid's as their voices blended in heartfelt song. Her eyes were brighter than the candle flames. Brighter than the stars.

It was nearing midnight when the celebration ended. For the duration, Nell had been able to forget her two remaining problems. By the following afternoon the *Pride of Paradise* would be riding at anchor in Antigua's turquoise waters. There had to be some way to get around the fact of her missing papers. To have come all this way only to be sent back would be so cruel!

Hugh Kincaid had been mulling over the very same thing. ''I believe there is a way to get you cleared to disembark in Antigua," he said as they strolled along the upper deck beneath a dazzling canopy of stars. "You might find it rather difficult, Nell. In fact, you might find it utterly repugnant, but I sincerely hope not. I'm certain that it would work."

"Oh, Hugh! I will do anything!"

He tilted her chin up with his finger. "Even marry me?"

"M-marry you?"

"You needn't sound so horrified." He kissed her nose. "Is it such a terrible fate? I know you would probably prefer a proper courtship first, but there is not the time for it. As the wife of an American citizen, you would be entered on my passport and could disembark quite legally."

She eyed him doubtfully. "Would you really go through such a sham in order to help me?"

For answer, he pulled her into his arms. "I intend no sham, my dear. If we marry, it will be valid and binding. The courtship can come after. I want you for my wife, darling Nell, without the slightest delay. To have and to hold, till death do us part, et cetera. You see, I knew the moment I first saw you that you were the only woman for me."

His kiss told her that he meant every word of it. Nell was desperately, deliriously happy. She felt like the heroine of a very strange fairy tale, in love with a dashing and most unorthodox prince.

"Tell me," he said, after several more kisses, "did you know the first time you saw me that we were fated to be together?"

Nell laughed. "At our first meeting you had on a red wig and thick spectacles and were muffled up to your chin in plaid wool. I thought you were insufferable."

"I am. But that is neither here nor there." He kissed her again. Then, suddenly, he was pulling her across the deck and back toward where they'd left Captain Creighton. "Hurry," Kincaid told her, laughing. "It's almost midnight. We can't be married on Christmas day. It wouldn't be legal. We have less than ten minutes to join the captain in his quarters and exchange our vows."

And so, Ellen and Hugh Kincaid were married on Christmas Eve by Captain Creighton of the *Pride of Paradise*, with Olga and Lady Culpepper for witnesses, while the bells chimed out the blessed hour.

Afterward, in Kincaid's suite of staterooms, Nell and her husband celebrated their wedding vows and their first Christmas together. "I don't have a wedding gift for you," he told her. "What would you like? Diamonds? Rubies?"

"Something not nearly so expensive," Nell replied, "but worth more than all the jewels in the world, as our song said. I will be content with truth and love."

Kincaid drew her close. "They are yours for all eternity, along with my heart." He kissed her brow, the tip of her nose, her soft lips. "But I still intend to deck you in gems and pearls."

She shivered as he drew off her jacket and undid the tiny buttons of her shirtwaist, one by one. "Are you afraid, Nell?"

"Oh, no. Never with you."

He crushed her in his arms and kissed her. Then he carried her to the bed. Nell soon discovered all the marvelous things that had been left out of the fairy tales she'd read. Later, while the candles guttered in their sockets, she fell asleep with her head cradled against her husbands broad, bare chest, lulled by the strong rhythm of his heart.

The following noon, the newlyweds stood on deck, hand in hand. Antigua's harbor was a deep blue-green, like watered silk. It was ringed with clusters of pastel buildings and crowned by velvet hills. Despite the beauties of the isle, Mr. and Mrs. Hugh Kincaid had eyes only for each other. Olga joined them, breaking their lovers' trance.

"If you come to Merkelstein," she announced happily, "I shall throw a great ball in your honor."

"So you truly *are* the Lady Levitskaya," Nell said, shaking her head. "And you were never in any danger of being thrown into the dungeon, or worse."

"Vell, for an hour or two, perhaps. I am cousin to poor Irina Christina, and you know vat a temper she has. But no, I vas in no danger. She is all talk, that one. Piffle. Then she forgets."

"Then," Nell asked sternly, "why did you tell me such a faradiddle?"

Olga looked at her innocently. "Vhy, because you vould not have gone along vith my plan otherwise."

When she saw Nell's shock, her eyes lit with laughter and she blushed all the way to the tip of her nose. "Dear Nell, I knew your so sad story... like the beginning of a fairy tale. And you vere such a perfect heroine, making your vay alone in the cruel vorld. I thought it vould be fun to be a fairy godmother, you see. And if anyone ever needed vone, it vas you! Besides, Irina vas being tiresome and needed to be taught a lesson. I knew she had only sprained her leg, not broken it, you see. She is as bad as 'Professor Smith' vas."

Nell was stunned. "I can scarcely believe that you planned it all."

"Vell, not the donkey cart. That vas good fortune, however, and I alvays take advantage of good fortune." As she said the last words, she cast a speculative glance in Captain Creighton's direction. "Did you know that Captain Creighton vill be here avhile?"

"Poor man," Kincaid whispered in Nell's ear. "Creighton stands no chance at all of escaping if she sets her cap in his direction."

Nell started to laugh, but her chuckle was cut off halfway. She stared at a young man strolling down the pier with a friend, idly eyeing the disembarking passengers. Nell leaned over the rail. "Harry? *Harry!*"

Grabbing her husband's hand, she ran down the gangplank to the wharf. The young man looked up as Nell and Kincaid joined them, and tucked his cane beneath his arm. "What the dev—*Nell?* What on earth are you doing here?"

She threw her arms around her brother's neck. "I thought something dreadful had happened to you! Where have you been?"

"Why, sailing the islands with friends. I've discovered the most remarkable fern, Nell. I shall name it after you. The opportunity to go on the expediton came up rather suddenly." Harry flushed. "By Jove, I was sure I'd written you about it. I must have forgotten to post it, in my hurry."

"But my letters to you were all returned."

"A mistake on my landlord's part," Harry said quickly. "He couldn't decipher the note I'd scribbled for him in my haste. I say, Nell, I hope I haven't put you to any trouble."

Kincaid stepped forward, arms akimbo. "That you have, you young scamp. Your sister has sailed half-way around the world, at considerable risk to herself, because she thought you'd vanished from the face of the earth."

Harry's flush deepened. He drew himself up with youthful dignity. "And who might you be, sir?"

"Your brother-in-law."

"Oh. Quite." Harry looked from Kincaid to Nell and back. "Er...did I know about this happy event?"

"We were married aboard ship yesterday," Nell told him. There was no use explaining. Harry's brain had already returned to the subject most important in his mind.

"About this fern," he said earnestly, his eyes glowing with enthusiasm. "It's quite a capital little thing. I have written an article for the Scientific Society, and it has been accepted for publication. Would you care to stop by my lodgings and see it?"

"No," Kincaid said.

"Yes," Nell replied simultaneously. "But not just at the moment." Her glance fell on Gwendolyn Boyton. "If you have no objection, I shall bring a friend along. She is very fond of flowers and plants."

"Well, then," Harry said, suddenly aware that he was intruding on a honeymoon, "I'm sure you have any amount of unpacking to do. I'll take myself off. I've an appointment to meet with the director of the botanical garden."

"Well," Nell exclaimed in exasperation. "Harry certainly has taken my arrival calmly."

Kincaid laughed and shook his head. "Your brother will go far in scientific circles. He has the fervor and single-mindedness necessary to succeed. Speaking of which..."

Taking Nell's arm, he led her back up the gangplank. "Where are we going?" she asked in bewilderment. "Everyone else is leaving the ship."

"Exactly, Mrs. Kincaid." He pulled her into a convenient alcove and kissed her soundly. "The *Pride of Paradise* will be here two weeks for refitting and loading. And I can't think of a better place to spend our honeymoon undisturbed. Unless you have some objection?"

Nell wound her arms around his neck. "Not in the least."

Olga was the last passenger to leave. She turned on the dock and saw the newlyweds embrace. Really, everything had turned out delightfully, as she had expected all along. Just like a fairy tale.

"And," she said merrily beneath her breath as she got into the waiting carriage and drove off toward her hotel, "they lived happily ever after."

* * * * *

A Note from Marianne Willman

Dear Reader,

Christmas is one of my favorite times of the year: family, friends, Christmas carols and beloved traditions, the anticipation of joy—and the blessed message of Peace on Earth, Good Will to All. Old hurts are put aside, new promises made. The world is reborn in love.

At least two weeks before Christmas we get the whole family together to put up our tree, and decorate it with ornaments that reflect out diverse heritage, from both the Old World and the New. On my side, Polish, Scots, Irish, Dutch and Sioux Native American. On my husband's side, French, Alsatian, German, Scots, Irish and Seneca Native American. By marriage and blood, we've added English, Finn and more Irish.

We are, in ourselves, a wonderful little United Nations. Perhaps the next generation will enrich us with the heritage of other continents, other peoples. Although we are of varying backgrounds and several different religions, we all celebrate the same joy and the same wish: Peace on Earth, Good Will to All.

We celebrate with Christmas Eve Mass at our favorite church and leave wrapped packages for the St. Alexander's Mitten Tree, which provides gifts for the homeless, the elderly, the mentally impaired and those who have no family. We join in prayer for world peace and understanding, for the end of wars and suffering, for the homeless, the hopeless, the oppressed and those in need—and for those who work to make the world a better place. I thank God for my family and friends, for good health, for the wonderful readers, editors, booksellers and publishers who enable me to make a living doing what I love to do.

Home again, we curl up before the fire to give quiet thanks for our blessings, and to conserve our energy for the wonderful, noisy confusion of Christmas Day.

If the angels have a pillow fight, we'll wake up to a Currier and Ives snow scene. The world will be fresh and new, reborn on this Holy Day. It wouldn't be Christmas at the Willmans' without friends dropping by, family gathering, children running around laughing and screaming, babies cooing or crying, carol singing and our traditional feast: roast turkey stuffed with sage dressing, apples, onions and sausage, kielbasa, mashed potatos and giblet gravy, yams, corn, baked beans and biscuits. The youngest child says grace.

Afterward, we totally destroy the family room with shiny ribbons and glitter and gay wrapping paper... smiles of delight and happy exclamations... toys everywhere... a toddler falling asleep beneath the tree, clutching an old blanket and a new teddy bear... much laughter... much love.

Dessert comes after. The holiday isn't official unless I make my famous sugar pies. Also pumpkin pies, cheesecake, pumpkin cheesecake and cupcakes or cookies. Tomorrow we'll go back to watching calories and cholesterol. Tomorrow we'll worry about our problems and the world's. This one special day is a gift to us all, wrapped up in love, tied with bows of laughter and music. In the morning we'll vacuum, knowing that we'll still be picking silver tinsel out of the carpet in July. Grateful that the work of the celebration is over, hopeful that the meaning of Christmas will carry us all through the year. Looking forward eagerly to next year all over again. And, when the house is clean, we reward ourselves with another helping of sugar pie.

My Christmas wish for you, dear readers, is that your lives will be filled with love. That peace and goodness are yours. That your hearts will be filled year-round with the joy, the wonder and magic of Christmas, the fairytale season.

Merry Christmas and Happy New Year,

TIDINGS OF JOY
Victoria Pade

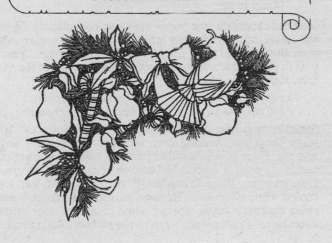

Although I bake a lot throughout the year, I like to do something fancy and a little special at Christmastime. This recipe fits the bill nicely. Be sure to use a high-quality chocolate. White chocolate in particular has a tendency to taste like wax if you don't.

TRIPLE CHOCOLATE PATÉ

8 oz bittersweet chocolate　　*½ cup plus 2 tbsp heavy cream*
　¼ cup butter

Melt the chocolate and butter together; cool slightly. Whip the cream until stiff; fold into the chocolate/butter mixture. Butter a loaf pan, then line with plastic wrap. Spread paté in pan. Press a second sheet of plastic wrap to the surface. Refrigerate 1 hour.

　¾ cup heavy cream　　*6 oz white chocolate*
　　1½ tsp gelatin　　*½ cup heavy cream*

Sprinkle the gelatin over the cream and let sit 5 minutes. Add white chocolate, heating over very low temperature until smooth. Place pan in another pan of ice water, stirring occasionally until it reaches the texture of egg white. Remove from ice water. Whip ½ cup heavy cream until stiff, fold into cooled white chocolate. Remove plastic wrap from bittersweet chocolate layer. Spread white chocolate over bittersweet layer. Press plastic wrap to the surface. Refrigerate 1 hour.

8 oz milk chocolate　　*¼ cup butter*　　*½ cup heavy cream*

Follow same procedure as for bittersweet chocolate. Refrigerate 1 hour or until set.

To serve:

Thirty minutes before serving, place in freezer. Then, lift free, using the plastic wrap that lined the pan. Peel away the plastic wrap. Heat a large knife and cut into slices (the knife will probably need to be reheated after every few slices).

This dish is particularly elegant served with a few fresh raspberries.

Chapter One

Pinewood, Colorado
1853

Standing on a stool, Linnie Rhodes glanced down at the skirt of the gown she was having fitted. "The hem needs to be just a little shorter," she told Molly MacGregor, the seamstress and owner of the shop.

"I can't believe how perfect this color is for you!" the dressmaker said as she adjusted her pins. "Ice blue—it's the very color of your eyes. There isn't another soul in town who could do it justice."

Linnie couldn't resist rubbing her hand over the velvet of the opposite sleeve. "It is beautiful cloth, isn't it? The minute it came in, I just had to have it."

"One of the advantages of you and your sister owning the store. How is Mary Alice? That baby of hers is due any time now, isn't it?"

"A few more weeks."

"I wish her an easy time of it. Why, with my first..."

It seemed to Linnie that she'd heard the childbirth stories of every mother in Pinewood since her sister and brother-in-law had announced they were expecting a baby. She knew it was part and parcel of life in a small town, but that didn't help her concentration any, and as her mind wandered, so did her gaze—right out the storefront window.

Light flakes of snow fell beyond the shop's overhang, adding to the nearly two feet that had fallen on the mountain community in the past few days. They'd have a white Christmas on the following Sunday, there was no doubt about it. But Pinewood was accustomed to snow, and this close to the holiday, it didn't keep much of anyone from going about their business.

Linnie watched as people she'd known all her life made their way along the boardwalk across the street, bundled up in coats and hats and bonnets. Then someone she was slower to recognize stepped out of the widow Mordine's restaurant, causing her eyes to widen in disbelief.

"That isn't Drew Dunlap..." she fairly whispered, more to herself than to the seamstress.

Molly stopped what she was doing to glance from behind Linnie's skirt for just a moment. "That's him, all right," she said before going back to work. "I was down at the depot meeting my husband's cousin, and I saw him come in on the morning train. Here we've all been wondering who it was bought the old Hayes place and was fixing it up, bringing in so much fancy furniture, and it wasn't a stranger at all. It was Drew Dunlap!"

Drew Dunlap.

Linnie closed her eyes, as if denying the sight of him would make him go away.

"He looks mighty different than he did when he left six years ago, doesn't he?" Molly said.

Linnie swallowed, clenched her teeth and slowly opened her eyes.

He was still there, standing just outside the restaurant, glancing up and down Pinewood's main street as if assessing it.

Molly was right; he was much changed from the rangy seventeen-year-old she remembered. He had a man's body now—taller even than the six feet he'd been when he'd left—and . . . fuller. In fact, his shoulders were so broad inside his sheepskin coat that he'd had a pretty tight squeeze through the restaurant's door.

His face had changed, too, though from this distance Linnie couldn't tell quite how. Sharper, maybe, more angular. More handsome. If that was possible.

Molly was chattering on about something, Linnie suddenly realized, but she took little note of the woman's ramblings, as all her attention was still trained on the man across the street.

The sheriff walked by just then, recognized Drew and extended a hand for him to shake. Even from far away, Linnie could tell that Drew's hand, like the rest of him, was bigger than it had been before, stronger, more powerful. . . . Would it still feel the same if he cupped her face with it?

"Don't raise your arm, Linnie, it'll make the hem uneven," the seamstress admonished from below.

Only then did Linnie realize that her fingertips were on her cheek, in just the spot where Drew used to lay his palm. She dropped her hand immediately.

Look away! she told herself.

But she couldn't take her eyes off Drew as the sheriff clapped him on the back.

The new Drew Dunlap didn't wear a hat, and his hair was shorter than he'd kept it as a boy, though she could tell it was just as thick and wavy, and the color still reminded her of rich coffee beans.

"Can you imagine?" the dressmaker said, her voice barely penetrating Linnie's reverie. "Drew Dunlap took his drunkard father out of town without a penny to either of their names, and now here he is, back again, rich as you please. Why, I can remember him hiring himself out to anyone who'd have him, shoveling manure, digging privies, mopping the barroom floor, unloading grain for your daddy—"

The seamstress stopped short. "Oh, my, look who I'm talking to," she said in a rush. "I'm sure you don't care one whit about anything to do with Drew Dunlap anymore. Why, you two were so young.... Puppy love, that's all it was."

Linnie didn't say a word. In her mind's eye, she could see Drew unloading those grain sacks for her father as clearly as if it were happening in front of her that moment. She could see his hair forming damp curls against his nape, his young muscles bulging beneath a thin, clinging white shirt, the streak of sweat down his spine that had made her want to trail a finger along the same path....

He'd seemed all grown to her then. Looking at the man he was now made her realize how wrong she'd been.

But then, she'd been wrong about many things six years ago. And all of them to do with Drew Dunlap.

"Everyone is wondering if you and Will Larson might be making a wedding announcement this

Christmas,'' Molly said then, as if to make amends for having spoken so freely about Drew. "He's quite a catch, that one. In line for the bank and all, when his mother finally decides to hand it over to him. You've been mulling his proposal a long while now, haven't you?"

"Not so long," Linnie answered vaguely, forcing herself to think of Will. Tall, handsome Will...

"Just a few more minutes and we'll be finished," Molly said, launching into the details surrounding the turkey she'd be cooking for Christmas dinner.

Linnie tried harder to concentrate on what the seamstress was saying, just as hard as she was trying to keep her eyes from straying out that window again.

But somehow Molly's voice seemed to grow fainter and farther away, and all on its own, Linnie's gaze drifted across the street to where Drew still stood visiting. It was as if she were in a tunnel, and the only thing she was really aware of was him, standing at the other end, connected to her in some intangible way.

But they weren't connected. There was nothing at all between them. Except some long-ago times they'd shared when they were little more than children.

Yet she still couldn't look anywhere else. Not even when he turned away from the sheriff and headed up the boardwalk.

Linnie told herself not to watch him go. But she'd told herself the same thing six years ago, and now, just like then, she couldn't seem to help it.

For a moment she thought she could even hear the strong, hollow sound of his bootsteps.

But that wasn't what she was hearing at all, she realized with a bit of a jolt. What she was hearing was the beating of her own heart.

Just like six years ago.

The long-vacant Hayes house had a curved lane off Main Street all to itself. Though it had been sadly neglected by its absentee owner, the building was still an impressive and sound structure; it was two stories of white clapboard and gabled roof, with big bay windows all around the first level, and a cupola jutting out from the second floor over the front door.

It wasn't the biggest house in Pinewood, or the fanciest—Will Larson's mother owned that—but it was the one home in the small town that Linnie had always fancied.

The house also wasn't exactly on her way from the dressmaker's shop back to the general store she and Mary Alice had inherited from their folks. But whenever Linnie passed the entrance to the lane, she always took that small detour anyway, just so she could look at it.

And today was no different.

Except maybe that now, since she knew who the new owner was, she probably should have avoided it altogether.

But here she was, being carried along by feet that wouldn't listen to reason, up Hayes Lane to the house, which sat nestled among mountain pines and bare-branched aspens. *Her* house, she'd always considered it.

Ever since the deaths of Pinewood's founders, William and Mary Hayes, their son, who'd had no desire to live in the small town, had ignored the house in which he'd grown up, leaving it to dust and cobwebs and target practice for rock-throwing boys.

But no matter how dilapidated it became, no matter how many of the windows were broken, Linnie had still coveted it. Something Drew Dunlap knew all too well, since they had planned to marry and raise a whole passel of children there.

Remembering that elicited a mirthless chuckle from Linnie.

Dreams. That was all those plans had been, no matter how real they'd seemed at the time. The foolish dreams of a fifteen-year-old who had been the lovestruck sweetheart of the town drunk's son.

But, oh, how real those dreams had seemed!

And how much it had hurt to accept that they'd never come to be.

But Linnie had accepted it. And put it behind her and gone on with her life. Just the way Drew Dunlap had. As if they'd never meant anything at all to each other.

Still, though, she'd suffered a minor jolt to hear a month back that local craftsmen were getting orders from some lawyer in Denver to go to work on the place.

Word had spread that someone had bought the house, and Linnie had watched as the windows and the gingerbread trim were replaced, the carved balusters were reset to bolster the porch rail again, and new shutters were added around the windows.

She'd heard tell that the dust and cobwebs had been swept away from the inside. She knew that fresh paint had been ordered at the store. But she hadn't seen more than a glimpse of what was being done beyond the front door.

And until today, until finding out that the new owner was Drew Dunlap, she hadn't really felt as if the place were completely lost to her, silly as that seemed.

Well, it *was* lost to her, she told herself sternly as she stood staring at her dream house. And there was no sense crying over spilled milk.

Jamming her hands deeper into her muff, Linnie spun on her heel to get away from what was suddenly a painful sight, and ran nose first into a broad, hard male chest.

"Whoa! Slow down!" Big hands shot to her arms to steady her.

Linnie knew who she'd run into even before she looked up. Drew's voice had changed long before he left Pinewood, but it had a deeper timbre to it now, a richer resonance—and the sound of it set off a cascade of little tingles across the surface of her skin.

Trying to escape the unsettling sensation, she stepped back in a hurry.

"Linnie? Linnie Rhodes, is that you?"

For one brief moment, she considered denying it. Then she gathered her dignity and raised what she hoped was a pleasantly impassive expression to him. "Hello, Drew. I heard you were back in town."

At that first close look at him, Linnie felt her heart give a kick. She didn't want to notice how handsome he was, but she couldn't help it. He stood not far away, a slight sprinkling of snow dusting his dark hair and the collar of his coat. She'd been right when she watched him from the dressmaker's shop—his features were more defined, as if a thin layer of immaturity had been absorbed as the man emerged.

His eyes were the same, though, not quite green and not quite brown, but a mixture of the two; and they still seemed to be able to penetrate right to the core of her.

"Lord, but it's good to see you," he said, in a voice so soft he seemed to be thinking out loud, rather than actually talking to her.

Those eyes of his searched her face, as if to relearn it, and into her mind, unbidden, came the memory of the last time she'd seen him, six years before. For all his youth, there had been harsh lines between his thick eyebrows as he told her he was leaving Pinewood. His father had been caught trying to steal a delivery of whiskey, and Drew had been given the choice of taking him away for good or seeing him tried as a thief and sent to jail.

Now, just thinking about that scene made Linnie want to crawl into a hole and hide.

She'd begged Drew to take her with him. *Begged* him.

And he'd refused.

He hadn't known where he'd end up or what he'd do once he got there, and he'd had his father to look after.

"But I'll come back for you," he'd said earnestly. "A year's time. Just give me that long to find work and a place for the three of us to live. Then I promise I'll come for you."

The memory left a sour taste in Linnie's mouth.

Six years without so much as a note from him told her clearly that the empty promise had been given just to extract himself from the silly girl who'd lost her pride right there in front of him.

"I went over to the store to say hello, and instead of finding you there, I bump into you here, standing out front of the old Hayes house, just like always," he said, bringing her back to the present.

"Yes, well..." she answered, not knowing what else to say, and feeling her pride tweaked yet again. He probably thought she was still pining for the house, all these years later. And maybe for him, too. "I was just at the dressmaker's, and she told me the house had been fixed up. She said I should take a look, so..." Linnie had never been a good liar, and she knew she was bungling this. She stopped short.

"I suppose the dressmaker also told you I bought the place."

"Yes." But Linnie didn't want to talk about that, and so she went on quickly. "If you've been to the store, you know a lot of things have changed around here."

Drew's expression turned serious. "I was sorry to hear that your father passed on. I lost my own not long ago."

That sobered her. "I didn't know," she said, her tone soft, sympathetic. "Did he ever get over your mother's death?"

"And stop drinking? No. She was the love of his life. He just couldn't forgive himself for not being able to get a doctor out to her in time. He said drinking was the only thing that dulled the pain, and he kept at it right up until he was killed in a knife fight over a bottle of rye. When he was dying, he was the most peaceful I ever saw him. Said he knew he'd be with her again."

A single lock of Drew's coffee-colored hair had fallen over his forehead, and Linnie had a sudden urge to brush it back, the way she might have once, long ago. She clasped her hands tightly together inside her muff and stiffened her spine a bit to resist the impulse.

"And I was surprised to find my old friend Carl as the new storekeeper, married to Mary Alice, and with a baby on the way." He shook his head in disbelief. "Carl always was sweet on your sister, but she'd never give him the time of day before. And here they are together."

"As I said, a lot has changed."

"Including you." He leaned back just a little, so that his hazel eyes could run from the top of her head all the way down to her toes and back up again.

It made no sense, but just that simple glance sent a wave of warmth over her. Linnie fought the sensation by telling herself that standing there with Drew Dunlap was no different from standing there with Pinewood's paunchy, balding, sixty-year-old mayor.

Then Drew's deep voice surrounded her again and made the effort useless.

"You were something when I left, but now . . ." He shook his head and smiled a slow, crooked smile that tilted his mouth to one side.

His chin was prominent, and had a dent right down the middle, and suddenly there flashed through Linnie's mind a memory of a warm summer day's picnic when she'd drawn a stick of straw through that crease while he slept, tickling him awake and inspiring that same kind of smile, just before he rolled her over and tickled her back.

The thought set off a strange fluttering in her stomach. The last thing in the world Linnie wanted was to have anything at all stirred up in her by this man. But the stirrings were there just the same, poking up from where she'd buried them.

She took a deep breath of the frigid air. "So you mean to make your home in Pinewood again," she said, very formally.

"I wouldn't have bought the house if I didn't."

"But you must work somewhere else, to afford the Hayes place, and having it fixed up."

Something about that made him grin, and the grin drew deeper lines around his wonderful mouth and crinkled up a few from the corners of his eyes, too. "Let's just say I got lucky and don't have to worry about there not being many high-paying jobs around Pinewood."

And what did that mean? she wondered. But she wouldn't let herself show interest by anything more than a raising of her eyebrows. Still, she was disappointed when he didn't elaborate.

"I plan to settle down and spend the rest of my days right here."

"Have you come back alone?" she heard herself ask, the words slipping out on their own and making her wish she could bite off her tongue. Why should it matter to her if he had a wife he was bringing here with him? It shouldn't. It didn't.

He grinned again, as if he saw right through her. "Yes, I've come back alone." Then one of his own eyebrows rose. "I understand you're keeping company with Will Larson."

Why did he seem to find that amusing? Linnie tilted her chin up at him. "Yes, I am. We've been seeing each other for some time now. He started to come around to the apartment to see Carl after the wedding, and we discovered how much we have in common."

"Is that right?" He kept on staring at her, those hazel eyes seeming to hold her pinned in place. But he didn't say any more about Will. Instead, after a moment, he glanced over her shoulder at the house. "I don't have anything unpacked or set up yet, but would you like to come in and see what I had done to the place?"

She was dying to. But to give in to her curiosity would be to admit that she wasn't as impervious to him or his buying her house as she wanted him to think. So she drew herself up straight and said, "No, thank you. I really need to get back to the store to help Carl. I've been away too long already."

"Maybe another time, then."

"Maybe." She moved to step around him.

"It's been good to see you, Linnie," he said, in a tone that was suddenly tinged with more intimacy than it should have been.

"Six years is a long time," she answered, only because it was the first thing to come to mind that didn't concede that it was good to see him, too.

She took two steps past him, but that was as far as she got before he caught her arm and drew her up short.

Linnie looked down at his hand, wondering how she could possibly feel such intense heat through her coat sleeve. Then she glanced up at his face; it was much nearer than it had been before.

"Aren't you going to welcome me back?" he asked, in a tone that melted over her like warm honey.

It wasn't easy to find her voice for the wellspring of unwanted feelings and sensations erupting inside her at his touch. When she did find it, it wasn't strong. "I hope living here will work out better for you now than it did before," was all she could manage, and that very stiltedly.

He smiled a secret smile. "I hope so, too," he said softly before letting her go.

For a moment, Linnie couldn't move on, frozen as she was, her eyes locked on his.

Then she remembered herself and broke off the contact. "Goodbye," she said, as courteously as if he meant no more to her than anyone else she might meet on the street, for that was all he was to her, she lectured herself on the way back to the store. Drew Dunlap was nothing more than another citizen of Pinewood.

It didn't mean a single thing to her that he was back. After all, she wasn't a fifteen-year-old girl anymore, a girl who thought all that mattered in a man was a pair of penetrating eyes and muscles like mountains.

She was a full-grown woman now, a woman who knew and appreciated the value of a man who was kind and reliable and could be trusted to keep his word. A good man. A man like Will Larson.

Chapter Two

When Drew woke the next morning, it was to the sight of the sky through his bedroom window. Gunmetal gray clouds hung low, and snow fell as thick as soap flakes. But to him it was a glorious sight. It was the look of home.

He rolled onto his back and stretched, grabbing for the brass spindles of the headboard with both hands and causing the blanket to slip down his chest. The air was cold against his bare skin, but he didn't pay much attention to it, as his thoughts had already turned to Linnie.

He was used to waking up thinking about her. And falling asleep thinking about her. He'd done it often enough in the past six years.

But there were two differences today. She wasn't hundreds of miles away this time. And she was no longer the young girl he'd remembered her as, the young girl he'd left behind.

Six years ago, she'd been as sweet and pretty as a summer sunrise. Now she was more than that. In fact, that first look into her face the day before had taken his breath away.

As he lay in bed, he had a crystal-clear image of the grown-up Linnie in his mind's eye, and he savored it. If any woman on earth had longer, thicker lashes, he'd never met her. They were like sable around eyes as luminous as the reflection of a cloudless sky in new-fallen snow. Ice blue, but with a softening look of serenity to them, a serenity that was contradicted by her slightly unruly brows.

He pictured her skin—as flawless and clear and smooth as fresh cream. And her nose, small and thin. Somewhere along the way, he'd forgotten how perfect was the shape of her lips, with their gentle curve at the corners, and how they puckered up, almost as if she were ready to be kissed, when she said certain words—like *no* for instance; it was almost worth being refused something just to see it.

Her jaw was still as stubborn as ever, and slightly square for a woman, but lovely nonetheless. In fact, it gave her a kind of beauty that was all her own.

Oh, yes, she was beautiful, all right. In fact, he'd say she was exquisite.

Had her cheekbones always been so high? he wondered as he tried to figure out what exactly made her prettier than she'd been before. As a girl, she'd had round apples for cheeks. Now her face was more refined, and her features were more delicate.

And what about her hair? Yesterday she'd worn a bonnet that covered all but a few wisps of the dark, licorice-colored waves he remembered so well falling down to the middle of her back. Had she cut it? He hoped not. Would that wild shock of curls still fall over the left side of her forehead when she left it unpinned? Did it still feel like spun silk and smell like wildflowers?

Lord, how he wanted to find out.

But it wasn't just the physical parts of her that he wanted to know again. It was everything. He wanted to know all about her. What she'd done in the past six years. What she'd thought about. How she'd felt. What had shaped her into the woman she was.

Six years.

They seemed like sixty when he thought about all he'd missed with Linnie. Actually, it seemed like a lifetime when he thought about all the things that had happened to him.

But, somehow, all the years apart had fallen away the second he set eyes on her yesterday. Just the way he'd hoped they would when he'd run into his old schoolteacher in Denver a few months back and learned that Linnie had never married. She hadn't exactly welcomed him back with open arms, though.

Not that he deserved it, he reminded himself.

But would she give him the second chance he'd come back for? In spite of the promise he'd broken?

It didn't seem quite as likely today as it had before he got to Pinewood. Before he saw the coolness in her eyes. Before he asked about her and discovered she was keeping company with Will Larson.

"Will Larson and Linnie," he said out loud.

Just the thought of the other man with her made the muscles across Drew's shoulders bunch up and his grip around the headboard spindles tighten.

Not that there was anything wrong with Will. Drew had known him fairly well growing up, though their main connection had been through Carl, Linnie's brother-in-law now. Carl and Will were cousins, and since Carl and Drew had been best friends, there had been a lot of times when Will tagged along with them.

Tagged along, but not joined in.

Drew and Carl had been little hell-raisers as boys, snitching old Doc Melrose's underwear off the clothesline and hooking them to the back end of his buggy, pouring honey on every door handle on Main Street, catching all the cats in town and putting them in the spinster sisters' backyard....

They'd been full of mischief and pranks. But when Will Larson had been with them, he'd stood back, disapproving and clearly too worried about getting into trouble to share in the fun.

Then they'd all gotten older, and Drew and Carl had had their turn smoking behind the livery barn and tasting whiskey purloined from Drew's father. Will hadn't even stuck around to watch those antics.

No, Will Larson had been as dull as dirt. That was Drew's greatest memory of him. But he was a decent enough sort.

Drew almost wished he weren't.

Because one thing was certain—it wasn't Will Larson who had made Linnie a promise and then not kept it. So if it was a choice between him and old Will, Linnie probably had plenty of cause to choose Will.

Drew gave the headboard a mighty shake.

"Damn!"

He wondered for a moment if he would have come back to Pinewood had the schoolmarm let him know about Linnie and Will Larson.

He would have, he realized.

Because keeping company wasn't the same as being married. Or even betrothed.

And even if a second chance at winning Linnie seemed slimmer than it had before, he still had to try— Will Larson, or no Will Larson.

* * *

By the middle of that afternoon, Linnie's temper was short. If she had to listen to one more person talk about Drew Dunlap, she thought, she'd go out of her mind. There hadn't been a single customer the whole day who had said much about anything else.

And the last thing Linnie needed was help bringing Drew Dunlap to mind.

Replacing a bolt of satin on the fabric table, she unwittingly slammed it down so hard she knocked over a box of thimbles that clattered all over the wooden floor. Muttering to herself, she bent over to retrieve them. When she stood up again, she noticed her brother-in-law watching her intently.

Carl Martin was a stocky man of medium height, with warm blue eyes, a gentle smile, and a nose that had been broken when he was a child. His nose had healed at a somewhat crooked angle, giving his appearance a fighter's roughness. He reminded Linnie of a bear. A great big burly—and gentle—bear.

"Are you all right today?" he asked.

"I'm fine. Just fine," she assured him as she replaced the thimble box.

Linnie's and Mary Alice's mother had passed away when they were no more than children, and when their father had died three years ago, the sisters had inherited the store the family had owned ever since moving to Pinewood. Having been raised in the apartment on the second floor, they'd been taught early to tend to the business. But never could Linnie remember having had a day as vexing as this one. If Mary Alice weren't too far along in her pregnancy to work beside Carl, Linnie would have feigned a headache and escaped to her own room.

The bell over the door rang, announcing yet another customer, and Linnie felt as if her nerves jangled right along with it. But then she looked up to find Will coming in behind his mother, and not even the appearance of Louise Larson dimmed her pleasure at seeing him.

Tall and thin, he was, as always, dressed impeccably, in a high-buttoned suit beneath a gray overcoat. As she watched him, he removed his beaver hat and clasped it in the same hand that held his gloves. Then he smoothed his short blond hair.

His aquiline nose was his best feature, Linnie thought. It might have been carved by an artist's hand.

When he caught sight of her, he smiled; it was a soft smile that didn't quite reach his brown eyes. But it did show small white teeth framed in pale lips.

He headed straight for her then, but was waylaid by his mother before he got more than two steps into the store.

Louise Larson.

As owner of the bank, she was Pinewood's most prominent citizen. A tiny white-haired woman who carried a cane even though she had no need for one. Its function was more that of a city policeman's nightstick: she pointed with it, pushed doors open with it—even poked people with it when the mood struck her.

"Carl?" Will called over Louise's head from where they still stood near the door. "Do you think you might help Mother so that I may have a word with Linnie?"

Linnie saw Louise cast her son a dour look, but the elderly woman released her grip on his arm anyway. Linnie didn't care whether his mother was pleased or not. Stealing a few minutes of peace with Will was just what she needed at this moment.

"I'm so glad you came in today," she said in greeting as he approached.

But rather than returning her enthusiasm, a slight frown pulled his pale brows together. "Can we go in back to talk?"

"Of course."

At the rear of the store were boxed-in steps that led up to the apartment Linnie shared with her sister and brother-in-law. It was into the relative privacy of the stairway that Linnie led Will.

"Is something wrong?" she asked once they were there.

"Drew Dunlap is back," he said under his breath.

Linnie's uplifted spirits plunged again. Was there no escape from this today? "Yes, I know."

"Have you seen him already?"

There was a note of accusation in Will's tone that she didn't appreciate. "I saw him yesterday, when I was walking back from the dressmaker's shop."

For a moment, Will just stared at her, as if he expected her to say more. When she didn't, his frown deepened. "How do you feel about him being back?"

"How do I feel? I feel sick to death of hearing his name, that's how I feel."

Will drew back indignantly, and Linnie was instantly sorry for her tone. "I'm sorry. I didn't mean to snap at you. I just don't know what you or anyone else expects me to say about this."

"Did you know he was coming back?"

"No, I didn't. I didn't know any more about who had bought my—the Hayes house than anyone else in town. I was as surprised as you are."

"And it doesn't matter to you?"

Oh, it mattered to her. It mattered a whole lot. She didn't want to meet the man she'd shamed herself in front of on the street every day for the rest of her life. She didn't want to have to wait on him when he came into the store and know that he was probably laughing at her behind her back, that he'd probably laughed at her all these six years.

But she knew that wasn't what Will meant. "I don't care one whit about Drew Dunlap," she said with conviction.

"I know you were very smitten with him, Linnie," Will went on dubiously. "Everybody in town knew how heartbroken you were when he left, and how much hope you had pinned on him coming back for you."

Well, that cut right to the heart of the matter, didn't it? Of course, she'd always assumed that the whole of Pinewood knew about Drew's unfulfilled promise, and how hard it had been for her, but since she'd been spared the talk, she'd been able to pretend that her shame had been a private affair. It wasn't easy to be faced with the truth.

"I was just a girl then, Will. A silly child. And I got over it all. Would I have been seeing you if I hadn't? Would I have been so happy to have you come in today if I had feelings for Drew Dunlap?"

That made him smile again, if only slightly. "Are you happy that I came in today?" he asked, placing his hands on her shoulders.

"Happier than I was to see another single soul step through that door."

His grin broadened even more, and he pulled her toward him, so that her cheek rested against his chest. "I'm so glad, Linnie."

She wrapped her arms around his waist and closed her eyes, wanting badly to anchor herself to the present.

But there in her mind was the image of Drew Dunlap, looking just the way he had the day before—amused that she was keeping company with Will Larson, and too handsome for anyone's good.

She opened her eyes in a hurry and pushed herself far enough away that the sight of Will's face would block out the image.

"I should be feeling sorry for him for losing you to me," he said as he began a slow descent to kiss her.

But before his mouth reached hers, Louise Larson's strident voice came from just around the corner.

"Will, we have to be on our way if we're to finish all our errands."

Will pulled back, hands and all, as if he's been caught doing something he shouldn't. "I'll be right there."

Linnie had wanted him to kiss her. And hold her. And do whatever it took to wipe away the thoughts of Drew that had been bedeviling her since she'd first set eyes on him from the dressmaker's shop the day before.

But it wasn't to be.

"I guess I'll see you tonight, then," she said, forcing more brightness into her tone than she felt.

"Tonight..." Will repeated tentatively. "You did tell me you'd have to carry most of the hostess duties for Mary Alice, didn't you?"

"Yes, but that won't be so bad. You and I will still have time together."

"Well, the thing is, since you said you'd be busy, I didn't think you'd mind if I didn't come."

"Why wouldn't you come?"

"Oh, Mother's in one of her moods," he said, rolling his eyes as he did. "She says she's suffering the pre-Christmas melancholia and she needs my company to take her mind off it. I'm sorry, Linnie."

Linnie didn't get to respond before Louise Larson stepped into the stairwell. "Willie? Now, please."

"I knew you'd understand," he said to Linnie, reaching over to squeeze her hand. "I'll make it up to you."

"We really have to be on our way," Louise said. The older woman turned her side to her son and held out her elbow.

Will hesitated for a brief moment, but in the end he took her arm.

"We'll see you soon, dear," Louise said over her shoulder.

Above the tiny woman's head, Will made an exasperated face.

But he went along just the same.

By the time the guests were to arrive for the party that evening, the sideboard in the dining room of the apartment above the store was laden with punch and food. Pine garlands hung over all the doorways and draped the corners of mirrors and pictures, and pomanders made from oranges stuck with cloves and rolled in spices scented the air.

For the final touch, Linnie climbed on a chair beneath the arch between the dining room and parlor to hang a pine-and-berry kissing ball tied with red ribbons. As she did, Mary Alice and Carl came out of their bedroom, both of them dressed in their party finery.

"Don't you two look nice!" she said as she finished the chore and stepped down.

Carl held his wife's hand as she curtsied, somewhat cumbersomely. Mary Alice's features were similar to Linnie's, but her coloring was less striking; her hair was a dark brown, rather than Linnie's raven black, and her eyes were a plainer blue. She was no taller than Linnie, and normally no heavier, but at present she was great with child.

"And what about you, Linnie?" Mary Alice returned. "That dress is so pretty on you, it's a shame Will won't see you."

"Especially since he asked me to wear it," Linnie said with a laugh, brushing at the full overskirt of silver satin, which opened in an inverted vee to show a deep blue underskirt. The ruche at the neckline rested at the very tips of her shoulders, leaving her throat and collarbones bare.

"I'm sure he's disappointed not to come tonight," Mary Alice added.

"I wonder when he's going to learn to say no to that aunt of mine," Carl put in.

Linnie wondered the same thing, but didn't say it. "I don't suppose it matters. We've invited so many people, we won't even notice that there's one less."

Carl made a scrunched-up, sheepish face and scratched behind his ear. "There, uh . . . won't exactly be one less."

"Why is that?" Mary Alice asked.

Linnie felt a cold knot of dread form in the pit of her stomach even before her brother-in-law answered.

"I invited Drew."

The party was well under way by the time Drew arrived. Linnie was busy serving punch at the buffet table, and yet she was aware of him the moment he came into the apartment.

The dining room and parlor were connected by an opening so large the two rooms were almost one. Glancing up, she could see him standing just inside the door. He wore gray wool trousers and a jacket over a black brocade waistcoat that fitted him snugly, leaving nothing of his broad shoulders, his narrow waist or his long, thick legs disguised.

Linnie wished more fervently than ever that Will hadn't stayed at home with his mother.

With what looked to be a singular purpose, Drew crossed from the door in a few long strides, and before she could think what to do to get away from him, there he was, on the other side of the table.

"Linnie," he said in a barrel-deep voice that wrapped around her as if the past six years hadn't happened at all.

She swallowed with some difficulty, forced her chin up and said levelly, "Hello, Drew," hoping as she did that she was only imagining that the whole room had grown hushed and that all eyes were on the two of them.

And then she murmured that she'd forgotten something in the kitchen and beat a hasty retreat, promising herself that she would stay as far away from him as she could this evening.

Blindman's buff started the games, not long afterward. As they all played, Linnie could feel Drew's gaze on her, as surely as if it were hot water on her bare skin. She kept her distance, even disappearing into her bedroom when the blindfold was tied around his eyes, lest he instinctively seek her out in the course of the game and have an excuse to lay those big hands of his on her.

They played snapdragon next. As Linnie poured brandy on a silver tray and set a raisin in the center, Drew appeared beside her, offering to set the liquor on fire for her before taking the first turn trying to pluck out the raisin without getting burned.

Was it only the heat from the flaming brandy that made her feel flushed? she wondered as she watched him take off his coat and roll his snow-white shirtsleeve up to his elbow.

She hoped so. But she was a little afraid to stay around and find out, so she dragged her gaze away from his thick, bare wrist and again escaped into the kitchen, this time throwing a window wide open.

Deep breaths of icy air were just beginning to cool her off when Mary Alice poked her head in through the door. "The mayor's son has a new game he's going to teach us. It's called cutlets. Come and see."

"I'll be right out," Linnie assured.

Why was she being so silly? she asked herself. Why couldn't she just think of Drew as one of Carl's friends, no different from any of the others?

She had to. That was all there was to it.

And if Drew sought her out or watched her with eyes that bored into her, well, she'd learn to ignore it, to act as if she didn't notice.

Thus bolstered, Linnie took a last deep breath of winter air and rejoined the party.

One of the dining room chairs had been placed in the center of the parlor, and the mayor's son was perched on the very edge of the seat. "Now we form a chain, with each person sitting on another's knees," he explained.

Four people joined in as Linnie watched, not sure where Drew was. And then, suddenly, he stepped out of the hallway to her right and took her hand.

"Come on, let's get in on this," he whispered in her ear, pulling her forward before she could balk.

Drew sat gingerly on the knees of the undertaker's wife, and then set Linnie down on his.

That first contact with Drew set off flutters in her stomach. She was grateful when the undertaker took his place on her own knees and she could try concentrating on the game instead of thinking of being so near to sitting in Drew's lap.

Five more people joined the chain before the mayor's son called out, "Are you a believer in the Great Muddle?"

"Yes," they all called out, as they'd been instructed.

"So am I," shouted the mayor's son, just before he stood up and threw everyone off balance.

With arms and legs flailing, the whole chain toppled in a clamor of surprise. Linnie landed with her back against Drew's chest. His arm was all the way around the front of her, and his hand was on her shoulder, big and warm, slightly callused and very masculine.

She felt as if her bare skin had come to life, and for a moment, as everyone lay collapsed, laughing, she just couldn't move.

Then his fingers pulsed against her, sending lightning bolts of pleasure shooting through her with a force that frightened her. Linnie lunged to her feet, getting there long before anyone else.

All that mattered to her was that she escape—both Drew and feelings she wanted more than anything not to have. This time the kitchen wasn't far enough away, and she went through it to the stairs that led down into the store.

So much for bolstering, she thought, as angry with herself as with Drew for not leaving her alone.

Welcoming bayberry candles lined the two front display windows, casting the only light in the large cluttered space, where stacks of stock and merchandise hanging from the ceiling and the supports cast deep shadows.

With her arms wrapped tightly around her middle, Linnie went as far as the candy counter and leaned back against it to catch her breath.

Drew Dunlap be damned. Why did he have to come back?

"Are you all right?"

The deep bass voice that came to her from the bottom of the stairwell was the last one she wanted to hear.

For a moment, she considered not answering Drew, hoping he might think she wasn't there after all and rejoin the party. But she knew it was useless. He'd been right behind her all evening.

"I'm fine," she said coolly. "I just wanted a little time to myself."

But rather than go back up the stairs the way she silently willed him to, he crossed the room, his footfalls strong on the wooden floor, stopping just in front of her.

He didn't look at her. Instead, he stood in profile to her, glancing around the store at the big red coffee grinder at the other end of the counter, the barrels of pickles, sugar and flour, the bolts of cloth, the corner where overalls and long johns hung, the grain sacks stacked not far from the front door.

"It's exactly the way I remember it," he said after a time. "People may change, but not this place.... It even smells the same." As if to prove it, he closed his eyes, lifted his nose into the air and turned, pointing. "The tobacco and cigars are there." Another turn. "That's the perfume counter, chock-full of Christmas sachets." A third turn. "The coffee beans are that way." He tilted his head farther back and pointed toward the ceiling. "Pine boughs trussed up for kissing balls." Yet again he turned. "And there are the spices—cloves and nutmeg and cinnamon are the only ones I know the names of."

Then he opened his eyes and turned one last time, to face her. "Did I miss anything?"

His silliness made her smile in spite of herself. "You know you didn't."

He went to the potbellied stove, not far away in the center of the room, put his back to it and hooked his boot heel on the fender, crossing his arms over his chest as he did. The light in the store was too dim for Linnie to make out details, but she could tell he was looking her up and down by the way his head was tilted to one side.

"So, where's Will Larson tonight?" he asked after a moment.

"He couldn't come."

"Why not? The bank's not open, and as far as I know there wasn't anything but this party going on. Is he sick?"

"No."

"Illness in the family? A death?"

"No."

"I can't think of anything else that would keep me away from your side tonight if I were him. Where is he?"

"He didn't want to leave his mother," she answered, softly, reluctantly.

"He chose sitting with his mother over coming to a party with you?"

"You chose your father over me, once upon a time," she shot back without thinking about it. She regretted the words the moment they were out.

Silence filled the air, thick with tension, before he said, "That was different."

"Was it?"

"I didn't have a choice, Linnie. I couldn't see him go to jail. He wasn't a bad man, just a heartsick one."

"Well, maybe Will's mother is feeling heartsick tonight."

"That woman is tough as shoe leather. She put her husband in the ground the same day he died, and took his chair at the bank the next morning, business as usual. More likely she just wanted to see if she could make Will stay."

There was too much truth in that. Instead of addressing it, Linnie pushed herself from the counter and went to straighten some pots and pans on a table not far away.

"I heard he's proposed to you."

This time it was Linnie who didn't answer with any speed. "He has."

"I also heard you haven't given him an answer one way or'another. Why is that?"

She shrugged, as if it were of no import. "We haven't been courting that long. I wanted time to think about it." And time to be sure her feelings for him were the marrying kind. But Drew was the last man on the face of the earth she'd admit that to.

"Do you love him, Linnie?" he asked, in a voice so soft she barely heard him.

"Will is a good man."

"There are a lot of good men. That doesn't mean you love them."

Linnie couldn't bring herself to answer that. She believed she did love Will. But what she felt seemed bland next to what she'd felt for Drew all those years ago.

"Are you going to say yes to his proposal?" Drew said challengingly when she didn't respond.

"It's Will who'll be hearing my answer before anyone else."

From the corner of her eye, she saw Drew push away from the stove and saunter toward her. Quick sidesteps took her farther away to the hat table.

Instead of coming any nearer, Drew stopped at the checkerboard, which was set atop a barrel with two round-backed chairs on either side of it, and lined up the pieces.

The candlelight was less diffuse there and Linnie watched every movement of his hands, remembering all too vividly how it had felt to have one of them on her shoulder not long before. "Why did you come back?" she fairly whispered.

He seemed to think that over before he said, "I've lived a lot of places in the past six years, most of them just the same—too many people, too much soot, too much noise, not enough familiar faces. I discovered that I missed this little town. And since I can afford to choose where I live ... well, this was as good as any, and better than most."

Curiosity got the better of her. "How is it that you can afford to choose where to live and not worry about work?"

"I hooked up with a prospector two years ago. An old man with a map he claimed led to a mother lode. He wasn't strong enough to mine the claim alone, and no one else believed him. I thought it might be good to get my father up into the mountains, away from the saloons, so I agreed to go for a full half share, and we went gold hunting."

"And you found it?"

"We found it."

"Then you really are a rich man, the way folks have been speculating."

"Rich enough. In money, anyway."

Again he took a few steps closer. This time Linnie crossed his path to straighten some bottles on the patent-medicine counter. "What about the four years before that? What were you doing all that time?"

He followed her, stopping beside her with his back to the counter, the heels of his hands hooked on the edge, staring straight ahead rather than at her. "You want to know why I didn't come back for you, don't you?"

She felt her spine straighten in response. "I know why you didn't come back," she said, as if it didn't matter to her at all.

"Do you?"

"You never had any intention of it. You made the promise because I . . . because I didn't leave you any other choice."

"I made the promise because I thought I could keep it."

She put down a bottle of stomach bitters. Hard.

"That's the truth, Linnie."

"Then why didn't you?"

He made a sound like a chuckle, but without the mirth. "I didn't have any idea what my life would be like when I left Pinewood. Growing up in a small town didn't prepare me for what was outside of it, for scarce work that earned little pay that got sucked up in higher costs for everything. I didn't plan on my father turning cantankerous and getting us run out of town after town, but not before he'd started barroom brawls that were ultimately settled with what little money I'd put aside. How could I have brought you to one shabby room after another, most of them over a saloon, some of them having to be shared with four men besides my father and me?"

Linnie felt him turn to look at her. "How could I have brought you to a life like that?" he repeated.

She swallowed back the tightness in her throat and swung around into an alcove formed by bookcases. "Why didn't you just come back here, then, if things were so hard?"

He leaned a shoulder against the end of one of the shelves. "And do what? Hand my father over to the sheriff? Or should I just have abandoned him? I couldn't do either of those things. He was like a child, Linnie, a sick child. He couldn't take care of himself."

"And what was it kept you from writing?"

The silence came again, longer this time than either of the other two, until it became clear he wasn't going to answer that.

Then he swung into the alcove as if his shoulder were a hinge, and said, "You'll never know how much I wanted to keep that promise to you."

Her mouth had suddenly gone very dry. She pretended he wasn't a scant foot away, and straightened the books on the shelf directly in front of her, not saying anything at all.

"There wasn't a day went by that I didn't think about you," he said in a soft, thick voice.

One of the pins that held her hair coiled at the back of her head must have come loose in the fall, for when he reached and pulled it free, she felt her hair tumble down her back. She grabbed for it, jerking as she did, and coming face-to-face with him.

"I missed you so much it was like a fist in my stomach the whole time," he said in a quiet, husky voice.

She didn't believe him. And she wanted to tell him that. To shout that if he'd thought so much about her, if he'd missed her so much, he would have written to her, he would have let her know where he was, what he was doing, why he couldn't keep his promise, instead of leaving her hanging, wondering, worrying, feeling ashamed.

But the words wouldn't come out, and all she could do was raise her gaze to his face, which was gilded by the faint candlelight, and so near above her own, and slowly, slowly, coming nearer still. . . .

She realized all at once that he was going to kiss her.

"No!" She stepped away, and came up against the shelves with enough force to set the books to rocking.

Drew stood up straight, but he didn't take his penetrating eyes off her. "Linnie—"

"I have to get back to the party," she said in a rush, her voice much stronger than she felt inside.

For a moment he stayed where he was, blocking her path. Then he gave her back her hairpin, and while she refastened the long, black strands, he left the alcove.

"I won't let this be the end of it," he said.

But when she came out from the alcove, he was gone.

It was just as well. She hadn't wanted him to follow her downstairs in the first place.

Taking a shaky breath, Linnie crossed the store to where three hand mirrors were for sale, and used one of them to make sure she was presentable again. Then she headed back to the party.

She'd show Drew Dunlap, she thought on the way. She wouldn't do any more running from him. She'd look right through him when he sought her out. She'd laugh at everyone else's funny stories and ignore his altogether. She'd be bright and witty to all the guests but him. She'd act as if she didn't even know he was there.

But once she got upstairs again, she realized he'd left.

Good! What a relief, she told herself. Now she could genuinely enjoy the party.

And if something inside her felt alarmingly like disappointment?

She'd pay it no mind.

No, none at all.

Chapter Three

By the time the silver light of dawn crept in under the curtains of her bedroom the next morning, Linnie had stopped even trying to sleep.

She got up and scrambled across the cold wooden floor to start a fire in the small fireplace in the corner. Then she light-footed it back to bed.

Sitting against the pine headboard, she drew her knees to her chest, the blankets over them, wrapped her arms around her shins and stared into the dancing yellow flames.

Never in her twenty-one years of life had she felt so out of touch with herself. So confused.

What was wrong with her?

She had been right not to let Drew kiss her the night before, of course. But why had she spent the hours since then regretting it? Especially when even a small part of the shame she'd carried for the past six years should have done just the opposite, and confirmed how right she'd been to resist?

A shiver shook her, even though the room was warming, and Linnie closed her eyes, dropping her forehead to her upraised knees.

It wasn't easy to think that she might still be as foolish when it came to Drew Dunlap as she had been six years before.

Even the memory made her cringe, though this time what was plaguing her wasn't the thought of his leave-taking. It was the vivid image of an evening just days before that.

He'd come to see her, needing to escape the uproar over his father's attempted theft while the townsfolk decided what to do about it. She'd taken Drew down into the storeroom, where they could be alone.

Sitting amid the grain sacks that night, he'd confided his concerns over what was going to happen. Discussing it had seemed to make him feel better, and before too long, talking had turned to kissing.

Oh, how Linnie had loved the way he kissed her! Warm, tender kisses that had drawn her out of herself and left her aware of nothing but the sensation of his mouth on hers, of his sweet, gentle lips.

In his arms she'd felt as if she were in a different world, removed from reality, safe, secure, where she was meant to be. And when passion ignited in them both, it had seemed only natural and right.

Natural and right.

How could she have been so wrong?

Sitting in her bed, Linnie suddenly buried her face in her palms at the mere memory of that night.

His hands had shyly slipped inside her bodice, and then, tentatively, underneath her chemise, finding the hard crest of her breast. Nothing had ever felt so wondrous as his exploring, untutored hand closing over her bare, sensitive skin. Kneading, learning, growing slightly bolder. She'd thought she would die if he took his hand away and stopped the magic shards of light that were shooting all through her.

But after a while he had taken his hand away. He'd moved it to her hip, then lower, finding the hem of her skirt and petticoat, where they had already ridden up to her knees.

Linnie had groaned out loud when he slid his hand under, to her stockinged leg, trailing a hot caress up her thigh....

Now, in the emptiness of her bedroom, she groaned out loud again, only this wasn't a sound of pleasure, of passion, of love. It was a sound of pure humiliation.

She'd wanted him to go further. And she'd let him know that. She'd told him that she didn't care if they were married or not. She didn't care about anything but loving each other and showing it—

Linnie swallowed the tightness in her throat, a tightness that was part shame, part desire aroused by the simple thought of what she'd felt that night. She dug her hands into her hair, pressing her chin all the way to her chest.

The one final act that would have taken her virginity hadn't happened.

But only because Drew had stopped short, because *he* had pulled away.

To have given herself so freely...to have wanted to give even more...and then to have been left, that night, and again, two days later, for good...

The shame hadn't set in until she finally accepted that he wasn't coming back for her. But when it had, it had been as heavy and oppressive as July heat, a dark secret she carried right to the present.

And yet, in spite of all that, here she was, wondering, as she had been all night, what it would have been like had she let him kiss her in the book alcove. Wondering if his kiss had changed the way the rest of him had. Wondering how it would have felt to be held by those bigger arms. How it would have felt to be up against the strapping man's body that had grown out of the youth's.

She hit the mattress on either side of her with balled-up fists.

Stop it! Stop thinking about it! Stop thinking about him!

How many other women had he kissed in the past six years? she asked herself, as if that would wipe away the yearnings inside her. How many others had he let that deep voice roll over with sweet words? How many others had he touched? Maybe even loved?

And all while she'd waited and worried and dreamed of the day when he'd come back for her. All while she'd suffered the agony of knowing she'd thrown herself at him. *Twice.*

Linnie lunged out of bed and stormed the washstand, splashing frigid water from the pitcher into the bowl. She plunged her hands in and cupped as much as she could to her face, holding her breath until her lungs burned.

Fool! Silly fool!

But she hadn't let him kiss her last night, she reminded herself. No matter what she'd felt then, no matter what she'd felt since then, she hadn't let him kiss her.

There was solace in that. Not much, but some.

She let the water fall back into the basin, took a towel from the bar beside the table and pressed it against her cheeks. Then she stared at her stark reflection in the mirror.

Memories and thoughts and even yearnings didn't have to mean anything. She was finished and done with Drew Dunlap. She'd gone on with her life. She had friends and family and the store. She had Will, and a future with him, if only she said yes to his proposal.

And nowhere in any of that was there a place for Drew. Nor would she let there be.

She shucked off her nightgown, opened the trunk that sat at the foot of the bed, and pulled out clothes for the day.

No matter what it took, she was going to forget the past and ignore him as much as she could in the present. That was all there was to it, she swore as she shook the folds out of a navy blue wool dress.

Seeing him again had just raised the old memories and feelings to the surface, was what had happened. But before long she'd get used to his being in Pinewood. It would become commonplace, and she wouldn't give him a second thought. It wasn't as if she still loved him, after all.

And whatever was the purpose of this cat-and-mouse game he was playing with her, if he was rebuffed enough times, he'd give that up, too. He'd realize she wasn't in love with him the way she had been as a fifteen-year-old girl, and he'd leave her alone.

And then life would go on just the way it had for the past six years. Calmly. Quietly. Safely.

Sadly.

She stopped in the act of pulling on her chemise, closed her eyes and willed the thought out of her mind, and the feeling along with it. Not sadly. Just calmly. Quietly. Safely.

And then she went on with her dressing with a vengeance, deciding that an early start on a hard day's work would do wonders.

"I haven't seen you since the party last night," Mary Alice said to Linnie as they sat down to dinner that evening. "I don't know what time you must have gotten up this morning, but thank you for cleaning everything."

"She was in the store before I got downstairs today, too," Carl chimed in, helping himself to mashed potatoes. "Something wrong, Linnie?"

"I just didn't want to leave a dirty apartment for Mary Alice to clean, and when I finished I thought I might as well open the store early, is all."

"We were awfully tired last night," Mary Alice said, smoothing her enormously round stomach to include the coming baby in the statement. "But I wanted to talk to you."

Linnie raised her eyebrows questioningly, because her mouth was full of home-baked bread.

Mary Alice didn't need any more prompting to go on. "I saw you hightail it downstairs after that joke the mayor's son played with that so-called game. And I saw Drew follow right after you. What happened?"

Linnie took a sip of tea, avoiding her sister's eyes. "Absolutely nothing."

"You were gone a long time, and then he left the party altogether when he came back upstairs. Something must have happened."

"He just talked about some of the things he'd done since he left Pinewood. I don't know why he went home after that, and I don't much care."

"Well, I'm glad of that," her sister said. "I would hate to think he could just sashay back in here, bold as you please, and take up where he left off. I spent this whole day wishing you were already married to Will so Drew Dunlap wouldn't have a chance."

"What's wrong with Drew?" Carl asked.

"Are you saying you'd rather see Linnie with a man who deserted her and broke her heart than with your own cousin?"

Carl frowned and mashed some squash with the back of his fork. "I'm not taking sides one way or the other. How could I when Drew is one of my best friends and Will is blood? I just don't think Drew should be judged by something that happened so long ago, and under circumstances that none of us can understand, since we haven't been faced with what he was."

"I'll grant you that it was commendable for him to take care of his father," Mary Alice conceded ungraciously. "But that doesn't change what he did to Linnie. I don't want him hurting her again."

"Now, don't get upset with each other over this," Linnie put in. "There's nothing to be bothered about, because what was between Drew and me is long over with. It doesn't even bear discussing."

"I hope that means you're going to say yes to Will, then," Mary Alice said.

"It doesn't mean that, either. I'm still thinking about Will's proposal."

"If you take too much longer, he's liable to get away. Have you considered that?"

As a matter of fact, Linnie hadn't. But she did now, wondering how she'd feel if Will were to rescind his offer and turn his back on her.

Not good, was the answer. She cared for Will.

But did she want to marry him?

The mantel clock chimed just then, giving her a reprieve. "I'm sorry to leave you two with the dinner dishes, but I'm late for choir practice," she said, standing suddenly.

"I'll do them tonight," Carl offered.

Linnie gave him a sisterly peck on the cheek. "Thank you. You're a good brother-in-law."

"And Will is just as good a man," Mary Alice put in as Linnie took her coat from the hall tree beside the front door. "It runs in the family. He'll make you a fine husband, the same as Carl has made me."

"No doubt," Linnie called back. "Good night."

The crisp scent of snow was in the air, even though there was none falling. Linnie buttoned her heavy winter coat all the way to where it fell just inches short of her wool skirt as she descended the wooden staircase alongside the store to the boardwalk.

She didn't realize she'd forgotten to bring gloves or a muff or even a hat until she reached the street, and she decided against going back for them. Instead, she plunged her hands into her coat pockets and went quickly on her way down the half mile of Main Street to Vine.

Once she rounded the corner, she saw the Larson house, which took up the whole first block of the cross street. It was a large three-story brick Georgian with a carriage house in back—the only carriage house in all of Pinewood. The main house sat several yards from the street, surrounded by a tall wrought-iron fence between brick pillars.

There were Christmas pine boughs draped between each pillar and hung with wreaths. As she passed by, Linnie looked through them for signs of Will. All she found were his footsteps in the inch of snow that covered the ground leading from the gate to the church.

She followed them all the way to the white clapboard structure, with its tall spire running right up the center front, and two arched windows on either side. Tied to the posts in front of the church were horses hitched up to wagons, their backs covered with blankets as they stood breathing out clouds of steam.

Practice had already begun, and Linnie made quick work of taking off her coat before going into the chancel to climb onto the end of the middle riser and join in.

From her position, she had a clear view of Will, standing first in line on the highest riser on the opposite side of the curve the choir formed. He sang with vigor, his mouth forming a wide oval, his chin raised high, his voice a clear tenor.

He enjoyed singing in the choir as much as she did. It was something they had in common. And it was good to have things in common, she told herself as she sang, picturing herself and Will married, sharing a meal and then walking to the church for practice or for the service on Sunday morning.

Thoughts began to flit through her mind as the lyrics came on their own.

She'd have a good life with Will. Decent and upstanding. Like Will himself.

She'd be the banker's wife. Will would be a considerate husband. Like Carl.

Will loved her.

Mary Alice thought she should marry him.

Any number of marriage-minded ladies would jump at his proposal.

She and Will would have a home of their own, children. He'd be a patient father.

Linnie could see Will at the head of a dining table, carving a Christmas turkey while she watched from the other end, proud of him and their family.

Afterward she and Will would sit in the parlor as the children played with their new toys until it was bedtime. She'd get them into their nightclothes, and he'd read them a story before tucking them in. And then he'd circle his arm around her waist and guide her to their bed....

That was where the daydream ended.

Linnie had difficulty picturing Will behind the bedroom door.

But then, of course she did. They'd never done more than embrace and steal a few kisses. That was no reason not to believe that they wouldn't have a full and satisfying intimate life. They would. Certainly they would. In private Will would relax, and so would she, and everything would be just fine. Better than fine. Wonderful. Perfect.

So what was there to even think about? Why didn't she just accept his proposal and begin making wedding plans?

The loud clap of the choir director's hands brought Linnie out of her reverie and made her realize that the whole practice had passed without her paying much attention to anything but what was on her mind. Chatter began all around her. The other members of the choir began to file out of the chancel, but Will made his way to her side.

"I waited for you tonight, but you never came. I had to leave so I wouldn't be late," he said as he helped her down from the riser and they headed for the rear of the church.

"The store was even busier than usual today. We couldn't close until late, and then Mary Alice had dinner ready, and I lost track of the time."

"I thought as much," he said congenially.

They both slipped on their coats, and as she buttoned hers, she watched him do the same. His fingers were long and thin, almost feminine looking, as he fastened the buttons down the front. It was the first time she'd noticed them, and she couldn't tear her eyes away as he set his beaver hat on his head, cocking it at just the right angle, and then slipped on his kidskin gloves. She wasn't sorry when his hands were out of sight, and that made her feel a little guilty.

"Shall we go?" he said.

Linnie answered with a smile and turned toward the door.

Will held it open for her and then followed her outside. The other members of the choir were saying their good-nights, and Linnie and Will chimed in, following in the tracks left by the last wagon.

As they walked, Will told her about his day, and again Linnie had trouble paying attention. And then, before she knew it, they were at the Larson house.

Will cleared his throat, and his tone took on a hint of awkwardness. "Would you mind very much if I didn't walk you home tonight?"

That took her by surprise. Even though walking her home meant passing his own house and then back-tracking, Will always did it. "Is something wrong?"

"Not really. It's just that Mother worked hard today. She wants to get to bed early, and you know she can't sleep until I'm home. She asked that I come straight in tonight."

"Oh." Was she imagining it, Linnie wondered, or had Louise Larson's dictates been on the rise since Will's proposal?

Will went on. "I hate to make you walk alone, but—"

"I'll keep her company."

Both Linnie and Will turned abruptly as Drew stepped from the shadow of the pillar that marked the corner of the Larson property.

It seemed to take Will a moment to recognize him. "Drew Dunlap?"

"Hello, Will," Drew said, coming to stand with them. "I couldn't help but overhear you say you couldn't walk Linnie home. I'm going past the store anyway. We might as well walk together."

Linnie's heart had picked up speed at the first sound of his voice. The sight of him didn't calm it. And suddenly all her attention was focused on the present, with an alertness she hadn't been able to summon the whole evening. It was as if she'd just been awakened from a daze.

Drew was wearing the big sheepskin coat she'd seen him in that first day. It was made with the leather side out, the fleece showing at the collar and the front openings and around the cuffs. His face in the gray-white winter light looked ruddy, as if he'd been out in the cold a long time. And all in all, though she didn't want to notice it, he was so handsome it made her heart skip.

Will's brow was beetled as his eyes bored into hers. "Did you know he'd be here?"

"Of course not."

"No way she could have known," Drew put in, congenially enough. "I was just out walking off my dinner, heard the music coming from the church and thought I'd pass by. But now I'm on my way back home."

Will went from scowling at Drew to scowling at Linnie again. "Maybe I should get the carriage out and drive you to the store," he said, his indecision ringing clearly in his voice.

"That's silly, man," Drew said forcefully. "I can have her home by the time you hitch the horse."

Just then the front door to the Larson home opened and Louise called out, "Will? Are you coming in?"

Linnie watched Will's expression cloud over even more as he glanced in his mother's direction.

"Go on in," Drew urged him. "No reason not to."

"Please, dear," the older woman called beseechingly.

Linnie felt herself losing ground. Worried that Will really would leave her alone with Drew, she said, "It's not that far. You could be back before you know it."

"Will!" This time Louise Larson's tone was that of a mother with a recalcitrant child.

Will sighed disgustedly and turned to Linnie again. "I can't upset Mother," he finally said, as if Linnie were somehow at fault. "But I'll want to see you tomorrow." It sounded like a threat.

Before Linnie could even say good-night, he bobbed down to peck a quick, hard kiss on her cheek, and trotted up the walk to his mother.

And that was that. Linnie was left standing with Drew.

His hand closed around her elbow. "Come on, Linnie love, let me get you home and out of this cold."

"Don't call me that!" she snapped, and started walking, leaving him behind.

But Drew caught up in two strides and fell into step beside her. "Does he always put his mother before you?"

"Of course not." She could feel Drew's gaze on her, but she refused to look his way, keeping her eyes straight ahead.

Then, suddenly, one of those big hands caught her shoulder and stopped her in her tracks, turning her to face him. "No hat, no muffler, no gloves—a person would think you hadn't lived here all your life." He pulled her coat collar up around her neck.

For a moment, her face was bracketed by his hands, and heat went through her like a flash fire, even though he wore heavy gloves that matched his coat. "I'm fine," she told him, trying to step back. But only when he was finished with her collar did he let her go.

Taking off his gloves, he held them out to her. "Put these on." When she opened her mouth to protest, he stopped her. "Or I'll put them on for you."

Knowing he was as good as his word, she impatiently took the gloves and slid her hands into them. The soft fleece lining was warm from his own hands having just been in them, and the sensation sent goose bumps up her arms.

Trying to ignore the feeling, she squared her shoulders and began to walk again.

For a short time, the only sound was that of their footsteps on the ice-encrusted snow. Slow footfalls that adjusted themselves to each other and seemed in no hurry, as if this were a summer stroll.

He kept a little distance from her, but Linnie couldn't have been more aware of him if he'd been inside her coat with her.

"It's hard for me to imagine you and Will together," he said into the quiet.

"Everyone says we look very well together."

"Does that matter—how you look together?"

She only shrugged. It didn't matter. It had just been something to say.

"Is he good to you, Linnie?"

"Of course he is. Will is a kind, caring man."

When Drew didn't respond, she sensed that he didn't want to hear about the other man's qualities. And it was disconcerting to discover that she didn't much want to talk about them, either.

Instead of saying anything more, she watched Drew from the corner of her eye.

His own collar was up around his neck, the pale fleece accentuating his dark hair and brushing against his strong jawline, leaving his dented chin to poke out from between the two sides. In profile, his nose had a slight bump on the bridge; it was not at all symmetrical and aquiline, the way Will's was. But that didn't stop her from wanting to follow the line of it with her finger, maybe dropping that same finger down to his lips, just to see if he might kiss it once it was there. Or maybe those lips would part and he would flick his tongue against the tip....

Linnie forced her gaze down to the ground.

But into this line of vision came his big, booted feet, and she had a sudden memory of them, bare on a picnic blanket, long ago. The image did nothing to steady her erratically beating heart.

All of a sudden she tore his gloves off and shoved them at him. "My hands are too hot in these."

He took them from her, his long, thick fingers brushing hers as he did.

And why should she be so conscious of such a thing?

Linnie jammed her hands into her coat pockets as he put the gloves in his. She ducked her head lower into her upturned collar, as if that would keep her straying eyes and thoughts in line.

They rounded the corner onto Main Street, which was lined with tall black iron lampposts spilling golden light on the snow.

"I don't believe you were just out for an after-dinner stroll and happened by the church," she told him.

"No reason for you to believe it. It was a lie," he admitted, without any sign of remorse. "I heard there was choir practice tonight, and I figured you still belonged. I was waiting for you to come out so I could walk you home. What I didn't bargain for was Will being with you. But he took care of that."

They climbed up onto the boardwalk in front of the funeral parlor, the sound of their steps changing to those of heels echoing on hollow wood.

From the corner of her eye, Linnie saw Drew glancing slowly around as they walked, taking in the shops and stores and other establishments on Main Street. There was a small, contented smile on his lips.

He took a deep breath that raised his chest within the big coat, and the smile grew. "Mountains and pine—there's no smell quite like it. Much better than the sea." Then he sighed elaborately. "It's good to be home."

"Is it?"

"You'll never know how good. I was going to sneak into the church tonight—the way I used to when you had choir practice before—but it was so nice to look around and know I was finally where I belonged that I just listened from outside so I could soak up all of Pinewood. You know, the folks here are really as close as I've ever come to having a family."

His words were so heartfelt that they made her feel small for wishing he hadn't come back after all this time. His mother had died when he was only a boy, and from then on his father had taken to drink and not made much of a family for him. Without the kindness of some of the townsfolk, there would have been times when the young Drew didn't have a decent meal or boots for winter. And here she was, nestled snugly in the bosom not only of her own family, but of all of Pinewood, and she'd begrudged him coming back.

Guilt chastened her and softened her tone. "It must have been lonely, traveling from town to town."

"Mmm... A man full of whiskey isn't good company." He took another hearty breath of air and blew it out with a shout at the stars. Then he laughed at himself and turned back to Linnie. "Tonight I thought I could hear your voice alone, even from outside, singing Christmas songs."

"You couldn't have picked out my voice from all the rest."

"I like to think I could."

For a moment, the only sound was their footsteps. Then Drew said, "We used to take a lot of walks like this, remember?"

"I remember." Though she didn't want to.

"I liked the winter ones the best, because it was quiet, we'd have the street to ourselves—like this—and since there weren't many people out to see us, we'd hold hands."

Before she realized his intention, he pulled her hand from her coat pocket and enveloped it in his own. It was big and warm and strong.

Why did it have to feel so good?

Somehow she couldn't find the will to pull away. Instead—all on their own—her fingers curved around the heel of his hand and her palm settled against his.

Drew raised her hand to his face and rubbed the back of it along his jaw.

Linnie's glance wandered upward, too, and she found his eyes on hers again. Warmth from them bathed her, and washed away the years for just a moment, until she remembered herself and pulled free of his grip to plunge her hand back into the isolation of her pocket and stare straight ahead again.

"I wish you would leave me alone," she whispered, because it was all she could manage.

"I can't do that."

They'd reached the staircase leading to the apartment by then, and Linnie stopped at the foot of it. "Why can't you?" she asked, more strongly, though she had failed to achieve the stern tone she was trying for, and she sounded more bewildered than anything.

"Could be I've finally come back for you."

She would once have given her life to hear those words, now her pride asserted itself. "You're too late," she said, not a trace of uncertainty or weakness in her voice. Then she went up the stairs as if he weren't there.

But he followed her, and when she reached the landing she had no choice but to turn to him again.

There were Christmas candles burning in both the windows that bracketed the door, and they cast a faint yellow glow that, together with the moonlight, seemed to christen his features. Frost dusted his wavy hair, and the sight of him made something inside her waver again.

"I don't think I'm too late." His words were every bit as strong as her denial had been.

"Then maybe you should think again."

He held her with his eyes for the longest time, and then, all at once, he grasped the sides of her throat and pulled her forcefully into a kiss.

His lips were cold and firm and just slightly parted, in a way that was at once familiar and new. Gone was the tentativeness of youth, the uncertainty, replaced by the strength and confidence of a man who knew what he wanted and was taking it because he had no doubt she wanted it, too.

And she did want it! Lord help her, she did!

He opened his mouth a little more, urging her to do the same. When she complied, he did something unexpected; he touched the sensitive underside of her upper lip with his tongue.

Surprised, thrilled, curious, she let her lips part as wide as his were, and sure enough, his tongue found its way inside, touching hers, teasing it, inviting her to play.

Feeling wicked, Linnie took a tentative twirl with her own, trying the dance he was teaching her. And then he went on, plundering, exploring—the roof of her mouth, the soft insides of her cheeks....

There was hunger and urgency in his kiss. And maybe in hers, too, because before Linnie knew it she was learning a bit herself, following his lead and actually finding the very tips of his teeth with her tongue, learning what it was like even farther inside his mouth.

And all the while her heart was racing with excitement, with exhilaration, and it was as if something were sparkling inside her, raining brilliant, glittering shards down through her, waking her up, bringing her to life.

Then Drew's hands left her face, and he wrapped her in his arms, pressing her close against him.

Something about that change in position brought her back to reality.

Linnie broke off the kiss and pushed away from him. "Don't do that," she said, but the order had little power because of the feebleness of her voice, and because she'd participated so fully in the kiss.

Drew shook his head, just once, as if nothing she could say was going to stop him. Then he pulled her to him again for one more brief, searing kiss before he released her on his own. He pressed his thumb to her burning lips then, as if branding her as his, and held it there for a moment before he turned and walked away.

Linnie grasped the railing to steady herself, and watched him go, trying unsuccessfully as she did to stamp out those sparks that were still alive within her.

How could he cause such feelings in her? And so easily? Why wouldn't he do as she asked and leave her alone? Leave her in peace?

But it suddenly occurred to her that peace was just what she had as she stood there alone.

And the thought made the night air feel so much colder than it had moments before.

Chapter Four

The following evening was Louise Larson's weekly whist game. It was the only night Linnie could be certain of seeing Will. And, sure enough, he'd sent her a message early in the day he'd be by after supper to take her for a sleigh ride.

When she finished with the dishes that night, she went into her room to brush her hair. While she did, she wondered if Will was mad at her. She'd been wondering it all day.

As a rule, he showed up at the store himself to ask her to spend the evening with him. Sending a messenger instead, and not with a request, but with a straight statement that allowed nothing in the way of a choice, was not like him. And then, too, there was his parting attitude the night before, when he'd left her to go in to his mother.

Well, he had no call to be mad, Linnie thought as she tied her hair at her nape with a plum-colored ribbon that matched her dress. Just once he could have put off his mother in favor of her. It wasn't as if she'd gone with Drew Dunlap willingly. Will had abandoned her to him.

If he hadn't, none of what had gone on at the end of that walk home would have happened.

And, oh, how she wished it hadn't.

She leaned closer to the oval mirror above the washstand, but ended up stepping back without pinching her cheeks for color. They had enough of it just from the thought of the previous night.

But she didn't want to think about that kiss, and she wasn't going to. Better to think about Will being upset with her.

When she heard the knock on the front door, she assumed it was Will and headed out of her bedroom. She was halfway across the parlor by the time Carl let Drew into the apartment.

"What are you doing here?" she blurted out, stopping short.

Carl frowned at her curiously, and Mary Alice glanced up from her knitting with a startled expression, but Drew only smiled benignly.

"I came to visit Carl. He invited me."

"We have a lot of catching up to do," Carl added.

Linnie felt her cheeks grow hotter. It hadn't even occurred to her that Drew would be there to see Carl and not her. She had treated one of her brother-in-law's invited guests rudely, and she was at a loss as to what to say for herself.

Luckily, a second knock on the door spared her.

"That'll be Will," she said, anxiously rounding the two men to let him in.

It was indeed Will, standing straight and tall on the landing outside, a somber expression on his face. He barely spared her a glance before catching sight of Drew.

"Dunlap," he said, in a wholly unfriendly way. Without so much as a glance or a word for anyone else, he stepped inside, bringing tension with him like a hostess gift.

"I'll get my coat, and we can be on our way," Linnie announced, a little too brightly.

Will was in her line of vision as she took her coat down from the hall tree. As always, he wore a suit, overcoat, hat and gloves, looking every inch the conservative banker.

Linnie had always admired how well he tended to himself, so very different from the rustic way Drew was dressed—flannel shirt tucked into close-fitting denim britches, the vee at the neck of his long johns showing at his throat, and big boots.

But for the first time Will's garb struck her as stuffy, and it occurred to her that she couldn't remember when she'd last seen him dressed casually. He'd even worn banker's clothes to the church picnic at the end of the summer.

Not that he didn't look good, she amended guiltily. He did. And actually, the more formal attire better suited his face than Drew's rugged garb would have. After all, Will's features were so perfect, he was almost pretty. Well, *refined* was probably a better word for a man's looks, she thought.

Once her coat was buttoned, she snatched her hat and muff and nearly ran for the apartment door, calling out a general goodbye without looking at anyone in particular.

Will followed her outside, and not until Linnie heard the door close after him did she breathe.

The cold, bracing air helped clear her head, and the tiny flakes of fresh snow that were falling felt good against the lingering warmth of her skin. Holding on to the railing, she headed down the steps, with Will close behind her.

His cutter was waiting beside the boardwalk. A courting cutter, the small two-seater sleigh was black, decorated with a gold scroll design that wrapped around the curved back. The runners and supporters were hickory wood, the black leather seat was tufted with brass buttons, and a single gray gelding was hitched to the front.

Will took her elbow as she got in, and then he climbed in beside her to sit in the space left on the narrow seat. He pulled a red plaid blanket up over their knees, tucking it cozily in around them both, and then retrieved the reins, all without saying a word to her.

But once the horse set off at a slow trot, Will broke his silence. "So, tell me about your walk home last night."

He was mad, all right. Or at least upset.

"There's nothing to tell," she said, hoping no one had seen Drew holding her hand or kissing her and spread the word.

"Did you enjoy it?"

"Enjoy it?"

"Being with Drew Dunlap again."

"If you'll recall, I asked you to put off going inside rather than leaving me with him."

"So you did enjoy it."

Guilt poked at her like a pitchfork—guilt over her curtness, which had put hurt in Will's tone, and guilt because, yes, she had enjoyed the walk with Drew, and the hand holding, and the kiss. Even if she wished it weren't so.

"I didn't want to be with Drew last night," she said in a kinder voice. "I wanted to be with you. I wasn't happy to be left in the street out front of your house alone with him, Will."

But there was still accusation in his eyes when he glanced over at her, and there was even more hurt in his voice when he said, "I heard he held your hand."

Gossip was the bane of a small town. "He took my hand at one point, yes. I took it back." And the kiss? Had anyone seen that and reported it? Linnie held her breath and waited for the other shoe to drop.

But Will just said, "Do you still care for him, Linnie?"

She wasn't quick to answer his question. She'd spent the past twenty-four hours wondering the same thing. She didn't want to care for Drew. But could that kiss have done what it had to her insides if she was really over him? And in light of that, was it fair to Will to swear she didn't care about Drew, even though she wished it were true? She didn't think so.

She took a deep pull of the chill night air, and watched the snowflakes, white against the blackness of the sky, for a moment as she chose her words. "I can't tell you his being back hasn't confused me," she said, fairly whispering.

She could feel Will jolt.

"I don't want to be made a fool of if you're starting things up with him again," he said. His voice, too, was painfully quiet.

"Oh, Will..."

"Say you'll marry me," he demanded, suddenly, desperately.

"Oh, Will, don't!"

"Then you *are* starting up with him."

"I don't want to!"

"Then don't. Say you'll marry me, and we'll announce it, and that'll be that."

If only it were that easy. "I can't," she said, her voice quieter still.

"You can't marry me, or you can't give me your answer?"

"I can't give you my answer. Not yet."

For a time, the only sounds were the gliding of the runners, and the horse's hooves on the hard-packed snow. Then Linnie said, "I care about you, Will. Too much to make a decision about marrying you when I'm not thinking straight."

"And how long will it take you to start thinking straight?"

"I'm trying."

"You still love him, don't you?"

"No." But was that true? Or was it love that Drew had stirred up again? She honestly didn't know. And how could she say she'd marry Will when the mere touch of Drew's hand could send hot sparks all through her? She didn't want to feel anything for Drew, and she was doing all she could not to. But until she knew if that was possible, she wouldn't feel right agreeing to marry Will.

"I told you before that I needed time to think, to be sure, and that's still true," she said reasonably.

"You've had three weeks already. And now, with Dunlap back..." His voice trailed off ominously. "I've waited long enough, Linnie. I want an answer."

"Don't, Will. Don't do this to me. I told you I'm confused. I need to sort through my feelings."

They'd reached the edge of town, and ordinarily they'd have gone out to the lake just beyond. But Will turned the horse and headed back the way they'd come. For a long time, he didn't say anything at all, and Linnie wasn't sure whether that meant he was sticking to his demand for an immediate answer or not.

Then, out of the blue, he said, "Christmas Eve. I'll give you until then."

"That's just the day after tomorrow."

"And if the answer is yes, we can announce it at the Christmas service the next morning."

"But, Will—"

"I won't wait longer and have people talking behind my back about you and Dunlap. Mother and I have a reputation to uphold in this town. When she came to me with the news that you'd been seen holding hands with him last night, she wanted me to march straight over to the store and call back my proposal that minute. She was embarrassed to even show her face the rest of the day today. And I can't say I felt much better. She won't be happy to know I've even given you until Christmas Eve to choose between us."

"I'm not choosing between you!" Linnie fought a rise of anger at the mention of Louise Larson's part in this, and reminded herself that it was Will who was the wounded party here. "I just want to be sure of my feelings before I agree to marriage, Will. You don't want a wife with doubts."

"Doubts," he repeated, as if she'd struck him with the word.

"I do care for you, Will. You must know that. But this is a big decision. I have to be sure."

For a moment, he made no comment. Then, in a formidable tone, he said again, "Christmas Eve."

There didn't seem to be anything more to talk about, and they spent the rest of the ride back to the store in a silence so heavy that it seemed to press Linnie into the seat.

Once the sleigh was stopped in front of the store again, Will frowned up at the apartment. "Do you suppose he's still up there?"

Linnie hoped not. "I don't know. Why don't you come and see for yourself? I'll make hot cocoa, and we can sit in front of the fire. Drew only came to see Carl, anyway."

Will looked undecided. But then he shook his head. "I can't. Mother said her game wasn't going to last long tonight, what with everyone tired out from getting ready for the holiday. She wants me in early."

"Just like last night."

"No, not just like last night. I'm not leaving you alone with Drew Dunlap tonight. You said yourself, if he's up there, he's with Carl."

This time it was Linnie who didn't say anything.

Will climbed out of the cutter and took her hand to help her do the same. At the foot of the stairs, he again glanced up at the apartment, as though he might catch sight of Drew from there. But he didn't offer to walk her any farther.

Instead, he faced her, taking her by the shoulders and staring earnestly into her eyes. "I love you, Linnie. I still want you to marry me, and if you do, I'll never mention Drew Dunlap, or anything about him, again."

Linnie smiled weakly, wondering if he could make the same promise for his mother. But she didn't say that. "You're certain you have to have my answer on Christmas Eve?"

"It would be wonderful for the three of us to go to the service together the next morning and announce our engagement," he repeated. "It would be the best gift I've ever gotten."

Linnie nodded very slowly.

He bent down to her and kissed her on the mouth, letting his lips linger for a moment. It was a sweet kiss, warm and loving. Nothing at all like the forceful way Drew had kissed her the night before.

And somewhere deep inside her she longed for Will to part his lips the way Drew had. To boldly send his tongue courting, exploring, tormenting. To leave her feeling as kissed as she had then.

But after a moment of that firm, closed mouth on hers, Will ended it and straightened. "We can be happy, Linnie. I know it."

She smiled again, even more weakly than before. "Good night, Will."

"Good night."

She watched him get back into the cutter and send the horse into a gallop to get him home in a hurry. Then she trudged up the stairs, wondering what would have happened if she'd opened her lips and thrust her tongue into Will's mouth, wondering if he would have been scandalized or if he would have followed her lead and sparks would have flown between them after all.

She was still wondering about it when she opened the apartment door and found Drew inside, putting his arms into the sleeves of his sheepskin coat, while a frantic-looking Carl fidgeted beside him.

"Oh, thank goodness!" her brother-in-law nearly shouted when he saw her.

Immediate concern ran like lightning through Linnie. "What's wrong? Has something happened to Mary Alice?"

"It's the baby! The baby's coming!" Carl said. "Linnie, you and Drew go find the midwife. And hurry!" he said, nearly shoving them out the door.

"Is Mary Alice all right?" Linnie asked Drew on the landing outside.

"She's not feeling like running a footrace. Seems the pains came on fast and hard. That's part of what has Carl so rattled. Let's get that midwife. I think your sister *and* your brother-in-law will feel better when she's with them."

Linnie didn't need any more urging. With Mary Alice and the coming baby on her mind, she hurried down the stairs, crossed Main Street and headed toward the houses east of there.

The midwife was just going to bed when they knocked on her door. Linnie paced while they waited for her to dress, and then the three of them walked briskly back to the apartment, where the woman disappeared into the bedroom with Carl.

For a moment, Linnie stared at the closed door, wanting to be inside with Mary Alice. But in the end she decided the birthing room had enough occupants already, and she turned away, just in time to see Drew taking off his coat.

"There's nothing else either one of us can do. You might as well go home," she told him, her stomach jittery at the thought of being alone with him again.

"I don't want you to wait by yourself."

"This could take all night. You can't stay that long."

"Why can't I? There's no one telling me I have to be home. And even if there was, it wouldn't matter. I want to stay with you."

"There's no need," she insisted, trying to think quickly of some way to convince him to leave. She took off her own coat and threw it over the back of the sofa. "I'll probably go down to the store and do some work to pass the time. The storeroom needs straightening."

He shrugged. "I'll help."

She took in the sight of his britches, cut tight over narrow hips, the broadness of his shoulders in the flannel shirt, that dent in his chin, and knew she should insist he not stay.

She opened her mouth to do just that, but before she could, he shook his head. "I'm not leaving, so save your breath."

She considered pitching a real fit to get him to go, but deep down she didn't want to be left alone to wait through the birth, and in the end she gave in.

"Suit yourself," she said, as if it didn't make any difference to her one way or another. Then she headed for the kitchen, grabbed up an oil lantern to light, and took it with her down the back steps to the store.

The storeroom was a small space at the rear of the store, under the stairs, extending half the width of the building. Most of the merchandise was kept out front, but extra grain sacks and other items that would soon need to be replaced or replenished were kept there.

Linnie hung the lamp on a hook beside the door. "You can stack those flour sacks against the wall," she told Drew as she picked up a bag of cinnamon sticks, intending to go out to the store with it.

But her retreat was stalled by the sight of him rolling up his sleeves, exposing the long johns that clung to his thick forearms, stopping just above his wrists.

She tried not to notice the pure masculinity of those wrists, speckled with dark hair, or those big hands as they worked at turning up his cuffs. She tried not to remember how those hands had felt cupping her face last night, pulling her to him, holding her to his kiss....

Linnie shook herself, forcing her gaze away from him, and went out to the spice counter, where she took deep breaths until she felt in control again.

When she returned a few minutes later, he had a fifty-pound sack of wheat flour slung over his left shoulder. He was headed to the rear corner of the storeroom with it, and Linnie's gaze ran down his straight spine to the narrowing vee of his waist and on to a taut backside that almost seemed to taunt her.

Suddenly feeling very warm, she grabbed the broom and went to work on the flour-dusted floor with a vengeance. "You can take that last sack out to the front," she ordered, in a voice that was too husky.

He didn't say anything, but she could feel his eyes on her as he walked past, and the sensation didn't do anything at all to lower her temperature.

She applied the broom with even more vigor, wishing she could believe the lies she was telling herself that the only reason she was feeling unnerved was that Mary Alice was giving birth upstairs, and that it had nothing at all to do with Drew.

"Now that's a sight...." His deep voice washed over her out of the blue. She hadn't realized he'd come back. Glancing up, she saw him leaning against the doorjamb, his arms folded across his chest, each hand clamped under the opposite armpit, with his thumbs sticking out and pointing up at that face that was so handsome it turned her knees to mush.

"I don't know what you're talking about," she told him stiffly.

"Seeing you sweep reminded me of the first time I took notice of you."

"Is that right?"

"It was a day in spring. Carl dragged me along to the store to buy fishing line, even though we didn't have any intention of going fishing—he just wanted an excuse to see Mary Alice. But she always made you wait on him. I was supposed to go in ahead of him and get you busy so she'd have no excuse."

Linnie was interested in spite of herself, but she went on sweeping as if she weren't.

"We waited across the street for over an hour, watching for your father to go down to the widow Mordine's for lunch, like he always did. While we were there, you came out to sweep in front of the store.

"Carl was pacing and worrying that this one day your daddy wouldn't leave and fretting over how he was going to get a word with Mary Alice, but there you were, and I couldn't take my eyes off you."

His voice washed over her like warm honey, slowing up her sweeping.

"You had on a yellow gingham dress, and your hair was tied down low on your neck." She caught him pointing his chin at the strand that had worked loose and fallen over the left side of her forehead. "But that same shock of curls was bobbing on your brow, and even though I'd seen you around town and school and church all my life, there was something about that wild hank of hair and the way the sun made your skin look like fresh cream. It was as if I was seeing you for the first time."

Caught up in her own memories of that day, Linnie picked up the story. "You were standing with your shoulder against the lamppost, a lot like now, only your hands were hooked in your pockets and you were chewing on a piece of straw."

"So you did see me! You didn't show it."

She'd noticed him long before that day, noticed him when he came around with Carl or to work for her father, noticed him every time their paths crossed anywhere else in town. And she'd wished for him to notice her, but he'd never seemed to. She didn't tell him that.

Instead, she said, "You pushed off the lamppost and headed across the street, and poor Carl nearly had a fit, yelling, 'What're you doing? Not yet! Not yet!'" Linnie laughed. "But you just ignored him and kept on coming." And even then her pulse had danced a jig, and she'd only pretended she wasn't aware of his every movement.

"It was the oddest feeling I've ever had," Drew went on. "Up until that one second, you were just another girl around town, and all of a sudden it was like a door opened up in my heart and you walked through it. I knew you were the one for me. I knew it as surely as I knew my own name."

Something skittered across her nerve endings, and she fought to ignore it. "We were just children."

"I thought I was a man."

"You were only sixteen."

"I felt like a man."

"And I was only fourteen."

"A wisp of a girl. You've filled out some."

Without her realizing it, her swooping had taken her close to him. He reached out and inserted one index finger in the curl that fell in a coil down her forehead.

"You ran me a worse chase than Mary Alice did Carl. For a time, anyway."

She hadn't wanted him to know how much she liked him. Maybe, just like now, she hadn't even wanted to feel as much for him as she did. It had scared her, him being older and so sure of himself. "Girls around this town made it too easy for you. I wasn't going to be one of them."

"And the challenge of that just whetted my appetite all the more. Here was the prettiest girl in Pinewood, and she made the bottom of my stomach drop out every time I set eyes on her from that minute onward, and she wouldn't give me the time of day. Carl and I wondered what there was about you two Rhodes girls that made you so stuck-up."

"Stuck-up? I beg your pardon!" But she smiled, for all her pretense of being affronted.

"Yes, stuck-up. We wanted coy flirting and a chance to show off, and you both looked right through us as if we weren't even there."

"It was good for you. Took you down a peg."

"But you came around," he said smugly. "Runyon's barn dance."

"Someone spiked the punch."

"Carl and I did it. Poured half a bottle of rum in when no one was looking."

"And I didn't 'come around,' as I recall. I was outside, trying to get my head to stop spinning, and you—"

"Took you on a walk in the moonlight and charmed you."

"You just weren't strutting around for a change, is all."

"I got you to take off your shoes and stockings and dangle your bare feet in Runyon's pond."

"They were tired from dancing."

"They danced a lot more later that night. And all with me."

"You wouldn't turn me over to anyone else."

He laughed then. It was a deep, full-barreled rumble of a laugh that filled the small space. "No, I wouldn't, that's the truth. Then I walked you home and kissed you for the first time."

"On the ear, of all places."

"I wanted to show you that I respected you. And to catch just one more whiff of your hair—it smelled like spring rain and roses. I thought I was the happiest man in the world that night."

"And poor Carl..." Linnie laughed. "Mary Alice still didn't give him a second look. She was pining for Runyon's farmhand, that tall, skinny stick of a man, remember him?"

"But look where Carl is now. He got all he ever wanted. And me? I'm still having to work at it."

Mention of where Carl was at that moment brought Mary Alice and the baby back to Linnie's mind, and gave her an excuse not to pay too much attention to Drew's last statement.

She realized with some surprise that she'd stopped sweeping, and she went back to work. "I hope everything is all right upstairs and that baby doesn't take too long to get here," she said, both because it was true and to change the subject from remembrances of all those years ago, remembrances that were fonder than she wanted them to be.

Out of the corner of her eye, she saw Drew push away from the doorjamb. He picked up a box of three-penny nails and moved it to the corner where the other hardware supplies were kept, beside the grain sacks.

"How about you, Linnie? You still want a whole passel of babies now that you're grown and know what motherhood involves?"

"Maybe not a whole passel, but one or two would be nice."

"With your eyes and hair..."

And the dimple in your chin... That was what they'd always said when they talked about having children of their own.

"Who would've ever guessed that Mary Alice and Carl would get together and beat you and me at having a family?" he mused.

"Yes. Well," was all Linnie could think to say to that.

She paid renewed attention to her sweeping, but even as she did, she could see Drew leaning against the grain sacks, running one of those big hands over the supple burlap as if it were a living thing.

"I remember one of our last nights, too," he said then, in a deep, reverent voice. "Here in the store-room, sitting against the flour sacks. I've carried that memory around with me like a picture in a locket all this time."

"You have?" she asked, in a small, stunned voice.

"Of course I have."

This time she stopped sweeping on purpose, to search his expression for signs that he wasn't telling the truth. But all she found was a frown. He almost looked hurt that she would think anything different.

"Haven't you?" he demanded.

Linnie swallowed, with some difficulty. "No. I haven't," she admitted quietly. "I was afraid that—"

But she didn't finish, because just then came a baby's cry.

Linnie glanced up at the ceiling and then at Drew. His wonderful face erupted into a grin as broad as if he were the child's father. Without another word passing between them, she propped the broom in the corner and grabbed up the lantern, and they both headed upstairs.

For a time, they waited in the parlor, just a few feet from the bedroom door, listening to the strong wailing of the newborn. And then, finally, Carl came out, carrying what looked like just a bundle of blankets, except that he was handling them so carefully, eggs might have been wrapped inside.

His face was beaming, and his eyes were wet. "It's a girl. We have a daughter," he whispered, as if he couldn't believe it. "And Mary Alice is fine. Just fine."

Linnie's own eyes filled as she stepped to peek inside the bundle. "Oh, Carl, she's so beautiful," she said through a full throat.

"Hold her, Linnie," he offered, as if sharing a miracle.

She accepted the tiny, mewling infant, and when his arms were free, Carl turned to Drew. With wordless joy, they first shook hands, then clapped each other on the back, and finally came together in a brawny hug.

"Congratulations," Drew said afterward, his voice sounding shaky.

"I'm a lucky man," Carl allowed. "Hold her. See how she feels," he suggested. "You don't mind, do you, Linnie?"

"No, I don't mind," she said through a soggy laugh at her brother-in-law's awestruck elation.

She stepped near to Drew and handed him the baby, her eyes staying glued to him even as she moved back again. There was something very touching about seeing the tiny tangle of blankets held against that big, broad chest.

"Did you ever feel anything so wonderful?" Carl asked.

"It's pretty wonderful, all right," Drew answered.

Linnie could only think that the sight was almost as good.

Then the baby wailed even louder, and Drew laughed. "But maybe you'd better take her back in to her mother now."

Carl scooped up his daughter, pausing long enough for Linnie to have one more look at the rosy-faced cherub before slipping back through the bedroom door.

"I think he's proud of her," Linnie said unnecessarily, around a lump in her throat.

"I think he has reason to be," Drew answered.

They stood there, face-to-face, and Linnie had the strongest urge to step into his arms, to wrap her own around his waist and press her cheek to his chest, to partake fully of a moment that seemed somehow very intimate.

He must have had the same inclination, because he raised his hands as if to reach for her, but seeing that, she backed up, knowing that to step into those arms right then would be the end of her.

She cleared her throat and tried for a decorous tone. "You should go home and get some sleep."

"Should I?"

"It's very late."

Those hazel eyes of his stayed on her, holding her as surely as his arms would have had she not moved away, and for a fleeting second she wondered if he was going to pull her into his embrace anyway.

But he didn't, and there was a sharp spot of disappointment deep down inside her because of it, in spite of the fact that she knew it was better this way.

Instead, he turned and went to the hall tree for his coat.

Linnie followed, but only as far as the middle of the room, keeping some distance between them. As he shrugged into the big sheepskin jacket, he again looked at her. "Come to supper tomorrow night," he said. "The house is finished, and I'd like you to see it."

She shook her head.

"I'll be on my best behavior. I only want to show you what I've done to the place."

"I can't."

"You aren't engaged to him yet, Linnie. Come and see your house now that it's all fixed up."

Her house.

The temptation was great. But was it only the house?

"Just a simple supper. I'll expect you at seven."

"I haven't said yes."

"Then say it now."

She told herself to refuse the invitation. To make it clear that she wanted nothing to do with him. To declare her allegiance to Will.

But the truth of it, in her heart of hearts, was that she wasn't sure she wanted nothing to do with Drew. Not after the evening they'd just spent. Not after the kiss the night before. Not when such strong feelings could wash over her when she wasn't on guard against them.

And she needed to be sure before she could give Will an answer to his proposal.

"A simple supper, and you'll behave yourself?" she heard herself say, as if it were someone else speaking.

"I'll be a perfect gentleman."

"All right," she said, her voice little more than a whisper.

He stepped to her in two strides and bent low, nearly pressing his cheek to hers, as if he were going to tell her a secret. "Tomorrow night. Seven."

The words sounded as if they held a promise of some sort, and his breath was a warm gust against her skin. Then he kissed her ear, just the way he had the first time he ever got that close, only this time he lingered with his lips pressed to her lobe for a moment before straightening again.

He made it all the way to the door and opened it, but he didn't go out. Instead, he looked back at her, nodding in the direction of the bedroom, from which the baby's cries still came. "I can't help thinking that she could have been ours, Linnie," he said, in a voice that sounded tight.

Her eyes were so full he was only a blur. She couldn't say anything.

Instead, she turned her head sharply away so that he wouldn't see that it was something she, too, couldn't help thinking.

Chapter Five

"I'm not surprised," Mary Alice said the next morning when Linnie told her and Carl about Will's ultimatum.

Linnie sat perched on the edge of the bed while Mary Alice ate the breakfast she'd brought in to her. Carl was in the rocking chair alongside, holding his new daughter.

"Will really has been patient with you, Linnie," her sister went on. "I don't know what you've had to think about that could be taking you so long. I said yes to Carl before his whole proposal was out of his mouth, didn't I, Carl?"

"That you did, sweet. But maybe my cousin just isn't as wonderful as I am."

"Oh, it isn't that," Linnie was quick to put in. "Will is a man any woman would be lucky to have. He's kind and considerate and—"

"But do you love him?" Carl asked straight out.

When she answered her voice faltered slightly. "I do, yes. . . ." But not passionately. And until he actually proposed, that had seemed preferable to her. She'd experienced passion, all those years ago. And she'd also suffered the pain of the fall when that passion wasn't borne out. A comfortable, steady, reliable love had felt better. But would that be true forever? That was what she was trying to decide. Or would she one day regret that her marriage was more practical than passionate?

"If you love him, I can't see that there's a problem," Carl said.

"I'd say it was Drew Dunlap coming back to town, but you put off giving Will an answer even before that," Mary Alice added.

"Drew being back has complicated things, though," Linnie admitted.

"Oh, Linnie..." her sister fairly groaned. "You can't mean that."

"There have just been so many memories and old feelings."

"*Old* feelings," her sister reminded her. "That's the important part. They don't mean anything now."

Was that true? Linnie wondered. Were the things she was feeling about Drew just part of remembering the past, and not the present at all? It was possible. In fact, it was an explanation she wanted to believe.

"You're probably right."

"Of course I am. I think you're just letting memories of the good times overshadow what came afterward. Don't make that mistake, Linnie. I saw how much you suffered when you realized Drew wasn't coming back for you the way he promised."

"That was a terrible, terrible time," Linnie agreed in a quiet tone, remembering that part of the past more vividly than she had in the last few days.

"And keep in mind that marriage is a promise. You already know that Drew doesn't keep his, and Will does," her sister went on.

"Drew hasn't asked me to marry him."

"All the more reason to be wary of him. He could just be toying with you."

"Drew wouldn't do that," Carl put in, as if he was only entering the conversation to keep things fair.

"Well, even if he does propose, do you want a man who's already left you once? Who made you a promise he didn't keep? Who didn't even have the decency to write and tell you what was going on, and instead left you to figure it out for yourself and feel like a fool for waiting in the meantime?"

"No, I don't," Linnie answered without hesitation, because her sister was only repeating her own sentiments to her. Somehow she just lost sight of it all whenever she was with him.

"On the other hand, there's Will," Mary Alice put in.

"And his mother." The words slipped out of Linnie's mouth before she even knew she was thinking them. But since the subject had been raised, she decided to go on. "I can't help wondering if marriage will finally cause Will to put me first now and then."

"You remember what Grandmother used to say? A man who treats his mother well will treat his wife well, too. That's the kind of husband you want."

"If he's not too busy taking care of his mother even to notice Linnie is alive."

"Carl!"

"Don't get me wrong, Will is my cousin, and he loves Linnie, and I don't want to see him hurt. But I know my aunt too well, and it worries me that in marrying Will, Linnie is taking her on, too."

"Linnie will just have to have a firm hand in setting some boundaries with her, is all."

Linnie wondered if anyone had a firm enough hand to set boundaries with Louise Larson, but she didn't say it.

"Frankly," Mary Alice said, "I can't see why you even need to think until tomorrow about marrying Will. You should invite him over to see the baby tonight and tell him then."

Linnie agreed that that seemed like the logical thing to do, but only if she could forget the feelings that rose within her when she was with Drew. And since she couldn't, she decided they had to be considered.

"I can't have Will over tonight," she finally said to her sister. "I told Drew I'd have supper with him."

"Linnie! Why would you do such a thing?"

"He invited me so I could see the house now that it's finished."

"Oh, Linnie, no! I know how much you've always wanted that house. Don't go. It doesn't matter what's been done to it, it isn't as nice as anything Will will build for you."

Carl's head shot up. A frown pulled his brows down as he glanced at Linnie. "Has Will told you he'll build you a house?"

"No, not really. We've never actually talked about it. But there isn't room for more of us in the apartment," she said with a laugh.

Carl didn't smile. He just shook his head. "I think you ought to talk over where you'll be living with Will before you assume anything."

Linnie sobered. "Has he said something to you about where we'd live?"

"Not exactly. But over the years he's let it be known how he feels about his family home, and it one day being his."

"Are you trying to tell me that you don't think he intends for us to live in a place of our own if I marry him? That he means for me to just move in with him and his mother?"

"You'd best talk to him before figuring on anything else."

"Tonight," Mary Alice said anxiously. "Invite him over tonight and talk to him. Just, please, don't go to Drew's house."

The thought that Will might even consider their living with his mother weighed heavily on Linnie's mind. But when she measured that concern against her reasons for going to Drew's house, it came up just slightly short. This was the last chance she had to sort through her feelings and decide if they really were nothing but remembrances of what she'd felt long ago. "Having supper with Drew tonight is something I think I should do before I make up my mind about a future with Will."

"Then it isn't only the house you're going to see," Mary Alice said.

"Leave Linnie alone, sweet. She's doing what she needs to."

"What if Will finds out?" her sister said ominously.

That thought was not a pleasant one. But Linnie was on the cusp of making the most important decision of her life, and she had to risk it. "I just have to hope that he won't. It'll be all right, Mary Alice."

"Will it?" her sister asked dubiously.

But the only further reassurance Linnie could offer was "I hope so," because even she wasn't so sure.

The air was bracingly cold that evening as Linnie stood across the street from Drew's house, stalling for time, her heart racing and her palms damp despite the winter temperature. She was wondering again if she was doing the right thing.

But after reminding herself of all the reasons she'd decided to do this, she took a deep breath of air that bit her lungs and crossed the last few yards to the house, denying the guilt that taunted her over wearing her ice blue velvet Christmas dress two days early and fashioning her hair with a ribbon at her nape and a coy tug of curls on the left side of her brow.

Daffodil-colored lamplight spilled from the first-floor windows onto the unmarred blanket of snow. It was a welcoming sight and Linnie couldn't help feeling that her house was happy to finally accept her into it.

But it wasn't her house, she reminded herself.

A path had been shoveled to the big porch, and walking up it between two knee-high walls of snow made Linnie feel as if she were walking up the center aisle of a church. And with her hands tucked into her muff in front of her, she might have been carrying a bridal bouquet.

Silly thought. Linnie pushed it aside as she climbed the cleared steps. The hollow sound of her heels on the porch was knock enough to alert Drew, or else he'd been watching for her, unseen, because the front door opened just as she reached it.

And there he was, dapper in dark trousers and a starched white shirt, with the button on his banded collar open and his sleeves rolled up to his elbows.

He smiled at her, smooth and confident, but with a warmth as bright as the light through the windows. "I'm glad you came," he said, holding out his hand to her as if to help her over the threshold.

Linnie took it without first judging the wisdom of the action. And it wasn't wise. Those strong fingers closed around hers in a way that melted some of the unease that should have remained to keep her cool and aloof. The result was that, when she stepped into the foyer, she lacked some of the protective reserve she'd come bolstered with.

"Let me take your coat," he said, his voice seeming loud in the quiet house.

As he did, she glanced around at what was clearly her dream made real. They'd climbed in through broken windows many times all those years ago, and, like a symphony conductor, she'd stood in each doorway and outlined what she'd do when the house was hers. And now here it all was.

Every spindled baluster of the wide oak staircase directly in front of the door had been restored. And wound up the banister were pine boughs with red ribbons, just the way she'd said she would do it for all the Christmases she'd been so sure they'd have here together.

To her right was the den. Without going into it, she could see that it was done in dark, rich paneling, its centerpiece a huge desk with a high-backed tufted-leather chair. The room for the man of the house, she'd told Drew when she'd daydreamed aloud all those years ago.

Then she glanced into the parlor to her left and was drawn there without waiting for Drew or an invitation to look around.

The wall directly opposite the entrance had always been taken up by an oak fireplace that the original owners had brought over from France. It looked new again. In awe, she ran her fingertips over the center carving, a fan that branched out on either side into leaves and scrollwork that followed the firebox all the way to the ornate columns on either end. Cleaned and polished, it was as glorious as she'd imagined it could be.

Here, too, were pine boughs, all along the mantel-shelf, and in the corner was a Christmas tree decorated with tiny white candles and strings of holly berries.

Linnie had been barely eleven when a German family moved to Pinewood and brought with them the town's first Christmas tree. The custom had gained in popularity, but the apartment over the store had always been too small to accommodate a tree.

But when the Hayes house was hers, she'd bragged to Drew so long ago, she'd have a tree every year, and she'd put it in the corner next to the fireplace....

This, too, was as wonderful as any of her fantasies had been.

"I waited to light the candles because I thought you might like to do it," Drew said as he joined her.

He took a long stick of kindling from the iron log holder on the hearth, lit it from the fire and held it out to her.

Linnie hesitated. Should she really do something so proprietary?

But she couldn't resist.

As she set each candle wick aflame, she could feel Drew's eyes on her, but she tried not to think about it. When the task was finished, she stood back to stare at the tiny lights flickering amid the verdant needles and the bright red berries, feeling like a child in her delight.

"Isn't it beautiful?" she said.

"Mmm...beautiful," he responded. But when the intimacy in his tone made her glance at him, she found that he wasn't looking at the Christmas tree at all. He was staring unabashedly at her, his hazel eyes aglow and appreciative, his handsome mouth quirked up at the corners.

And a tiny wick seemed to have been lit inside of her, too.

Linnie spun around to look at the rest of the room, though in truth she could have described each piece of furniture and its placement with her back turned, it was all so near to what she'd always said she would do.

A long, overstuffed sofa and two wing chairs around a low claw-footed oak table. A rocking chair near the fireplace. A small desk off in the corner for letter writing. A tufted pillow in the window seat for comfortable darning in the morning light. A tall, small table for Drew's chessboard, with two straight chairs on either side. And a huge grandfather clock just to the right of the entrance from the foyer.

It occurred to her that she didn't need to see the rest of the house to know what had been done to each and every room. The kitchen would be dominated by a trestle table with ladder-back chairs on either side. The dining room would have two sideboards stocked with china, and an oval table, with a thick pedestal, surrounded by spindle-backed chairs.

Upstairs there would be a big brass bed in the master bedroom, with two armoires facing it like sentries. One of the three smaller rooms would be a nursery, and the other two would have sleigh beds of burnished mahogany, and bureaus to match. All the windows would have French lace curtains with heavier velvet draperies over them that tied back on either side. And the hardwood floors would be polished to a mirror sheen.

Her ideas. Her tastes. But none of it belonged to her.

Linnie felt something stab her deep inside. "Maybe I shouldn't have come."

"You don't like the place?"

"No, it isn't that." She liked it too much. "It's . . ." But she couldn't think of what to say to explain herself. After a moment he spared her the struggle. "Let's go in to supper before it gets cold."

Drew took her elbow and guided her back into the entranceway and down the hall that ran alongside the staircase. Linnie didn't know whether to laugh or cry when she stepped into the dining room. Every detail was her own design, just as she'd expected.

But it was laughter that came out when she opened her mouth. "You have a truly astonishing memory."

Grinning at her, he held her chair out. "You've forgotten how much you talked about this house and what you'd do to it if it was yours. When I ordered the work done and the furniture bought, I had only to repeat what I'd heard enough times to recite it myself."

When Linnie sat down, he took the seat nearest to her, just around the curve of the oval. Straight ahead was the open archway that connected the dining room to the kitchen—also refinished to her specifications. An image flashed through her mind of herself carrying a flaming Christmas pudding from that room to this one. And for a moment it was difficult for her to remember that she was only a guest here.

She shook her head slightly to chase away the thought and concentrated on Drew as he uncovered two plates of roast beef, browned potatoes, glazed carrots and thick slabs of fresh-baked bread.

"I had the food brought over from the widow Mordine's restaurant."

And no doubt the talk of Pinewood tomorrow would be speculation on who the second plate was for. Unless someone had seen her, and then the gossip would keep Christmas Eve buzzing.

"I didn't tell Will I was coming here tonight."

"I doubt he'd have approved." Drew nodded toward her meal as he took the first bite of his own. When he'd swallowed, he said, "I heard he gave you until tomorrow night to answer his proposal."

Today's town talk, no doubt. "Someone told his mother you were holding my hand on the way home from choir practice the other night."

He nodded as he ate. Linnie took a small piece of potato but found her stomach in too many flutters to want food.

"I met Carl coming out of the barbershop this afternoon," he said then, leaving behind the other subject. "He's so pleased with the new baby, I was afraid he might bust. Not that I blame him. Funny how we've reached that time in our lives when a baby can make a man jealous."

Linnie didn't comment on that, for fear of revealing her own feelings of envy. Instead, she glanced around the room. "Does it seem strange to actually live here?"

"It does, yes. Today I went by my old house. I guess because I spent the last six years in some pretty seedy places, I remembered it as better than it was. Truth is, it's not so different from where I've been—ramshackle and falling down. And then I came back here, and I couldn't believe this house was really mine." He broke off a piece of crusty bread and added, "Though it does seem like the place echoes with only me here."

She was wondering about him bringing a wife to her house to keep him company when she heard herself say, "Have there been other women—?" But she stopped cold when she realized where her ponderings had led her.

"I'd be lying if I said there hadn't been one or two who'd helped me pass the time along the way," he said, sitting back in his chair to pierce her with those eyes of his.

Linnie reminded herself that she'd taken the occasional buggy ride or twirl across the dance floor herself in the past six years. And now there was Will. But somehow that didn't ease the pang she felt at Drew's admission, and she couldn't keep from wondering which of those one or two other women had taught him to kiss the way he had two nights before.

Drew took her hand, where it rested on the linen tablecloth. "But none of them could chase away the memory of a blue-eyed girl with hair the color of licorice."

His hand was a warm blanket, and she slipped her own out from under it before she could get too accustomed to the comfort of it.

"So what will you do with yourself now?" she asked, a little too brightly, tearing her gaze from that handsome face.

"First off, I thought I'd see about building a new school. We need one, no doubt about that, and I'd like to share some of my good fortune with Pinewood. Of course, I'll have to get the permission of the town council."

"They're not apt to turn down an offer like that."

"And I was thinking of buying those ten acres south of here and raising racehorses."

"To race yourself?"

"A time or two a year. Might be fun to travel to a race here and there and show off."

"You and Carl and your horse races."

His grin was disarmingly devilish. "I wonder if the reverend thinks any more kindly about horse racing than he used to."

Linnie couldn't resist smiling back. "I'm sure he doesn't. Will that give you pause?"

His grin stretched a little wider. "Do you think a bell for the church might keep him quiet?"

"What if it doesn't?"

Drew shrugged those wide shoulders of his. "I'll impress upon him the fact that I'm raising and training the horses here but racing them somewhere else."

"Except when you and Carl have a mind to go off running one yourselves down Easley Road on Sunday morning instead of going to church, and half the men in Pinewood go with you."

"That only happened twice, to my recollection. And on both occasions it was because there was a good horse in from out of town and we just didn't have another time to do it." He narrowed his eyes at her. "And as I recall, one of those Sundays we caught the Rhodes sisters spying from behind that old willow instead of saying their prayers. Not that they didn't hightail it back to town when we spotted them and stick their uppity noses in the air to deny it."

"Scandalous goings-on," she agreed with a little devilishness of her own.

He held her eyes with his as they both smiled at the memory of childhood mischief, and for a moment Linnie lost herself in those hazel depths. Then she slipped down that thin nose to lips that were more sensual than they had any right to be.

It would be so much easier for her to resist him if she just didn't enjoy his company. If he couldn't make her laugh and feel just a little wicked. If the simple sight of him didn't bring something to life in her that nothing else could.

She tore her gaze free and pushed away her plate, just for something to do.

Then, without warning, Drew took her hand again. "Come and dance with me the way you did in Runyon's barn that first night you paid me any attention," he said, tugging her to her feet.

"Do you have Runyon and his fiddle hidden away in a closet somewhere?"

"No, but I have something else that'll work."

He led her into the parlor once more, leaving her standing in the middle of the floor while he went to the mantel. From behind the pine-bough garland, he took what looked like a cigar box, except that instead of a half-dressed woman on the top, there were blue columbines. And when he opened the lid, a lilting waltz played from flute pipes that made a sound like an organ.

Then he turned back to her and pulled her into his arms. "I never danced with a woman who fit me so well," he said into her hair.

He held her close, and Linnie knew she should resist it, but she didn't. Instead, she gave in to the urge to lay her cheek against his chest. She felt guilty for it, she really did. But she couldn't help indulging herself. It was only a dance, after all.

She could hear his heartbeat, steady and strong, and somehow she felt as if her own heart were keeping the same rhythm. He smelled of soap, the clean, woodsy one she sold in the store that lathered up for shaving, and his shirtfront felt like clean sheets against her skin.

He was right about how they fit together, her hand in his much bigger one, his chin perched atop her head. She could feel the hard muscles of his shoulder beneath her palm, rolling slightly as he guided her in a small circle in the firelit parlor. And there was something about the way his arm wrapped around her that made every curve flow into every hollow.

"I never stopped loving you, Linnie," he said in a smoky voice, ruining her guilty pleasure.

"Don't say that!" she almost groaned, pulling away as she should have done in the beginning. But he wouldn't let her go far, and he went on dancing as if she hadn't budged.

"It's true."

She looked up at him, at his dark hair, his full brows, his thick eyelashes. She took in the sight of those lips that had such power over her, those high cheekbones, that dent in his chin. This was the face she knew so well. The face she'd dreamed about since she was a young girl. The face she'd loved. And suddenly everything inside her grew weak.

"You could forgive me, you know," he suggested quietly, as if he could sneak the idea into her mind. "You could love me again. We could have what we should have had six years ago."

Could they? she wondered, feeling very removed, as if she'd somehow lost touch with herself.

The music stopped then, and so did their dancing. But Drew didn't let go of her. Instead, he kept holding her, staring down into her eyes.

Slowly he bent to take her lips with his, and at that first touch of his warm, barely moist mouth, Linnie took her arm from his shoulder. Meaning to push herself away, she clasped the crook of his elbow.

But his lips played over hers, parting them, and then his tongue came calling, and somehow her hand slid slowly up the bulge of his bicep and around to his back.

Never before the night he'd walked her home from choir practice had she been kissed like that, and now she found in herself a deep curiosity, as well as a desire to taste more.

Her tongue danced with his, circled his, led his a merry chase before she let him catch her. How strange the texture, the shape. And, oh, the wicked delight of having a part of him inside her!

Linnie raised both her hands to the back of his head, wanting to feel his hair, to know if it was still as silky to the touch. And when that deepened the kiss, she didn't mind.

He didn't, either, if the fact that his arms tightened around her was any indication. She was pulled up close against him now, her breasts pressed to his chest, and the feel of that hard, masculine body against the softness of hers sent sparks skittering all through her.

She felt his mouth open wider still and his arms wrap so far around her that one of his hands was at her side, his fingers just reaching the beginning swell of her breast. And she knew she should pull away, but somehow she didn't care. She was too lost in the feeling of her body melded with his.

Drew ended the kiss, only to rain smaller, passionate ones on her chin and its sensitive underside. He pressed her head back and went on down the arch of her neck into the hollow of her throat, tracing the contour with the tip of his tongue and sending chills of pleasure spiraling outward from there.

Desire was a living thing, and what had begun as sparks ignited to become much more, running through her like a brush fire and arching her backward.

A small, answering groan sounded from deep inside Drew, and he slipped one arm from around her to take her breast fully in his big, powerful hand, gently kneading and teasing the crest into a taut kernel that longed to feel his touch without the barrier of clothes.

The fire flamed hotter inside her, and everything ceased to matter, everything but Drew and the magic he was working. Completely carried away, Linnie felt immersed in sensual pleasure the likes of which she'd experienced only once before...such need, such wanting, such...

But that once before had been in the storeroom, six years ago.

That thought was like a bucket of cold water thrown on her. And in that instant panic replaced pleasure, and she pushed away from Drew with so much force that she rocked backward and almost lost her balance. "No!" she shouted. "I didn't come here for this!"

His hair was tousled from her hands in it, and he raked his own through it, as if using that moment to gain some control. "Why did you come, Linnie?"

"I shouldn't have...."

"But you did. You wanted to know if there was still anything real between us. You wanted to know if I could still do to you what I just did, still raise the feelings and the longings and the abandon that Will can't.''

''I have to go!''

''No, dammit!'' His hand shot out to her arm and stopped her. ''He can't do to you what I can, can he, Linnie? He won't.''

''He also won't break promises or leave me behind.'' She yanked free of him and nearly ran to the foyer, throwing open the closet door to find her coat, not sure whether it was Drew or her own feelings for him that she was trying to run from.

''I didn't break the damn promise or leave you behind because I wanted to!'' he shouted, following her.

''And why didn't you write once you had? I still haven't heard a reason for leaving me waiting and wondering and worrying that you might be sick or hurt or dead.''

''I couldn't write!'' The words erupted from him. ''I loved you too much, and it would have meant setting you free for some other man to have you. I could no more do that than I could turn you over to dance with anyone else that first night in Runyon's barn.''

That gave her a moment's pause. Linnie stared at him as what he had said sank in.

''I know. It was selfish,'' he went on. ''I admit it. But I loved you too much to let you go.''

''If you loved me so much, you'd have wanted me with you, no matter where you were,'' she cried, hating the pain she heard in her voice.

She saw his anger in the flex of his jaw that jutted his chin forward and deepened the indentations in his cheeks. ''You wouldn't say that if you'd seen where I was. But now I'm back. Now we can start up where we left off."

"Maybe you can, but I can't."

"Why not? Because you're too mad at me for not keeping my promise? For not writing? Scream and holler and get it out of your blood, then. Do whatever you need to to put it behind us so we can go on."

"On to what?"

"To marrying me. To coming to live in this house I fixed up for you. To having babies and a life like we dreamed of."

"To waiting and wondering if there are other promises you'll break? To worrying that one of those times when you go off racing horses you might not come back, the way you just didn't come back six years ago?"

"That isn't likely."

"Likely. I didn't think it was likely before, either. But that's what you did, and if you could do it once, you could do it again."

He didn't say anything to that, and in the silence that was left she realized for the first time just how loud both their voices had been.

Then, very quietly, he said, "I'm here to stay, Linnie."

But as she looked at him, she saw only danger in believing him the way she'd believed him so long ago. Danger in letting herself feel what she felt for him. Danger in kisses so powerful they could wipe away all thought, all reason, all sense, all memory. Memory of the agony she'd suffered, the shame—things it wasn't safe to forget.

Up against that, Will seemed like a haven. Like sanity in the face of insanity. Will was security and peace and steadiness. Comfort instead of calamity.

"No!" was all she said. She pulled her coat around her as if it were armor that would protect her from him.

"Don't do this. Give us a second chance," he beseeched her.

This time she didn't have to think about it. "I can't," she said with finality.

Then she turned and ran, as fast as she could, away from him and all he could do to her.

Chapter Six

The church was lit only with bayberry candles on Christmas Eve. Most of Pinewood's citizens were there, and when the choir finished the final song, everyone rose and began to spread their wishes for a merry Christmas as they bundled up and made their way out into the winter night.

Will hurried through the crowd to Linnie's side, urging her to cut short her chatter so that they could leave.

Linnie understood his impatience. The time had come for her to give her answer to his proposal, and goodness knew she'd put him off long enough.

So, feeling as tightly wound as a watch spring, she let him maneuver them into their coats and then outside without stopping to say anything to their friends.

In fact, Will paused only once, at the foot of the church steps, to speak to his mother. As he did, Linnie stood off a ways, busying herself with her muffler and gloves.

"Merry Christmas!"

"Merry Christmas to you!"

The voices all around her were familiar, and yet Linnie found herself listening hard, and looking hard,

too, past what she was hearing and seeing. It was as if
she expected to hear one particular voice, to see one
particular face.

But Drew hadn't come to the concert.

She was glad. She was. She hadn't seen him since
the night before, when she'd run from his house. And
she didn't want to. She wished she never had to see him
again.

"You don't mind if we walk Mother home first, do
you, Linnie?"

Engrossed in her thoughts, Linnie didn't hear Will
come up until his words startled her. She turned to
find he had Louise in tow. Or maybe Louise had him
in tow.

"The ground has iced up while we were inside, and
I can't have Mother slipping and sliding," he explained.

"No, of course you can't," Linnie agreed, reminding herself that the Larson house was only a block
away, and then she and Will would be alone and she
could tell him she'd marry him. That she wanted the
wedding to be soon. Very soon. Maybe even before she
had to set eyes on Drew again.

Louise didn't seem to need help then, as she set off,
tugging her son along with her hand in the crook of his
arm.

Linnie was left to follow as the older woman discussed the evening's music with Will. It was exactly as
if the two of them were all by themselves.

Several times Will threw Linnie an exasperated
glance over his shoulder, and, to his credit, he did
hurry his mother as much as he could. But still Linnie
felt shut out from their walk home.

Just a few minutes more, she thought, and then she'd have Will all to herself.

She waited at the gate while he walked Louise to the door and saw her inside. Standing in the long, dark shadow cast by the big house, Linnie could hear the older woman's reminders to him that they needed to get up early in the morning to open their gifts, that she wouldn't be going to bed until he got home.

And then Will was back beside her. "There now," he said, clasping Linnie's arm and steering her on their way again. "That didn't take too long, did it?"

"No." Just long enough for her to have the feeling that the Larson house was looming ominously over her. "There's something I have to ask you, Will."

"It was answers I was hoping for tonight," he said teasingly, his mood ebullient. "But ask away, anything you want to know."

"I was just wondering where you were planning on us living." Glancing up at him, she found him grinning as broadly as if her question told him she was accepting his proposal.

"Why, in my house, of course."

"Your house. Do you mean your mother's house?"

"My mother's house, my house, the same thing. It's where all the Larsons have lived since they came to Pinewood."

"Yes, but it wouldn't be *our* house."

He laughed. "Well, it certainly would be."

"Wouldn't you want a new home for us to start out in? Someplace that was all our own?"

"Why would I want a new home, when I already have the best one in town?"

"Because that's your mother's house," Linnie said slowly, as if he might understand better if she did.

"You already said that," he answered, a little peevishly.

For a moment, Linnie wondered how to put what was on her mind. In the end, she decided honesty was best. "What if I told you I don't want to live with your mother?" she said quietly.

Will's grip on her arm tightened. "You want me to leave Mother?"

"That's very often how it happens—when a couple marry, they go off to start their life on their own."

"Mary Alice and Carl didn't," he reminded her curtly.

"They didn't really have the wherewithal."

"Maybe they didn't want to leave you alone."

The accusation in his tone was unmistakable. "They didn't stay on my account," Linnie protested. "I wouldn't have minded if they'd gone to live somewhere else, and I've been very careful of their privacy."

"Are you saying Mother wouldn't be?"

"Will—"

"No, I want to know. Are you saying that you think my mother would intrude on our life?"

Linnie watched the path in front of them. "She can be very demanding of your time."

"She needs me."

"I'm not saying that I would expect you to abandon her. Not at all. It just seems to me that it would be better for all of us if we had a home of our own. You could still see to her needs."

Will didn't respond to that for a long time, and as they turned onto Main Street and climbed to the boardwalk, Linnie had a sudden memory of taking this same walk with Drew just a few nights before. Her feelings had been so different then. Despite everything, she'd felt lighter than she did at this moment with Will. She'd felt excited and alive and—

She stopped the thought and pushed the image of Drew out of her mind. "Will? Did you hear what I said?" she asked, to draw them both back into the conversation.

"Mother wouldn't hear of my leaving home," he finally said. "She doesn't even like it when I have to go to Denver on business and stay overnight."

"I don't think it should be up to your mother."

Will stopped short, turning to frown down on Linnie. "Mother was afraid of this."

"Of what?"

"She said you gave her the feeling that if you married me, you wouldn't be joining our family, but trying to take me away from it."

Linnie didn't say anything to that. Instead, as she looked up at Will, she remembered the night before, with Drew at his house. What had she thought? That Will had seemed like a haven. Like security and peace and steadiness. Like comfort instead of calamity.

But how much of a haven would there be, living in the same house with Louise Larson? How much peace would there be? And comfort? Wouldn't Will always choose to comfort his mother over her?

Linnie suddenly realized that it wasn't only that Louise Larson was demanding and overbearing, but that Will accommodated those things in her, that he chose to be malleable, that he always defended her behavior.

And just as suddenly, Linnie knew with clear certainty that in marrying Will she would not only be settling for practicality instead of passion, but also for a life in which she would take a back seat to his mother, because that was as much what Will wanted as what Louise wanted.

"It isn't going to work, Will," Linnie said then, quietly.

"What isn't going to work?" he demanded, sounding more like a petulant child than ever.

"A marriage between you and me."

"Why not? Is it such a terrible thing to want to bring you to my family home? To expect you to go from some tiny little rooms over a store to a grand and beautiful house?"

"Tiny little rooms over a store. I didn't know where I live seemed so shabby to you."

His eyes narrowed at her. "You're just looking for an excuse not to marry me, aren't you? It's Dunlap that's really the reason."

Just the mention of Drew made her heart clench. "I can't marry you, Will. That's all there is to it."

"You mean you won't."

"I'm sorry."

"Is he waiting for you? Are you going to run off now and meet him?"

The appeal of those two thoughts was so strong it almost hurt. "I'm just going home," she said wearily.

"You're making a mistake!" Will shouted at her as she turned from him. "Dunlap left you once before, and he'll leave you again!"

Linnie felt as if he'd kicked her. "Good night, Will."

"Mother knew it all along! She said she could see you were still pining for him! She warned me!" he yelled after her.

Linnie just kept on walking, but as she did, Will's words seemed to repeat themselves in her mind.

Pining for Drew? Somehow that term seemed so mild for what she'd been feeling ever since he came back.

But what was it, if not pining? She couldn't stop thinking about him. Wanting him. Wondering where he was every minute, what he was doing. Being jealous of the time he wasn't with her.

"You love him! Admit it," Will shouted.

Linnie closed her eyes for a brief moment and tried to swallow a lump in her throat at just the mention of love for Drew.

It *was* love she felt for him, Lord help her. Love as strong as she'd felt six years ago. Love as deep and as all-encompassing as if no time at all had passed.

"You're a fool, Linnie Rhodes! A pure fool!" Will's voice was growing more distant as she kept walking, never looking back or acknowledging that she heard him.

But she definitely heard him. And, worse than that, she agreed with him. She was a fool. A pure fool, to love a man who had left her and had not so much as written to tell her he wasn't coming back for her.

I loved you too much, and it would have meant setting you free for some other man to have you. I could no more do that than I could turn you over to dance with anyone else that first night in Runyon's barn....

"You're making a big mistake!" Will's voice barely reached her now.

Had she made a mistake in running away from Drew the night before? Could she ever really run from her feelings for him? From the passion that he sparked inside of her? From the dreams of so long ago, dreams he said he wanted to make come true now?

He'd asked her to forgive him, so that they could go on, so that they could have a future together. Was it only a matter of not having forgiven him? Of believing in him? Of believing what he'd told her?

Or was everything so muddled up in her mind that suddenly it all just seemed simple? Were her feelings just confused by all that had gone on with both Drew and Will in the past week?

Linnie reached the steps to the apartment without noticing whether Will had stopped calling out to her or she'd simply gone too far to hear him anymore.

The night was still and quiet, and she felt too exhausted to think about any of it one minute longer. Drew. Will. It didn't seem as if she'd thought of anything but the two of them for so long. It had worn her out. She just wanted to get up those stairs and crawl into her bed and pull the covers over her head.

Because at that moment all she was sure of was that she wasn't sure of anything.

Drew didn't know how long he'd been sitting in the dark. Long enough for Christmas Eve to turn into the first hours of Christmas morning. But acceptance wasn't an easy thing for him.

He'd come back to Pinewood for Linnie. To finally have with her what he'd always wanted.

But he'd seen so much more anger and hurt and stubbornness in her the night before than he'd realized she felt. And it had begun to make him think that the chasm between them might be too deep to bridge.

Sighing into the quiet of the night, he pushed himself up from the chair and headed for the stairs, picturing in his mind's eye all he'd seen earlier in the evening.

He'd stood in the shadows at the back of the church where no one would see him, watching Linnie, longing for her, loving her, wondering what he could do to win her back.

But when the service ended, he'd watched her allow the other man that possessive hand on her arm. He'd watched her smile at Larson the way she had once smiled at him.

He'd followed them, keeping far enough away that they didn't notice, as Will let Linnie lag behind him and his mother like some mangy dog.

Don't let him do that to you! he'd been silently screaming. He'd wanted to rush to her, yank her back and shake her, shake some sense into her, force her to see that he loved her, that he'd never treat her like that, that no one had the right to.

But her words of the night before had kept him away—she didn't want him. In fact, it was clear that she hated him so much that she preferred playing second fiddle to Louise Larson to anything he could offer her.

And then Will had left Louise and gone on with Linnie, holding her arm again, happiness radiating from him.

She'd done it, Drew had known in that instant. She'd said yes to the other man's proposal. She'd closed the door on Drew forever, on any future for them together.

At the top of his stairs, Drew turned into the master bedroom on his right. The curtains were still open, and moonlight fell across the bed.

Staring at it, he hated the memories of all the nights he'd dreamed of carrying Linnie to that bed. And suddenly he knew he couldn't face it alone, not now that there wasn't even a hope that she would ever come to it.

And what about the rest of the house? he asked himself.

Her house. Every inch of it was hers.

He didn't want it without her.

Drew lit the bedside lamp and gave up any idea of sleeping. His thoughts were heavy with wondering how he could stay in Pinewood and watch her marry Will Larson. Watch her have a life with the other man. Watch her have the other man's babies.

Something inside him clenched, hard and sharp, and he knew what he had to do.

Crossing to one of the two armoires at the foot of the bed, he took his valise from underneath it, tossing it on the feather ticking so hard it bounced open.

He couldn't have Linnie. He had to accept that. But he couldn't stand by and watch Will Larson have her, either.

So, with a heart heavier than it had been when he left Pinewood six years before, Drew began to pack.

Christmas morning dawned with a clear sky and a sun so bright it made the snow on the ground glitter like diamonds. And Linnie faced it with just as clear and bright a knowledge of what she wanted and what she had to do.

She'd fallen asleep the moment she slipped into bed the night before, but she had managed to stay that way only half the night. By three she'd been awake and thinking. By six she'd been up and dressed. By a quarter of seven, she couldn't make herself wait any longer.

"Where are you going so early?" Mary Alice called from her bed, where she sat propped up, feeding the baby and looking out her open door at Linnie as she donned her coat.

"I'm going to see Drew," she answered, buttoning the coat with nervous fingers.

"No, Linnie, don't—"

"Hush, sweet." Carl came from inside the bedroom to stand in the doorway. Then, to Linnie, he said, "You've made up your mind, haven't you?"

"Yes, I have."

"And you're going to him."

"Yes."

Her brother-in-law grinned as broadly as he had when he introduced his daughter to her. "Tell my friend I'd wish him a merry Christmas, but I know he'll be having one now, regardless. And be careful on the ice."

Linnie smiled back at him and swept out the door.

His cautionary words had merit, she realized as she made her way down the outside steps. Even the boardwalk was slippery, and she had to walk slowly and with care. It made her feel the way she did in nightmares—wanting, needing, to run, yet unable to move at anything but a snail's crawl.

Drew would still be asleep, she told herself, trying to believe that there was no hurry, when inside she felt that if she could fly, she still wouldn't get to him quick enough, not now that she'd finally made up her mind.

Lying in the dark in the middle of the night, she'd found herself in such abject misery that she'd been forced to search her heart of hearts about Drew. And what she'd found was that she didn't really believe that if she was married to him, he would leave again and never come back. She'd discovered that she believed he loved her. That he hadn't come back for her because he couldn't. That he hadn't written because it would have set her free, and he'd loved her too much to do that.

And most of all, she'd realized that she loved him. That she loved him with a fuller, more mature love than she'd felt for him all those years ago. A love that was stronger than any she'd ever known, a love that could forgive him anything now, even if it couldn't have before. A love that would not be denied.

When she finally reached Hayes Lane, she took to the street, where the snow-packed road made walking easier. Looking up through the bright glare of the sun, she focused on the house. Her house. Hers and Drew's. And she nearly broke into a run to reach it. But dignity prevailed, and she only walked more quickly, all the while feeling her pulse racing and butterflies fluttering in her stomach.

Just a few more steps. Just a few. And then she'd be with him, now and forever.

Linnie climbed the stairs to the porch. Her heart was beating so hard she could hear it. It was silly to feel so nervous, so afraid, so worried, she told herself. After all, Drew had said he had come back to Pinewood for her. Why wouldn't he welcome her with open arms?

She raised her hand to knock on the front door.

And that was when she saw the folded paper slipped into the frame of the screen, her name written on it in Drew's hand.

Swallowing back the lump of dread in her throat, she reached for it. Inside was written "Congratulations, Linnie. Consider the house and everything in it my wedding gift to you and Will."

And it was signed "Drew Dunlap." The formality had a painful finality to it.

No, it couldn't be, a voice in her mind shouted.

Linnie opened the screen and pounded on the oak door. "Drew? Drew! It's me."

But there was no answer.

She tried the handle and, finding it unlocked, opened the door to the stillness of an empty house. But she called inside anyway, to no avail.

Hot tears sprang to her eyes, but she wouldn't let them fall. "Oh, Drew, no...."

Over her lament came the sound of the train whistle announcing the arrival of the early run.

Linnie remembered the dressmaker saying that Drew had come in on the train. Wouldn't that be how he'd leave? Maybe there was still time!

Forgetting all about dignity, she went as fast as she could, back the way she'd come, only this time when she turned onto Main Street she ignored the boardwalk and headed up the street, having to step off into the drifts when wagons and carriages came along on their way to church. But the snow filling her shoes and covering her hem didn't matter to her. All that mattered was Drew, and getting to him before he could leave.

The train whistle sounded once more just before she reached the station. The last call, she knew.

Linnie picked up her skirts in both hands, holding them high enough that she could break into a run. She didn't care who saw her or what the talk would be. She could only think that if that train took Drew away, she'd never see him again.

Bounding up onto the platform, she rounded the station house to get to the rear, searching frantically for some sign of him. But all she discovered was the steward disappearing into one of the cars as the wheels made their first turns to take Drew out of her life forever.

"Wait! Wait!" she shouted desperately, as if that would halt the big black beast.

But, of course, it didn't.

"Drew!" she cried, stopping dead in her tracks, her heart breaking.

And then she was running again, faster than she'd ever run in her life, after the train, after Drew, after her Christmas dream.

The blood seemed to pound in her head with the same rhythm as the chugging of the engine, which was slowly building speed. With each thrust she heard his name—Drew! Drew! Drew!—pumping fuel to her own feet to carry her faster, faster, faster.

The parting whistle blew, and it came to Linnie as a taunt. She'd never catch up. She'd lost him. Forever.

Her lungs burned, and still she ran, harder, faster. The caboose rail grew closer. Maybe she could reach it....

She stretched out her arm, but she was inches short.

Faster, faster, she ran, with no thought but getting to him.

And then her hand closed around the cold iron railing.

But the train picked up more speed, half dragging her behind it as she hung on for dear life, fighting just to keep from stumbling, to keep from losing her grip.

She tried to pull herself nearer, but she couldn't. She tried to swing her other arm to the rail so that she could hold on with both hands, but she couldn't manage that, either.

And then her hand began to slip. . . .

"My God, Linnie!" Drew's voice seemed to come out of nowhere, and with it a long, strong arm that circled her waist, lifting her up onto the platform and against his solid, familiar chest.

"Drew!" Her heart was beating so hard, she was sure he must be able to feel it as she gasped for breath.

"What the devil were you trying to do?" He sounded like a man who'd just had the wits scared out of him.

But Linnie couldn't say anything. She was laughing and crying up into a face so wonderful to her that she had to press her fingertips to his cheek to make certain he was real.

He stared into her eyes, his expression full of disbelief, shaking his head just before he took her face in both of his hands and captured her mouth with his in a quick, fiercely possessive kiss.

"Oh, Drew, I'm sorry!" she told him breathlessly when he released her mouth so that he could hold her tight against him, as if he was afraid he might lose her yet.

"You should be sorry for trying to chase down a train and nearly getting killed."

"No, you don't understand."

"If that isn't what you're sorry for, then no, I don't understand."

"I'm sorry for the other night. For not forgiving you before. For—"

A helpless chuckle rumbled from deep inside his chest. "For agreeing to marry Will Larson?"

"I didn't say I'd marry him. I said no. And then this morning I went to the house to see you, and—"

"It better not have been just to tell me you were sorry. And you'd better not have chased this train only for that, either." His voice softened. "You better be here to tell me you love me, that you'll marry me."

The train was moving fast by then, and the cold winter air was nipping at their skin. But all that mattered was that they were together, that they'd snatched happiness out from under the train wheels that might have separated them. And all Linnie could do as she stared up into that handsome face was nod her head.

"Tell me you love me, Linnie."

"You know I do. I always have."

"Tell me you'll marry me and live with me in the Hayes house and have my babies."

"I will. I will. Yes. You know I will," she said, with a laugh that sounded a little hysterical even to her own ears.

Drew breathed a sigh of relief into her hair. "I love you, Linnie Rhodes."

"I love you."

"This is the best Christmas gift anyone has ever given me, you know."

"Or me."

"Can we finally put the past behind us?"

"Far behind us."

"And go on to the future we planned to have?"

"Oh, yes. Yes!"

Her arms were around his waist now, and she held on tight, loving him with all her heart and soul. She'd never really stopped, only hidden away true feelings somewhere where it didn't hurt so much to love him when he wasn't with her. And then he'd come back, and the love had sneaked out all on its own, blossoming once again, growing into the fullness that filled her so completely now.

But suddenly she realized that the train had taken them from Pinewood. From home. That it was pirating them farther away with every passing moment.

She looked up at Drew. "Where are we going?" she asked, laughing.

He glanced around at the open countryside as if he, too, had just noticed that they were on a speeding train, and laughed with her. "The next stop is Denver. We'll have to get off there and take the night train back."

"We'll spend our first Christmas together in a train station," she said, laughing even harder.

"But I'll have you all to myself, so it doesn't matter where we are."

Still holding her close, he stared down into her eyes once more before lowering his lips to hers, taking her mouth fully, hungrily, with his.

And even with frigid air whipping around them, Linnie felt warm. She was where she belonged, where she wanted to spend the rest of her life—with Drew, in his arms. None of what had happened so long ago was important anymore. All that mattered was the present and the future. That they'd be together for the rest of their lives, for the rest of their Christmases.

And that some dreams did come true.

* * * * *

A Note from Victoria Pade

Dear Reader,

Christmas is my favorite time of year. I particularly love the decorations. Our tree goes up the day after Thanksgiving, and in that week just before, my daughters—Cori, 17, and Erin, 13—and I shop for new ornaments to add to the old. We never buy fewer than two so the girls can each choose one. I've done this since they were born, which makes for a very full tree.

I like most to take out the whole slew of them each year and remember what stages the girls were in when they picked them. There are a variety that range from Baby's First Christmas (I chose those) through tiny stuffed animals, Sesame Street characters, a lot of mice and on up to Santa sporting a surfboard.

But not all of our ornaments were bought.

One of my favorites that wasn't (though it makes her roll her eyes every time I mention this or put it in my special place on the tree) is the very first ornament that Cori made in preschool and gave to me as a gift. It's a walnut panda bear with a hazelnut head. The eyes and ears are lopsided. The arms and legs are at odd angles. And the black and white paint barely covers the color of the shells. But to me it's beautiful.

Erin, the younger of my kids, loves a project and is a wellspring of creativity and talent. Over the years I've looked forward to watching what she can come up with to fashion Christmas ornaments out of. My favorite was the year she uncoiled small springs into spirals and wrapped them in bright ribbons to hang like twirling icicles from the branches.

When the girls move on to homes of their own I'll pack up the ornaments they've chosen to buy each year and give them to them to take along.

But those special ones they've made will stay behind with me. I suspect it will make for a funny-looking tree, though not as funny as the year Cori stuck first-grade drawings to every branch, or the year Erin tossed colored pencil shavings all over it.

But I don't think I'll mind too much. I look at these child-crafted ornaments as my own private Christmas treasures. Things that make up for the messes left on the counter every morning; and the disappearance of anything they lay their hands on into their Bermuda Triangle of bedrooms; and having to hide in the pantry when they unexpectedly bring friends home late at night and catch me without a bathrobe; and replacing the contents of the spray bottle so that when I finally find it, I dampen the ironing with shampoo instead of water; and . . .

Well, you get the idea.

Merry Christmas and the best of new years.

Victoria Pade

Fifty red-blooded, white-hot, true-blue hunks
from every State in the Union!

Look for MEN MADE IN AMERICA! Written by some
of our most poplar authors, these stories feature fifty of
the strongest, sexiest men, each from a different state in
the union!

Two titles available every other month at your favorite
retail outlet.

In November, look for:

STRAIGHT FROM THE HEART by Barbara Delinsky
(Connecticut)
AUTHOR'S CHOICE by Elizabeth August (Delaware)

In January, look for:

DREAM COME TRUE by Ann Major (Florida)
WAY OF THE WILLOW by Linda Shaw (Georgia)

You won't be able to resist MEN MADE IN AMERICA!

Relive the romance...
Harlequin and Silhouette
are proud to present

by **Request**™

A program of collections of three complete novels by the most-requested authors with the most-requested themes. Be sure to look for one volume each month with three complete novels by top-name authors.

In September: **BAD BOYS**　　　　Dixie Browning
　　　　　　　　　　　　　　　　　Ann Major
　　　　　　　　　　　　　　　　　Ginna Gray
No heart is safe when these hot-blooded hunks are in town!

In October:　**DREAMSCAPE**　　　Jayne Ann Krentz
　　　　　　　　　　　　　　　　　Anne Stuart
　　　　　　　　　　　　　　　　　Bobby Hutchinson
Something's happening! But is it love or magic?

In December: **SOLUTION: MARRIAGE**　Debbie Macomber
　　　　　　　　　　　　　　　　　Annette Broadrick
　　　　　　　　　　　　　　　　　Heather Graham Pozzessere
Marriages in name only have a way of leading to love....

Available at your favorite retail outlet.

REQ-G2

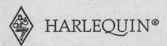
HARLEQUIN®

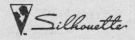
Silhouette

Harlequin® Historical

Nora O'Shea had fled to Arizona seeking freedom, but could she ever find love as a mail-order bride?

MARIANNE WILLMAN

PIECES OF SKY

From the author of THE CYGNET and ROSE RED, ROSE WHITE comes a haunting love story full of passion and power, set against the backdrop of the new frontier.

Coming in November 1993 from Harlequin

Don't miss it! Wherever Harlequin books are sold.

Harlequin® Historical

From *New York Times* bestselling author

The powerful story of two people as brave and free as the elusive wild mustang which both had sworn to capture.

A Harlequin Historicals Release
December 1993

HHRLOVE